Marianne and the Rebels

Juliette Benzoni was born and educated in Paris, studying at the Collège d'Hulet, then at the Institut Catholique, where she obtained a BA degree in Philosophy, a Licentiate in Law and a Licentiate in Letters. She was married to Dr Maurice Gallois in 1941 and had two children. Widowed in 1950, she moved to Casablanca and lived there for two years. Back in Paris she married Count André Benzoni di Costa in March 1953. She has been in charge of the historical section of the French paper *Confidences* since 1960. Juliette Benzoni is the author of the famous 'Catherine' series of historical romances, set in medieval France, and of the successful 'Marianne' series, set in Napoleonic France.

Also by Juliette Benzoni in Pan Books

Juliette Benzoni

Marianne and the Rebels

Translated by Anne Carter

Pan Books in association with
William Heinemann

First published 1972 as *Toi, Marianne* by Opera Mundi, Paris
First published in Great Britain 1973 by William Heinemann Ltd
This edition published 1975 by Pan Books Ltd,
Cavaye Place, London SW10 9PG,
in association with William Heinemann Ltd
© Opera Mundi, Paris 1972
Translation © Opera Mundi, Paris 1973
ISBN 0 330 24409 4
Printed and bound in England by
Hazell Watson & Viney Ltd, Aylesbury, Bucks

Contents

Principal Characters

Marianne Elisabeth d'Asselnat, now Princess Sant'Anna. The daughter of a French marquis and his English wife, both of whom perished in the French Revolution. She was rescued as a baby by her godfather, Gauthier de Chazay, and taken to England to be brought up by her spinster aunt, Ellis Selton. In 1809 she married Francis Cranmere who, on her wedding night, gambled away both her fortune and her virginity to an American privateer, Jason Beaufort. Much later, after many adventures in France and Italy, first as the mistress of Napoleon, and then, when she discovers she is about to bear the Emperor's child, as wife to the mysterious recluse, Corrado Sant'Anna, Marianne has come to realize that Jason is, after all, the man she really loves.

Adelaide d'Asselnat. A French cousin of Marianne's, an elderly spinster, and devoted companion.

Jason Beaufort. The man to whom Francis Cranmere lost Marianne's fortune and virginity. He generously failed to claim the second but reappeared later in Paris to become first her friend and then her lover, although not until he himself was unhappily married to another. He was determined to renounce Marianne, but his jealous wife, realizing the situation, contrived to enmesh him in a plot of Francis Cranmere's which brought him to prison and almost to death. Marianne followed him with the chain-gang to Brest and engineered his escape, only to find that Napoleon had contrived to part them at the last moment. Jason sailed away after making a tryst with her: six months later, in Venice.

Pilar Beaufort. The daughter of a Spanish-American colonist, whom Jason married out of chivalry when her estates were sequestered and she herself was put in danger of imprisonment. With all the pride and passion of her race, coupled with a jealous and vindictive temper, she schemed for Jason's death and at one time kidnapped Marianne (who escaped) with the same objective.

Gauthier de Chazay, a French Abbé, later Cardinal San Lorenzo, Marianne's much-loved godfather, who rescued her as a baby and was responsible for arranging her marriage to Prince Sant'Anna.

Francis, Lord Cranmere. Marianne's dastardly first husband. She fought a duel with him and left him for dead in the blazing wreck of Selton Hall, but he reappeared in Paris as an English spy, tried to blackmail her, and later concocted the plot of which Jason was the victim. He failed, and Napoleon had Marianne brought to Vincennes in order that she might witness the preparations for his execution by the guillotine.

Matteo Damiani. Agent of the Sant'Anna estates, one of the few people in contact with the Prince, but with a sinister history connecting him with the dead witch-princess, Lucinda, Corrado's beautiful but evil grandmother. Marianne crossed swords with him at the Villa dei Cavalli, near Lucca.

Fortunée Hamelin. A Créole lady and a leading figure in Paris society. Devoted to the Emperor, she was entrusted by him with the task of introducing Marianne to the polite world, and the two women became firm friends.

Arcadius, Vicomte de Jolival. A French aristocrat and one of Marianne's staunchest friends. Formerly her theatrical manager, now her business agent.

Donna Lavinia. Housekeeper and devoted retainer of Prince Sant'Anna.

Gracchus-Hannibal Pioche. A former Paris errand-boy and now, at the time of the action, Marianne's faithful coachman, factotum and self-appointed guardian.

Prince Corrado Sant'Anna. Marianne's second husband. The heir to great Italian estates and scion of a powerful but strangely accursed family. Suffers from some unspecified condition which makes him live the life of a recluse. He married Marianne because she was carrying Napoleon's child, but has not set eyes on her since she returned to Paris and lost the baby as a result of a fire at a ball she was attending. He has been demanding her return, both directly and by application to Napoleon who, characteristically, has compromised by sending her as a special envoy to his sister, the Grand Duchess Elisa, in Florence, thus ensuring diplomatic protection for her.

Part One
Venice

Chapter One
Florentine spring

Gazing at Florence, spread out in the sun in its nest of soft grey-green hills, Marianne asked herself why it was that this city drew her and yet irritated her at the same time. From where she stood, she could see only a part of it, framed between the dark spire of a cypress and the rose-coloured bank of laurels, but this fragment of the city hoarded beauty as a miser hoards gold : provided only there was enough of it.

Before the long gold streak of the Arno, spanned by the bridges that seemed almost on the point of collapsing under their burden of medieval shops, was a huddle of old-rose tiles tossed at random on a background of warm ochre-coloured, pale grey or milky-white walls. Here and there a special jewel emerged : the Duomo, a coral bubble poised on a glittering, inlaid ground; a half-open lily, frozen for ever in silvery stone on the old Palazzo della Signoria, plain, square towers blossoming into crenellations like so many butterflies, and campaniles gay as Easter candles in many-coloured marbles. More often than not, this beauty soared in a random way out of some dark and twisted alley, between the blank wall of a palazzo, double-locked like a strong-box, and a peeling, malodorous slum. And sometimes the stonework was breached by a scented riot pouring from an overgrown garden which no one had had sufficient bad taste to prune.

Florence lay warming its old gold and tarnished embroideries in the sun, basking under a sky of indigo in which a single small white cloud floated aimlessly, as if the future had no meaning for it and it had forgotten the inexorable passage of time; content only to feed its dreams upon the past.

It may have been something of this aspect of Florence that caught an element of Marianne's own nature on the raw. To her the past was important only in so far as it affected the present, and in the ominous shadow it cast over her future, that vague, almost impenetrable future towards which she was straining with her whole being.

True, she could have wished to share this moment, lulled by the beauty of the garden all around her, to share this fleeting moment with the man she loved. What woman would not? But two long months were yet to pass before she could meet Jason Beaufort in Venice, where his ship was to cast anchor in the lagoon, according to the promise made between them on that strangest and most tragic of all Christmas nights. Always supposing that they would ever meet again, for between Marianne and that meeting of her life stood the dread shadow of her unseen husband, Prince Corrado Sant'Anna, and the unavoidable, possibly even dangerous explanation which she owed him, and which she would have to cope with before long.

In a few hours' time, she must leave Florence and the comparative safety it had offered her and continue her journey to the white palazzo whose gentle, singing fountains had no power to exorcise its evil ghosts.

What would happen then? What compensation would the masked prince exact from one who had failed in her part of the bargain, to bring him the child of the imperial blood, the hope of which had prompted the marriage? What compensation ... or what punishment?

For it was true, wasn't it, that for several generations the Sant'Anna princesses had come to evil ends?

In the hope of making sure of the best possible counsel for her defence, the most understanding and also the best informed, she had written, immediately on arrival in Florence, to her godfather, Gauthier de Chazay, Cardinal San Lorenzo with an urgent appeal for help, and despatched it by a messenger. Gauthier was the man who had married her to the Prince in such strange circumstances, thinking to ensure a more than enviable life for her and for her child, while at the same time obtaining for a wretched, self-condemned hermit the heirs he either could not or would not produce for himself. It seemed to Marianne that the little cardinal was the best person to unravel a situation which had become worse than tragic and to find some acceptable solution.

But after several days' wait, the messenger had returned empty-handed. He had not found it easy to make contact with the restricted entourage of the Pope, whom Napoleon's men hardly allowed out of their sight, and the news he brought back was disappointing: Cardinal San Lorenzo was not at Savona and no one knew where he could be found.

Marianne had been disappointed, naturally, but not otherwise surprised. Ever since she had been old enough to understand, she had known that her godfather spent most of his time travelling mysteriously in the service of the Church, one of whose most active secret agents he appeared to be, or else for the exiled King Louis XVIII. He might now be at the ends of the earth, with nothing further from his mind than the fresh troubles besetting his god-daughter. She must get used to the idea that this hope had failed her.

The days to come, then, were not without their promise of clouds, Marianne reflected with a sigh: far from it. Yet she had long known that the generous gifts which fate had bestowed on her birth – beauty, charm, intelligence, courage – were not given for nothing, but were weapons with whose aid she might yet succeed in winning happiness. It remained to be seen if the price would be too heavy to pay . . .

'What have you decided, my lady?' The well-bred, courteous voice held an impatience ill-concealed.

Roused from her wistful reverie, Marianne shifted the pink sunshade that was supposed to protect her delicate complexion from the heat of the sun and lifted to Lieutenant Benielli an abstracted gaze which yet held a disquieting green glint of anger.

God what a bore the man was! In the six weeks since she had left Paris with the military escort under his command, Angelo Benielli had dogged her footsteps unmercifully.

He was a Corsican: stubborn, vindictive, jealous of the least bit of his authority, and possessed, besides, of a most unamiable character. Lieutenant Benielli admired only three people in the world: the Emperor, of course (and all the more so because

they were compatriots); General Horace Sebastiani, because he
hailed from the same village; and a third soldier, also a native
of the Beautiful Isle, the General the Duke of Padua, Jean-
Thomas Arrighi de Canova, because they were cousins and also
because he was a genuine hero. Apart from these three, Benielli
had scant regard for any of the great names of the imperial
armies, even for Ney, Murat, Davout, Berthier or Poniatowski.
The basis of this indifference was the fact that none of these
marshals had the honour to be Corsicans, an unfortunate but,
in Benielli's view, disqualifying fault.

It went without saying, in the circumstances, that the duty of
acting escort to a woman, even a princess ravishingly lovely and
honoured with the especial regard of his Majesty the Emperor
and King, was to Benielli nothing more than a tiresome chore.

With the fine frankness which constituted the most delightful
side of his character, he had let her understand as much before
they reached the Corbeil stage, and from that moment the
Princess Sant'Anna had begun seriously to wonder if she were an
ambassadress or a prisoner. Angelo Benielli watched her like a
law officer pursuing a pickpocket, arranged everything, decided
everything from the length of the stages to the room she occupied at the inns (there was a soldier on guard outside her door
each night), and might almost have required to be consulted on
her choice of dress.

This state of affairs had not failed to provoke the antagonism
of Arcadius de Jolival, who was not remarkable for patience at
the best of times. The evenings on the early part of the journey
had been punctuated by a series of verbal duels between the
Vicomte and the officer. But Jolival's best arguments only came
up against the single principle on which Benielli took his stand :
it was his duty to watch over the Princess Sant'Anna until a
certain date fixed in advance by the Emperor himself, and to do
so in such a way that not the slightest accident of any kind
should befall her. To this end he meant to take all necessary precautions. Beyond that there was nothing to be got out of him.

From initial irritation Marianne became at last resigned to
having the lieutenant as her shadow and she even soothed Jolival. It had occurred to her that this surveillance, however irk-

some at present, might have its very real advantages when, flanked by her dragoons, she came to cross the threshold of the Villa Santa'Anna for the interview which lay ahead. If Prince Corrado Sant'Anna was contemplating any vengeance on Marianne, the obstinate bulldog Napoleon had fastened to his friend's heels might well guarantee her life. Nevertheless, it was extremely trying . . .

Half-annoyed and half-amused, she looked at him for a moment. It was a pity the lad should carry about with him that angry cat-like glare, because he had it in him to attract a woman, even one not easy to please. He was not tall but strongly built, with a stubborn face, tight-lipped and given an added arrogance by the jutting beak of a nose which projected from the shadow of his helmet. He blushed with a readiness surprising in one of his dark ivory complexion, but the eyes revealed beneath the bushy black brows and the lashes which rivalled Marianne's in length were, curiously, of an attractive light grey, flecked with gold in the sunshine.

Partly, perhaps, out of a very feminine desire for conquest, Marianne had amused herself on the journey by making occasional idle attempts to win him, but Benielli had remained as impervious to her charming smiles as to the flash of her green eyes.

One evening, when the inn they were dining at was less than usually grimy, she had offered him the bait of a white gown cut low enough to have done credit to Fortunée Hamelin, with the result that throughout the meal the lieutenant had performed a succession of astonishing ocular gymnastics. He had looked everywhere, from the strings of onions hanging from the beams, to the great black andirons in the hearth, or concentrated his attention on his plate or on endless pellets of bread rolled on the cloth, but he never once regarded the golden curves revealed by her gown.

On the following night, more vexed and angry than she cared to admit, Marianne had dined alone in her room, wearing a dress whose frilled muslin collar came up almost to her ears, to the unspoken delight of Jolival who was deriving intense amusement from his friend's performance.

For the present, Benielli's attention was directed to a snail which had ventured out from beneath the friendly shade of a bay tree and was crossing the stone desert of the balustrade on which Marianne was leaning.

'Decided, Lieutenant? What should I have decided?' she asked at last.

The note of irony in her voice could not have escaped Benielli, who promptly flushed beetroot-coloured.

'But – what are we to do, Princess! Her Imperial Highness the Grand Duchess Elisa is leaving Florence tomorrow for her villa at Marlia. Do we go with her?'

'I don't see what else we can do, Lieutenant. Do you expect me to remain here alone? By alone, of course, I mean in your own delightful company ...' As she spoke she snapped shut her sunshade and pointed with it in the direction of the imposing frontage of the Pitti Palace.

Benielli shrugged. It was evident that this cavalier reference to what was in effect an imperial residence had shocked him. A great respecter of persons, he had an inbred reverence for all things connected with Napoleon, even his houses. But he prudently held his peace, knowing that this strange Princess Sant'-Anna could, when so inclined, make herself as disagreeable as he.

'We are leaving, then?'

'We are leaving. Besides, the Sant'Anna estates, to which you are to escort me, are quite close to her Imperial Highness's villa. Naturally I shall go with her.'

For the first time since Paris, Marianne saw on her bodyguard's face something which might, at a pinch, have been described as a smile. Her news had given him pleasure. At once, however, he clicked his heels, very correctly, and gave a military salute.

'Then with your permission, Princess, I'll make the necessary arrangements and inform his Grace the Duke of Padua that we shall be leaving tomorrow.'

Before Marianne could open her mouth, he had swung on his heel and was heading for the palace, apparently in no way discommoded by the sabre banging against his legs.

'The Duke of Padua?' Marianne murmured in astonishment. 'Whatever has he to do with it?'

She could find no possible connection between her own affairs and this admittedly remarkable man, who had arrived in Florence two days previously. Until yesterday, she had never met him in her life, although Benielli, who regarded him as one of his three household gods, had been visibly delighted by his appearance.

A relative of the Emperor and also inspector general of cavalry, Arrighi had arrived at the Grand Duchess's court with no more than a single squadron of the fourth Colonne Mobile, destined for the service of the Viceroy of Italy, Prince Eugene. His real business was to enforce the laws concerning recruitment and to hunt down deserters and those avoiding military service. Ostensibly, his journey into Tuscany had been undertaken for no more serious purpose than to visit his cousin Elisa and renew old ties with the Corsican members of his family, whom he had not seen for years but who were now to make the journey expressly to meet him. No one at the court of Tuscany had the faintest inkling of the deeper reason underlying this family reunion in the midst of military duties.

The Grand Duchess, who had accorded a most gracious welcome to the Princess Sant'Anna, the ambassadress charged with the news of the birth of the little King of Rome, now welcomed Arrighi with enthusiasm, being almost as enamoured as Benielli of heroes and glory and Napoleon. At the grand ball held the previous night in honour of the Duke of Padua, Marianne had found her hand being bowed over by this distinguished, grim-faced person – a man who was still one of the finest horsemen in the world, despite the countless serious wounds received in the Emperor's service, almost any single one of which in another man might well have proved fatal.

Drawing on information gleaned from Elisa and from Angelo Benielli, Marianne had stared with a very natural interest at this man who had had his skull cracked open by a scimitar blow at the battle of Salalieh in Egypt, his external carotid artery severed by a shot before Acre, and suffered a terrible wound in the neck from a sabre at Wertigen, not to mention innumerable 'minor scratches', the man who, when half-decapitated by shrapnel, had still risen from his bed to charge at the head of his dragoons –

only to return to it more shattered than before. In the interim, though, he had been a lion, saving countless lives and swimming unnumbered rivers – including recently the torrents of Spain.

Marianne had experienced a curious shock as their eyes met. She had the extraordinary impression, fleeting but real, that she was face to face with the Emperor himself. In Arrighi's eyes there was the same steely glint which seemed able to pierce through her like a knife. But her new acquaintance's voice broke the spell : it was low and hoarse, broken perhaps from yelling orders above the heat of charging cavalry, and utterly different from Napoleon's clipped accents, and Marianne had felt strangely relieved. An encounter with such a faithful image of the Emperor was certainly the last thing she wanted now, at the very moment when she was preparing to disregard his orders and flee from France, far away with Jason.

That first meeting with Arrighi had gone no further than an exchange of polite commonplaces which gave no hint that the general might be in any way concerned in Marianne's affairs. Consequently Benielli's oracular remark left her somewhat at a loss. Why on earth did he have to go and tell the Duke of Padua that she was leaving?

Too much put out to feel any inclination to await the return of her impetuous bodyguard, Marianne left her vantage point and began to descend the terraced slopes towards the palace, intending to go to her own rooms and give her orders to her maid, Agathe, regarding the morrow's departure. As she reached the Artichoke Fountain, she repressed a gesture of irritation. Benielli was coming back. But he was not alone. A few paces in front of him walked a man in the blue and gold uniform of a general, wearing an enormous cocked hat decked with white plumes. The Duke of Padua himself was coming hurriedly to meet her.

A meeting was unavoidable. Marianne paused, waiting, feeling vaguely uneasy and yet at the same time curious to know what the Emperor's cousin might have to say to her.

As he came within reach, Arrighi pulled off his cocked hat and bowed correctly, but his grey eyes were already boring inexorably into Marianne's. He spoke, without turning.

'You may leave us, Benielli.'

The lieutenant clicked his heels, about-turned and disappeared as though by magic, leaving the general and the Princess alone.

Not best pleased at finding her way thus effectively blocked, Marianne coolly folded her sunshade and setting the point to the ground, leaned both hands on its ivory handle as though she meant to consolidate her position. Then, with a little frown, she prepared to move in to the attack. Arrighi was before her.

'From your expression, madame, I deduce that this meeting is not to your liking. I must ask you to forgive me if I've interrupted your walk.'

'I had finished my walk, General. I was just about to go in. As to my pleasure or otherwise, I shall be able to tell you that when you have told me what you wish to say. You have something to say to me, have you not?'

'Certainly. But ... may I ask you to take a turn with me in these magnificent gardens. They appear to be quite deserted, whereas the palace is thrown into confusion by preparations for departure – and this court rings like a bell!'

He bowed courteously, offering his arm. The injuries to his neck, concealed by the black stock and high gold-embroidered collar, prevented him from bending his head, but this stiffness suited his large frame.

He continued to watch her closely and Marianne found herself blushing under his regard, without quite knowing why. It might have been because it was hard to know what was going on behind those eyes.

With dignity, therefore, she accepted the proffered arm and as she laid her gloved hand on his braided sleeve she was suddenly aware of contact with something about as solid as a ship's rail. The man must be made of granite.

They walked on a little way in silence, avoiding the lawns and pavements of the big amphitheatre and making instead for the peace of a long avenue of oaks and cypresses where the glaring sunlight was diffused into single shafts.

Marianne sighed.

'I collect you don't wish to be overheard? Is our conversation of such importance?'

'The Emperor's commands are always important.'

'Ah ... commands! I thought the Emperor had given me all his commands at our last meeting.'

'So it is not your orders but mine I wish to discuss. It is only natural that you should be informed since they concern yourself.'

This approach made Marianne uneasy. She knew Napoleon too well not to feel some alarm at the idea of orders concerning herself and given to no less a person than the Duke of Padua. This was unusual. Still dwelling on what the Emperor of the French might have in store for her now, she merely remarked 'Indeed?' in a tone so preoccupied that Arrighi stopped dead in the centre of the avenue, obliging her to do the same.

'Princess,' he said concisely, 'I am aware that you find this interview tiresome and would ask you to believe that I should greatly prefer to engage you in idle talk. A stroll in your company and in such pleasant surroundings would be most enjoyable. However, I regret that I must request you to give me your full attention.'

Why, thought Marianne, more amused than embarrassed, the man is angry! What a hot-tempered race these Corsicans are, to be sure!

But because she knew that she had been less than polite, she bestowed on him a mollifying smile of such brilliance that the soldier's stern face flushed.

'Forgive me, General. I did not mean to offend you, but I was deep in thought. It always makes me anxious, you know, when the Emperor goes to the trouble of giving special orders which concern me. His Majesty's ... er ... solicitude is apt to be somewhat demanding.'

As abruptly as his earlier move to anger, Arrighi now gave a bark of laughter and, repossessing himself of Marianne's hand, he carried it to his lips before tucking it back within his own.

'I quite agree,' he said cheerfully. 'It is always unnerving. But if we are friends?'

Marianne smiled again. 'We are friends.'

'Then, if we are friends, listen to me for a moment. My orders are to escort you personally to the Sant'Anna palace and, once within your husband's domain, not to let you out of my sight. The Emperor told me that you had some private matter to settle with the Prince, but one in which he too should have a say. He wants me, therefore, to be present at the interview with your husband.'

'Did the Emperor tell you that it is highly unlikely that you, any more than I myself, will be privileged to see Prince Sant'-Anna with your own eyes?'

'Yes. He told me. Nevertheless, he wants me to hear at least what the Prince says to you, and what he wants of you.'

'He may,' Marianne said hesitantly, 'he may simply want me to stay with him?' This was her deepest and most dreadful fear, for she did not see how the Emperor's protection could prevent the Prince from keeping his wife at home.

'Then that's precisely where I come in. The Emperor wishes me to convey to the Prince his express wish that your meeting today shall be a brief one – a few hours at most. It is designed merely to show him that the Emperor accedes to his request and to allow you both to reach some agreement about the future. For the present—'

He paused and taking a large white handkerchief from his pocket mopped his brow with it. Even under the green roof of trees the heat made itself felt and in the heavy uniform, made heavier still by its weight of gold braid, it must have been very nearly intolerable. But Marianne pressed him to go on. She was beginning to find their conversation more and more interesting.

'For the present?'

'The present, madame, belongs neither to the Prince nor to yourself. The Emperor has need of you.'

'Has need of me? But what for?'

'I think this will explain.'

A letter sealed with the imperial cipher had appeared, as if by magic, between Arrighi's fingers. Marianne regarded it for a moment before taking it with an expression of such deep distrust that the general smiled.

'Don't be afraid. It won't explode.'

'I'm not so sure.'

Marianne took the letter to an old stone seat at the foot of an oak tree and sat down, her dress of rose-pink lawn spread like a graceful corolla around her. She slid nervous fingers under the seal of wax, unfolded the letter, and began to read. Like most of Napoleon's letters, it was brief.

'Marianne,' the Emperor had written, 'it occurs to me that the best way to protect you from your husband's resentment is to enlist you in the service of the Empire. You left Paris under cover of a somewhat vague diplomatic mission, now you have a real one, of great importance to France. The Duke of Padua, who is under orders to see that nothing occurs to interfere with your departure, will convey to you my detailed instructions concerning your mission. I look to you to prove yourself worthy of my trust and that of all Frenchmen. I shall know how to reward you. N.'

'His trust? The trust of all Frenchmen? What does it all mean?' Marianne managed to ask.

There was a world of bewilderment in the eyes she lifted to Arrighi's. She was half inclined to think Napoleon must have gone mad. To make sure, she re-read the letter carefully, word by word, under her breath, but this second perusal only confirmed her in the same dismal conclusion, which her companion had no difficulty in interpreting from her expressive face.

'No,' he said coolly, seating himself beside her. 'The Emperor is not mad. He is merely trying to gain time for you, once your husband has made his intentions clear to you. The only way to do that was to enrol you in his own diplomatic service, which is what he has done.'

'Me, a diplomat? But this is absurd! What government would listen to a woman?'

'The government of another woman, perhaps. In any case, there's no question of making you an official plenipotentiary. The service his Majesty requires of you is of a more ... secret nature, such as he reserves for those most in his confidence and for his closest friends ...'

'I dare say,' Marianne broke in, fanning herself irritably with the imperial letter. 'I have heard a good deal about the "immense" services which the Emperor's sisters have rendered him in the past, in a sphere which I find less than attractive. So let us come to the point, if you please. Just what is the Emperor asking me to do? And, more important, where is he sending me?'

'To Constantinople.'

If the great oak under which she sat had fallen on her, Marianne could not have been more astonished. She stared up at her companion's expressionless face, as though searching for some reflection of the brain fever to which, she was persuaded, Napoleon must have succumbed. But not only did Arrighi appear perfectly composed and self-possessed, he was also taking her hand in a grasp that was as firm as it was understanding.

'Hear me calmly for a moment and you will see the Emperor's idea is not so foolish after all. I might even go so far as to say that it's the best thing for you and for his policies in the present circumstances.'

Patiently, he outlined for his young hearer's benefit the European situation in that spring of 1811, and in particular the relations between France and Russia. Relations with the Tsar were deteriorating rapidly, despite the great maritime reunions at Tilsit. The barque of understanding was adrift. Although Alexander I had practically refused his sister Anna to his 'brother' Napoleon, he nevertheless regarded the Austrian marriage askance, nor had his view been improved by the French annexation of his brother-in-law's grand duchy of Oldenburg and of the Hanseatic towns. He had expressed his displeasure by reopening his ports to English shipping and by slapping heavy duties on goods imported from France, and prohibitive dues on the ships which carried them.

Napoleon had countered by taking notice at last of the precise activities in which the handsome colonel Sasha Chernychev was indulging at his court, maintaining a satisfying network through the agency of various pretty women. The police had descended without warning on his Paris house. Even so, they were too late. The bird had flown. Warned in time, Sasha had elected to disappear, without hope of return, but the papers found there had told their own tale.

These circumstances, combined with the lust for power of two autocratic rulers, made war appear inevitable to attentive observers. Russia, however, had already been at war, since 1809, with the Ottoman Empire over the Danube forts: a war of attrition but one which, thanks to the strength of the Turkish forces, was keeping Alexander and his army fully occupied.

'That war must go on,' Arrighi said forcefully. 'It will keep a large part of the Russian forces busy on the Black Sea while we march on Moscow. The Emperor does not mean to wait until the Cossacks are on our doorstep. This is where you come in.'

Marianne had listened with considerable relish to the tale of her old enemy Chernychev's present troubles, aware that his barbarous treatment of herself had probably played its part in bringing those troubles upon him, but this was not enough to make her bow to the imperial commands without further question.

'Do you mean that I'm to persuade the Sultan to continue the war? But you must have thought that—'

The general interrupted her with some impatience.

'We have thought of everything. Including the fact that you are a woman and that, as a good Muslim, the Sultan Mahmud regards women in general as inferior creatures with whom it is not proper to negotiate. Consequently, it is not to him you go but to the Haseki Sultan. The Empress Mother is a French-woman, a Créole from Martinique and own cousin to the Empress Josephine, with whom she was for some time brought up. There was a great bond of affection between them as children, a bond which the sultana has never forgotten. Aimée Dubucq de Rivery, whom the Turks call Nakshidil, is not only a woman of great beauty but also an extremely active and intelligent one. She has a long memory too, and has never accepted the Emperor's repudiation of her cousin and his remarriage. Since she has great influence over her son Mahmud, who worships her, this has led to a distinct chill in our relations. Our ambassador, Monsieur Latour-Maubourg, is at his wits' end and crying out for help. He can no longer even obtain an audience at the Seraglio.'

'And you think the doors will open more readily to me?'

'The Emperor is sure of it. He has not forgotten that you are in some degree related to our erstwhile Empress, which makes you kin to the Sultana also. It is on those grounds that you will seek and obtain audience. In addition, you will have in your possession a letter from General Sebastiani, who defended Constantinople against the English fleet when he was our ambassador there. His wife, Françoise de Franquetot de Coigny, who died in the city in 1807, was the Sultana's close friend. You will be armed with the best possible introductions and I don't think you'll have any difficulty in gaining admittance. You can mourn with Nakshidil over the fate of Josephine as much as you like; you may even blame Napoleon since you will not be there in an official capacity ... but never lose sight of French interests. Your own charm and skill will do the rest. But Kaminski's Russians must remain on the Danube. Are you beginning to understand?'

'I think so. But forgive me if I seem slow – all this is so new to me, and so very strange ... this woman of whom I have never heard, yet who is a Sultana! Can't you tell me anything about her? How did she get where she is?'

Marianne's chief object in getting Arrighi talking was to gain time for herself. This thing she was being asked to do was very serious for her since, although it had the advantage that it offered a way of avoiding Prince Corrado's vengeance, for the time being at least, it was also more than likely to make her miss her appointed meeting with Jason. This she would not, could not do at any price. She had waited too long and with such agonizing impatience for the moment when she would be in his arms at last and could set out with him for the land and the future which fate and her own stupidity had so far denied her. With all her heart, she desired to help the man she had once loved and whom she would always love in a way ... but if it meant the loss of her true love and the destruction of a happiness she felt that she had earned ...

At the same time, she was listening, with half an ear, to the story of the little fair-haired, blue-eyed Créole girl who had been captured at sea by Barbary pirates, as the culmination of an extraordinary series of adventures, and taken to Algiers, from where she had been sent by the dey of that city as a gift to the Grand Signior at Constantinople. She heard how Aimée had charmed the last days of the old sultan Abdul Hamid I, and had a son by him, and had then gone on to win the love of Selim, the heir to the throne. By means of this love, which for her had gone as far as the supreme sacrifice, and that of her son Mahmud, the little Créole had become a queen.

In Arrighi's colourful phrases, the narrative took on such an irresistible vividness that Marianne found herself longing to know this woman, to meet her and perhaps to win her friendship. The extraordinary life that she had led seemed to Marianne more exciting than anything she had read of in the novels she had devoured in the schoolroom – stranger even than her own history. Even so, who could outweigh Jason in her thoughts?

Cautious as ever and determined to make quite sure of what Napoleon had in store for her, she asked, after the slightest of hesitations:

'Have I . . . any choice?'

'No,' Arrighi told her bluntly. 'You have not. The Emperor gives no one any choice where the good of the Empire is concerned. He commands – myself, as well as you. I am to escort you – to be present at your – encounter with the Prince and to make sure the outcome is in accordance with the Emperor's wishes. You'll be obliged to put up with my presence and act in all things as I shall direct. I've had a copy of his Majesty's detailed instructions regarding your mission left in your room so that you may study them tonight. You would do well to learn them by heart and then destroy them. With them is Sebastiani's letter of introduction.'

'And . . . when I leave the Villa Sant'Anna? Do you go with me to Constantinople? I understood that you have business here?'

Arrighi did not answer immediately. Instead, he studied Marianne's averted face. As always when she was unable to betray her real thoughts, she preferred not to meet his eye, and because of this she missed the smile which flickered across his face.

'By no means,' he said at last, in an oddly detached tone. 'I am merely to escort you to Venice.'

'To—?' Marianne could scarcely believe her ears.

'Venice,' Arrighi repeated blandly. 'It is the most convenient port, being both the nearest and at the same time the most likely.

Besides, it is just the place to attract a young and lovely woman who is bored.'

'That's as may be. Yet it seems odd to me that the Emperor should want me to take ship from an Austrian port—'

'Austrian? What gave you that idea?'

'But I thought – that is, I have always understood that Bonaparte gave Venice back to Austria by the treaty of – what was it?'

'Campo Formio,' Arrighi supplied. 'But Austerlitz and Pressburg have happened since then. There is the marriage with Vienna, true, but Venice is ours. Otherwise how could the Emperor have called his daughter, if he had one, the Princess of Venice?'

It seemed obvious enough, and yet something was not quite right. Even Jason, the sea-rover who generally knew what he was talking about, had given her to understand that Venice was Austrian, and Arcadius, that universal fount of information, had not corrected him ... Marianne did not have to wait long for the explanation.

'I dare say you were misled,' the Duke of Padua was saying, 'by the strong rumours that Venice was to be returned to Austria at the time of the marriage. In any case, the city charter is still rather special. In practical if not in political terms it enjoys a kind of extra-territorial status. That is why there has been no official replacement yet for General Menou, who died recently. He was an odd fellow, by the way, a convert to Islam. The city is altogether much more cosmopolitan than French. You'll find it much easier there to play the part of a rich lady with nothing to do and desirous of travelling than in the stricter atmosphere of other ports. You can wait quietly for a passage on a neutral vessel bound for the east – many such put in to Venice.'

'A – a neutral vessel?' Marianne said faintly, feeling her heart thud as her eyes, this time, sought those of her companion. But Arrighi appeared to have developed a sudden interest in a butterfly which was hovering conveniently at hand.

'Yes ... American, perhaps ... The Emperor has heard that they are known to anchor in the lagoon.'

This time Marianne had no answer. Surprise had left her

speechless. Speechless, but not without the power of thought.

Reaching her own apartments, a few minutes later, she made praiseworthy efforts to recover the shreds of her dignity. She was well aware that this had suffered greatly as, oblivious of time, place, and even the most elementary decorum due to her position, it had finally sunk home what was meant by the junction of those three words : *Venice* and *American vessel*. She had quite simply flung her arms round the Duke of Padua's august neck and planted two smacking kisses on his clean-shaven cheeks.

To tell the truth, Arrighi had not shown any undue surprise at this startlingly familiar assault. He had laughed heartily and then as, blushing furiously, she had attempted to stammer some kind of apology, had hugged her back and kissed her in a most fatherly way, saying :

'The Emperor warned me you would be pleased but I hadn't hoped to find my mission so pleasantly rewarded. All the same, one final word : you must realize the gravity of your mission. It is very real and important. His Majesty is counting on you.'

'His Majesty is perfectly right, Duke. As always, surely ? For my own part, I would rather die than disappoint the Emperor when he not only takes such pains for my welfare but even concerns himself for my future happiness.'

Sweeping him a final curtsey, she had left Arrighi to enjoy the delightful shades of the Boboli Gardens on his own. She was overflowing with gratitude and sped back towards the palace, her feet in their pink satin slippers barely touching the sanded paths.

With three words Arrighi had ripped apart the storm clouds, banished her nightmares and opened a great shining passage through the looming mists which hid the future, enabling her to step out confidently towards it. Everything had become wonderfully simple.

With General Arrighi to protect her, she need have nothing to fear from her strange husband and, more to the point, she could stop worrying about how to get rid of the tiresome Benielli.

She was to be delivered practically into Jason's arms, and Jason, she knew, would not refuse to help her to carry out a mission laid on her by the man to whom they both owed so much. They would have such a wonderful voyage together, on that great ship which she had watched with such an aching heart as it vanished into the mist off the coast of Brittany. But now the *Sea Witch* would soon be heading for the scented shores of the east, bearing its cargo of lovers lightly over the blue waves, through days of burning sun and nights ablaze with stars. How good it must be to make love underneath the stars!

Lost in her shining dream, her imagination already slipping its cable, Marianne did not pause to wonder how Napoleon could have come to know of her most secret thoughts, a plan whispered hastily into her ear in that last passionate embrace with her lover.

She was quite used to his habit of knowing everything without having to be told. He was a man endowed with superhuman powers of reading what lay in men's hearts. And yet ... ? Was it possible, after all, that this miracle too was the work of François Vidocq? The ex-convict turned policeman seemed possessed of a remarkably acute hearing, when he took the trouble to use it.

Wholly wrapped up in themselves and in the grief of this fresh separation, neither Jason nor Marianne had thought to notice whether Vidocq had been within earshot. Well, true or not, this betrayal, if betrayal it were, was the source of too much happiness for Marianne to feel anything but heartfelt gratitude.

She reached the palace still bubbling with happiness and floated up the great stone staircase without paying the slightest attention to the activity going on all around her. Footmen and waiting-women hurried up and down, bearing everything from leather travelling cases and carpet-bags to curtains and articles of furniture. The staircase echoed to the din and clatter of a removal on a princely scale.

The Grand Duchess would not return to Florence before the winter and in addition to an extensive wardrobe she liked to carry with her all the familiar objects of her everyday life. Only the guards on the doors maintained their accustomed rigidity, in hilarious contrast to the domestic upheaval going on around them.

Marianne was almost running by the time she came to the three rooms which had been assigned to her on the second floor. She could not wait to find Jolival and tell him of her happiness. She could scarcely breathe for excitement and she had to share it with someone. But she looked for him in vain. Both the Vicomte's own room and the little sitting-room they shared were empty.

She was both irritated and downcast when a servant informed her that 'Monsieur le Vicomte was at the museum'. She knew what that meant. In all probability, Arcadius would not be back until very late and she would have to keep her glad news to herself for hours.

Ever since their arrival in Florence, Jolival had been spending a great deal of his time officially visiting the Uffizi Palace and, unofficially, frequently a certain house in the via Tornabuoni where the play was high and the company exclusive. The Vicomte had been introduced into this circle by a friend on a previous visit and had retained nostalgic memories, stimulated to some extent by the intermittent smiles of Fortune, but rather more by recollections of the languishing and extremely romantic charms of the hostess, a violet-eyed countess with a claim to Medici blood in her veins.

All in all, Marianne could not in justice blame her old friend for paying a final visit to his enchantress. After all, he was to leave Florence with Marianne in the morning.

Postponing her confidences, therefore, until later, Marianne went into her own room, where she found her maid, Agathe, up to her neck in a sea of satins, laces, gauzes, lawns, taffetas and fripperies of all kinds which she was stowing away methodically in big trunks lined with pink *toile de Jouy*.

Flushed with exertion, her cap askew, Agathe nevertheless put down the pile of linen she was carrying to hand her mistress the two letters which were waiting. One was a formidable, official-looking document sealed with the Emperor's personal cipher, the other a much smaller affair, artistically folded and adorned with a frivolous seal of green wax impressed with a dove. Since she had a very good idea of what to expect from the big letter, Marianne turned first to the little one.

'Do you know who brought this?' she asked her maid.

'A footman belonging to Baroness Cenami. He came soon after your highness went out. He made a great thing of its being urgent.'

Marianne nodded and went to the window to peruse her new friend's letter. Zoe Cenami was, in fact, the only friend she had made since coming into Italy. She had been given a letter of introduction to her by Fortunée Hamelin before leaving Paris.

The young Baroness was a fellow-Créole and before entering the Princess Elisa's household, where she met her future husband, had been a frequent visitor at the house of Madame Campan, where Fortunée's daughter Léontine was receiving her education. A common origin had created a bond of friendship between Madame Hamelin and Mademoiselle Guilbaud, a friendship continued by letter after Zoe's departure for Italy. Not long after her arrival there, she had married the charming Baron Cenami, brother of the Princess's favourite chamberlain and one of the best placed men at court by virtue of his elder's attractions. Zoe's own wit and elegance had soon won her Elisa's regard and she had been entrusted with the upbringing of the Princess's daughter, the boisterous Napoléone-Elisa, whose tomboyish ways put a severe strain on the young Créole's patience.

Marianne, aided by her friend's good offices, had found herself naturally drawn to the charming woman who became her guide through Florence and had introduced her to the pleasant circle of friends who met most afternoons in the pretty drawing-room in the Lungarno Accaiuoli.

There the Princess Sant'Anna had been welcomed in a simple and comfortable way which, little by little, made her feel at home there. It was strange that Zoe should have bothered to write, since she was expecting her as usual that evening.

The note was short but disturbing. Zoe seemed a prey to some strong anxiety.

'My dear Princess,' she had written in a scratchy, nervous hand, 'I must see you, but not at my house. For the sake of my own peace of mind and perhaps of the life of one dear to me. I shall be in the church of Or San Michele at five o'clock, in the right aisle, which is the one with the Gothic tabernacle. Wear a veil so that you will not be recognized. You are the only person who can save your unhappy Z.'

Marianne re-read the letter carefully in a good deal of bewilderment. Then, crossing to the hearth where owing to the prevailing dampness of the palace a fire still burned even at that late season, she tossed Zoe's missive into the flames. It was gone in a moment but Marianne continued to watch it until the last white ashes had fallen apart. She was thinking hard.

Zoe must be in dire trouble to have called on her for help like this, for she was noted for her shyness and discreet behaviour, as well as for her talent for making friends. There were many of these of far longer standing than Marianne, so why call on her? Because she inspired more confidence? Because they were both French? Because she was a friend of that indefatigable help in trouble, Fortunée Hamelin ... ?

Whatever the answer, Marianne, glancing at the clock on the mantelpiece, saw that it was not far off five already and called to Agathe to come and dress her.

'Give me my olive-green dress with the black velvet trimmings, my black straw hat and a Chantilly-lace veil to go with it.'

Agathe's top half emerged slowly backwards out of the trunk which had all but swallowed her and she stared at her mistress blankly.

'Wherever is your highness going in that gloomy get-up? Not to Madame Cenami's, surely?'

Agathe enjoyed all the devoted servant's freedom of speech, and normally Marianne was ready to indulge her. Today, however, was an exception. Marianne's temper was sharpened by her anxiety for Zoe.

'Since when has it been any business of yours where I go?' she snapped. 'Do as I ask, that is all.'

'But if Monsieur le Vicomte should return and ask for you?'

'Then you will tell him all you know: that I have gone out. And ask him to wait for me. I don't know when I shall be back.'

Agathe said no more but went in search of the required garments, leaving Marianne to slip hastily out of the rose-pink lawn which she felt was rather too conspicuous for a discreet assignation in a church, especially since Zoe had asked her to come veiled.

Helping her mistress on with the plain dress, Agathe, still bridling from her set-down, inquired through pursed lips whether she was to order Gracchus to bring the carriage.

'No. I'll walk. The exercise will do me good and it is only on foot that Florence is to be seen to the best advantage.'

'Very well, my lady, if you don't mind going up to your ankles in mud . . .'

'Never mind. It will be worth it.'

A few minutes later, Marianne was dressed and making her way out of the palace. The full lace veil placed a delicate screen of leaves and flowers between her and the sparkling daylight as, walking quickly, with her skirts lifted a little to keep them from the dirt of the streets, where patches of wet mud still lingered here and there in the shade, left over from the last shower of rain, Marianne made her way in the direction of the Ponte Vecchio. She crossed it without a glance at the jewellers' shops ranged in picturesque clusters on either hand.

In her gloved hands she held a fat morocco-bound missal with gilt corners. Agathe had seen her take it, eyes bulging with curiosity but her lips discreetly sealed. Thus armed, Marianne had the perfect air of a well-bred lady going to evening service. It had the added advantage of preserving her from the un-wanted gallantries which every Italian male worth the name felt in honour bound to address to any personable woman : and the streets, at that hour, were always full of men.

A few minutes' brisk walk brought Marianne within sight of the old church of Or San Michele, formerly the property of the rich Florentine guilds, which had adorned it with the priceless statuary standing in its Gothic niches. She was hot in her en-veloping black lace and heavy cloth. There was sweat on her forehead and trickling down her spine. It seemed a sin to be muffled up like this when the weather was so warm and the sky a canopy of exquisite and everchanging hues. Florence seemed to be floating in a huge and iridescent soap-bubble lifting to the whim of the setting sun.

The city, so shuttered and secretive in the heat of the day, opened its doors and spilled out into the streets and squares a throng of chattering humanity, while the thin sound of convent bells called to prayer those men and women whose conversation was henceforth dedicated to God.

The church struck surprisingly chill, but its coolness did her good: it was a reviving coolness. It was so dark inside, with only the dim light that filtered through the windows, that Marianne had to pause for a moment by the holy-water stoup until her eyes grew accustomed to the gloom.

Soon, however, she was able to make out the double nave and, in the right-hand aisle, Orcagna's masterpiece, the splendid medieval tabernacle aglow with soft dull gold in the trembling flames of three altar candles. But no figure, male or female, prayed before it. The church appeared empty and the only sound which echoed beneath its great roof was the shuffling footsteps of the verger making his way back to his sacristy.

The emptiness and silence made Marianne uneasy. She had come with a strange reluctance, torn between her real wish to help her charming friend in her trouble and a vague foreboding. Moreover she knew that she was on time and Zoe was the soul of punctuality. It was odd and disquieting: so much so that Marianne had half a mind to turn round and go home. It was thoroughly unnatural, this meeting in a dimly-lighted church ...

Without thinking, almost, she took a step or two towards the door but then the words of the letter recurred to her:

'... for the sake of my own peace of mind and perhaps the safety of one dear to me ...'

No, she could not leave that call for help unanswered. Zoe, who had given her this extraordinary proof of confidence, would never understand, and Marianne would blame herself for the rest of her life if a tragedy occurred which she had not done everything in her power to prevent.

Fortunée Hamelin would never have known that impulse to retreat, that moment of distrust: she was always ready to leap into the fire for a friend, or throw herself into the water to save a cat. The church was empty. Very well. All that meant was that something had happened to delay Zoe ...

Thinking that the least she could do was to wait for a few minutes, Marianne advanced slowly towards the appointed meeting place. She gazed at the tabernacle for a moment before sinking to her knees in fervent prayer. She had too much to thank heaven for to neglect so excellent an opportunity. It was, in any case, the best way of passing the time.

Deep in her prayers, she failed to notice the approach of a man draped from chin to calves in a black cloak with triple shoulder-capes, and she started suddenly when a hand was laid on her shoulder and an urgent voice whispered in her ear.

'Come, madame, come quickly! Your friend has sent me to find you. She implores you to come to her . . .'

Marianne had risen swiftly and was studying the man before her. His face was strange to her. It was the kind of face, moreover, which gives nothing away, broad, placid and unremarkable, but imprinted now with desperate anxiety.

'What's happened? Why does she not come herself?'

'Something terrible. Only come with me, madame, I beg of you! Every moment counts . . .'

But Marianne stayed where she was, struggling to understand first this strange meeting and now this stranger . . . It was all so unlike the tranquil Zoe.

'Who are you?' she asked.

The man bowed with all the marks of respect.

'A servant, Excellenza, that's all . . . but my family have always served the Baron's and my lady honours me with her confidence. Must I tell her that your highness will not come?'

Quickly, Marianne put out her hand and detained the messenger, who seemed on the point of withdrawal.

'No, please don't go! I'm coming.'

The man bowed again but in silence and followed her through the shadowy church to the door.

'I have a carriage close by,' he said when they had emerged into the light and air again. 'It will be quicker.'

'Have we far to go? The palace is very near.'

'To the villa at Settignano. Now, if you will forgive me, that is all I am allowed to tell you. I'm only a servant, you understand . . .'

'A devoted servant, I'm sure. Very well. Let us go.'

The carriage which was waiting a little farther on proved to be an elegant brougham with no crest visible on the panels. It was standing underneath the archway connecting the church with the half-ruined Palazzo dell'Arte della Lana. The steps were already down and a man dressed in black stood by the door. The driver on his box, seemed to be dozing, but Marianne was no sooner inside than he cracked his whip and the horses moved off at a brisk trot.

The devoted servant had taken the seat beside Marianne. She frowned a little at this familiarity but said nothing, attributing the solecism to his evident distress.

They left Florence by the Porte San Francesco. Marianne had not spoken since leaving Or San Michele, but cast about anxiously in her mind for the explanation of this sudden disaster which had befallen Zoe Cenami. She could hit on only one. Zoe was attractive and she was courted ardently by many men, some of them of great charm. Was it possible that one of them had succeeded in winning her favours and that some indiscretion, or malice, had made Cenami aware of his misfortune? If that were so, then Marianne did not see what help she could give her friend, except perhaps in calming the outraged husband. Certainly, Cenami had a high opinion of the Princess Sant'Anna. It was not a theory very flattering to Zoe's virtue, but what else could justify a cry for help so urgent and so fraught with extraordinary precautions?

It was as hot as an oven inside the closed carriage and Marianne was driven to lift her veil. She leaned forward to lower the window, but her companion held her back.

'Better not, madame. Besides, we're already there.'

It was true. The carriage had left the main road and was jolting along a narrow way between the ivy-clad ruins of what appeared to have been a convent. Below, at the end of the track, the Arno shone like brass in the setting sun.

'But – this is not Settignano!' Marianne exclaimed. 'What does this mean? Where are we?'

She turned to her companion, fear struggling with anger in her face, but the man only answered with impassive calm:

'Where I was ordered to take your highness. A comfortable travelling coach is waiting. You will be quite comfortable. Necessarily so, since we shall travel through the night.'

'A travelling coach? Travelling ... where to?'

'To where your highness is awaited with impatience. You will see ...'

The carriage stopped amid the ruins. Instinctively, Marianne clutched at the door with both hands, as though clinging to her last refuge. She was frightened now, horribly frightened of this man with his smooth, over-polite manners and his eyes which she now saw to be both shifty and cruel.

'Who awaits me? And whose orders? You are not a servant of the Cenami?'

'Correct. I take my orders from his Serene Highness, Prince Corrado Sant'Anna.'

Chapter Two
The ravisher

With a little scream, Marianne shrank back into the carriage, staring with eyes of horror at the peaceful, romantic scene, all bathed in the glorious sunset light which was framed in the open door. To her it might have been a prison.

Her companion got out and stood beside the man who had lowered the steps, bowing respectfully as he offered his hand.

'If your highness will descend . . .'

Hypnotized by the two black-clad figures who seemed to her suddenly like the ambassadors of fate, Marianne got out, moving like an automaton, knowing that it was useless to struggle. She was alone in an isolated spot with three men whose power was all the greater because they represented one whose authority she was not entitled to ignore. Her husband's rights were paramount and she now had every reason to fear the worst. If it were not so, Sant'Anna would never have dared to have her abducted like this by his servants, right in the middle of Florence and almost under the nose of the Grand Duchess herself.

Beneath the ruined arch of a ghostly cloister, which in any other circumstances would have charmed her, Marianne saw that a large travelling berlin was in fact standing ready waiting. A man was standing at the horses' heads. The berlin itself, while not new, was well-made and evidently designed to spare its occupants as much as possible the discomforts of the road.

And yet, like Dante at the gate of hell, she seemed to see written above it the words : Abandon hope, all ye who enter here. She had thought to cheat the man who had trusted her, only to find she had been cheated in turn. Too late she realized that Zoe Cenami had never written that letter, that she did not need her help and must be quietly occupied at that very moment in welcoming the usual company of friends to her house. As long as Marianne could rely on the powerful protection of Napoleon, she had turned to it as to a cliff-girt isle against which the most terrifying waves must break in vain. And finally she had believed that her love for Jason made her somehow invulnerable and could only end in triumph. She had gambled and she had lost.

The unseen husband had claimed his rights. Deceived, he had a brutal way of making himself felt, and when the fugitive found herself face to face with him at last, even if what she faced were still a blank mirror, and she would stand alone, with her hands tied and her soul defenceless. There would be no Duke of Padua, with his powerful form and voice accustomed to command, to stand as a bulwark, proclaiming the inalienable rights of the Emperor.

Suddenly a faint glimmer of light penetrated Marianne's despair. Her disappearance would be noticed. Arcadius, Arrighi, even Benielli would look for her. One of them might guess the truth. Then they would go straight to Lucca to check, at least, that the Prince had no part in her abduction, and Marianne knew them well enough to be sure that they would not readily abandon hope. Jolival, for one, was perfectly capable of taking the Villa dei Cavalli apart, stone by stone, to find her.

Nothing on earth could have made her betray her fears to the servants, whom she saw as nothing more than tools, so she sat with apparent calm, concealing the raging anxiety in her heart, watching the preparations for this new departure as if it did not concern her. She watched the man who held the horses hand them over to the coachman, before setting off at a tranquil pace with the brougham, back in the direction of Florence. Then the berlin itself moved off slowly, driving back up the track between the ruins to the road. It was this road which had dragged Marianne out of her state of apathy.

Instead of heading straight for the red disc of the setting sun, now about to sink behind the city's campaniles, so as to skirt the town and come out on the Lucca road, the heavy coach was continuing eastward in the same direction as that taken by the brougham a little earlier. They were making for the Adriatic, in quite the opposite direction from Lucca. It might, of course, be a ruse intended to throw pursuers off the scent, but Marianne could not help risking an oblique question.

'If you are my husband's people,' she observed coldly, 'you must be taking me to him. Yet you are taking the wrong road.'

Without deviating from a politeness which, however necessary, Marianne was beginning to find overdone, the black man answered in the same oily voice :

'Many roads lead to the master, Excellenza. One has only to know which way to choose. His highness does not always reside at the Villa dei Cavalli. We are going to another of his estates, so please your ladyship.'

Marianne was chilled by the irony in the last words. It did not please her in the slightest, but what choice had she? A cold sweat prickled unpleasantly at the roots of her hair and she felt the colour drain from her face. Her slender hope that Jolival and Arrighi would find her evaporated. She had known, of course, from Donna Lavinia, that her husband did not live at Lucca all the time but was sometimes found at his other properties. To which was she now being taken? And how could her friends discover her there when she herself did not know the first thing about these places?

By not listening to the reading of the marriage contract on her wedding night, she had lost a good opportunity of learning ... but that was only one of so many opportunities already lost in the course of her short life. The best and greatest of all had been at Selton Hall when Jason had asked her to fly with him; the second in Paris when she had refused once more to go with him.

At the thought of Jason, grief threatened to overwhelm her and she became a prey to bitter depression. This time fate was against her, and nothing and nobody was going to come and put a spoke in its wheel on her behalf.

Her husband's was to be the last word. The little hope that remained to her now was all in her own charm and intelligence, in the kindness of Donna Lavinia who was always near the Prince and who at least would plead for her, and perhaps in the occurrence of some chance to escape. If such a chance did present itself, Marianne was, of course, fully determined to grasp it and to use it, to the best of her ability. It would not be the first escape she had contrived.

She recalled with some pleasure and no little pride her escape from Morvan the Wrecker, and, more recently, from the barn at Mortefontaine. Luck had been with her both times, but even so she had not managed so badly!

Her need to find Jason, a deep, visceral longing which came from the inmost parts of her being to fill her heart and brain, would act as a stimulant, supposing any were needed beyond her own passionate desire for freedom.

Besides ... she might be wrong: there might be no need to torment herself about Sant'Anna's plans for her. All her fears stemmed from Eleonora Sullivan's hair-raising confidences and from the drama surrounding this abduction, but she had to admit that she had left her invisible husband little alternative. Perhaps, after all, he would be merciful, understanding ...

To boost her courage, Marianne went over in her mind the moment when Corrado Sant'Anna had rescued her from Matteo Damiani, on that dreadful night in the little temple. She had almost died of fright when she saw him burst from the shadows, a dark, ghostly figure masked in pale leather and mounted on the plunging white shape of his horse, Ilderim. And yet this terrifying apparition had brought rescue and life.

Afterwards, too, he had tended her with a solicitude that might easily have suggested love. Suppose he did love her ... No, better not to think of that, but make her mind a blank and so try to recover a little calm, a little peace.

Yet, in spite of herself, her thoughts would keep turning to the enigmatic figure of her unknown husband, caught between fear and a queer uncontrollable curiosity. Perhaps this time she would penetrate the secret of the white mask ...

The coach was still travelling into the oncoming dark. Soon enveloping darkness lay all around, and the coach pressed on through the mountains, from stage to stage, on its journey to the end of the night.

Marianne slept at last, exhausted, after refusing the food

offered her by Giuseppe – for this she learned was her kidnapper's name. She was in too much anguish of mind to swallow a bite.

Daylight woke her, and the sudden jolt as the berlin pulled up for fresh horses outside a small hostelry smothered in vines and climbing plants. They were on a hillside at the top of which a little red-walled town clustered round a squat castle, its towers almost hidden behind the red roofs. The sun revealed a landscape of neat rectangular fields, intersected by irrigation ditches on the banks of which a variety of fruit trees served to support great swags of vines, while far in the distance, beyond a broad band of darker green, a sheet of silvery blue spread to the horizon. The sea.

Giuseppe, who had got out when the coach stopped, now poked his head in the door.

'If your ladyship cares to descend for refreshment, I should be happy to be your escort.'

'Escort me? It does not occur to you, I suppose, that I might prefer to be alone? I wish, yes, I wish to restore my appearance a little. Surely you must see that I am covered with dust?'

'There is a room in the house where your ladyship may retire for that purpose. I shall be satisfied to remain outside. The window is very small.'

'In other words, I am a prisoner! Hadn't you better admit it openly?'

Giuseppe bowed with exaggerated courtesy.

'A prisoner? There's a nice word for a lady in the care of a devoted servant! My duty is merely to see that you reach your destination safely, and it's for that reason only that I have orders not to leave you for any cause whatsoever.'

'Suppose I shout and scream?' Marianne exclaimed with exasperation. 'What will you do then, master gaoler?'

'I should not advise it, Excellenza. In the event of any shouts and screams my orders are clear ... and far from pleasant.'

Marianne was outraged to see the black muzzle of a pistol gleaming in her so-called servant's plump hand.

Giuseppe gave her a moment to ponder this before tucking the weapon back unconcernedly in his waistband.

'In any case,' he went on, 'screaming will do no good. This place belongs to his highness. The people would not understand why the Princess should be calling for help against the Prince.'

Giuseppe's face was as bland as ever but Marianne knew from the cruel glint in his eye that he would not hesitate to kill her in cold blood in the event of a struggle.

Beaten, if not resigned, she decided that for the present her best course was to submit. For all the undoubted comfort of the coach, her body ached from the bad roads and she was longing to stretch her legs.

With Giuseppe, in his role of faithful family servant, close behind her, Marianne went inside the house. A peasant girl in a red petticoat and bright blue kerchief made her best curtsy, and later, when Marianne had withdrawn for a moment to the room he had mentioned, to wash and comb her hair, the girl brought her brown bread, cheese, olives and onions, and sheep's milk, on all of which the traveller fell hungrily. Her refusal of food the night before had been largely a gesture of bravado, mixed with sheer temper, but had been foolish because she needed all her strength. Now, in the fresh morning air, she discovered that she was famished.

Meanwhile fresh horses had been harnessed, and as soon as the Princess declared herself ready the coach resumed its way down to a low, level plain which seemed to go on for ever.

Strengthened and refreshed, Marianne elected to wrap herself once more in lofty silence, despite the questions which burned on her lips. In any case, she had no doubt that she would soon arrive at her destination, when her questions would be answered. They were heading straight towards the sea, without turning aside to right or left, so that the place they were making for must be on the coast.

At about midday they came to a large fishing village, its low houses clustered along the banks of a sandy watercourse. After the cool shade of the thick belt of pines through which they had just passed, with its tall dark wide-spreading trees, the heat seemed much greater than it really was and the village more forsaken.

Here was a realm of sand. As far as the eye could see, the shore was a vast sandy beach, patched here and there with clumps of marram grass, while the village itself, with its crumbling watch-tower and occasional fragments of Roman wall, might have emerged directly from the encroaching sands.

Alongside the houses, great nets hung drying on poles in the still air, like giant dragonflies, and a handful of boats lay at anchor in the canal which served as a harbour. The largest and smartest of these was a slender tartane. A sailor in a stocking cap was busy setting the red and black sails.

The berlin drew up on the edge of the water and the fisherman beckoned with a sweep of his arm. Once again, Giuseppe invited Marianne to descend.

'Have we arrived?' she asked.

'We have reached the port, Excellenza, but not the end of our journey. The second stage is by sea.'

Amazement, alarm and anger were stronger than Marianne's pride.

'By sea?' she cried. 'Where are we going? Do your orders include keeping me in ignorance?'

'By no means, Excellenza, by no means,' Giuseppe responded, bowing. 'We are going to Venice. This way the journey involves less discomfort.'

'To Ve—'

In other circumstances Marianne might well have laughed at the way the jewel of the Adriatic seemed to have the lodestone drawing all and sundry. It was certainly important to Napoleon that she should take ship from Venice, even if his reason had been partly kindness, and now here was the Prince, her husband, also selecting Venice as the place in which to make his wishes known to her! But for the nameless dread which hung over her, it would have been funny.

She got out and took a few turns beside the water to calm herself. The little sand-locked harbour was lapped in a profound peace. In the absence of a wind, nothing stirred, and everything in the village seemed asleep except for the sound of the cicadas. Apart from the fisherman who had jumped ashore to meet the travellers, there was not another human being in sight.

'They are having a siesta and waiting for a wind,' Giuseppe remarked. 'They will come out in the evening. All the same, we shall go aboard at once to allow your highness to settle in.'

He preceded Marianne across the plank joining ship to shore and helped her over the swaying bridge with all the respect of the perfect servant, while the coachman and the other servant bowed and turned back to the coach, which soon vanished with them into the pines.

To any casual observer, the Princess Sant'Anna would have presented the total appearance of a great lady travelling peacefully. The casual observer, however, would not have known that the devoted servant carried a large pistol in his belt, and that this pistol was not intended for possible highway robbers but for his mistress, should she take it into her head to resist.

For the moment, though, the only observer was the fisherman. Yet Marianne caught his eye as she stepped aboard, and the look of admiration it held. He was standing by the gangway, watching her come aboard with the wondering expression usually associated with supernatural visions, and he was still in his daze a good minute later.

Marianne studied him in her turn without appearing to, and her examination led her to some interesting conclusions. Although not tall, the fisherman was a fine figure of a man, with the head of a Raphael painting on the body of the Farnese Hercules. His yellow canvas shirt was open to the waist, revealing muscles which seemed carved in bronze. His lips were full, his eyes dark and brilliant, and the hair that curled thickly from under his tilted red stocking cap was black as jet.

Appraising him, Marianne caught herself thinking that Giuseppe's plump and oily person would be no match for such a man in a fight.

As she settled herself in the cubby-hole prepared for her in the stern of the boat, Marianne's imagination was busy picturing the advantages which, with a little ingenuity, might be gained from the handsome fisherman. It should not be hard to twist him round her finger. Then he might be persuaded to overpower Giuseppe and afterwards land Marianne herself at some point on the coast whence she might seek a hiding place and get a message to Jolival, or make her way back to Florence. Besides, if he too was in the Prince's service, it ought to be possible to win his allegiance by using her status as the Prince's wife.

It certainly looked as though Giuseppe was taking a vast deal of trouble to preserve appearances. The fisherman must be aware that his lovely passenger was nothing more nor less than a prisoner on her way to judgement ... and looking forward to it with less and less enthusiasm.

The truth was that if her natural honesty and courage urged her to a confrontation and a final settling of accounts, her pride could not brook the thought of being dragged to it by force and appearing before Sant'Anna in this humiliating state.

The tartane was not built to carry passengers, especially women, but a kind of berth had been fitted up for Marianne, where she could be comfortable enough. There was a straw mattress and a few crude toilet articles of rough earthenware. The handsome fisherman brought her a rug and she smiled at him, well aware of the devastating effects of that smile. This time it was instantaneous. The tanned face seemed to light up from within and the young man stood stock still, clutching the blanket to his chest, quite forgetting to give it to her.

Encouraged by this success, she asked softly:

'What is your name?'

'Jacopo, Excellenza,' Giuseppe broke in quickly. 'But you will find it a waste of time to talk to him. The poor fellow is deaf and almost dumb. It takes practice to make oneself understood, but if your highness desires speech with him I will interpret for you ...'

'I thank you, no,' Marianne said quickly. Then she added, more softly, and this time perfectly sincerely:

'Poor boy. What a shame ...'

Compassion came to her aid and helped to hide the disappointment she felt. She understood now the odious Giuseppe's apparent carelessness in embarking alone with his prisoner on board a ship whose single crewman seemed to be so susceptible to feminine charms. In fact, if he was the only person able to communicate with Jacopo, then it was exceedingly well contrived. But the man had not done speaking.

'You need not pity him too much, Excellenza. He has a house, a boat and is affianced to a pretty girl . . . and he has the sea. He would not exchange these for any more risky adventures.'

The warning was clear and told Marianne that her winsome smile had not gone unnoticed. It was better not to try anything risky, which would certainly be doomed to failure. Another round to the enemy.

Angry, tired and on the verge of tears, the unwilling passenger sat down on her mattress and tried to make her mind a blank. No point in brooding over one defeat : better to get some rest and then look for some other way of escaping from a husband who, she could not help fearing, had no intention of letting her go so soon – always supposing he had no worse punishment in mind for her.

She closed her eyes, obliging Giuseppe to withdraw. A slight breeze had sprung up and through her half-closed lids she saw him telling Jacopo, with a wide range of gestures, to hoist sail. The boat slipped down the canal and slowly out to sea.

Except for a slight squall which got up during the night, the crossing was uneventful, but late the following afternoon, as a pink line appeared, hovering capriciously, like a lacy scarf flung around the neck of the sea, on the bluish horizon, Jacopo began taking in sail.

As they advanced, the mirage seemed to fade and gave place to a long, low island, beyond which it looked as if there were nothing but a green desert. It was a dismal enough isle, bare but for a few trees, and made up for the most part of a long fringe of sand. The boat drew nearer, sailed along the shore for a little way and then, as the beach seemed to turn inland in a kind of channel, hove to and dropped anchor.

Marianne leaned on the rail, striving to recapture the mirage of a moment past. The island was hiding it from her, she knew. Their anchoring had taken her by surprise.

'Why have we stopped?' she asked. 'What are we doing here?'

'By your leave,' Giuseppe said, 'we shall wait until nightfall before we enter harbour. The Venetians are an inquisitive race and his highness wishes your arrival to be as private as possible. We shall cross the Lido channel as soon as it grows dark. Luckily moonrise is late tonight.'

'My husband wishes my arrival to be private? Don't you mean *secret*, perhaps?'

'Surely they are the same thing?'

'Not to me! I dislike secrets between husband and wife! My husband seems very fond of them.'

She was frightened now and trying to hide it. The terror she had felt when she realized that she was in the Prince's power returned, irresistibly, despite all her efforts to fight it off during the journey. Giuseppe's words, his ingratiating, would-be reassuring smile, even the reasons he gave her, all added to her fears. Why all these precautions? Why this furtive arrival, if all that awaited her was a simple calling to account, unless she were condemned in advance? She could no longer fight off the thought that what she was to find at the end of this watery journey was a death sentence, summary execution in the depths of some cellar – those Venetian cellars which must have such easy access to the water. If that were so, then who would ever know? Who would even find her body? She had heard often enough that the Sant'Annas held the lives of their womenfolk cheaply!

All at once, unreasoning panic swept over Marianne, naked, primitive and old as death. To perish here, in this city which had figured in her dreams for so many months as the magical place where her happiness was to begin, to die in Venice, where love was said to reign supreme! What a grim jest of Fate! When Jason's ship entered the lagoon, he might sail, all unwittingly, over the very place where her body lay disintegrating slowly . . .

Appalled by this hideous vision, she flung herself forward in an almost convulsive movement, intending to jump overboard from the prow. This fishing boat carried her death, she knew that, she could feel it! All she wanted was to get away from it.

Even as she was about to plunge over the side, she was caught and held roughly by an irresistible force. Arms were round her body and she found herself held fast, in total impotence, against the broad chest of the fisherman, Jacopo.

'Tut, tut!' said Giuseppe's voice softly. 'How very childish! Does your ladyship seek to leave us? Where would you go?

There is nothing here but grass and sand and water ... whereas a luxurious palace awaits you ...'

'Let me go!' she moaned, struggling with all her strength, her jaws grimly clenched to keep her teeth from chattering. 'Why should you care? You can say I hurled myself into the water – that I am dead! Only let me off this boat! I'll give you anything you want! I am rich—'

'But not so rich as his highness ... and much less powerful. My life is a poor thing, Excellenza, but important to me. I do not want to lose it. And I am bound to answer with my life for your ladyship's safe arrival!'

'This is absurd! We are not living in the Middle Ages!'

'Here, in certain houses, we are,' Giuseppe said, suddenly grave. 'I know your ladyship is going to mention the Emperor Napoleon. I was warned of that. But this is Venice, and the Emperor's power is exercised lightly and with discretion. So, be sensible ...'

Marianne was sobbing now, still held fast in Jacopo's arms, her spirit broken and her resistance at an end. She was not even conscious of the absurdity of crying in the arms of a perfect stranger: she merely leaned against him as she might have done a wall, with one thought only in her mind: everything was finished. Now nothing could prevent the Prince from wreaking what vengeance he liked on her. She had only herself to rely on, and that was little enough.

Yet at the same time, she was aware of something odd happening. Jacopo's arms were little by little tightening round her and his breath was growing shorter. The young man's body, pressed against her, was beginning to tremble. She felt one hand move surreptitiously upwards from her waist, seeking the curve of her breast ...

Suddenly it was borne in on her that the fisherman was trying to take advantage of the situation, while Giuseppe had moved a yard or two away and was waiting, with an air of boredom, for her to dry her tears.

The fisherman's caress acted on her like a tonic, restoring her courage. If this man's desire for her was strong enough to make him take such an insane risk right underneath Giuseppe's nose, then he might be prepared to take still more risks for the promise of another reward.

Therefore, instead of slapping Jacopo's face, as she would have liked to do, she pressed herself more closely against him. Then, making sure that Giuseppe was not looking, reached up on tiptoe and brushed the boy's lips swiftly with her own. It was only an instant, then she pushed him away, at the same time gazing into his eyes with an expression of earnest entreaty.

As she moved away he watched her with a kind of desperation, evidently struggling to understand what it was she wanted of him, but Marianne had no means of expressing her wish. How could she convey to him by gestures that she wanted him to knock Giuseppe down and tie him up securely, when Giuseppe was at that moment moving towards them? A hundred times in the course of the last twenty-four hours she had hoped to find some implement on the boat which might have enabled her to do the thing herself. After that, to reduce Jacopo to a state of total obedience would no doubt have been child's play. But the servant was no fool and took care of himself. Nothing was left lying about on board that might have served as a weapon, and he scarcely ever let Marianne out of his sight. He had not closed his eyes all night.

Now was there anything within reach that could be used to write with? It was not even possible to scratch a message to the fisherman on the side of the boat, asking for help. Besides, he probably could not read.

Daylight faded and still Marianne had found no way of communicating with her unusual admirer. For an hour or more, Giuseppe sat on a heap of ropes between the two of them, turning his pistol round and round in his hands, as though he guessed the threat which hung over him. Any attempt would certainly have proved fatal to both.

With a sinking heart, Marianne watched as the anchor was hauled up and the tartane slipped out into the channel in the dusk. In spite of the terror which gripped her, she could not help a gasp of wonder, for the skyline had been transformed into a fantastic fresco of blue and violet colours, intermingled with

lingering traces of red gold. It was like a fantastically ornamented crown lying on the sea, but a crown already fading into
the dark.

Night fell quickly and by the time the tartane had rounded
the Isola di San Giorgio and entered the Canale della Giudecca
the darkness was almost complete. She sailed close-reefed, feeling her way, seeking perhaps to attract as little attention as
possible. Marianne held her breath. She felt Venice closing
round her like a clenching hand, and gazed with painful longing
at the tall ships which, once past the white columns and gilded
Fortune of the Dogana di Mare, rode sleepily with riding lights
aglow, off the airy domes and alabaster volutes of la Salute,
awaiting for tomorrows of salt winds to carry them far from
this perilous siren of water and stones.

The little vessel tied up away from the quay, beside a group
of fishing boats, and when Giuseppe momentarily turned his
back at last to lean over the side, Marianne seized the opportunity to move quickly to where Jacopo was furling the sails
and lay her hand on his arm. He trembled and looked at her then,
dropping the sails, made as if to draw her to him.

She shook her head gently and with a fierce movement of her
arm towards Giuseppe's back, endeavoured to make him understand that she wanted to be rid of him . . . at once!

She saw Jacopo stiffen and glance first at the man whom he
no doubt considered his master, then at the woman tempting
him. He hesitated, clearly torn between conscience and desire . . .
His hesitation lasted a moment too long, for already Giuseppe
had turned and was making his way back to Marianne.

'If your ladyship pleases,' he murmured, 'the gondola waits
and we should not delay.'

There were two more heads visible now over the side of the
boat. The gondola must be close alongside the tartane and it
was too late : Giuseppe had allies.

With a scornful shrug, Marianne turned her back on the
young sailor. She had completely lost interest in him now, although a moment before she had been ready to give herself to
him as the price of her freedom, with no more hesitation than
St Mary the Egyptian to the boatmen she had need of.

A slim black gondola lay waiting alongside. Escorted by Giuseppe, and without a single backward glance at the tartane, Marianne took her place in the *felze*, a kind of curtained black box in which the passengers sat on something like a low, broad sofa. Then, sped by long oars, the gondola slid over the black waters. It nosed its way into a narrow canal beside the church of la Salute, whose golden cross still watched silently over the health of Venice as it had done ever since the great plague in the seventeenth century.

Giuseppe bent forward as though to draw the black leather curtain.

'What are you afraid of?' Marianne asked with contempt. 'I do not know this city and no one here knows me. Let me look, at least!'

Giuseppe hesitated for a moment before sighing resignedly and resuming his seat beside her, leaving the curtains as they were.

The gondola turned into the Grand Canal and now Marianne saw that the splendid ghost was indeed a living city. Lights shone in palace windows, driving back the darkness here and there and making the water sparkle with reflections of spangled gold. Sounds of voices and music floated out of open windows, filling the soft May night. A tall gothic palace was ashimmer with light, and a waltz tune sounded above a garden which dripped luxuriant greenery into the canal. A cluster of moored gondolas danced to the rhythm of the violins below the steps of a noble stair which seemed to rise from the very depths of the waves.

Huddled in her dark retreat, Giuseppe's prisoner saw women in brilliant gowns and well-dressed men mingling with uniforms of every colour, the white of Austria prominent among them. She could almost smell the scents and hear the bursts of laughter. A party! ... Life, joy ... Then, suddenly, all was gone again and there was only the darkness and a vague musty smell. The gondola had turned aside abruptly into a little cut walled in by blind house walls.

As in a bad dream, Marianne glimpsed barred windows, emblazoned doorways, and now and then walls with crumbling plasterwork, as well as graceful arched bridges under which the gondola glided like a ghost.

At last they came to a small landing-stage below a red wall topped with black ivy, in which was the ornately carved lintel of a little stone doorway framed by a pair of barbaric wrought-iron lanterns.

The fragile craft came to a halt and Marianne knew that this time it was really the end of the journey, and her heart missed a beat. She had come again to the house of the Prince Sant'Anna.

But on this occasion no servant waited on the green-stained steps leading down to the water, or in the slip of a garden where plants sprang thickly round the ancient carved-stone well, as though out of the very stones. Nor was there anyone on the handsome stairway which led up to the slender pillars of a gothic gallery, at the back of which the red and blue glass of a lighted window shone like jewels. But for that light, the palace might have been deserted.

Yet, as she climbed the stone steps, Marianne found all her courage and fighting spirit come flooding back. As always with her, the imminent prospect of danger galvanized her and restored the equilibrium which waiting and uncertainty invariably drained away. She knew, could feel, with an almost animal instinct she had, that danger lurked behind the delicate old-world graces of that building, even if it were no more than the horrible memory of Lucinda the Witch, whose house this might once have been. For, if Marianne's recollections were correct, this must be the Palazzo Soranzo, the birthplace of that terrible princess. She nerved herself for the fight.

The vestibule which opened before her was so sumptuous as to take her breath away. Great gilded lanterns of exquisite workmanship, which must have originated in some ancient galley, threw moving patterns on the many-coloured marble floors, flowery as a Persian garden, and on the gilding of a ceiling with long, painted beams. The walls were covered with a succession of vast portraits and lined with imposing armorial benches, alternating with porphyry chests where miniature caravels spread their sails. The portraits were all of men and women dressed with unbelievable magnificence. There were even two of doges in full dress, the *corno d'oro* on their heads, pride in their faces.

The seafaring associations of the gallery were plain and Marianne was surprised to catch herself thinking that Jason or Surcouf might have liked this house, so dedicated to the sea. Alas, it was as silent as a tomb.

There was not a sound to be heard except the newcomers' own footsteps. In a little while this had become so ominous that even Giuseppe seemed aware of it. He coughed, as though to reassure himself, and then, going to a double door about halfway along the gallery, he whispered, as though in church:

'My mission ends here, Excellenza. May I hope that your ladyship will not think too hardly of me?'

'And of this charming journey? Rest assured, my friend, that I shall dwell on it with the greatest of pleasure – supposing I have the time to dwell on anything, that is!' Marianne spoke with bitter irony.

Giuseppe bowed without answering and withdrew. Yet the double doors were opening, creaking a little but to all appearances without human aid.

Beyond lay a room of impressive dimensions, in the centre of which was a table laid for a meal, with an almost unbelievable magnificence. It was like a field of gold: plates and dishes of chased gold, enamelled goblets, jewelled flagons, the whole adorned with wonderful purplish roses, and tall branched candlesticks spreading their burden of lighted candles gracefully over this almost barbaric splendour, while outside the ring of light the walls hung with antique tapestries and the priceless carved chimneypiece lay in deep shadow.

It was a table set for a banquet, and yet Marianne shivered as she saw that it was set with only two places. So . . . the Prince had decided to show himself at last? What else could be the meaning of those two places? Was she to see him, at last, as he was, hideous as that reality might be? Or would he still wear his white mask when he came to take his seat here?

Despite herself, she felt fear clawing at her heart. She knew now that however much her natural curiosity might urge her to

penetrate the mystery with which her strange husband surrounded himself, since that night of magic she had always feared,
instinctively, to find herself alone and face to face with him. Yet
surely that table, with its flowers, could not portend anything
so very terrible! It was a table laid to please, almost a table
for lovers.

The double doors through which Marianne had entered closed
with the same creaking. At the same time another door, a little,
low one at the side of the hearth, opened slowly, very slowly,
as though at some well-timed dramatic highlight in the theatre.

Marianne stood rooted to the spot, her eyes wide and her
fingers tensed, sweat starting on her brow, watching it as it
swung on its hinges, so much as she might have stared at the
door of a tomb about to deliver up its dead.

A glittering figure appeared in silhouette, too far from the
table to be seen clearly. Lit only from behind, by the light in the
next room, it was the figure of a stockily-built man dressed in a
long robe of cloth of gold. But Marianne saw at once that it
was not the slender figure of the man who had mastered Ilderim.
This man was shorter, heavier, less noble. He came forward into
the huge dining-room and then, with anger and disbelief, Marianne saw Matteo Damiani, dressed like a doge, step forward into
the pool of light surrounding the table.

He was smiling . . .

Chapter Three
Slaves of the Devil

Prince Sant'Anna's steward and trusted agent advanced with measured tread, hands folded in the wide sleeves of his dalmatic, and coming to one of the tall, red chairs drawn up to the table laid one beringed hand on its back while with the other he made what was intended as a gracious gesture towards the remaining place. The smile was like a mask affixed to his face.

'Be seated, I beg, and let us eat. You must be tired after the long journey.'

For a moment it seemed to Marianne that her eyes and ears must be deceiving her but it was not long before she knew that this was no evil dream.

The man who stood before her was indeed Matteo Damiani, the dangerous and untrustworthy servant who, on one night of horror, had almost been her murderer.

She had not seen him since that dreadful moment when he came towards her, hands outstretched, like a man in a trance, with murder in his eyes from which all human feeling had gone. But for the appearance of Ilderim and his tragic rider—

But at that fearful recollection, Marianne's fear very nearly became panic. She had to make a superhuman effort to fight it off and even to succeed in concealing what she felt. With such a man, whose frightening past history she knew, her one chance of escape lay precisely in not letting him see her terror of him. If he once knew she feared him, her instinct told her, she was lost.

Even now she still did not understand what had happened, or by what species of magic Damiani was able to parade himself like this, dressed up as a doge (she had seen the same costume on one of the portraits in the hall), in a Venetian palace where he gave himself all the airs of being master, but this was no time to indulge in speculation.

Instinctively, she attacked.

Folding her arms coolly, she eyed him with unconcealed scorn. Her eyes narrowed to glittering green slits between the long lashes.

'Does carnival in Venice continue into May?' she asked bluntly. 'Or are you going to a masquerade?'

Taken unawares, perhaps, by the sarcastic tone, Damiani gave a short laugh but, unprepared for an attack in this direction, he glanced uncertainly, almost with a shade of embarrassment, at his costume.

'Oh, the gown? I donned it in your honour, madame, just as I had this table set for your pleasure, to make your arrival in this house a celebration. I thought—'

'I?' Marianne broke in. 'I do not think I can have heard you correctly, or you so far forget yourself as to put yourself in your master's place. Recollect yourself, my friend. And tell me where is the Prince? And how comes it that Dona Lavinia is not here to welcome me?'

The steward drew out the chair before him and sank into it so heavily that it groaned under his weight. He had put on flesh since that terrible night when, maddened by his occult practices, he had attempted in his rage to kill Marianne. The Roman mask, which had then lent his face a certain distinction, was now melted into fat, and his hair, once so thick, was thinning alarmingly, while the fingers loaded with such vulgar profusion of rings had become like bloated sausages. But there was nothing in the least laughable or absurd about the pale, impudent eyes in that fat, ageing body.

'Eyes like a snake,' Marianne thought with a shiver of revulsion at the cold cruelty they revealed.

The smile had faded, as if Matteo no longer considered it worth while to maintain the fiction. Marianne knew that the man before her was her implacable enemy, and it came as no surprise to her to hear him say:

'That fool Lavinia! Pray for her, if you like. Myself, I had enough of her lectures and her pious airs – I—'

'You killed her?' Marianne exclaimed furiously, conscious of both outrage and a wave of grief as bitter as it was unexpected. She had not known that she had allowed the quiet housekeeper become so dear to her. 'You were base enough to murder that good woman who never did anyone any harm? And the Prince did not shoot you dead like the mad dog you are?'

'He might have done so,' Damiani growled, 'had he been in a position to.' He started to his feet with a violence that set the heavily laden table rocking and the golden vessels clinking. 'I did away with him first. It was time,' he added, thumping the table with his fist to emphasize his words, 'high time I took my rightful place as head of the family!'

This time, the blow went home, with such force that Marianne reeled as though she had been struck, and uttered a moan of horror.

Dead! Her strange husband was dead! The prince in the white mask, dead! Dead, the man who on that stormy night had taken her trembling hand in his, dead, the wonderful horseman whom even from the depths of her fear and uncertainty, she had admired! It was not possible! Fate could not deal her such a scurvy trick.

'You're lying,' she said in a voice that was firm, though drained of all expression.

'Why should I? Because he was the master and I the slave? Because he forced on me a life of humiliation, servile and unworthy of me? Can you tell me any good reason why I should not have done away with the puppet? I did not hesitate to kill his father because he slew the woman I loved! Why should I spare him who was the prime cause of that deed? Until I was ready, I let him live, so long as he did not get in my way. Then, a little while ago, he did get in my way.'

A dreadful feeling of horror and revulsion, mingled with a sense of disappointment and, strangely, with pity and grief also, was creeping over Marianne. It was absurd, grotesque and profoundly unfair. The man who had voluntarily offered his name to a stranger pregnant by another man, whether emperor or no, the man who had made her welcome, heaped riches and jewels on her, and even saved her life – he did not deserve to die at the hands of a sadistic madman.

For a moment she saw again, clear in the unfailing record of her memory, the shapes of the great white stallion and his silent rider flying through the shadowy park. Whatever the man's secret shame, at that moment he and the animal had made an extraordinarily beautiful picture, a combination of power and grace which had remained graven in her mind. The thought that this unforgettable picture had been destroyed for ever by a creature so sunk in evil and depravity seemed to her so intolerable that her hand went out instinctively to feel for a weapon with which to deal justice on the murderer then and there. She owed it to one who had perhaps loved her and from whom, she knew now, she had never had anything to fear. Who could tell whether he had not paid with his life for his intervention that night?

But the dainty gold knives that gleamed on the table offered no help. For the present, the Princess Sant'Anna had nothing but words with which to flay the villain, and words could have little power over such as he. Yet a time would come. To that Marianne swore a solemn oath in her heart. She would avenge her husband.

'Murderer!' she spat at him at last, with utter distaste. 'You dared to slay the man who trusted you, one who placed himself so unreservedly in your hands, your own master!'

'I am the only master here now!' Damiani cried in a curiously falsetto voice. 'Justice has come full circle, because I had far more right to the title than that pitiable dreamer! You poor fool, you do not know, let that excuse you,' he added, with a complacency that added the last straw to Marianne's indignation, 'but I too am a Sant'Anna! I am—'

'I know everything! And the fact that my husband's grandfather got a child on a poor, half-mad creature who could not fight for her honour is not enough to make you a Sant'Anna! You need a heart, a soul, class! You, you are a low thing unworthy even of the knife that will kill you, a stinking animal—'

'Enough!'

The word was roared out in a paroxysm of rage and the man's congested face had turned white with evil marks of venom, but the blow had gone home, as Marianne saw with satisfaction.

He was breathing hard, as though he had been running, and when he spoke again it was in a low, muffled tone, like one suffocating.

'Enough,' he repeated. 'Who told you this? How – how do you know?'

'That is my business! It is enough that I know.'

'No! You will tell me – one day, you will have to tell me. I shall make you talk – because you will obey me now. Me, do you hear?'

'You are out of your mind. Why should I obey you?'

An ugly smile slid, like a slick of oil, across the ravaged features. Marianne braced herself for a foul answer. But Matteo Damiani's anger evaporated as suddenly as it had come. His voice resumed its normal tone and sounded neutral to the point of indifference as he went on :

'I beg your pardon. I lost my temper. But there are things I do not care to speak of.'

'I dare say, but that does not tell me what I am doing here. If I have understood you correctly, then it would seem that I am a – a free woman, and I'd be glad if you would conclude this pointless interview and arrange for me to leave this house.'

'By no means. You don't think I took all that trouble to bring you here, which cost me a great deal of money, besides all the business of bribing agents, even among your own friends, simply for the doubtful pleasure of informing you that your husband was no more?'

'Why not? I can't exactly see you writing me a letter telling me you'd murdered the Prince. For that is what you did, isn't it?'

Damiani did not answer. He plucked a rose from the centre vase and began twisting it nervously between his fingers, as though seeking inspiration. Abruptly, he spoke.

'Let us understand one another, Princess,' he said in the dry voice of a lawyer addressing a client. 'You are here to fulfil a contract. The same contract that you made with Corrado Sant' Anna.'

'What contract? If the Prince is dead, then the only contract which existed, that concerning my marriage, is null and void, surely?'

'No. You were married in exchange for a child, an heir to the name and fortunes of the Sant'Annas.'

'I lost the child, accidentally!' Marianne cried, with a sharp pang of anxiety beyond her control, for the subject was still a painful one.

'I am not disputing the accident and I am sure it was no fault of yours. All Europe knows of the tragedy of the Austrian ambassador's ball, but as regards the Sant'Anna heir, your obligations remain. You must give birth to a child who may, officially, carry on the line.'

'You might have thought of that before you killed the Prince.'

'Why? He was useless in that line; your own marriage is the best proof of that. Unfortunately I am not myself in a position to assume publicly the name which is mine by right. Therefore, I need a Sant'Anna, an heir . . .'

Marianne seethed with anger, hearing him speak with such cynical detachment of the master he had killed, while at the same time she was becoming aware of an indefinable fear. Perhaps because she was afraid to let herself understand, she fell back on sarcasm.

'There is only one thing you have forgotten. The child was the Emperor's. I don't suppose you'd go so far as to kidnap his majesty and bring him to me, bound hand and foot . . .'

Damiani shook his head and began to move towards her. Marianne stepped back.

'No. We must do without the imperial blood which meant so much to the Prince. We'll make do with the family blood for this child – a child I'll bring up as I please and whose lands I'll administer gladly for many long years – a child who will be all the more dear to me because he'll be my own!'

'What!'

'Don't look so surprised. You understand well enough. You called me a low thing just now, madame, but no insults can wipe out, or even humble such blood as mine. Like it or not, I am the old Prince's son, and uncle to the poor fool you married.

And so, Princess, it is I, your steward, who will give you a child.'

Choked by such effrontery, it was a moment or two before Marianne was able to speak. She had been wrong in her first estimate. This man was nothing but a dangerous lunatic. It was enough to see his fat fingers working, and the way he licked his lips with the tip of his tongue, like a cat. He was a madman, ready to commit any crime to slake his overwhelming pride and ambition, and to satisfy his baser instincts!

She was suddenly very conscious that she was alone with this man. He was stronger than she and must no doubt have accomplices hidden somewhere about this too-silent house, if only the loathsome Giuseppe. She was in his power. He could force her. Her one chance might be to frighten him.

'If you think for a moment, you will see that you could never carry out this insane plan. I have come back to Italy under the Emperor's especial protection for a purpose which I may not disclose to you. But you may be quite sure that there are people looking for me, concerned about me at this very moment. Soon the Emperor will be told. Do you think you can fool him if I vanish for several months and then turn up with an unaccountable baby? It is plain you do not know him, and if I were you I should think twice before making such an enemy.'

'Far be it from me to underestimate the power of Napoleon. But it will all be very much simpler than you seem to think. In a little while the Emperor will receive a letter from the Prince Sant'Anna thanking him warmly for restoring to him a wife who is now infinitely dear to his heart and announcing their imminent departure together to spend a delightful and long-deferred honeymoon on distant estates of his.'

'And you expect him to swallow that? He knows all about the strange circumstances attending my marriage. Be sure he will have inquiries made, and, however remote our supposed destination, the Emperor will get at the truth. He had his suspicions about what awaited me here—'

'Maybe, but he will be obliged to rest content with what he is told. Especially as there will be a note, expressed, naturally, in glowing terms, assuring him of your happiness and begging forgiveness. I have paid, among other things, for the services of a very competent forger. Venice is seething with artists, most of them starving. Believe me, the Emperor will understand. You are lovely enough to explain away any folly, even my own at this moment. The simplest thing, of course, would be simply to kill you and then, in a few months' time, produce a new-born infant, claiming that the mother died in childbed. With a little care, that should go off without a hitch. But I have desired you, ever since the day that old dodderer of a cardinal brought you to the villa, desired you as I have never desired anyone before. That night, you may recall, I concealed myself in your closet while you undressed ... your body holds no secrets from my eyes, but my hands are still strangers to its curves. Ever since you went away I have lived in expectation of the moment which would bring you here – at my mercy. I shall get the child I want on your fair flesh ... It will be worth a little risk, eh? Even the risk of displeasing your Emperor. Before he finds you, if he ever does find you, I shall have known you tens of times and shall see my child growing in you! ... Then shall I be happy indeed!'

Slowly, he had resumed his advance towards her. His be-jewelled hands reached out, quivering, towards the girl's slender form. Revolted by the mere thought of their touch, she moved back into the shadows of the room, seeking desperately for some way of escape. But there was none : only the two doors already mentioned.

All the same, she made an effort to reach the one by which she had entered. It was just possible that it might not be locked, that if she moved fast she might be able to get out, even if she had to throw herself into the black waters of the cut. But her enemy had guessed her thought. He was laughing.

'The doors? They open only at my command! Do not count on them. You would break your pretty nails for nothing ... Come, lovely Marianne, use your common sense! Isn't it wiser to accept what you can't avoid, especially when you have every-thing to gain? Who is to say that by yielding to my desires you will not make of me your most devoted slave ... as Dona Lucinda once did? I know love – know it in all its ways, and it was she who taught me. If you cannot have happiness, you shall have pleasure—'

'Stay where you are! Don't touch me!'

She was frightened now, really frightened. The man was beside himself, past listening, or even hearing. He was coming for her mindlessly, inexorably, and there was something appalling in the machine-like tread and gleaming eyes.

Marianne retreated behind the table for shelter and her eye fell on a heavy gold salt-cellar standing near the centre-piece. It was a piece like a single carved gem, representing two nymphs embracing a statue of the god Pan : a genuine work of art and probably from the hand of the matchless Benvenuto Cellini. But to Marianne, at that moment, it had only one quality : it must be extremely heavy. She thrust out her hand and grabbed it and hurled it at her attacker.

He side-stepped in time and the salt-cellar flew past his ear and crashed on the black marble floor. The shot had missed but, giving her enemy no time to recover, Marianne had already got both hands round one of the heavy candlesticks, regardless of the pain as the hot wax spilled over her fingers.

'One step nearer and I'll hit you,' she threatened through clenched teeth.

He stood still as she commanded, but it was not from fear. He was not afraid of her; so much was clear from his salacious smile and quivering nostrils. On the contrary, he appeared to be enjoying the moment of violence as if it were a prelude to some voluptuous satisfaction. But he did not speak.

Instead, he raised his arms, the long sleeves slipping down to reveal broad golden armlets fit to have adorned a Carolingian prince, and clapped three times clearly, while Marianne stood speechless, still holding the candlestick ready to bring it down on him.

What followed happened very quickly. The candlestick was wrested from her hands and something black and stifling came down over her head while a hand forced her irresistibly backwards. Then she felt herself lifted by her feet and shoulders and borne away like a parcel.

It was not far, but to Marianne, carried up and down several times, half-suffocated, it seemed interminable. The cloth in which she was enveloped had a peculiar smell, of incense and jasmine combined with another, more exotic odour. She tried to struggle free of it but whoever was carrying her seemed to be unusually strong and her efforts only made them tighten the grip on her ankles painfully.

She felt them climb one more flight of steps and walk forward a little way. A door creaked. Finally, came the feel of soft cushions underneath her and almost at the same moment the light returned. Not before time: the stuff in which she had been muffled must have been remarkably thick, since no air had penetrated it.

She took a few deep breaths before sitting up and looking round to see who had brought her here. The sight that met her eyes was strange enough to make her wonder for a moment if she were dreaming. Three women stood a little way from the bed, eyeing her curiously, but three such women as Marianne had never seen before.

They were all very tall and dressed identically in dark blue draperies with a silver stripe and a multiplicity of bangles, and they were all three black as ebony and so alike that Marianne thought exhaustion must be making her eyes play tricks.

Then one woman moved away from the group and gliding like a ghost towards the open door vanished through it. Her bare feet made no sound on the black marble floor and, but for the silvery tinkle that accompanied her movements, Marianne might have believed her an apparition.

The other two, taking no further notice of her, began lighting a number of tall candles made of yellow wax which were set in large iron candle-holders ranged about the floor. Slowly, the details of the room began to emerge.

It was a very large room, and at the same time sumptuous and sinister. The tapestries hung from the stone walls were picked out in gold, yet the scenes they portrayed were of an almost unbearable violence and carnage. The furniture comprised an enormous oak chest, massively locked, and a selection of ebony chairs covered in red velvet, all suggesting a positively medieval degree of discomfort. A heavy lantern made of gilded bronze and red crystals hung from the beamed ceiling, but was unlighted.

The couch on which Marianne herself was lying was nothing less than an immense four-poster bed, big enough for a whole family and draped all round with heavy curtains of black velvet lined with red taffetas, to match the gold-fringed counterpane. The hems of the curtains were lost in the black bearskin rugs that covered the two steps on which the bed stood raised up, like an altar dedicated to some savage divinity.

To shake off the dread which was creeping over her, Marianne tried to speak.

'Who are you?' she asked. 'Why have you brought me here?'

But her voice seemed to her to come from a long way off, faint and distant as in the worst nightmares. Nor did either of the negresses make the slightest sign to show that they had heard. By now, all the candles were alight, reflecting bunches of flames in the black tiles that shone like a lake beneath the moon. Another candlestick on the chest was also alight.

In a little while, the third woman returned bearing a heavily laden tray which she set down on the chest. But when she approached the bed, gesturing to the others to follow, Marianne saw that the resemblance between the three came largely from their being all much of a height and size and from their dress, for the third was by far the most beautiful. In her the negroid characteristics so marked in the other two were refined and stylized. Her eyes were cold and steely blue, almond-shaped, and despite the almost animal sensuality of her thick lips, the profile might have belonged to some ancient Egyptian queen. Certainly the girl had all a queen's proud grace and scornful assurance. Seen in the melancholy light of the candles, she and her companions made a strange group, but there was no doubt as to who was mistress: the other two were clearly there only to obey her.

At a sign from her, they seized hold of Marianne again and pulled her upright. The beautiful negress, ignoring her feeble attempts at resistance, which were quickly overcome, began to unfasten the girl's crumpled dress. When it was off, she also removed the undergarments and stockings.

Naked, Marianne was borne away by her captors, who seemed possessed of phenomenal strength, to a sunken bath. She was deposited on a stool in the middle and the negress proceeded to wash her with a sponge and scented soap, still without uttering a word. Marianne's attempts to break the silence had no effect whatever.

Suspecting that the women were as dumb as the handsome Jacopo, Marianne submitted without further protest. The journey had been a tiring one and she felt weary and dirty. The bath was invigorating and when, after energetic towelling, the woman began to massage her body with hands which were suddenly amazingly gentle, rubbing in a strangely pungent oil which soothed all the tiredness out of her muscles, Marianne felt much better. After that her hair was brushed and brushed again until it crackled.

Finally, washed and brushed, she was carried back to the bed, which had been turned down, revealing purple-red silk sheets. The chief of the women brought the tray and set it down on a small table by the bed, then, ranged in a line at the foot of the bed, the three strange waiting-women bowed slowly in unison, turned and filed out of the door.

Marianne had been too much astonished to make the slightest move, and it was not until the last one had disappeared that she became aware that they had taken her clothes with them, leaving her alone in the room with no other covering than her own long hair, except, of course, for the covers of the bed on which they had placed her.

The purpose for which she had been left lying naked on the turned-down bed was self-evident, and all Marianne's sense of physical well-being evaporated swiftly in a single furious gust of anger. She had been made ready, stretched on the sacrificial altar as an offering to the lusts of the man who called himself her master, like the virgins and the white heifers once offered up to the old pagan gods. All she needed now was a crown of flowers on her head!

The three negresses must be slaves, bought by Damiani from some African trader, but it was not hard to guess what relations the creature enjoyed with the most beautiful one. Gentle her hands might be, but her eyes, as she bestowed her skilled attentions on the person of the newcomer, betrayed her feelings unmistakably: that woman hated her, probably seeing her as a new favourite and a dangerous rival.

Marianne felt herself colouring with shame and anger at the word. Seizing one of the red sheets, she hauled it off the bed and swathed it round her, like the wrappings of a mummy. She felt better then, and much more confident. How could she retain any dignity before her enemy if she were obliged to face him naked as a slave in a slave market?

Thus swaddled, she set out to explore the room in search of a way out, a crack through which to slip to freedom. But apart from the door, which was low and forbidding, a real prison door sunk in walls more than a yard thick, there were only two narrow pillared windows giving on to a blind inner courtyard, and these were blocked on the outside by a kind of cage of criss-cross iron bars.

There was no escape in that direction, short of prising out the bars and risking a nasty fall to the paved bottom of the well, from which there might be no other exit. It smelled unpleasantly damp and mildewy.

Yet there must be some means of access down there, a door or a window perhaps, because she could see a leaf fluttering in a draught of some kind. But that was mere guesswork and in any case how could she possibly escape, stark naked, from a house which could only be reached by water? She could hardly swim in a sheet, but neither could she imagine herself rising like Venus from the waves of the Grand Canal to go knocking coolly on someone's front door.

So the motive in removing her clothes had been twofold: to deliver her, helpless, into Damiani's arms, and at the same time make it impossible for her to escape.

With a heavy heart, Marianne made her way back to the bed and sat down on it dejectedly, trying to collect her thoughts and overcome her fears. It was no easy task. Then her eye fell on the tray which had been left for her. Without thinking, she lifted the gilded cover from one of the two plates set on the lace cloth alongside a golden-brown roll and wine in a speckled carafe of Murano glass, slender and graceful as a swan's neck.

A savoury smell arose from the dish which contained a stew

of some kind that made Marianne's mouth water. She realized suddenly that she was ravenously hungry and, seizing the golden spoon, plunged it eagerly into the luscious-looking caramel-coloured gravy. Then, with the spoon half-way to her lips, she paused, struck by an unpleasant thought : suppose this delicious-smelling dish contained a drug which would send her to sleep and leave her a defenceless prey to her enemy, like a fly in a spider's web?

Fear was stronger than hunger. Marianne put down the spoon and turned instead to the other cover. The second dish contained rice but that too was served with such unfamiliar sauce that the prisoner renounced it also. She was already feeling quite sufficiently alarmed about that inevitable moment when, overcome with fatigue, she would be bound to fall asleep at last. There was no need to meet the danger half-way.

With a sigh, she nibbled at the roll, which alone looked really harmless, but it was not nearly enough to satisfy her hunger. The carafe of wine was rejected also, after a tentative sniff, and, sighing again, Marianne got out of bed, trailing festoons of red sheet, and drank from the big silver ewer which the black woman had used for her bath.

The water was warm with a disagreeably musty after-taste but it went some way towards quenching a thirst which was growing every moment more intolerable. The heat which had hung over Venice all day had not abated with nightfall. On the contrary, it seemed to have grown still more oppressive and not even the thick walls of the room could keep it out. The dark red silk of the sheet clung to Marianne's skin, and for a second she was tempted to take it off and lie down naked on the tiles which felt so cool to the soles of her feet. But that sheet was her only protection, her last refuge, and so, reluctantly, she resigned herself to returning to the sumptuous bed, which made her nearly as uneasy as the food on the tray.

She had scarcely got in before the beautiful negress was back and gliding towards the bed with her lithe tread, like some half-tamed jungle cat.

Marianne recoiled instinctively, shrinking into her pillows, but the woman ignored the movement, perhaps interpreting it as one of fear or dislike, and raised the covers from the two plates. Her eyes gleamed mockingly under their blue-painted lids and, picking up the spoon, she began to eat as calmly as if she were alone.

In a few minutes both plates and carafe were empty. A sigh of repletion greeted the end of the meal and Marianne could not help finding this quiet demonstration infinitely more mortifying than any quantity of reproaches, since it carried overtones of both mockery and contempt. The woman seemed positively to enjoy making her caution look like cowardice.

Stung, and seeing moreover no reason to go on starving herself voluntarily, Marianne said shortly:

'I do not care for those foreign dishes. Bring me some fruit.'

Considerably to her surprise, the negress acquiesced with a flicker of her eyelids and clapped her hands at once. When one of her companions appeared, she said something to her in a guttural foreign language. It was the first time Marianne had heard her voice: it was strangely deep and almost without inflexion, and went well with her enigmatic character. One thing, however, was quite certain. The woman might not speak Italian but she understood Marianne's. The fruit duly arrived in a very few minutes. And at least the woman could speak.

Encouraged by this success, Marianne selected a peach and then, in a perfectly normal tone, asked for her clothes, or at the least for a nightgown. But this time the negress shook her head.

'No,' she said simply. 'The master forbids.'

'The master?' Marianne took her up at once. 'That man is not master here. He is my servant and nothing in this house is his. It belongs to my husband.'

'I belong to him.'

It was said on the surface, quite calmly but with a curious throb of passion underlying the simplicity of the words. Marianne was not greatly surprised. From the first moment of seeing the beautiful negress, she had sensed that there was something between her and Damiani. She was both his slave and his mistress, ministering to his vices and ruling him, no doubt, through the sensual power of her beauty. There could be no other explanation for the presence of the three strange black women in the Venetian palace.

However, the prisoner had no time to ask the questions on the tip of her tongue, for at that moment the door opened to admit Matteo Damiani himself, still decked in his gold dalmatic, but terrifyingly drunk.

Lurching, he started to cross the shining expanse of tiles, one hand stretched out before him in search of support. He found it in one of the columns of the bed and clung there, gripping it with all his strength.

Marianne watched with disgust the nearer approach of that dark, mottled face, its once not ignoble features now dissolved in fat. The eyes which she remembered clear, insolent, even ruthless, were bloodshot and wandering like candle flames in a draught.

He was panting as if he had just run a long way, and the smell of his breath, heavy and sour, sickened her. He spoke thickly.

'Well, then, my beauties? Been – getting to know each other, have you?'

Her mind torn between disgust, fear and sheer astonishment, Marianne tried vainly to understand how the man had come to this. He had been strange, even frightening, but he had possessed a certain dignity and an overweening vanity. How could that devil, whom Leonora had painted in all the colours of the subtlest evil, and whom Marianne herself had seen practising the rites of black magic, have become this lump of lard soused in drink? Was it the ghost of his unhappy and too-trusting master haunting the faithless servant who had murdered him? Always supposing Matteo Damiani was capable of remorse.

Casting himself bodily on to the bed, he was clutching with trembling fingers at the red silken sheet which covered the cowering Marianne.

'Take this off, Ishtar! ... It's too hot ... and anyway, I told you I would not have you leave her any clothes! She ... she's a slave and s-shlaves go naked in that heathenish land of yours. S-shlaves and c-cattle! An' she's the brood mare on whom I'll get the princely foal I need.'

'You're drunk!' the black woman told him with contempt. 'If

you go on soaking yourself this way you'll never get your foal –
unless another does it for you. Look at you, sprawling there!
You're in no fit state to make love!'

The man gave a drunken laugh which ended in a hiccup.

'Give me some of your potion, Ishtar, an' I'll be s-shtronger 'n'
a bull! Bring me a drink to heat my blood, my lovely witch!
An' be sure you give her some as well . . . make her pull like a
she-cat on heat . . . But first, help me to get this off her! Let me
once see her body and I'll be strong again! I've dreamed of it . . .
night after night!'

He scrabbled at the sheet with clumsy, drunken hands, item-
izing her charms with a madman's concentration, while the
girl shrank away from him in horror. Within an ace of retching,
she sought desperately for some way of fending off the drunkard
and his black helper. Terror lent her unexpected strength.
Snatching the silky fabric out of the fat man's hands, she jerked
herself with a swift twist of her body sideways out of bed and
across the room, securing the sheet tightly under her arms as
she ran. As she had done earlier downstairs, she grasped the
iron candelabra on the coffer with both hands and held it poised,
with its load of lighted candles. Burning hot wax fell on her
arms and on her naked shoulders, but anger and fright redoubled her strength and made her insensible to pain. In the
uncertain light, her green eyes glittered like those of a panther
brought to bay.

'This is for the first of you that tries to touch me!' she hissed
through clenched teeth.

Ishtar, who was looking at her with awakened interest,
shrugged.

'Don't waste your strength. He'll not touch you tonight. The
moon is not at the full and the stars are contrary. You would
not conceive . . . and he is quite incapable!'

'He shan't touch me, tonight or ever!'

The dark face hardened into an expression of such implacable
rigidity that for a moment it looked like a statue carved of
ebony.

'You are here to bear a child,' the woman said harshly, 'and you shall do it. Remember what I said: I belong to him and when the time comes I shall help him.'

'How can you belong to him?' Marianne cried. 'Look at him! He is vile, loathsome – a lump of lard steeped in wine!'

Indeed, Damiani was slumped on the bed in his crumpled gold cloth, as though the matter had ceased to concern him. He was breathing heavily and so obviously sunk in a drunken stupor that Marianne began to take heart. The man was a confirmed toper and all Ishtar's efforts to restrain him had evidently failed. It might be a long time yet before the stars were 'favourable', and before then some way of escape from this madhouse might present itself, even if she had to jump stark naked into the cut and swim ashore in broad daylight in the middle of Venice. She would probably be arrested but at least she would escape from this nightmare.

Her arm muscles were trembling with the strain of holding up the candelabra and, slowly, she relaxed. She had no strength left and perhaps, after all, it was not really necessary. Across the room, Ishtar had grasped Matteo round the body and was hoisting him over her shoulder as if he were nothing more than a sack of meal. Not even bending under his weight, she bore him to the door.

'Get back to bed,' was her contemptuous advice to Marianne. 'For tonight, you may sleep in peace.'

'And – other nights?'

'You'll see. At all events, don't flatter yourself he'll drink as much in future. I'll see to that. Tonight, perhaps, he ... overdid the celebrations. He has been waiting a long time for this. Good night.'

The strange creature vanished with her burden and Marianne found herself alone again with the prospect of long hours ahead. The nightmare feeling lingered, even in her tired brain which no longer seemed to be working very well, so that it could not grasp the idea of her mysterious husband's death, or the incredible alteration in circumstances which followed from it.

In spite of the heat, she found that she was shivering, but with excitement, and she knew that, exhausted as she was, she would not be able to sleep. All she wanted was to escape, as soon as possible! The absurd and revolting scene which had just taken place had left her in a kind of daze from which only the sheer animal instinct of self-preservation had roused her briefly when she made her dash for the candelabra.

She knew that she must break out of this deathly fog and rid herself of the paralysing fear which held her. She had to get a grip on herself. After all, this was not the first time she had been a prisoner, and so far she had always managed to escape, however desperate her situation. Why should luck and courage desert her now? Her captor was half-mad and her gaolers half savages. With wit and patience she ought to be able to find a way out.

Comforted a little by these reflections, Marianne made a further bid to regain her self-possession by washing her face and then drinking a little water and eating some fruit. The fresh, fragrant scent of it did her good. Then, because its voluminousness still draped about her got in the way, she tore the sheet in half and knotted one of the pieces firmly round her chest. For all the thinness of the covering, the sensation of being more or less dressed was reassuring.

Thus prepared, she repeated the tour of her room with minute care, in the vague hope of finding something passed over during her first examination. She stood for a long time at the door, studying the complicated play of the lock, only to reach the dispiriting conclusion that it was impossible to open it without the key. The sinister chamber was as securely fastened as any strong box.

Next, the captive returned to the window and studied the bars. They were thick but not very close together, and Marianne was slim. If she could only get one out she might be able to slip through the gap and, with the help of her sheets, climb down into the little inner court from which there must surely be some way out. But how to shift the bars? And what with? The mortar welding them into the stone was old and might crumble easily enough if attacked with a strong tool. The difficulty lay in finding such a tool.

There was the tray, but the cutlery on it was made of fragile silver-gilt, quite unequal to the task. That was no use.

But Marianne, thirsting for freedom, was not to be so easily discouraged. What she wanted was a piece of iron and she continued her obstinate search for it in every nook and cranny, studying the walls and furniture attentively in the hope of finding some answer, some object she could use.

Her perseverance was rewarded when she came to the big coffer and saw that the lock was ornamented with dainty but thoroughly medieval volutes of wrought iron ending in sharp points. A quick reconnaissance with eager, careful fingers produced a gasp of joy, quickly stifled. One of them was loose, its nails rusted through. It might come off.

Trembling with excitement, Marianne took the cloth off the tray to save her fingers and sitting down on the floor by the chest began working at the iron to loosen the grip of the nails in the antique wood. It was harder than she had first thought. The nails were long and the wood sound. In fact, it was painful and tiring work, made no easier by the heat, but with her whole mind concentrated on her goal, Marianne was unaware of it, any more than of the bites of the mosquitoes which tormented her continually, attracted by the light of the candles at her side.

By the time the piece of metal she wanted dropped into her hand, the night was far advanced and Marianne was exhausted and perspiring. She looked for a moment at the heavy piece of ironwork in her hand and then, getting to her feet with an effort, went to have another look at the seating of the window bars. She sighed. There were several more hours' work there and it would be daylight long before she had finished.

As though in corroboration, a clock somewhere nearby struck four. It was too late. There was nothing more she could do that night. Besides, she was feeling so tired and so cramped from her long time crouching over the lock that it was doubtful if she could have managed the descent by the sheet. Prudence dictated waiting until the next night and praying that nothing disastrous happened in the intervening day. Meanwhile, she must sleep, sleep as much as she could to recoup her strength.

Having made her decision, Marianne calmly returned the piece of iron to its original position and replaced the nails which held it. Then, with a murmured prayer, she went and lay down on the big bed and, pulling the covers over her, for the chill mist of dawn was stealing into the room, fell sound asleep.

She slept for a long time, waking only when a hand touched her shoulder. Opening her eyes, she saw Ishtar, draped in a flowing black and white striped tunic with big gold rings in her ears, seated on the edge of her bed gazing at her.

'It is sunset,' she said simply, 'but I let you sleep on for you were weary, and there was little else for you to do. Now it is time for your bath.'

The other two women were already waiting in the centre of the room, surrounded by all the same preparations as on the previous night. But instead of rising, Marianne curled further down among the bedclothes and stared at Ishtar sullenly.

'I don't want to get up. I'm hungry. I can have my bath afterwards.'

'I think not. Food shall be brought to you afterwards. But if you are still too tired to rise, my sisters will help you.'

There was a threat, sardonic but unmistakable, in the soft voice. Remembering how easily the tall black woman had hoisted Matteo's huge bulk over her shoulder, Marianne realized that it was useless to resist; and rather than waste the strength which she foresaw might be desperately needed, she got up and submitted herself, with no more argument, to the ministrations of her strange attendants.

The ritual ablutions of the previous night were repeated with, if anything, still greater care. Instead of the oil, they anointed her body with some heavy scent which soon began to make her head swim unbearably.

'Don't use any more of that scent,' she protested, seeing one of the women pour another hefty dollop into the palm of her hand. 'I don't like it!'

'Your likes or dislikes are of no importance,' Ishtar retorted coolly. 'This is the perfume of love. No man, even on his death-bed, can resist one who wears it.'

Marianne's heart missed a beat. She understood now : tonight, this very night, she was to be delivered up to Damiani. The stars, it seemed, must be favourable ... A wave of terror swept over her, mingled with rage and disappointment, and she made a desperate attempt to escape from the hateful ministrations which made her feel suddenly sick. Instantly, six granite hands came down on her and held her fast.

'Be still!' Ishtar adjured her roughly. 'You are behaving like a child, or like a lunatic! You must be one or the other to fight against what can't be helped!'

That might be true but Marianne could not resign herself to being offered up, bathed and scented like an odalisque for her first night with the sultan, to the revolting creature who desired her. Tears of rage filled her eyes as, her anointing completed, they dressed her this time in a flowing tunic of black muslin, wholly transparent but scattered here and there with strange geometric figures in silver thread. Her hair was dressed in innumerable tiny plaits, like black snakes, and on it Ishtar placed a silver circlet at the front of which was a coiled viper with emerald eyes. Then, taking a pot of kohl, she set about exaggerating the girl's eyes enormously while Marianne, momentarily accepting defeat, let her have her way.

This done, Ishtar stepped back a pace or two to review her handiwork.

'You are beautiful,' she said flatly. 'Not Cleopatra or the mother-goddess Isis herself was ever more so. The master will be pleased. Come now, eat ...'

Cleopatra? Isis? Marianne shook her head, as though to rouse herself from some bad dream. What had ancient Egypt to do with it? This was the nineteenth century and they were in a city full of ordinary people, under the protection of her own country's army! Napoleon was master of the better part of Europe! How dared the old gods raise their heads?

She felt the breath of madness touch her cheek. In an effort to bring herself back to earth, she tried the food which was brought her and drank a little of the wine, but the dishes seemed tasteless and the wine without flavour. It was like food eaten in a dream, tasting of nothing ...

She was embarking, without relish, on the fruit when it happened. The room began to revolve slowly about her, it tilted unnaturally and everything in it seemed suddenly withdrawn to an immense distance, as though she had been sucked into a long tunnel. Her sense of hearing and of touch became infinitely detached ... Before she was borne away on the great blue wave which rose up suddenly before her, Marianne had just time to understand in a lightning flash what had happened: this time, her food had been drugged.

Yet she was conscious of neither anger nor alarm. Her body seemed to have broken all its earthly moorings, including all capacity for fear, suffering or even disgust, and to be floating weightlessly, marvellously airborne amid a brilliantly coloured universe made up of all the glowing hues of dawn. The walls had fallen away. She was no longer in prison: a vast, shimmering world, shot through with all the colours of Venetian glass, opened up before her, full of rippling light and movement, and in a kind of trance, Marianne sped towards it. She seemed to find herself all at once on a tall ship ... perhaps the very ship whose coming had for so long figured in her dreams, steered by a green siren? High up on the prow, she sailed towards strange shores where fantastically-shaped houses shone like metal, where the plants were blue and the sea purple. The sails sang and the ship drove on over a richly-coloured Persian carpet, while the sea air carried the scent of incense, and Marianne, breathing it in, was no longer astonished at the strange sense of animal well-being which spread through every fibre of her being.

It was a weird sensation, a joy which tingled in the minutest nerve-endings, even to her fingertips. It was a little like the moment after love when the body, satisfied, wrought to the ultimate pitch of sensation, wavers on the very verge of oblivion. It was a kind of oblivion. For all at once everything changed, darkness was everywhere. The fabulous landscape melted into thick night and the soft, scented warmth gave way to an air cool and damp. Yet still Marianne floated on in the same tranquil happiness.

The darkness through which she moved was gentle and

familiar. She could feel it all about her like a caress: the darkness of the prison, squalid but wonderful, where for that one, only time in her life, she had given herself to Jason. Time rolled back. Once again, Marianne could feel the rough boards of their nuptial couch beneath her bare back, their harshness an apt counterpoint to the touch of her lover's hands.

She could feel that touch now. It slid over her body, lapping her in a web of fire beneath which her own flesh flamed and opened like some hothouse flower. Pressing her eyes shut, Marianne held her breath in the effort to hold on to the miraculous sensation which was yet only a prelude to the supreme delight to come ... She felt her throat swell with unuttered moans and cries of pleasure but they died unvoiced as the dream changed again and plunged into the absurd.

Far off at first, but growing nearer, moment by moment, there was the sound of a drum beating slowly, terribly slowly, like some dreadful knell. It quickened gradually until it was like the pulsebeat of some gigantic heart, throbbing faster as it came nearer, beating faster and faster, louder and louder.

For a moment, it seemed to Marianne that it was Jason's heart she heard, but then, as the sound grew clearer, so the amorous darkness thinned and melted like a fog and became tinged with a red light. And suddenly she was hurled from the heights of her dream of love into the very midst of the nightmare from which she had seemed to have escaped.

She seemed in some strange way to have become two people, for she could see herself stretched out in her transparent black draperies which lay like a dark veil over her nakedness. She was lying on a low table made of stone, like an altar, beyond which rose a brazen serpent with a golden crown.

The place itself was a grim, windowless cavern, with moisture dripping from the low, vaulted roof and slimy, pitted walls lit by great black wax candles which gave off a greenish light and an acrid smoke. Below the altar sat two of the black women in their sombre draperies, holding small round drums between their knees, on which they were beating rhythmically. Only their hands moved: everything else remaining perfectly still, even their lips which yet emitted a kind of musical humming, a strange, wordless melody. To this weird music, Ishtar was dancing.

She was quite naked, except for a slim, golden snake which was coiled about her loins, and the candlelight shone blue-black on her gleaming skin. Eyes closed, head flung back and arms upraised, stressing the curve of her heavy, pointed breasts, she was turning in circles on the spot, whirling faster and faster, like a top . . .

Abruptly, Marianne's wandering spirit which had been floating in a kind of limbo of detachment above this extraordinary scene, re-entered her prostrate body. And with the return came fear and dread, but when she tried to move, spring up and run away, she found that she could not stir. Nothing bound her to the stone table, no bonds that could be seen or felt, yet her head and limbs refused to obey her, as though she were in a trance.

The sensation was so terrifying that she tried to cry out but no sound came. Beside her, Ishtar was now whirling madly. Sweat ran in shining trickles down her black skin and her overheated body gave off an almost unbearable wild beast odour.

Marianne was unable even to turn away her face.

Then she saw Matteo Damiani loom up out of a dark corner of the cavern and she wished that she could die. He came towards her slowly, his eyes wide open and staring blankly, bearing in both hands a silver cup containing some bubbling liquid. He was dressed in a long, black gown, not unlike the one Marianne had seen him wearing on the dreadful night at the Villa Sant'Anna when she had snatched Agathe from his devilish rites, but this one was patterned with long snakes in green and silver thread and was open down the front to reveal a fat, grey, hairy chest, breasted almost like a woman's.

At his approach, Ishtar ceased her frantic dance abruptly. She dropped, panting, to the ground, pressing her lips to the man's bare feet. Matteo continued to advance as though he had felt nothing, pushing the woman aside with the toe of his black sandal.

Reaching Marianne, he stretched out a hand to grasp the muslin tunic, and ripped it off in a single movement. Then, taking a small tray from the floor, he placed it on her stomach and set the silver cup upon it. After this, he dropped on to his knees and began chanting strange verses in some foreign tongue.

From the depths of her paralysing trance, Marianne realized with sick horror that he was going to perform on her the same satanic rites which she had witnessed in the ruins of the little temple, only this time she was at the very centre of the black magic. It was her own body which was to be made the altar for this sacrilege.

Ishtar had risen and was kneeling beside Matteo, playing the role of acolyte in the infernal ceremony, chanting the responses in the same unknown language.

As her master seized the cup and drained it to the last drop, she uttered a wild shriek blending into an incantation, as if she were invoking for him the protection of some dark and terrible deity, probably the gold-crowned serpent whose emerald eyes seemed to glitter with ominous life.

Matteo had begun to shake. He seemed to be possessed by some kind of religious mania. His eyes were dilated and rolled in their sockets and there was foam on his lips. He was making a low rumbling sound in his chest, like a volcano about to erupt. At this point, Ishtar handed him a black cockerel and he severed its neck at a stroke with a great knife. The blood flowed, splashing over the girl's naked body.

At that, the horror that welled up in Marianne broke through the paralysing power of the drug that held her in thrall. She found her voice in the utterance of one fearful, inhuman shriek which seemed to tear itself from her rigid throat. It was as if her vocal cords had come to life of themselves and in this feeble effort had used up all her strength, for scarcely had the echoes of that dreadful cry died away in the cavern than Marianne mercifully lost consciousness.

She did not see Matteo, at the height of his madness, cast off his robe and lean over her with outstretched hands. She did not feel him throw himself with all his weight upon her blood-stained body, possessing her with all a madman's fury. She was far away in a world without colour or sound where nothing could reach her.

There was no way of knowing how long she remained unconscious like this, but when she surfaced at last in the real world again she was lying in the great pillared bed and she felt deathly ill.

Possibly, in order to subdue her resistance, they had given her a dose of the drug too strong for her constitution, or perhaps the mosquitoes which, as soon as night fell and the candles were lighted, filled Venice with their whining hum had already injected their stagnant fever into her veins, but she was tormented by agonies of thirst and stabs of pain drilled through her temples.

She felt too ill to be very much aware of what was going on around her. What little thought remained was concentrated on the single, fixed and obstinate idea of flight. She had to get away ... as far away as possible, out of reach of these devils!

In fact, her brain had cleared sufficiently for her to realize that her long dream, which had foundered at the end so catastrophically in the worst practices of black magic, had not been entirely a dream but, in its last stages at least, a horrible reality. With the help of his black sorceress, Damiani had succeeded in violating her without the least resistance.

The thought was at the same time revolting and destructive for Marianne knew now, beyond all doubt, that short of starving herself to death there was nothing she could do to escape from the degradation forced upon her by Damiani. There was nothing and no one to prevent her captors, whenever they chose, from employing the mysterious drug which rendered her powerless to resist the steward's lust.

Marianne's thoughts chased one another round and round, increasing her fever and with it her thirst. She had never known such thirst. It was as though her tongue had grown to twice its normal size, filling her mouth with its swelling.

With a painful effort, she managed to raise herself on her pillows, trying to measure the distance between herself and the water jug. The movement brought fresh stabs of pain to her head and she uttered an involuntary groan. At once a black hand put a cup to her lips.

'Drink,' said Ishtar's quiet voice. 'You are burning hot.'

This was true, but the presence of the black witch produced

a shudder of revulsion in Marianne. She raised one hand to push away the cup but Ishtar did not move.

'Drink!' she commanded. 'It is only tisane. It will bring down your fever.'

Slipping one arm underneath the pillows to lift the girl, she brought the vessel once more to the parched lips, which this time took in the tepid fluid instinctively. Marianne had no more strength to resist. Besides, it smelled pleasantly of good, familiar things, of woodland plants, mint and verbena. There was nothing suspicious there and when at last Ishtar laid her back on the pillows, Marianne had drunk it all to the last drop.

'You will sleep again now,' she was told, 'but it will be a good sleep and you will feel better when you wake.'

'I don't want to sleep! I don't ever want to sleep again!' Marianne burst out tearfully, seized by a fresh terror of dreams which began beautifully only to end in ugliness.

'Why ever not? Sleep is the best medicine. And you are too tired to resist it . . .'

'What about . . . him? That – that beast?'

'The master is asleep also,' Ishtar responded placidly. 'He is glad because he came to you at a propitious hour and he trusts the gods will accept his sacrifice and give you a fine son.'

At this tranquil evocation of the ghastly scene in which she had played a principal role, Marianne was overcome by a violent spasm of nausea which left her gasping and sweating on her pillows. She was suddenly aware of the violation of her body and recoiled from it in disgust. A kindly providence had taken away her senses at the crucial moment but the shame and humiliation remained, and with it the loathing of her own flesh possessed by the other.

How, after this, could she ever look Jason in the face, supposing that God ever allowed her to see him again? The American sea captain was everything that was open, clean-cut and straightforward in mind, in no way given to superstition. Could he accept the evil conspiracy to which Marianne had fallen victim? He was jealous, and in his jealousy violent and unbridled. He had accepted, though not easily, the knowledge that Marianne had been Napoleon's mistress. He would never bear to think of her subject to Damiani. He might even kill her ... he would undoubtedly leave her, overcome with revulsion, and never return.

These thoughts jostled and battered in Marianne's aching head with a frenzy that brought an increase of suffering and despair. Her shattered nerves broke suddenly in a burst of convulsive sobbing to which the big black woman, seated silent and motionless a little way from the bed, listened with a little frown.

Her knowledge of potions was powerless in the face of such despair and in the end she could only shrug and tiptoe from the room, leaving her prisoner to weep her heart out, with the reflection that she must ultimately cry herself to sleep.

In this she was right. By the time Marianne had reduced herself to the last stages of nervous exhaustion she ceased to struggle against the beneficent effects of the tisane and fell asleep with her face buried in the tear-soaked red silk of her sheets, and the last dismal thought in her head that she could always kill herself if Jason rejected her.

Thanks to three more cups administered by Ishtar at regular intervals, the fever had subsided by the morning and Marianne found herself still weak but clear-headed and very much awake, unhappily, to the desperate nature of her situation.

However, the despair which had overtaken her at the height of her fever had dissipated itself like a breaking wave and Marianne was herself again, with all her old zest for battle in her heart. The greater the power and wickedness of her enemies, the greater was her own determination to triumph at any cost.

Forcing herself to begin by considering her problem calmly from all angles, Marianne attempted to get up and try her strength. The piece of metal which she had succeeded in detaching from the lock of the antique chest seemed to shine brighter than the rest and drew her like a magnet. But when she sat up in bed she saw that she had a nurse: one of the negresses was seated on the steps of the bed, with her blue tunic spread out over the bearskins.

She was not doing anything, but simply squatting with her arms about her knees which were drawn up almost to her chin.

In her dark draperies she had the air of some strange brooding bird.

Hearing a movement, she merely turned to look at the girl and, seeing that she was awake, clapped her hands. Her companion, so like her that she might have been her shadow, entered with a tray which she set down on the bed and then seated herself, in exactly the same attitude, in the place of her sister, who bowed and went out.

For hours the woman sat there, as though rooted to the ground, uttering no word and appearing not to hear any that were addressed to her.

'You cannot be left alone,' Ishtar said later when Marianne complained of the guard mounted at the foot of her bed. 'We cannot have you giving us the slip.'

'Give you the slip? From here?' Marianne cried, disappointment at finding herself thus closely guarded whipping up her anger. 'How could I? The walls are thick and there are bars at my windows – and besides, I have no clothes!'

'There are other ways of escaping from a prison, even when the body is secured.'

Then Marianne understood the real reason for the watch kept on her. Damiani was afraid that in her humiliation and despair she might take her own life.

'I shall not kill myself,' she said. 'I am a Christian and Christians believe that suicide is both a coward's way out and a sin.'

'Perhaps. But I do not think you one to balk at flouting the gods. In any case, we can leave nothing to chance. You are too precious to us now.'

Ignoring the implications of this, Marianne let the matter drop. Let the future take care of itself! For the present, she was well aware that it was useless to insist on the removal of her watchdog, but it cost her an effort to conceal her chagrin. The woman's presence made things much more difficult. How could she make the smallest attempt to escape under that brooding black eye? Unless she could ensure that she was helpless, by stunning her first.

The idea worked away quietly in Marianne's brain and she,

who a moment before had been proclaiming herself a Christian, now coolly considered the possibility of killing her guard in order to escape. It all depended, of course, on whether she had the strength to do it and the turn of speed to surprise a creature with the reflexes of a wild cat ...

In this way, the day passed, monotonously but not without interest, in concocting any number of plans, some more practicable than others, for getting rid of her gaoler. But when night fell, Marianne knew that she had little chance of carrying out any of them, for after supper Matteo returned, walking into the room with a candlestick in his hand : a Matteo so altered from the one she had seen hitherto that for a second Marianne forgot her anger.

It was not simply that the mad sorcerer of the other night had vanished as if he had never been, or that the man no longer showed the slightest hint of drunkenness. He had also bestowed an unaccustomed degree of care on his appearance. He was shaved, brushed, pomaded, his nails gleamed like agate and he wore a dressing-gown of heavy dark-blue silk over a dazzling white shirt. There floated about him such a powerful smell of eau-de-Cologne that for a moment Marianne was reminded of Napoleon. He, too, was in the habit of drenching himself in eau-de-Cologne like that when—

Her brain recoiled from the horrid comparison which suggested itself. Yet Matteo certainly looked just like any rustic bridegroom on his wedding night – only without the inevitable look of embarrassment, for his face bore a triumphant smirk and he seemed highly pleased with himself.

Marianne drew her brows together, suddenly on her guard. When she saw him set his candle down on the bedside table she uttered an indignant protest.

'Take that candle away, and yourself too! How dare you come to me like this! What do you think you're doing?'

'Why ... I've come to sleep with you! After all, you are, in some degree, my wife now, Marianne, aren't you?'

'Your—'

Words failed Marianne but only for an instant. Then the torrent of her rage burst forth in a stream of abuse in several languages, borrowed indiscriminately from the stable oaths of old Dobs, her groom, and the vocabulary of Surcouf's seamen. She even succeeded in astonishing herself, and the steward fell back stupefied before the storm.

'Out!' Marianne commanded. 'Get out of here at once, you murderous brute! You miserable, sneaking cur! You're nothing but a lackey, the swinish offspring of a sow and a he-goat! Even your weapons are a lackey's weapons! The snare and the knife in the back! That's how you killed your master, isn't it? Cowardly, from behind? Or did you cut his throat while you were shaving him? Or was it a drug, like the one you used on me to get me in your power? And do you think, now, that your mumbo-jumbo has made me like yourself? Do you imagine I enjoyed the things you did to me? And do you think I must be so enamoured of your charms I'll share my bed with you, like any tradesman's wife! Take a look at yourself – and look at me! I'm no milkmaid to be tumbled in the hay, Matteo Damiani, I'm—'

'I know what you are!' Matteo cried, his patience at an end. 'You have told me often enough! Princess Sant'Anna! Well, like it or not, I'm a Sant'Anna, too, and my blood—'

'That is not proved, and you have yet to convince me! Easy enough to claim a great lord as your father when he is no longer there to confirm it. And, so far, the way you go about things tells against you. From what I know of the Sant'Annas, they at least killed openly. Theirs may have been a cruel and merciless kind of justice, but I do not think that they would ever have recourse to an African sorceress to help them get the better of a helpless woman—'

'Any means are fair with such a woman as you! Your own marriage was a cheat. Where is the child you pledged yourself to give your husband? Where is it, the one thing he married you for, you emperor's whore?'

'Miserable flunkey! One of these days, before I see you hanged, I'll have you flogged until you scream for mercy, until you wish you'd never dared to raise your hand against me – or your master!'

The room re-echoed with their rage as they confronted one

another, face to face, both gripped by an equal fury, if not of an equal quality.

Marianne, white-faced, her green eyes flashing, poured scorn on the apoplectic Damiani who, with bloodshot eyes and heavy, congested features quivering with rage, was clearly in a mood to kill, but she was past caring. Her anger was beyond all control now, and she spat out her hatred and disgust without even pausing to ask herself why this strange urge had come upon her to avenge a husband who, not so long ago, had inspired her with nothing but fear.

Matteo, beside himself, was on the point of hurling himself at Marianne to throttle her, but even as his hands went for her throat, Ishtar sprang between them.

'Are you mad?' she cried. 'You are the master and whatever she may say, she is yours! Why should you kill her? Have you forgotten what she means to you?'

Her words acted on Damiani like a douche of cold water. He stood for a moment, breathing heavily, striving to take hold of himself, and then, with unexpected gentleness, he put the negress aside and turned again to Marianne.

'She – she is right,' he gasped. 'Flunkey I may be, Princess, but this flunkey has got you with child, I doubt not, and when the child is born—'

'It is not born yet and you have no means of knowing whether your base treachery has borne fruit. And if it is true I am to bear your child, then you will have to kill me to keep me silent, for no power on earth shall prevent me delivering you into the Emperor's hands!'

'Then I shall kill you, lady. Why not, when you have done your part? In the meantime...'

'What in the meantime?'

For answer, Matteo set about removing his dressing-gown, which he laid over a chair, and then returned to the bed with the evident intention of getting in. But before he could so much as lay a finger on the sheets, Marianne had sprung out and, regardless of her unclothed state, had made a lightning dash for the curtains where she clung.

'If you dare to set foot in that bed, Matteo Damiani, then

you will sleep in it alone. Nothing shall make me share it with such a creature as you!'

As calmly as though she had not spoken, Matteo got into bed, plumped up the pillows and settled himself against them with obvious enjoyment.

'Like it or not, my lady, we shall be bedfellows for as long as I choose. What you said just now was very true. The best-laid plans can go astray and it may be that you are not yet breeding. So we'll do our best to make it certain. Come here!'

'Never!'

Marianne tried to run, to avoid the clutching hand which groped towards her, but she found Ishtar barring her way. The tall negress seemed enormous, standing there, as though the evil genie out of eastern tales had suddenly risen up before her to cast her back into the devil's power. Without apparent effort, not even seeming to notice Marianne's instinctive struggles, Ishtar picked her up bodily, screaming and kicking, and flung her on to the bed, straight into Damiani's arms, at the same time saying something in her strange tongue. The steward answered her in Italian.

'No, no hashish. She reacted badly and the child might suffer. We have other means. Call your sisters. You shall hold her down.'

At once, three pairs of black hands clamped down on Marianne, gripping her arms and legs and holding her flat on the bed, in spite of her screams and tears of rage. A gag was put in her mouth to quiet her and this time there was no merciful unconsciousness to spare her the shame and disgust.

For what seemed like endless minutes she was forced to suffer her tormentor, lying half-stifled and utterly helpless in the grip of those vice-like hands, and dying a hundred deaths of shame and sorrow. She felt as if she had fallen into the pit of hell itself, with the man's gross, scarlet, sweating countenance thrusting close to hers and the three black figures, standing still as stones, their blank eyes contemplating the rape with as much indifference as if it had been a mating of beasts. And that was what it was: she, Marianne, was being used like an animal, a brood mare to produce the right stock.

When they let her go at last, she lay unmoving on the ravaged bed, choking with sobs and drowned in tears, exhausted by her body's futile attempts at resistance. She had no more strength even to abuse her ravisher and when Matteo rose, still panting from his exertions, and began, grumbling, to put on his dressing-gown, she could only groan.

'She's so unwilling, there's no pleasure in it! But we'll keep it up, all the same, every night until we're sure. Let her be now, Ishtar, and come with me. That cold creature would put Eros off his stroke!'

So Marianne, broken and defeated, was left in her hated room, alone except for the other two women who remained as mute but watchful guards. No one even took the trouble to cover her. She had ceased to have any hope, even in God. She knew now that she would have to endure every step of this abominable martyrdom, until the time came when Damiani had what he wanted from her.

'But he shan't win – he shan't!' she vowed silently, out of the depths of her misery. 'I'll get rid of the child somehow, or if I fail I'll take him with me . . .'

Vain words, the desperate ravings born of fever and the paroxysms of humiliation she had suffered, yet Marianne repeated them over and over again in the nights that followed, nights in which even horror began to acquire a kind of monotony. Even revulsion became a kind of habit.

She knew that this was the witch Lucinda taking her revenge, that it was her power reaching out through Matteo from beyond the tomb. Sometimes, in the dark, it seemed to Marianne that she could see the marble statue from the little temple come to life. She heard its laughter . . . and would wake then in a bath of sweat.

The days were all alike, all dreary. Marianne spent them locked in her bare room under the watchful eye of one of the women. She was fed, bathed, even clothed after a fashion in a kind of loose tunic, like those worn by the black women, and a pair of slippers. Then, when night fell, the three she-devils bound her, for greater convenience, to the bed and left her so, naked and defenceless, to the tender mercies of Matteo. He, in point of fact, seemed to find increasing difficulty in performing what he appeared to regard as some kind of duty. More often than not, Ishtar was obliged to provide him with a glass of some mysterious liquid to revive his flagging powers. From time to time the prisoner's food was drugged, making her lose all sense of time, but she had ceased to care. In the end, overwhelming disgust had finished by inducing a kind of insensitivity. She had become a thing, an inanimate object incapable of reaction or of suffering. Her very skin seemed to have atrophied and grown dull to all sensation, while her sluggish brain held room for only one single, fixed idea : to kill Damiani and then die herself.

This idea, like a persistent, nagging thirst, was the one thing that remained alive in her. Everything else was stone and dead ashes. She no longer knew even if she loved, or whom she loved. All the people in her life seemed as strange and far-off as the characters on the tapestried walls of her room. She had ceased even to think of escape : how could she, guarded as she was by night and day? The she-devils who watched over her seemed incapable of sleep, fatigue or even inattention. All she wanted now was to kill, and then to do away with herself in turn. Nothing else mattered.

They had brought her some books, but she had not even opened them. Her days were spent seated in one of the high-backed chairs, as still and silent as her black guardians, staring at the hangings or at the marks of soot on the ceiling of her room. Words seemed out of place in that room where the silence was like that of the tomb. Marianne spoke to no one and did not answer when they spoke to her. She suffered herself to be cared for, fed and watered with no more response than a statue. Only her hatred was awake amid the silence and the stillness.

At last, this mute indifference began to have its effect on Damiani. As the days passed, Marianne could see the uneasiness growing in his eyes when he came to her at night. Little by little, the time he spent with her grew less until it was only a few minutes, and then, one night, he did not come at all. He had ceased to desire the marble being whose unblinking stare had perhaps power to disconcert him. He was afraid now, and soon Marianne did not see him at all except for the few moments every day when he came to inquire of Ishtar as to his prisoner's health.

He probably thought that by now he had done all he could to procure the child he wanted and that there was nothing to be gained from persisting in what had become a distasteful chore. Somewhere, beneath all her indifference, Marianne had felt a spark of joy at his fears, seeing them as a small triumph, though not enough to appease her hatred : that would only be satisfied with this man's blood, and she had patience to wait for that.

How long did this strange captivity continue, out of time, out of life itself? Marianne had lost all sense of hours and days. She no longer knew even where she was and scarcely who she was. Ever since her arrival she had seen only four people, and yet the palace was built to accommodate a huge staff, although now it was as secret and as silent as the tomb. Every sign of life, apart from the mere act of breathing, seemed to perish there, until Marianne began to think that perhaps death would come to her, creeping quietly of itself without her help. She would simply cease to be. The thing seemed, now, astonishingly easy.

Then, one evening, something did happen.

First of all, the usual watcher disappeared. There was a sound somewhere in the depths of the house, like a hoarse shout. The black woman heard it and, shuddering, left her accustomed place on the steps of the bed and went out of the room, not forgetting to close the door carefully behind her.

It was the first time for many days that Marianne had been left alone but she hardly noticed it. In a moment the woman would be back with the others, for it was near the time usually allotted for her bath. Without interest, she went and lay down on the bed and closed her eyes. The long imprisonment, with its enforced inactivity, was telling on her system. She often felt sleepy during the day and had got into the habit of following her own inclinations as meekly as the will of those outside herself.

She might have slept like that all night but for some instinct which woke her. She knew at once that something unusual had happened.

She opened her eyes and stared about her. It was pitch dark outside and the candles burned as usual in the great candelabra, but the room was as silent and empty as before. No one had come back and the hour for her bath was long past.

Marianne got up slowly and walked a little way across the room. A sudden draught, flattening the candle flames, made her turn her head towards the door and as she did so something stirred in her brain. The door was open.

The heavy oaken panel studded with iron swung back against the wall leaving a black hole between the tapestries. Hardly able to believe her eyes, Marianne moved forward to touch it, to convince herself that this was not simply another of the dreams which haunted her nights, in which, time and again, she had seen the door stand open on to limitless blue distances.

No, surely this time the door was truly open. Marianne could feel the faint draught it created. Even so, to make sure she was not dreaming, she went back to the candles and held one finger up to the flame. At once she gave a little cry of pain. The flame had burned her. Then, as she sucked her smarting finger, her eyes fell on the chest and she cried out again in surprise. There, neatly laid out on the lid, were the clothes in which she had arrived: the olive-green dress with the black velvet trimming, even her shoes and petticoat. Only the hooded cloak edged with Chantilly lace was missing. It was like a memory of another world.

Marianne put out her hand almost fearfully and touched the fabric, stroked it gently and then clutched at it like a drowning man at a straw. Something inside her seemed to snap and come away. She was suddenly alive again, capable of thought and action. It was as if she had been imprisoned in a block of ice and now the ice was broken and pieces were being chipped off and coming back to warmth and life.

With a surge of childlike joy, she tore off the hateful tunic they had put on her and fell on her own clothes as on something infinitely precious. She put them on, revelling in a sensation like feeling herself in her own skin after being flayed. She was so carried away that for the moment she did not even pause to wonder what it meant. It was simply wonderful, even if the heat made the garments uncomfortably hot to wear. She was herself again, from top to toe, and that was all that really mattered.

As soon as she was dressed, she marched determinedly to the door. Whoever had brought the clothes and opened the door must be a friend. She was being given a chance and she must take it.

Outside, everywhere was in total darkness and Marianne went back to fetch a candle to light her way. She saw that she was at the end of a long corridor with no other opening but another door facing her. It seemed to be shut.

Marianne's hand tightened on the candle and her heart missed a beat. Were they merely torturing her with false hopes? Was all this designed simply to bring her, helpless and more desperate than ever, face to face with yet another locked door?

But when she reached it, she saw that it was merely closed, not locked. It yielded to her hand and she found herself in an open gallery like a kind of long veranda, looking down on to a small courtyard. Overhead was a roof of broad, painted wooden beams supported on slender arched columns.

For all her haste to get away from the house, she paused for a moment in the gallery, drawing deep breaths of the warm night air. It carried with it a disagreeable smell of mud and decaying refuse, but she had not been out of doors for so long and able to see the sky. It made no difference that the sky in question was heavy with cloud with not a star in sight: it was still the sky and therefore the ultimate symbol of freedom.

Resuming her cautious advance, Marianne came to a second door at the far end of the gallery. It opened to her hand and she found herself in China.

All round the walls of the delightful little salon, slant-eyed princesses danced a mad fandango with a joyous troop of grinning monkeys, in and out among black lacquered screens and gilt whatnots bearing quantities of rose and yellow porcelain, over which a Murano lustre cast a shimmering rainbow brightness. It was, in truth, a very pretty room but so much festive illumination made an uneasy contrast with the stillness that reigned there.

This time, Marianne passed on without a pause. Beyond, all was again in darkness, but she was in a broad gallery from which a staircase led, apparently, down to ground level.

Marianne's feet, shod in thin leather, made no sound on the polished marble mosaic as she glided, ghostlike, past the bronze columns that emerged from the walls on either side like ships looming out of the fog, and past the blind stone warriors. Everywhere, on the long inlaid chests, miniature caravels spread their sails to a non-existent wind, and gilded galleys dipped their long oars in invisible seas. On all sides, too, were banners of curious shape bearing the often-repeated crescent of Islam. Lastly, at either end of the gallery, reflected in tall, tarnished mirrors, a great terrestrial globe stood still and useless, dreaming of the tanned hands which had once set it turning in its bronze rings.

Impressed, in spite of herself, by this kind of mausoleum to the warlike, seafaring Venice of other days, Marianne found her feet dragging unconsciously. She had almost reached the staircase when she came to a sudden halt, her heart thudding, and listened intently. Someone was walking about downstairs, carrying a light which was moving slowly along the wall of the gallery.

She stood, rooted to the spot, scarcely daring to breathe. Who was it moving down there? Matteo? Or one of her three sinister keepers? Marianne cast about her for a refuge in case the bearer of the light should come upstairs and catch her unawares. Selecting the statue of an admiral whose armour was partly covered by a cloak with ample folds of stone drapery, she slipped softly behind it and waited.

The light stood still. Whoever it was must have put it down somewhere, because the footsteps went on, growing fainter.

She was just beginning to breathe again when her blood froze. A groan had come from below. There was a muffled cry, as though of terror and surprise, and then, almost at once, the sound of two sets of feet, one running from the other. A crash like the clap of doom told of the collapse of some piece of furniture, evidently laden with bric-à-brac. A door slammed, and the noise of the pursuit dwindled rapidly. Marianne heard a second and much fainter cry followed by the faint but horrible sound of a death-rattle. Somewhere, in the house or garden, a person was dying ... After that, nothing. Only an overpowering silence.

Striving to still the thudding of her heart which seemed to echo through the silence like a cathedral bell, Marianne left her hiding place and tiptoed nervously towards the stairs, since there appeared to be no other way out. She reached them, but the sight which met her eyes froze her where she stood.

The stairs ran down to a noble hall sombrely furnished and hung with long tapestries and paintings in the style of Tiepolo, but to Marianne the room looked like a battlefield. A tall candlestick stood on a long stone table and nearby lay the bodies of the two black servants whose living voices she had never even heard. One was on the floor beside an overturned chair, the other lay across the table. Both had died in the same way, stuck through the heart with merciless precision.

But there was a third body, lying right across the lowest steps. Matteo Damiani sprawled with eyes wide open on an eternity of horror and the blood from his severed throat spreading in slowly widening pools over the dripping steps.

'He is dead!' Marianne said aloud, half-unconsciously, and the sound of her own voice seemed to come from an immense distance. 'Someone has killed him – but who?'

The horror of it was mingled in her with a savage joy that was almost painful in its intensity, the instinctive joy of the torture victim who finds the dead body of the torturer stretched suddenly at her feet. Some unknown hand had simultaneously avenged both the murdered Prince Sant'Anna and the sufferings of Marianne herself.

Abruptly, the instinct of self-preservation reasserted itself. There would be time to rejoice later, when she was safely out of this nightmare, supposing she ever got out of it, for there were only three bodies in the room. Where was Ishtar? Was it the black witch who had slain her master? She was certainly capable of it but, if that were so, why had she also killed the other two women of her own race whom she called her sisters? Then, there had been that other cry, the sounds of pursuit and that dying groan ... Was that Ishtar? And, if so, who was the author of this slaughter?

Since her arrival at this accursed place, Marianne had learned nothing of its inhabitants save for Matteo himself and the three negresses and the oily Giuseppe. Yet Giuseppe did not possess the physical strength to overcome a man like Damiani, far less Ishtar. Yet there might be other servants and it was possible that one of them had done this, for reasons of his own.

It occurred to her at this point that the murderer might well return and would not necessarily make any distinction between herself and his earlier victims. She fought off her sense of paralysing horror. She must not stay here. She had to escape from this charnel hell, walk down the stairs, past the red stains at their foot and past the body in its bloodstained golden robe with its hideous gaping wound and its staring eyes.

Shuddering, she crept down, flattening her back against the marble baluster, towards the dark red pools which now gleamed with an oily sheen as they congealed.

She gathered her dress up in trembling hands to keep it from contact with the blood, but could do nothing to save her shoes.

As she went down, she could not drag her eyes away from Matteo's body. They were drawn by the fascination of horror which afflicts imaginative minds, when they have not fainted outright.

So it was that she became aware of the nature of a curious heap of metal lying on the dead man's chest: it was made up of chains, a prisoner's chains and shackles. They were old and fairly rusty but they were unlocked and evidently placed there deliberately.

However, Marianne wasted no time on this latest mystery. A rush of panic swept over her and as soon as her feet touched the ground she began to run down the hall, too much in the grip of fear to care how much noise she made. She plunged through the double doors which stood half-open, without a thought for the murderer who might be lurking outside, and found herself in the entrance hall.

As it happened, it was empty. The two ship's lanterns she remembered were alight and the garden door was also open.

Not checking in her stride, Marianne sped towards it and went down the steps leading to the shadowy garden at breakneck speed in her haste to reach the door to the canal. That, too, stood open, giving a glimpse of the sheen on dark water.

Freedom! Freedom was there, within reach . . .

She was swerving to avoid the vague shape of the wellhead which loomed clearer as her eyes became accustomed to the dark, when she stumbled and fell headlong over something warm and soft. This time she almost screamed aloud, for the thing which had tripped her was a human form. Her hands encountered damp, silken cloth, and by the exotic scent, mingled with the sweet, sickening smell of blood, Marianne knew that it was Ishtar. So, that death cry had been hers. The mysterious killer had not spared her, any more than her sisters.

Choking back a hysterical sob, she was about to rise when suddenly she felt the body move under her and heard a feeble groan. The dying woman muttered something Marianne could not understand and, instinctively, she bent closer to hear, lifting the head a little as she did so.

In the dimness, she was aware of the black woman's hands moving, groping like a blind person's at the supporting arms, but she felt no fear. The woman was dying: nothing now remained of her phenomenal strength. Then, suddenly, she heard words:

'The . . . the Master! . . . Forgive . . . oh, forgive . . .'

The head fell back. Ishtar was dead. Marianne laid her down on the ground and got up quickly, but stopped dead as she turned towards the door.

Framed in the opening, two figures had appeared on the small landing. There was no mistaking their military outline and they were followed by others, less clear.

'But, officer, I heard screams, I assure you, frightful screams,' came a woman's voice. 'And now this door open – and that other, up there, at the head of the stairs. It's not right. I always thought there was something funny going on here. If people had only listened to me . . .'

'Quiet, everybody!' A rough voice broke in authoritatively. 'We'll search the house from top to bottom. If there's been a mistake made, then we'll apologize, of course. But it'll go hard with you, my good woman, if you've brought us on a wild-goose chase!'

'I'm quite sure I haven't, officer. You'll thank me, I daresay. I've always said that house was a wicked place.'

'Well, we'll soon see. Bring up a light, there!'

Slowly, holding her breath, Marianne backed away, half-crouching, into the shelter of the dark walled garden which lay beyond a stone arch. It seemed to run parallel with the canal. Her instinct told her that it would not do for her to be seen by the soldiers or by any of these people who, however well-intentioned, were a great deal too inquisitive. She could guess only too well what would happen if she were found, the only one alive in a house full of corpses. How could she expect them to believe her terrible but, on the face of it, improbable tale? At best they would take her for a madwoman and probably lock her up again, and in any case she would be detained by the police and questioned endlessly. Previous experience at Selton Hall, after her duel with Francis Cranmere, had taught her how easily the truth can be distorted. Her dress, her shoes, her hands were all stained with blood. She might very easily be accused of fourfold murder, and then what would become of her rendezvous with Jason?

She was conscious of faint surprise at the readiness with which her lover's name came to her mind, with no touch of fear or foreboding. It was the first time, since awakening from her long-drawn nightmare, that she had thought of the pre-arranged meeting in Venice. After her rape by Damiani she had experienced a dreadful sense of something irrevocable having occurred, and such a revulsion from her own body that death had seemed to her the only proper end. But now that she had her freedom so unexpectedly restored to her, her own spirit re-awakened and with it her passionate love of life and the accompanying instinct to fight.

She remembered now that somewhere in the world there was a ship and a sailor on whom all her hopes were concentrated, and that she wanted to see them again, the ship and the sailor, whatever else might come of it. Unfortunately, in this house of madness, the combination of drugs and despair had made her lose all count of time. The time for their meeting might have come or gone, or it might be still some days ahead : Marianne had no means of knowing. The first step towards finding out was to get out, but that was easier said than done.

Not knowing what to do next, Marianne huddled in the midst of a large flowering shrub and tried to think of a way out of the garden which, for all its scents of orange blossom and honey-suckle, was still a trap. The walls were high and smooth and in a little while the trap would surely be sprung.

Back towards the house, lanterns had been brought and flitted about in the darkness. What looked like a crowd of people poured into the courtyard, led by the two soldiers. From her hiding place, Marianne saw them bend over the body of Ishtar, lying near the well, uttering exclamations of horror. Then one of the soldiers went up the steps and disappeared into the house, followed by a train of interested spectators, only too glad of the chance to see inside the grand house and, maybe, pop something into their pockets on the sly.

It dawned on Marianne then that if she did not want to be discovered, she had very little time left. She crept out of her precarious shelter and stepped out into the garden, searching the wall for some other door, if any existed. It was as dark as the pit. The trees met in a thick roof overhead, making the night blacker than ever underneath.

Holding her hands stretched out in front of her, like a blind woman, she at last encountered warm brick and began following the wall with the intention of making a circuit of the garden. Then, if she did not find a way out, she would climb up into a tree and wait, though goodness knew how long, until the way was clear.

She traversed some thirty yards in this way before the wall turned a corner. A few more steps and the wall ended abruptly, giving way to emptiness and curved ironwork. By this time, her eyes were growing much more accustomed to the darkness and she was able to make out that she was looking at a small opening barred with scrollwork in wrought iron, which made a lighter patch in the surrounding black.

On the other side, contrary to what she had feared, was no canal but an alleyway lit faintly by a distant lantern. Here at last was her way of escape.

As ill-luck would have it, Marianne found herself no better off. The bars were strong and the gate fastened with a padlock and chain. It refused to open. Yet the breath of free air in her lungs was enough for Marianne. She would not despair. Besides, the noises from the house seemed to be coming nearer.

Stepping back a pace, she measured the height of the surrounding wall with her eye. What she saw satisfied her. The gate might not open but it looked a comparatively simple matter to climb: the ironwork offered plenty of footholds, not too far apart, while the piece of wall directly above was not more than eighteen inches high and the brickwork sufficiently ancient to provide a good grip. She thought she could get over it without difficulty.

The sounds were getting more distinct. Voices and footsteps. A light flashed under the trees at the entrance to the garden. However, climbing was out of the question encumbered by a long, thick skirt.

In spite of her haste and her alarm, she made herself take time to take it off and stuff it through the gate into the alley. Then, dressed only in her chemise and cotton drawers, she turned her attention to the climb.

It was, as she had foreseen, a fairly simple matter. This was just as well because her muscles, weakened by her long incarceration and inactivity, had lost much of their old elastic strength.

By the time Marianne had reached the top of the wall, she was sweating and gasping for breath. Her head was swimming and she felt so dizzy that she was obliged to sit on the ridge for a moment to recover from the pounding in her chest. She could never have believed that she was so weak. Her whole body was trembling and she had the alarming feeling that her sinews might give way at any moment. Yet there was no choice but to go down.

Marianne shut her eyes and, holding tight to the top of the wall, swung her legs over and groped for a foothold. She managed to move one foot, then the other, one hand, then the other, but as she tried to take the next step downwards her muscles gave way suddenly, she felt the bricks burn her clutching hands and then she fell.

Luckily it was not very far and she landed on the clothes she had pushed through the gate. The thick velvet-trimmed fabric broke her fall, so that she was able to get up at once, rubbing her bruised seat, and cast a swift glance up and down. As she had guessed, she was in a narrow passage, and at either end was a small hump-backed bridge. On one side, the left, there was a faint glimmer of light. In both directions the alley was completely deserted.

Marianne slipped her dress on again hurriedly, taking care to keep in the shelter of the wall, and then hesitated for a moment. As she did so, there came a distant roll of thunder and a gust of wind blew down the passage, lifting her unbound hair. The effect on her was electric. She flung both arms wide, as though to grasp the wind, and took a deep intoxicating breath. The breeze held more dust than it did sea air, but she was free! Free at last! Even if it was at the cost of four killings by a mysterious unknown hand, she was still free, and the dead who lay in the ancient splendours of their stolen palace were not worth a thought. To the newly-escaped prisoner it seemed a veritable judgement of God.

She paused for a moment, undecided which way to go, then, feeling suddenly lighthearted, she turned to the left and made her way towards the gleam of yellow light.

At the same instant, big, heavy drops of rain began to fall, making little coin-sized craters in the dust. The storm was reaching Venice.

Chapter Four
A sail on the Giudecca

Before Marianne had crossed the little bridge, she was caught in a torrential downpour. She saw people running for the doorway of the Soranzo palace and a cluster of gondolas nosing up to a small landing stage. Then, in a few seconds, everything was blotted out. Venice was drowned in a world of water, only pierced now and then by streaks of white lightning which brought the street into sudden sharp focus. The light for which Marianne had been making, probably an oil lamp burning before some holy statue, had vanished.

Drenched to the skin in no time, Marianne dashed on, without slackening her pace. The joy of being able to run, to forge straight ahead without thought for where her path might lead! So she simply put down her head and bowed her shoulders against the downpour.

For the storm which burst over the city was a good storm and the rain did her good, washing her more thoroughly than Damiani's slaves with their complicated ritual. It was as if the heavens had decided to send down a flood and wash away all trace of the blood and hate and shame, and Marianne revelled in the stinging rain with a blessed sense of release. She longed to scrub each fibre of her being clean of all memory of what had passed.

However, she could not go running about Venice all night long until she dropped with exhaustion. She had to find somewhere to go, and quickly, because, apart from the possibility of being picked up by the police, it was not unlikely that by daylight her strange appearance, and her sodden clothes and hair, would begin to attract attention.

It seemed to her that her best course was to look for a church where she could ask for help and succour, and also find out what the date was.

That was the one place where she could feel safe. The ancient right of sanctuary which had so often stood between the criminal and the law might also extend its inviolable shield to guard a woman, whose only crime was her desperate longing for happiness, from an authority which, she knew in her bones, would be both inquisitive and interfering. As a last resort, she could claim her kinship with the Cardinal San Lorenzo and hope that someone would believe her.

She ran on, between rows of greengrocers' stalls, closed at this hour, towards another bridge, and another alley. Blinded by the rain which streamed into her eyes, stumbling over leeks and cabbage stalks lying in the gutter, she nearly measured her length a dozen times in the mud.

It was pouring harder than ever by the time she came to a largish canal and, following it, crossed over another bridge to emerge breathless into an open square. In the glare of a flash of lightning, the graceful russet-coloured façade of a Gothic church loomed up out of the deluge on her right. But only for a moment. Then the pall of rain and darkness fell thicker than ever and the thunder cracked and rolled directly overhead.

Marianne veered and aimed herself by guesswork at the church glimpsed momentarily through the driving rain, only to be brought up short as she crashed painfully into a projecting corner of stonework. Her gasp of anguish changed to a startled scream as another lightning flash illumined the obstacle she was striving to circumvent. It was nothing but a statue, some equestrian warrior of the fourteenth century, but it reared over her with such vivid realism that it seemed to be plunging out of the very heavens, and, through the sculptor's skill, there was such brutal strength and power in the figure of the greenish-bronze horseman, and in the expression of the face and the jutting jaw outlined below the helmet's brim, that Marianne recoiled in spite of herself, as though the gigantic charger was about to trample her underfoot. On such a night of violence, nothing strange or supernatural seemed out of place, and the bronze condottiere surging unbidden out of the storm bore too much resemblance to the evil genius which dogged her. He reared up before her, crushing her with his pride and menace, as though daring her to try and pass him by . . .

Dragging herself away, she turned towards the church, which showed up again for a brief instant, and made a dash for the shelter of the porch. The door refused to open but she pressed herself against it in an effort to get out of the wet. Unhappily the porch was not deep and the rain beat down on her.

It had turned a lot colder since the rain, and Marianne was shivering now, with the water streaming in fountains from every stitch of clothing. She tried again and again to open the door, but without success.

'They always shut the church at night,' a quavering little voice spoke close beside her. 'But you can come over here if you like. It's not so wet and we can wait till the rain stops.'

'Who's that? I can't see.'

'Me. Over here. Stay where you are an' I'll come to you.'

There was a sound of splashing and then a small hand was slipped into Marianne's. So far as she could tell from his size, it belonged to an urchin of about ten years old.

'Come on,' he commanded her, towing her after him without further ceremony. 'There's more room in the porch of the Scuola and the rain's not coming that way. Your dress and your hair are sopping wet.'

'How do you know? I can hardly see you.'

'I can see in the dark. I'm like a cat, Annarella says.'

'Who is Annarella?'

'My big sister. She's like a spider. She makes lace. The finest lace in all Venice!'

Marianne laughed. 'Well, if you're hoping for a customer, you're wrong, my lad! I haven't a bean. But you sound like an odd family, I must say! The cat and the spider. It's like a fairy story.'

With the child leading, they ran together to the entrance of another building a few seconds away, to the right of the church. A brief flash revealed an elegant Renaissance front with curved pediments, on one of which was the lion of St Mark. As the boy had said, the broad pillared portal guarded by a pair of crouching beasts was very much more comfortable than the church porch.

Marianne had room to shake out her dress and wring the water out of her streaming hair. In any case, the rain was beginning to ease off. The child had not spoken again but for the sake of hearing his voice, which was pure and clear as crystal, she started to question him.

'Surely it's very late? What are you doing out at this hour? You ought to be in bed.'

'I had something to do for a friend,' the boy said vaguely, 'and I got caught in the rain, like you ... Where have you come from?'

'I don't know,' Marianne answered with a pang. 'I was locked up in a house and I escaped. I was trying to get into the church for shelter.'

There was silence. She could feel the child looking at her. He was probably thinking she was a lunatic and had escaped from some institution. She must look like it. But he only said, in the same matter-of-fact tone:

'The sacristan always locks San Zanipolo. In case of thieves. On account of the treasure. Lots of our doges are buried there – and he's there to keep guard over them,' he added, pointing to the bronze horseman who, seen from the side, seemed to be riding ahead of the church.

Lowering his voice suddenly, the boy whispered: 'Was it your lover who locked you up – or the police?'

Something told Marianne that her young friend would be more impressed by the latter. In any case, she could scarcely tell him the truth.

'The police! If they catch me, it's all up with me! Tell me, now – by the way, what's your name?'

'I'm called Zani – same as the church.'

'Well, Zani, can you tell me what day this is?'

'Don't you know?'

'No. I have been in a room with no light and no windows. It makes you lose count of time.'

'*Peccato!* You were lucky to get out! They're a bad lot, the police, and they've been worse than ever since Bonaparte's people came. Each trying to go one better than the other!'

'Very true, but please, please tell me what day ...' She clutched at his arm.

'Oh, yes, I was forgetting. It was the twenty-ninth of June when I set out. It must be the thirtieth now. It's not far off dawn.'

Marianne leaned weakly against the wall. Five days! For five days now Jason must have been waiting in the lagoon! He was so near, was probably spending his nights peering into the darkness looking for her, while she had been submitting in passive despair to Damiani's hateful caresses!

When she had left that dreadful house she had believed that she still had some time left to sort out her feelings, to think things over and try and wipe out the memory of the foul and shadowy time that lay behind her. She felt that she needed a breathing space before she faced Jason's penetrating eyes. She knew his perspicacity too well, and the unerring, almost animal instinct which made him invariably put his finger on the weakest spot. He would know at a glance that she was not the same woman he had said good-bye to aboard the *Saint-Guénolé* six months before. The blood which had been shed might avenge her shame but it could not do away with the living evidence that might remain inside her, although at this moment she could not bear to believe or even think of the possibility. Yet now, already, he was waiting for her!

In a few minutes, an hour perhaps, she might be with him. It was agony to think that the moment she had looked forward to so passionately for so long now held nothing but terror for her. She did not know now what awaited her beyond these watery streets and streaming domes, across this rain-drenched city which lay between her and the sea.

When she saw Jason, would it be as a happy lover, full of the joys of being reunited, or would he also be an inquisitor, nursing dark suspicions? He was expecting a happy woman, coming to him in the sunshine and in all the dazzle of beauty fulfilled, and he would see a hunted creature, as fearful and uneasy in herself as in her draggled clothes. What would he think?

'It's stopped raining, you know.'

Zani was pulling at her sleeve. She opened her eyes with a shiver and looked about her. It was true. The storm had ceased as suddenly as it had started. The thunder was rumbling away into the distance and the din and drenching rain of a moment ago had given place to a great calm, hardly broken by the trickle of water from the eaves. The exhausted air seemed to have paused for breath.

'If you've nowhere to go,' the child went on, his eyes shining like stars in the darkness, 'you can come to us. You can shelter there from the rain and the carabinieri.'

'But what will your sister say?'

'Annarella? Nothing. She's used to it.'

'Used to what?'

But Zani did not answer and Marianne sensed that his silence was deliberate. He simply walked on with his head held high and that air of innocent self-importance which denotes the bearer of weighty secrets. Forbearing to question him further, his new friend followed. The thought of a roof over her head was an agreeable one. A few hours' rest would do her good and might help her to dredge up from somewhere some semblance of the woman Jason was expecting to meet.

They set off in the direction from which Marianne had come but in the street of the vegetable stalls they turned left and were swallowed up in an infinity of narrow alleys broken by canals which appeared to Marianne a perfect maze.

The way they took was so circuitous that she could have sworn they had doubled back on their tracks a hundred times, but Zani never hesitated for so much as an instant.

The sky lightened to grey and somewhere a cock crowed, hailing the dawn, the only sound in the whole empty labyrinth where all human life lay hidden behind thick wooden shutters and the cats reigned supreme. These had lain snugly in some dry corner while the storm lasted but now they appeared on all sides, slinking past dripping gutters and leaping over puddles as they made their way home. Now, slowly, the houses were becoming visible: whimsical rooftops, pinnacles, balconies and weird funnel-shaped chimneys silhouetted against the first light of day. Everywhere was perfect peace and the two night-walkers might have thought they had the street to themselves when suddenly they ran into ill-luck.

They had just turned into the Merceria, a thoroughfare a little wider than most, although twisting, and lined with shops on both sides, when they came upon a patrol of National Guardsmen. A bend in the street made it impossible to avoid them.

In a moment, Marianne and the child were surrounded by soldiers, two of them bearing lanterns.

'Stay right where you are!' their leader ordered, with more force than logic since it was impossible for them to do anything else. 'Where are you off to?'

Taken by surprise and struck dumb by the sight of the uniforms, Marianne could only stare at him. He was a young officer with an arrogant expression, evidently well-pleased with his smart uniform and white leathers and sporting a moustache big enough for a small breastplate. He reminded her of Benielli.

But Zani, like a good Venetian, was already deep in a rapid stream of explanations. They poured from him at such a rate that his small, piping vice seemed to fill the street. He knew, of course, that this was no time for a boy of his age to be wandering round Venice but it wasn't their fault and the officer must please believe him because this was how it came about: he and his cousin had been called out last night to the bedside of Zia – that is, Aunt Lodovica who was sick with malaria. Cousin Paolo had sent for them before he went off fishing and of course they had gone at once because Zia Lodovica was old and so ill that her mind was wandering which was a terrible thing! She was such a clever woman, too, and the foster-sister and servant to Monsignior Lodovico Manin, the last doge. And, seeing her like that, himself and his cousin, they had not liked to leave her so they had stayed and watched by her and done what they could for her and so the time had gone by. And then, when the crisis was over and their aunt had gone to sleep it was very late. Since there was nothing more they could do and Cousin Paolo would be back in the morning, Zani and his cousin had set off home because his sister Annarella would be worrying about them. Then they had got caught in the rain and been obliged to take shelter until it was over. So now, if the noble soldiers would kindly let them go on their way ...

Marianne had listened to this extempore speech with fascinated admiration, nor did the soldiers make any attempt to interrupt, being probably too dazed by the flow of words. But neither did they stand aside and their leader asked again :

'What's your name?'

'Zani, Signor Officer, Zani Mocchi, and this is my cousin Appolonia—'

'Mocchi? Any relation to the courier from Dalmatia who disappeared near Zara a few weeks ago?'

Zani bowed his head, as though under the weight of great grief.

'My brother, signor. It's a dreadful thing because we still don't know what has become of him ...'

He seemed to be prepared to continue in this vein but one of the soldiers leaned across and said something in the officer's ear which made him frown.

'I understand that your father was shot in 1806 for making subversive speeches against the Emperor, and this sister Anna-rella, who will be worrying so, is the notorious lacemaker of San Trovaso who makes no secret of her dislike of us. Your family does not love us and there have been suggestions at headquarters that your brother may have gone over to the enemy ...'

Things were beginning to look awkward and Marianne cast desperately about for some way of assisting her small friend without betraying herself, but Zani spoke up bravely.

'What cause have we to love you?' he cried boldly. 'When your General Bonaparte came here and burned our Golden Book and proclaimed a new republic we thought he was going to give us real liberty! And then he handed us over to Austria! And now he's taken us back again, only he's not a republican general any more but an emperor, so all we've got out of it is a change of emperors. We could have loved you. It's your fault if we don't!'

'Ho ho! You've a long tongue for such a little shrimp! I wonder now ... but what about this one, your cousin is she? What has she got to say for herself?'

One of the lanterns, held up by an arm in a braided sleeve, shone full on Marianne's face. The officer whistled through his teeth.

'By heavens! What a pair of eyes! And what a rig-out for the cousin of such a ragged urchin! More like a fine lady!'

This time, Marianne knew it was up to her to take a hand in support of Zani's story. The officer was altogether too suspicious. Entering into the spirit of the thing, she favoured him with a saucy smile.

'Well and so I am a lady – almost! It's a real pleasure to meet with such a discerning gentleman, Signor Officer. It didn't take you long to see that I don't belong here even if I am Zani's cousin. I'm just on a visit for a few days to see my cousin Annarella. I live in Florence, really.' She smirked complacently. 'I'm a lady's maid to Baroness Cenami who's companion to her royal highness Princess Elisa, the Grand Duchess of Tuscany, God bless her!'

She crossed herself several times very fast as evidence of her devotion to so illustrious a princess. The effect, indeed, was magical. At the mention of Napoleon's sister, the officer's face relaxed. He drew himself up, ran a finger round the inside of his high collar and gave a twirl to his moustache.

'Indeed? Well then, my pretty dear, you can think yourself lucky to have met with Sergeant Rapin, a man that understands these things! Anyone else might have taken you in for question-ing—'

'You are letting us go?'

'But of course! But we'll see you on your way a step, just in case you should happen to run into another patrol that might not know how to treat a lady like yourself ...'

'But – we should not like to put you to any trouble ...'

'Trouble! Not a bit of it! A pleasure! If you're going to San Trovaso, our way is in the same direction. You'll not have to look far for a ferryman to take you across the Grand Canal if you're with us, and besides ...' he dropped his voice to a con-fidential whisper, 'Venice is not safe tonight. We've been warned to look out for conspirators! The south of Italy is full of them and they are sending their agents up here. Seems they call themselves Carbonari – charcoal burners, that is. Not that that makes it any easier to tell them in the dark.'

Delighted with this evidence of his own superlative wit, Sergeant Rapin gave a roar of laughter, dutifully echoed by his men, and then gallantly offered his arm to Marianne who was still gaping at the success of her diplomatic invention.

The patrol resumed its way, swelled by the addition of Marianne, walking ahead on Rapin's arm, and Zani who was so overcome with admiration for his new friend that he attached himself to her skirts and clung inseparably.

The light was growing swiftly, driving out the darkness with the eager haste of a summer morning. In the east the grey dawn was already tinged with pink. In a little while, people and things stood out clearly and the lanterns, now no longer needed, were put out.

Tired and anxious as she was, Marianne thought their curious procession certainly had its funny side.

'We must look like a village wedding gone wrong,' she told herself, as her unlooked-for gallant went on pouring nonsense into her ear, doing his best to obtain an assignation although it was not clear whether he was prompted by her personal charms or by her connection with the court.

The Merceria dived suddenly underneath a broad archway cut through the base of a tower supporting a vast clock surmounted by a bell. As they emerged on the other side, Marianne had a sudden sense that she had been transported into a fairytale, so beautiful was the spectacle which met her eyes.

She saw a cloud of white pigeons fly up into the pale violet morning, and go circling up, like spiralling snowflakes about a slender rose-coloured campanile. She saw the twin green domes and alabaster pinnacles belonging to a church that was like a palace, and a palace like a jewel : delicate, flesh-tinted stone, gold mosaics, lacework of marble and enamelled turrets. She saw a huge square fringed with a border of arcades and marked out in white marble like some outsize game of hopscotch. Last, between the splendid palace and another box-like building with a row of statues along the top, framed by a pair of lofty columns, one topped by a winged lion, the other by the figure of a saint with a kind of crocodile, there lay a wide expanse of silky blue that made her heart beat faster.

Lateen-sailed vessels moved like bunches of anemones over the silvery surface, and beyond them another dome, another campanile emerging from the misty distance. Yet it was the sea all the same, the roadstead of St Mark where Jason might be waiting for her . . .

Sergeant Rapin, for his part, had seen something rather different. He dropped Marianne's arm abruptly as they came out from beneath the clock-tower, for they were now in sight of the guards on duty outside the royal palace, formerly the Procuratie, and gallantry must yield to discipline. He saluted in correct military fashion.

'I and my men leave you here, Signorina, but you are not far from home now. But before we part, may I beg the favour of another meeting? It seems a shame that we should be such near neighbours and not see one another, don't you think?' He smiled engagingly.

'I'd be glad to, Sir!' Marianne simpered, with a readiness that did credit to her acting talents. 'But I don't know that my cousin—'

'You're not dependent on your cousin, surely? And you a member of her Imperial Highness's own household?'

Rapin's imagination was clearly as fertile as Zani's and in the short interval of time they had spent together he had contrived to do away with Marianne's supposed employer, the Baroness Cenami, whose name evidently meant nothing to him, and remember only her august mistress, the Princess Elisa.

'No, no, of course not,' Marianne said hastily. 'But I shall not be here much longer. Indeed, I am leaving—'

'Don't tell me you are leaving tonight,' the sergeant interrupted her, giving another twirl to his moustache, 'or you will oblige me to stop all vessels leaving for the mainland. Stay until tomorrow . . . then we can meet tonight . . . go to a theatre . . . I can get tickets for the opera, at the Fenice. You'd like that . . .'

Marianne was beginning to think her importunate soldier would be more difficult to be rid of than she had anticipated. If she were to rebuff him, he might turn nasty, and Zani and his sister might have to pay for it. So she controlled her irritation and glanced quickly at the boy who was observing the scene with a little frown. Then, her mind made up, she drew the sergeant a little apart from his men. They, too, were beginning to show signs of impatience.

'Listen,' she whispered, remembering suddenly his questions to the child. 'I can't go to the theatre with you, or ask you to come to my cousin's to call for me. Ever since my other cousin, the courier from Zara, disappeared we have been more or less in mourning. And Annarella hasn't the same reason to like the French as I have.'

'I see,' Rapin breathed back, 'but what is to be done? I like you, you see.'

'I like you too, Sergeant, but the family would never forgive me. It's much better to be quiet about it – meet in secret, you understand? We shan't be the first.'

Rapin's plain, honest face lit up. He had been long enough in Venice to have heard of Romeo and Juliet and now he was obviously seeing himself in a mysterious love affair with a spice of adventure about it.

'You can count on me!' he declared enthusiastically. Then, remembering to lower his voice to a conspiratorial mutter, he said in muffled tones: 'Tonight ... at dusk ... I'll wait for you under the acacia at San Zaccharia. We can talk there. You'll come?'

'I'll come. But take care! No one must know!'

On this promise, they parted and Marianne had to bite back a sigh of relief. She had felt for a moment as though she were taking part in one of the farces so beloved of the strollers in the Boulevard du Temple in Paris. Rapin saluted, but not without stealing a furtive and passionate handclasp with one whom he evidently regarded as his latest conquest.

The weary patrol marched off into the palace, trailing their weapons, and Zani led his supposed cousin, somewhat to her disappointment, away from the sea to the far end of the square where workmen were beginning to arrive on the site of a new series of arcades destined to fill up the fourth side.

'This way,' he hissed. 'It's quicker.'

'But – can't I have a look at the sea?'

'Later. We'll get to it sooner like this, and the soldiers would think it funny if we went any other way.'

The city was beginning to wake up. The bells of St Mark's rang out and women in black shawls, some of them made of lace, were hurrying to church for early mass.

When, after a short walk, they reached the waterfront, Marianne's heart missed a beat and she had a temptation to shut her eyes, hoping and yet fearing to see the proud lines of Jason's brig *Sea Witch* at anchor in the roads. However much she reasoned with herself, she could not help feeling as guilty as an adulterous wife returning to her husband.

But except for the little fishing boats, flitting out towards the Lido, the shallops laden with vegetables making their way up the Grand Canal, and the big barge which served as a passenger link with the mainland, there was no vessel worthy of the name in the pool. But before Marianne had time to feel disappointment, she caught sight of the tall mastheads of sea-going ships standing up behind the Dogana di Mare, on the other side of the Punta della Salute. The blood rushed to her cheeks and she grasped Zani by the arm.

'I want to go across there,' she said, pointing.

The boy shrugged and glanced at her curiously.

'We are. That's the way to San Trovaso, surely you know that?'

Then, as they made their way to the big gondola that ferried passengers across the Grand Canal, Zani voiced the question which must have been on his mind for some time.

Ever since their parting from the patrol, the young Venetian had been oddly silent. He had walked ahead of Marianne, his hands dug deeply into the pockets of his rather frayed blue canvas trousers, pushing up folds of the still-damp shirt of yellow wool which came down nearly to his knees. There was a stiffness in his attitude which suggested that he was not altogether happy about something.

'Is it true,' he asked, in a small, hard voice, 'that you are lady's maid to that Baroness ... thingummy? ... Close to Bonaparte's sister?'

'Of course. Does it worry you?'

'A bit. It means that you must be for Bonaparte too. The soldier knew that, he—'

Doubt and disappointment were written so clearly on the round brown face that Marianne forbore to add to his trouble.

'My mistress is for – Bonaparte, naturally,' she said gently. 'But for myself, I have no interest in politics. I serve my mistress, that's all.'

'Then where are you from? Not from here, at any rate. You don't know the city and you haven't the accent.'

Marianne's hesitation was scarcely perceptible. It was true that she did not speak with the Venetian accent but her Italian was a pure Tuscan which made her answer come quite naturally.

'I am from Lucca,' she said. It was, after all, not altogether a lie.

The result more than rewarded her. Zani's worried little face broke into a dazzling smile and his hand crept back into Marianne's.

'Oh, that's all right then! You can come to our house. But it's some way yet. You're not too tired?' he added anxiously.

'A bit,' Marianne confessed, conscious that her legs were numb with fatigue. 'Is it much farther?'

'A bit.'

A sleepy ferryman took them across the canal, which was almost deserted at this hour of the morning. It promised to be an exceptionally lovely day. The sky was a soft blue, washed clean by the night's storm, streaked across with flocks of pigeons. The wind off the sea was cool and smelled of salt and seaweed, and Marianne took deep rapturous breaths as they moved slowly on to where la Salute on its point hung like a gigantic seashell in the clear morning air. It was a day made for happiness, and Marianne dared not look ahead to what it might hold for her.

Once on the far side, there were more alleys, more little flying bridges, more half-glimpsed wonders and more prowling cats. The sun rose in a glory of gold and she was reeling with exhaustion by the time they came to a point where two canals met. The wider of the two, lined with tall pink houses with washing drying at their windows, flowed directly into the waters of the harbour. It was spanned by a slender bridge.

'There!' Zani said proudly. 'That's where I live. San Trovaso! The *squero* of San Trovaso is the hospital for sick gondolas.'

He was pointing across the water to where, beyond the orange peel and rotting vegetables, lay a number of brown wooden sheds with a dozen or so gondolas drawn up before them, lying on their sides like wounded sharks.

'You live there?'

'No, over there. The last house on the corner of the quay, right at the top.'

A masthead sticking up beyond the corner of the house showed where a tall ship lay at anchor. Marianne could not help herself. Her weariness was forgotten as she picked up her skirts and ran with the bewildered Zani hard on her heels. She could not wait to see if Jason was there waiting for her.

It had already occurred to her that he might be late for their meeting and this was the real reason why she had followed Zani so far.

Friendless and penniless, she had nowhere else to go if Jason had not come. Now, suddenly, the possibility seemed to have receded. She was sure he must be there.

She emerged, panting, on to the quay. Sunshine was all about her and there, all at once, on all sides, was a forest of masts. Ships were everywhere: serried ranks of slender prows on one hand and a solid mass of sterncastles with gleaming lanterns on the other. A whole fleet was there, connected to the shore by long dipping planks on which the porters moved up and down under their heavy loads as nimbly as acrobats. There were so many ships that Marianne felt dazed. Her brain reeled.

Orders rang out, mingling with the shrilling of bosuns' whistles and the striking of ships' bells. Music hung in the air, played by an unseen mandoline, and the tune was taken up by a barefoot girl in a striped petticoat carrying a shimmering basketful of fish on her head. The rose-coloured quayside was alive with people going about their business, as noisy and colourful as characters in a Goldoni play, while on board the moored vessels men stripped to the waist were swabbing down the decks with big buckets of clean water.

'What are you doing?' Zani's voice reproached her. 'You've gone past the house. Come in and rest.'

But the impatience of love was stronger than fatigue. At the sight of all those ships, Marianne felt the fever of anticipation stir in her again. Jason was there – not far away! She was certain, she could feel it! So how could she possibly think of going to sleep? Suddenly, all her earlier doubts and hesitations fell away, like so much dead skin. The only thing that mattered was to see him, feel him and touch him.

Resisting all Zani's efforts to detain her, she thrust her way through the busy crowd on the quay, gazing up at the vessels at their moorings, studying the faces of the men and peering at the silhouetted figure of a captain pacing the poop, but nowhere did she see the one she was looking for.

Then, quite suddenly, she saw it. The *Sea Witch* was there, right out on the Giudecca, several cables' length away from the vessels ranged along the quayside. She was veering gracefully on the calm waters while out ahead the men in the longboats bent manfully to the oars and barefoot sailors swarmed in the shrouds.

Marianne had a brief glimpse of the siren figure at the prow, twin sister to herself.

The sun gleamed on her brasswork and Marianne gazed, fascinated, at the lovely ship, scanning the moving figures on the deck for one she knew would be unmistakable. But the *Sea Witch* was putting on sail, as a gull spreads its wings, she was swinging round by the head, lifting to the wind, moving out to sea...

Understanding burst on Marianne. A wild cry broke from her:

'No!...No! Don't!...Jason!'

She began to run along the quay, screaming and shouting like a lunatic, hurling herself blindly through the crowd regardless of the knocks she received or of the stares that followed her. Dock hands, market women, sailors and fishermen turned to look after the dishevelled, tear-stained woman running with outstretched arms and uttering heartbroken cries, apparently on the point of casting herself into the sea.

Marianne herself was aware of nothing, she saw and heard nothing, only that the ship was going away from her. The thought was torture. It was as though an invisible thread, woven from her own flesh, had been drawn between her and the American vessel, stretching tighter and tighter, agonizingly, until it tore the heart out of her breast and drowned it in the sea.

A single sentence repeated itself endlessly in her brain, with cruel insistence, like an ironic refrain :

'He didn't wait for me . . . He didn't wait . . .'

Jason had sailed across two seas and an ocean for this meeting, yet his patience and his love had not endured beyond five days. He had not sensed that she, whom he claimed to love, was there, close at hand; he had not heard her desperate cries. Now he was going away, sailing out to sea, to the sea that was his other mistress, this time, perhaps, for ever. How could she reach him now, how call him back ?

She was gasping for breath and her heart was knocking painfully in her chest, but she ran on, her eyes, blinded with tears, fixed on the ever-widening dazzle of sunlight between ship and shore. It danced before her like an ultimate sign of hope, drawing her like a lover. A few more steps and she would plunge into it . . .

A strong hand grasped her just as she reached the very end of the quay.

She was on the point of casting herself, borne on an irresistible impulse, straight into the water, when she found herself pulled up short and overborne. She looked up and found herself face to face with Lieutenant Benielli, who was staring at her as if he had seen a ghost.

'You ?' he ejaculated, as he recognized the frenzied woman whom he had just saved from suicide. 'Is it you ? . . . It's unbelievable !'

But Marianne had reached the point where the sight of Napoleon himself could not have surprised her. She did not even recognize who was holding her, seeing him only as an obstruction to be circumvented. She struggled furiously in his arms, fighting desperately to escape.

'Let me go !' she screamed. 'Let me go !'

Fortunately the Corsican lieutenant had a firm grip, but his patience was short. It came to an end abruptly and he gave his prisoner a smart shaking in an effort to silence the screams which were attracting everyone on the quay. Some of those who approached were looking quite ugly, seeing only that a member of the 'occupying' forces was molesting a young woman. Conscious that he was in a minority, Benielli opened his mouth and yelled :

'Dragoons! To me!'

Marianne herself did not see the arrival of Benielli's reinforcements. She continued to scream and struggle until the exasperated lieutenant silenced her with a neatly delivered blow from his fist. Instead of into the waters of the harbour, Marianne plunged into merciful unconsciousness.

When she came round from the effects of this involuntary swoon, under the influence of a compress of aromatic vinegar held under her nose, it was to find herself looking at the lower half of a black and yellow striped dressing-gown and a pair of embroidered slippers which seemed somehow familiar. She had worked that design of roses on a black background with her own hands.

She raised her head, reviving the pain in her injured jaw, and almost bit the pad which a kneeling chambermaid was holding under her nose. She thrust the girl away automatically and gave a cry of joy.

'Arcadius!'

It was he indeed. Swathed in the striped gown, his feet thrust into the slippers, and his hair standing on end in two comical tufts which made him look more like a mouse than ever, the Vicomte de Jolival was earnestly supervising the restorative treatment.

'She's come round, my lord,' the chambermaid announced, with remarkable perspicacity, as the invalid sat up.

'Splendid. You may leave us now.'

Almost before the girl had got to her feet and made room for him to sit down on the edge of the sofa, Marianne had flung herself into his arms.

The return of consciousness had brought with it the recollection of her woes and she fell on his chest and wept, too much distressed to utter a single word.

Deeply pitying, but also deeply experienced, Jolival allowed the storm to wear itself out and confined himself to gently stroking the still-damp hair of the girl he regarded in the light of an adopted daughter. Gradually, the sobs diminished and in a lost, little-girl voice, Marianne murmured into her old friend's ear:

'Jason! ... He's gone!'

Arcadius laughed and raising Marianne's tear-blotched face from his shoulder, he drew a handkerchief from his dressing-gown pocket and wiped her red and swollen eyes.

'And is that why you were trying to throw yourself into the harbour? Yes, he's gone – all the way to Chioggia to take on fresh water and a cargo of smoked sturgeon. He'll be back tomorrow. In fact, it was for that very reason that Benielli was watching the harbour. I told him to be there as soon as the *Sea Witch* put to sea and I was to relieve him later on myself in case you should arrive while the ship was away, as indeed you did.'

A wonderful sense of relief stole over Marianne. She was torn between the desire to laugh and a strong impulse to cry again and she looked at Jolival with a good deal of respect.

'You *knew* I'd come?'

The urbane vicomte's smile faded and the girl saw that he had aged in her absence. There was a little more silver about his temples and lines of anxiety were deeply carved between his brows and at the corners of his mouth. Very tenderly, she kissed away the signs of worry.

'It was our one chance of finding you,' he said, sighing. 'I knew that if you were still alive, you would do your utmost to be here in time to meet Jason. And in spite of all our efforts, even the efforts of the Grand Duchess herself, who set her own police to work on the case, we could find no other clue. Agathe said something about a letter from Madame Cenami which might have something to do with it, because you had gone out in a hurry, and plainly dressed, as though to avoid notice. But Madame Cenami had sent no letter, of course – and you failed to leave the slightest hint.' The last words were uttered in a mildly reproachful tone.

'Zoe's letter begged for secrecy. I supposed she must be in some trouble. I never thought ... but if you only knew how I've regretted it!'

'Poor child. Love, friendship and prudence do not generally live easily together, especially where you are concerned. Naturally, both Arrighi and myself thought at once of your husband, that he had lost patience.'

'The Prince is dead,' Marianne said soberly. 'Murdered.'

'Hm.' It was Jolival's turn now to study his friend's face. How much she had endured was written clearly in its pallor and the haunted look in her eyes. He guessed that she had lived through some terrible experience and that it was, perhaps, still too soon to talk about it. So, postponing the inevitable questions, Jolival said merely:

'You shall tell me about it later. Obviously, that explains a good deal. But when you vanished, we were half out of our minds. Gracchus was threatening to set fire to the villa at Lucca and Agathe cried all day long and kept on insisting that the devil of the Sant'Annas had carried you off. The coolest person, as might have been expected, was the Duke of Padua. He went in person to the Villa dei Cavalli, with a strong escort, but found none there but servants, and no more of them than served to keep the place up. No one could tell him where the Prince was to be found. It seems that he is – or rather was – in the habit of going away suddenly, often for long periods, telling no one when he meant to return.

'We went back to Florence feeling thoroughly hopeless and wretched, because we no longer had the smallest clue. We were still very far from convinced that Prince Sant'Anna had no hand in your disappearance but we knew virtually nothing about his other estates, or where to begin the search. In what direction, even! The Grand-Ducal police were equally baffled. It was then I thought of coming here, for the reason I have told you, although I must say, ever since Beaufort arrived five days ago, my hopes have been dwindling hourly. I thought—'

Jolival's voice broke and he turned his head away to hide his feelings.

'You thought I was dead, didn't you? Oh, my poor friend, forgive me for the distress I've caused you. I wish I could have spared you. But did he – did Jason think that I—'

'No! He never had a moment's doubt. He absolutely refused to even consider it. He rejected the very idea. "If she were no longer in this world," he kept saying, "then I should feel it. I should feel as though I'd lost a limb, I'd bleed, or my heart would cease to beat, but I should know!"'

'Indeed, that was why he went this morning : so as to be ready to weigh anchor the moment you appeared. Although I suspect the waiting was preying on his nerves, though he would have had his tongue cut out before he admitted it. He was like a man possessed, never easy unless he was on the move, doing something. But where were you, Marianne? Do you feel able to tell me yet, or is it still too painful?'

'Dear Jolival! You have been through hell on my account and now you're dying to know ... And yet you've waited all this time to ask because you were afraid to awake unpleasant recollections! I have been here, my dear.'

'Here?'

'Yes. In Venice. At the Palazzo Soranzo, which once belonged to the Prince's grandmother, the notorious Dona Lucinda.'

'So we were right! It was your husband—'

'No. Matteo Damiani, the steward. It was he who killed my husband.'

And Marianne told Jolival all that had taken place since she had gone out, supposedly to meet Zoe Cenami, in the church of Or San Michele : her abduction, the journey and her degrading captivity. The telling of it was long and difficult because, greatly as she loved and trusted her old friend, she was obliged to recall too many things that did violence to her pride and modesty. It was hard for a woman both beautiful and much admired to have to confess that for weeks she had been treated no better than an animal, or a slave bought in the open market. But it was necessary that Arcadius should know the whole extent of her moral wreck, since he was probably the only person who could help her – perhaps even the only one who could understand.

He heard her out with a mixture of imperturbable calm and fierce agitation. Now and then, at the most painful moments, he got up and strode about the room, his hands behind his back and his head thrust forward, struggling to take in the extraordinary tale which, coming from anyone but Marianne, he would have found almost beyond belief. When it was over and Marianne fell back exhausted on the sofa cushions and closed her eyes, he went quickly to a marquetry side-table, poured himself a drink from a flask, and drank it off at a gulp.

'Would you like some?' he offered. 'It's the best cordial I know, and you probably need it more than I do.'

Marianne shook her head.

'Forgive me for inflicting all this on you, Arcadius, but I had to tell you everything. You don't know how badly I needed to!'

'I think I do. Anyone who had been through what you have suffered would feel the need to get some of it off their chest, at least. And you know that my chief function on earth is to serve you. As for forgiveness – my dear child, what have I to forgive you for? You could not have given me a greater proof of your confidence than this tissue of horrors. What we have to decide is what to do next. This villain and his accomplices are all dead, you say?'

'Yes. Killed. I don't know who by.'

'Personally I am inclined to think that executed would be a better word. As for who was the executioner ...'

'Some prowler, perhaps. The palace is full of treasures.'

Jolival shook his head doubtfully.

'No. There are those rusty chains you found on the steward's body. That suggests vengeance as a motive, or some kind of rough justice! Damiani must have had enemies. Perhaps one of them learned of your plight and set you free ... remember that you found the clothes that had been taken from you lying ready to hand! It's certainly a most peculiar story, don't you think?'

But Marianne had already lost interest in her captor of yesterday. Now that she had made a clean breast of it all to her friend, her next preoccupation was with her love, and her thoughts turned irresistibly to the man she had come to meet and with whom she still meant to make her life.

'But Jason?' she asked desperately. 'Should I tell him all this?

You are very fond of me, and yet even you found it difficult to accept my story, didn't you? I'm afraid—'

'Afraid that Beaufort, who loves you, will find it even more difficult? But, Marianne, what else can you do? How are you going to explain your disappearance during the past weeks except by telling the truth, however painful?'

Marianne sprang up from her cushions with a cry and running to Jolival took both his hands in hers.

'No, for pity's sake, Arcadius, don't ask that of me. Don't ask me to tell him those shameful things. It would make him loathe me ... he might even hold me in disgust ...'

'Why should he? Was it your fault? Did you go to the villain of your own free will? You have been abused, Marianne, first in your kindness and simplicity and secondly as a helpless woman, not to mention the base means employed: drugs and violence!'

'I know. I know all that but I know Jason, too. He can be jealous ... violent. He has already had much to forgive me. Remember what it must have done to his strict moral principles to find himself in love with Napoleon's mistress. Then remember that after that I was obliged to literally sell myself to a total stranger in order to preserve my honour. And now you want me to tell him ... to try and explain ... ? Oh, no, my dear friend! I can't. Don't ask me to do that! It's just impossible.'

'Be sensible, Marianne. You said yourself that Jason loves you enough to overlook a good deal.'

'Not that! Oh, he wouldn't blame me, of course. He'd ... understand, or try to look as though he understood to spare me pain. But I should lose him. There would always be that frightful picture between us, and if I kept anything back from him, he would imagine it! I should die of grief. You don't want me to die, do you, Arcadius? You wouldn't like that ...'

She was trembling like a leaf in the grip of a panic fear resulting partly from the terrors of the past days and partly from despair and the tormenting dread of losing her only love.

Arcadius put his arm round her, led her very gently to a chair and made her sit down. Clasping her suddenly ice-cold hands in his, he knelt beside her.

'Not only do I not want you to die, my child, I very much want you to be happy. Of course, it's natural for you to be frightened at the idea of telling the man you love a thing like this, but what can you tell him?'

'I don't know. That the Prince kidnapped me ... locked me up somewhere ... and I escaped. I'll think of something ... and you'll think too, won't you, Arcadius? You're so clever ... so intelligent ...'

'And supposing something comes of the affair? What will you say then?'

'Nothing will come of it. I won't let it! To begin with, there's no reason to think that monster's efforts were successful, and if they were ...'

'Well?'

'I'd get rid of it, if I have to risk my life to do it. I'd do anything to be free of that rotten fruit, and I will, if I ever find out that it's true! But Jason must never, never know! I told you: I'd rather die! You must promise me you'll not tell him, even on pledge of secrecy. You must swear to it. If you won't, I shall go mad!'

She was in such a state that Jolival saw it was impossible to reason with her. Her eyes were burning with fever and exhaustion and there was a shrill note in her voice that revealed nerves strained almost to breaking point, ready to snap at any moment.

'I promise, my dear, and now, for heaven's sake, calm yourself. You need rest and sleep ... to help you recover. You are quite safe with me. No one can harm you and I'll do all I can to help you to forget this time as quickly as possible. Gracchus and Agathe are here with me, you know. And now I'll call your maid and she shall put you to bed and take care of you and no one, I promise you, is going to ask you any more questions ...'

Jolival's voice flowed on in a gentle, reassuring murmur, soft and soothing as velvet, and it acted like oil on troubled waters.

Little by little, Marianne relaxed, and when, a minute later, Agathe and Gracchus burst into the room with cries of joy, they found her weeping softly in Jolival's arms.

But these, too, were healing tears.

Chapter Five
Dreams to reality

Late on the following afternoon, Marianne lay on a sofa pulled up to the open window and watched two ships come sailing through the Lido Channel. The first and larger of the two was flying the American colours from her peak but it did not need the stars on her flag to tell the watcher it was Jason's ship.

She had known from the confused and contradictory state of her own feelings, even when the tall, square-rigged brig was no more than a white dot against the sky.

The sun which all day long had blazed down on Venice was sinking in a welter of molten gold behind the church of the Redeemer. A breath of cooler air drifted through the window, bringing with it the sound of seabirds crying, and Marianne sniffed appreciatively, enjoying the fragile peace of these last moments of solitude, and wondering a little that she should be doing so when the thing she was waiting for was the arrival of the man she loved.

In a few minutes, he would come. She pictured his entrance, his first look, his first words and trembled with mingled joy and apprehension: apprehension that she might not be able to sustain the role she had decreed for herself, that she might not be sufficiently natural.

Waking that morning, after practically sleeping the clock round twice, she had felt much better, her mind easier and her body relaxed by her sleep which, thanks to Jolival, had been surrounded by more luxury than might have been expected.

Instead of putting up at one of the inns, Jolival had taken rooms in a private house on his arrival in Venice. In Florence he had been recommended to the house of a Signor Giuseppe Dal Niel, a polite, good-natured and cheerfully-disposed individual who, at the fall of the Republic, had rented the upper floors of the splendid old palace built for the doge Giovanni Dandolo, the man who had given Venice her coinage and had been responsible for striking the first golden ducats.

Dal Niel was a widely-travelled man and consequently deplored the poverty of contemporary inns and hostelries. He had the notion of taking in paying guests and surrounding them with a degree of comfort, even luxury, hitherto quite unknown. It was his dream to get possession of the whole of the mansion and turn it into the greatest hotel of all time, but in order to do so he needed the ground floor, and this, so far, he had failed to acquire, since the present owner, the old Countess Mocenigo, was violently set against any such commercial undertaking.*

He made up for it by taking in only hand-picked visitors in whom he took as much interest as if they had been his personal guests. Twice a day he would attend them in person, or send his daughter Alfonsina to make sure that they had everything they required. Naturally he could not do enough for the Princess Sant'Anna, in spite of her somewhat unconventional arrival, clad in a soaking wet gown, in the arms of an officer of dragoons, and he had given strict orders to his staff that no noise be allowed to disturb her rest.

As a result of his care, Marianne had succeeded, in a single day, in erasing the marks of her imprisonment, and she now presented a fresh and blooming countenance to the sun. If it had not been for the evil memories which still persisted, she would have felt gloriously well.

As soon as the *Witch*'s lines became clear beyond a doubt, Jolival had gone down to the harbour to tell Jason of Marianne's arrival and explain what had happened to her, or that version of it which had been concocted between them. Agreeing that the simplest was always the best, this was what they had decided upon together: Marianne had been carried off by her husband's orders and kept prisoner under strong guard in a house whose whereabouts she did not know, where she remained in total ignorance of the fate in store for her, a fate which her injured husband seemed in no hurry to reveal. All she knew was that

* He had to wait until 1822 before he was at last able to found the Royal Danieli hotel, still the most exclusive in Venice.

she was to be put on board ship for some unknown destination. One night, however, when her guards were unusually lax, she had succeeded in escaping and making her way to Venice where Jolival had found her.

It was Jolival, of course, who had applied himself to fabricating a sufficiently circumstantial account of her actual escape, and Marianne had spent much of the day going over her lesson until she was sure of being word perfect. Even so, she could not help feeling uncomfortable at telling a lie against which all her natural honesty and truthful instincts rebelled.

The story was a necessary one, certainly, because, as Jolival himself said, 'the truth cannot always be told', especially to a lover, but Marianne found it all the more distasteful because it involved the name of one who was not only innocent of any wrong but was actually the chief victim of the affair. It went against all her instincts to portray as a ruthless abductor the man whose name she bore and for whose death she was, indirectly, responsible.

She had always known that everything, in this imperfect world, had to be paid for, and happiness above all, but the thought that her own would be built upon a lie brought with it a superstitious dread lest fate should exact its penalty for the deception.

All the same, she knew that she was capable of enduring anything for Jason, even the hell of these past days ... even to live a lie.

A large mirror ornamented with glass flowers, hanging on the wall near her sofa, showed her her reflection looking charmingly graceful in a dress of white muslin, with her hair beautifully dressed by Agathe, but neither rest nor any amount of beautifying had been able to dispel the worried look in her eyes.

She forced herself to smile but the smile did not reach her eyes.

'Is there anything wrong, your highness?' asked Agathe, who had observed this manoeuvre from the corner where she was sitting quietly with her needlework.

'No, nothing at all, Agathe. Why should you think so?'

'Only that you do not look very happy, my lady. You should

go out on to the balcony. At this time of day the whole city is out there on the quayside. And you will be able to see Monsieur Beaufort when he comes.'

Marianne told herself she was a fool. What did it look like for her to be sitting here, skulking on a sofa, when she ought ordinarily to have been bursting with impatience to see him? The previous day's exhaustion made it natural for her to let Jolival go alone to the harbour, but not to be lurking here in-doors instead of looking out for him like any woman in love. She could hardly explain to her maid that she was afraid of being recognized by a sergeant in the National Guard or by a nice small boy who had helped her.

At the thought of Zani, she was aware of a twinge of remorse. The child must have watched in utter bewilderment as she was knocked out and carried off by Benielli. He must be wondering now what kind of a dangerous person he had been consorting with and Marianne felt some regrets for a promising friendship which had been broken off.

Nevertheless she got up from her couch and took a few turns up and down the loggia, while taking care to keep in the shade of the Gothic pillars that supported it.

Agathe had been right. Down below, the Riva degli Schiavoni was crowded with people. It was like an endless ballet, full of noise and colour, moving back and forth between the Doges' Palace and the Arsenal and offering an amazing spectacle of life and gaiety. Even defeated, uncrowned, occupied and reduced to the status of a provincial town, Venice still remained the in-comparable Serenissima.

'Which is more than I do!' Marianne muttered, remembering that she bore the same title. 'Much more than I do!'

A sudden swirl in the crowd dragged her from her melancholy thoughts. Down there, a few yards away, a man had jumped from a boat and was forging through the throng towards the Palazzo Dandolo. He was very tall, much taller than those he was thrusting out of his path. He cut through the crowd like an irresistible force, as easily as a ship breasting the waves, and Jolival, behind him, was having considerable difficulty keeping up. The man was broad-shouldered and blue-eyed, with a proud face and unruly black hair.

'Jason!' Marianne breathed, suddenly wild with joy. 'At last!'

In an instant, her heart had made its choice between fear and happiness. Everything but the glow of love had been swept away. Her whole being was irradiated.

As Jason, down below, vanished inside the palace, Marianne picked up her skirts with both hands and ran to the door. Speeding through the rooms like lightning, she flung herself down the stairs just as her lover was starting up them two at a time. With a shriek of joy that was almost a sob, she cast herself on his chest, laughing and crying at once.

He, too, cried out as he saw her. He roared out her name so loudly that the vaulted ceilings of the ancient palace rang again, making up for the many months of silence during which he had only been able to murmur it in his dreams. Then, his arms were round her, and he swung her off the ground, covering her with frantic kisses, devouring her face and neck like a starving man, regardless of the servants who, drawn by the noise, were hanging over the banisters to watch.

Jolival and Dal Niel stood, side by side, at the foot of the stairs and gazed upwards with approval.

'*E meraviglioso! Que belle amore!*' the Venetian sighed, clasping his hands.

'Yes,' agreed the Frenchman modestly. 'It's well enough.'

Marianne, her eyes closed, saw and heard none of this. She and Jason were alone together in a storm of passion, cut off as though by some strong enchantment from the world around them. They scarcely even noticed when their audience, good Italians for whom love is no light matter, was moved to express a connoisseur's appreciation of the scene. The applause rose to a climax when the privateer picked Marianne up bodily and, still without taking his lips from hers, bore her up the stairs. The door, kicked back by an impatient boot, slammed shut behind them to the cheers of the delighted onlookers.

'Will you do me the honour to drink a glass of grappa with me to the health of the lovers?' Dal Niel said, smiling broadly.

'Something tells me they will do quite well without you ... and such happiness deserves a little celebration.'

'I should be delighted to drink with you. But, at the risk of disappointing you, I shall be obliged to interrupt the lovers' meeting before long, because we have important matters to decide.

'Important matters? What matters can a pretty woman like that have to decide beyond the choice of her clothes?'

Jolival laughed.

'You'd be surprised, my friend, but her toilette plays only a very small part in the Princess's life. I spoke of decisions and here, I see, is one coming upon us now.'

Lieutenant Benielli, very smart in uniform, his hand resting on the pommel of his sword, had just marched into the hall. His entry, although somewhat less tumultuous than Jason's, nevertheless had the effect of bringing about the instant dispersal of the inquisitive servants.

He approached the two men and clicked his heels.

'The American vessel has returned,' he announced. 'I must see the Princess at once. I may say that it is of the utmost urgency. We have already wasted too much time.'

Jolival sighed. 'I see. You will have to excuse me, Signor Dal Niel, but I am afraid we must postpone the grappa. I shall have to take this impulsive military gentleman upstairs.'

'*Peccato!* What a pity!' was the understanding answer. 'Do not be in too great a hurry to disturb them. Leave them a moment longer. I will keep the lieutenant company.'

'A moment? Upon my soul, a moment to them could well mean hours! They have not seen each other for six months.'

However, Arcadius was mistaken. No sooner had Marianne allowed her love to overcome her fears than she was regretting it. She had not been able to resist the impulse which had made her fly into the arms of the man she loved, as soon as she set eyes on him, an impulse to which he had responded with equal passion. Too much so, perhaps. But even as he was carrying her upstairs two at a time and slamming the door behind them in his haste to be alone with her, Marianne was suffering a return of all the clearheadedness which had flown so deliciously to the winds a moment before.

She knew what would happen next: another moment and Jason, in an ecstasy of love, would cast her on to her bed; in five minutes, or even less, he would have undressed her and in a very short time after that, he would have made her his own, giving her no chance to stop the tender hurricane in which she was caught up.

Yet there was something inside her which refused, something she had not been aware of until now, and that something was the depth of her love for Jason. She loved him enough to crush down her own, fiercely urgent desire for him. In a lightning flash of understanding, she knew that she could not, must not be his while that doubt still hung over her unresolved, while her body was still horribly mortgaged to Damiani.

Of course, if some germ of life was beginning to grow inside her, it would be undeniably convenient, and even easy to throw the responsibility for fathering it on to her lover. Given a man of his passionate nature and so deeply in love, any goose could do it! But although Marianne might not be prepared to tell the truth about her six weeks' disappearance, she was even more determined not to make him her dupe – and in that worst way of all! No, until she was absolutely certain, she could not let him make love to her. On no account. It could lead them both into a morass of lies from which she would never escape. But, heavens, it was going to be difficult!

As he paused for a second in the middle of the room and stopped kissing her for long enough to get his bearing and find out the door of her bedchamber, she uncoiled herself smoothly from his arms and stood up.

'My God, Jason! You are quite mad! And I think I must be as mad as you.'

She walked across to a mirror and began putting up her hair which was falling down her back but he came after her at once, enveloping her once more in his warm embrace. Laughing, his mouth in her hair, he murmured:

'I sure hope so! Oh, Marianne, Marianne! For months I have

dreamed of this moment ... when I'd be alone with you again at last ... Just the two of us, you and me ... with nothing between us but our love. Don't you reckon we've deserved that much?'

His voice, so warm and yet with a sardonic undertone never far away, was roughened and he was putting her hair aside to kiss the nape of her neck. Marianne shut her eyes. Already she was in torment.

'We are not alone,' she murmured, disengaging herself once more. 'There is Jolival ... and Agathe ... and Gracchus – any one of them might come in at any moment. This house is practically public property! Didn't you hear them clapping on the stairs?'

'Who cares? Jolival, Agathe and Gracchus have all known for long enough how matters stood. They'll understand that we want to be together, now, this minute.'

'They will, yes – but they are not all. The people here are foreigners and I must respect—'

Abruptly he had had enough. In a voice sharpened perhaps by disappointment, he flashed back:

'Well, what? The name you bear? It's a good while since we heard much about that! And if Arcadius is to be believed, you'd be a fool to waste too much consideration on a husband capable of abducting you and keeping you prisoner! Marianne, what's come over you? You're playing propriety all of a sudden, aren't you?'

Marianne was spared the necessity of answering by the arrival of Jolival. Jason stood frowning, somewhat put out, it seemed, by this untimely interruption which appeared to support Marianne's previous arguments.

Taking in the scene at a glance, Jolival saw Marianne at the mirror pinning up her hair while Jason stood at a little distance with folded arms, looking broodingly from one to the other in evident displeasure. Arcadius's smile was a masterpiece of conciliation and fatherly tact.

'It's only me, my children, and, believe me, I hate to interrupt your first meeting. But Lieutenant Benielli is here and he insists on coming up at once.'

'That confounded Corsican again? What does he want?' Jason growled.

'I didn't stop to ask him, but it may be important.'

Marianne stepped quickly over to her love and, taking his head between her hands, stifled his protests with a swift touch of her lips.

'Arcadius is right, my darling. We had better see him. I owe him a great deal. But for him, I might be lying drowned in the harbour by now. Shall we at least see what he wants?'

The cure was miraculous. The captain calmed down at once.

'The devil fly away with the fellow! But if that's what you want ... Go and fetch the nuisance, Jolival.'

As he spoke, Jason turned away, straightening the dark-blue coat with the silver buttons which fitted so closely to his wiry, muscular form, and took up his stance at the window, clasping his hands behind his back, which he kept firmly to the unwanted visitor.

Marianne's eyes followed him lovingly. She did not know exactly why Jason should feel such antipathy towards her bodyguard but she was sufficiently well-acquainted with Benielli to guess that it had probably not taken him long to rub the American very thoroughly up the wrong way. So she respected his evident wish to have no part in the conversation and prepared to receive the lieutenant. His entrance and initial bow were punctilious enough to have wrung approval from the most exacting commanding officer.

'If your serene highness will permit, I have come to take my leave. I rejoin the Duke of Padua tonight. May I tell him that everything is now satisfactorily settled and that you are safely on your way to Constantinople?'

Before Marianne could reply, an icy voice spoke from behind her.

'It pains me to have to tell you that there is no question of this lady's travelling to Constantinople. She sails with me tomorrow for Charlestown where it is my hope that she will be able to forget that women were not made to be pawns on some political chessboard. That will be all, Lieutenant.'

Stunned by this uncompromising declaration, Marianne looked

from Jason, pale and angry, to Jolival who was chewing his moustache with an air of embarrassment.

'Arcadius, didn't you tell him?' she asked. 'I thought you would have explained to Monsieur Beaufort about the Emperor's orders?'

'And so I did, my dear, but without a great deal of success. Our friend simply refused to listen and I thought it best not to insist, relying on you to be better able to convince him than I.'

'Then why didn't you tell me at once?'

'Don't you think you had enough to trouble you when you came here?' Jolival said quietly. 'It seemed to me that such diplomatic arguments could wait at least until—'

'I don't see that there is any argument about it,' Benielli broke in harshly. 'To my mind, when the Emperor commands he is obeyed.'

'You are forgetting one thing,' Jason said. 'Napoleon's commands are no concern of mine. I am an American subject and as such answerable only to my own government.'

'So? Is anything being required of you? The lady does not depend on you. The Emperor desires merely that she sails on a neutral vessel and there are a dozen in harbour. We can do without you. Go back to America!'

'Not without her! Can you not understand what is said to you? Very well, I will spell it out for you. I am taking the Princess with me whether you like it or not. Is that clear?'

'So much so,' snarled Benielli, his slender patience at an end, 'that short of having you arrested for kidnapping and incitement to revolt there is only one answer—' He drew his sword.

Instantly, Marianne sprang to her feet and flung herself in between the two men who were measuring one another dangerously.

'Gentlemen, I beg of you! I suppose you'll allow me a say in the matter, at least? Lieutenant Benielli, be good enough to leave the room for a moment. There is something I wish to say to Mr Beaufort in private.'

Contrary to her expectations, the officer acquiesced without a word. He clicked his heels and gave a curt little bow.

'Come along then,' Jolival said amiably, leading the way to

the door. 'We'll go and try some of Signor Dal Niel's grappa to pass the time. There's nothing like a glass before a journey. A kind of stirrup cup, you know.'

Left alone again, Marianne and Jason stood and looked at one another with some amazement: she on account of the hard, stubborn line which had settled disquietingly between her beloved's black brows; he because, for the second time, he had encountered resistance from that soft and graceful creature with her deceptive air of fragility. He sensed that all was not well with her and in the hope of finding out what it was, he made an effort to overcome his bad temper.

'Why did you want to speak to me alone, Marianne?' he asked quietly. 'Are you hoping to persuade me to undertake this ridiculous voyage to Turkey? Well, don't. I haven't come all this way to indulge Napoleon's whims again.'

'You came to find me, didn't you ... so that we could begin a new life together? Then, what does it matter where we live it? Why won't you take me, if I want to go and it could be so very important to the Empire? I shan't stay long and afterwards I shall be free to go wherever you like ...'

'Free? Do you mean that? Have you finally broken completely with your husband? Have you persuaded him to a divorce?'

'No, but I am free because the Emperor says so. He has made this mission he has given me a condition of his help and I know that once I have performed it, nothing and no one will stand in the way of our happiness. It is the Emperor's wish.'

'The Emperor! The Emperor! Always the Emperor! You still talk about him as besottedly as when you were his mistress! Have you forgotten that I've rather less reason to love him? You may cherish an understandable nostalgia for the imperial bedchamber and for the life of princes and palaces. My own memories of La Force, and Bicêtre and the *bagne* at Brest are by far less alluring, I assure you.'

'You are unjust! You know there is nothing between me and the Emperor, and has not been for a long time, and that he really did his best to save you without upsetting a delicate diplomatic situation.'

'So I recall but I am not aware that I stand in Napoleon's debt in any way. I belong to a neutral country and I have no intention of becoming any further involved in his politics. It is enough that my country should be risking her peace abroad by refusing to take sides with England.' He took hold of her suddenly, cradling her close and laying his cheek against her forehead with a desperate tenderness.

'Marianne! Oh, Marianne! Forget all that ... everything but us two! Forget Napoleon, forget that somewhere in this world there is a man whose name you bear, forget, as I have forgotten, that Pilar is still living somewhere, hidden in some remote corner of Spain, believing me still in prison and hoping I'll die there. There is only the two of us, nothing else ... us two and the sea, there, right at our feet. If you will, it can carry us away tomorrow to my home. I'll take you to Carolina. I'll rebuild my parents' old house at Old Creek Town that was burned down. As far as anyone knows, you will be my wife ...'

Carried away by the touch and the scent of the slender form pressed close to his, he was enveloping her again in his disturbing caresses and this time Marianne was too weak and too much enslaved to fight against it. She recalled those dizzying hours in the prison. It could all happen again so easily. Jason was hers, wholly and completely, flesh of her flesh, the man she had chosen from all others, whom no one could replace. Why, then, should she refuse the thing he offered? Why not go with him, tomorrow, to his land of liberty? After all, he might not know it but her husband was dead : she was free.

In an hour she could be aboard the *Witch*. She could easily tell Benielli she was going to Turkey, when all the time the ship was really sailing to freedom in America, and she, Marianne, would be lying for the first time all night long in Jason's arms, rocked on the waves, and drawing a final curtain over her past life. She could take up her own life again from where it had left off at Selton Hall, at the moment when Jason had first begged her to go with him, and in a little while she would forget all the rest : the fear, the flights, Fouché, Talleyrand, Napoleon, France and the villa of the fountains where the white peacocks roamed but where no ghostly rider in a white mask would wake the echoes any more.

But once again, as it had done earlier, her conscience awoke, a conscience which was becoming a great deal more inconvenient than she would ever have thought possible. What would happen if, during the long journey to America, she were to find herself pregnant by another man? How would she be able to deal with the situation there, in a land where she would never be out of Jason's sight for a moment, for she refused categorically to deceive him? Assuming, of course, that he did not begin to suspect anything in the course of a voyage at least twice as long as that to Constantinople!

Besides, at the back of her mind she seemed to hear Arrighi's grave voice saying: 'Only you can persuade the Sultana to keep up the war with Russia, only you can calm her anger against the Emperor, because you, like her, are Josephine's cousin. She will listen to you ...'

Could she really betray the trust of the man she had once loved and who had sincerely tried to make her happy? Napoleon was relying on her. Could she deny him this one last service which was so important to him and to France? The time for love was not yet. It was still the time to be brave.

Gently, but firmly, she pushed Jason away.

'No,' she said. 'I can't. I must go. I have given my word.'

He stared at her incredulously, as though she had suddenly changed before his eyes into a different creature. His dark blue eyes seemed to withdraw more deeply beneath the black brows and Marianne's heart was wrung as she read the vast disappointment in them.

'You mean – you won't come with me?'

'No, my love, it's not that I won't come. All I am asking is for you to come with me for a little while, only a few weeks. A little delay, that's all. Afterwards, I shall be all yours, heart and soul. I'll go wherever you like, to the ends of the earth if I must, and I'll live exactly as you please. But I must carry out my mission. It is too important to France.'

'France!' he said bitterly. 'That's a good one! As though France, for you, didn't mean Napoleon.'

Pained as she sensed the underlying jealousy which still persisted, Marianne gave a little, hopeless sigh and her green eyes dimmed with tears.

'Why won't you understand me, Jason? Whether you like it or not, I love my country. I have scarcely begun to know it yet and the discovery is precious to me. It is a beautiful country, Jason, noble and great! And yet I shall leave it and without regrets or heartburnings, when the time comes to go with you.'

'But that time is not yet?'

'Yes ... perhaps, if you will agree to take me to meet this queer Sultana who was born so near to your own land.'

'And you say you love me?' he said.

'I love you more than anything in the world because for me you are the world, and not only that but life and joy and happiness. It's because I love you that I won't steal away like a thief. I want to stay worthy of you.'

'Words, words!' Jason shrugged furiously. 'The truth is that you can't bring yourself to give up, all at once, all the glittering life that was yours as someone close to Napoleon! You're young, rich, beautiful – and a Serene Highness – of all the God-damned stupid, pompous titles! And now they've sent you on an embassy to a queen! What can I offer to match that? A fairly humble existence, and not altogether respectable at that, so long as neither of us are free of our matrimonial ties. I can understand your hesitating.'

Marianne regarded him sadly.

'You're so unfair! Have you forgotten that if it hadn't been for Vidocq I would have given all that up without a moment's thought? And believe me, this voyage isn't an excuse or anything, it's a necessity. Why won't you?'

'Because it's Napoleon who sends you. Do you understand? Because I owe him nothing but humiliation, imprisonment and torture! Oh, I know, he gave me a guardian angel but if the guards had bludgeoned me to death or I'd died of my wounds, do you think he would have grieved overmuch? He'd have expressed polite regret, and then turned to something else. No, Marianne, I have no cause to serve your Emperor. Indeed, if I agreed, I should feel a fool. As for you, you may as well know that if you lack the courage to say no now, once and for all, to all that has been your life up to this moment, you'll not find it tomorrow. When this mission is accomplished, you'll find another – or another will be found for you. I'm not denying a woman like you is a valuable asset.'

'No, I swear it! I'll go away at once!'

'How can I believe you? Back in Brittany, you asked nothing better than to flee this man, yet now you want to serve him at all costs! Are you even the same woman? The one I left would have committed any madness for my sake. This one is hidebound by respectability and won't kiss me for fear of the chambermaid's coming in! I can't help noticing it, you know.'

'What are you after? I swear to you I love you and only you, but you must take me to Turkey.'

'No.'

Uttered without anger, the word was none the less final.

'You refuse?' Marianne said dully.

'Precisely. Or rather, no. I give you the choice. I'll take you, but after that I shall sail alone for my own country.'

Marianne recoiled as though he had struck her, knocking over a small table and smashing a fragile piece of Murano glass. She sank on to the sofa where she had lain so short a while ago – a century, it seemed! She stared at Jason wide-eyed, as though seeing him for the first time. He had never looked so tall, so handsome – or so inflexible. She had believed his love was like her own, equal to anything, ready to suffer and endure anything for the sake of a few hours' happiness, and how much more so for a lifetime of love. Yet now he could find it in his heart to offer her this ruthless choice.

'You could leave me – of your own will?' she asked incredulously. 'Leave me there and go away without me?'

He folded his arms across his chest and regarded her without anger but with a terrifying firmness.

'The choice is not mine, Marianne. It is yours. I want to know who is boarding the *Witch* tomorrow: the Princess Sant'Anna, official ambassadress of his Majesty the Emperor and King – or Marianne Beaufort.'

The sound of that name, coming so unexpectedly, when it had figured for so long in her dreams, cut her to the quick. She closed her eyes, her face as white as her dress. Her fingers curled and the nails dug into the silk upholstery, fighting off incipient panic.

'You're so hard . . .' she moaned.

'No. I only want to make you happy, in spite of yourself, if need be.'

Marianne gave a sad little flicker of a smile. The egotism of men! She could see it even in this man she adored, just as she had seen it in Francis, Fouché, Talleyrand, Napoleon, and even in the monster Damiani. All of them had this curious urge to make decisions about the happiness of the women in their lives, convinced that in this, as in so much else, they alone possessed the key to real wisdom and truth. They had both suffered so much from all that had come between them. Were the obstacles now going to come from Jason himself? Couldn't he subdue his overbearing pride for the sake of his love?

Once again there came the temptation, so powerful as to be almost irresistible, the temptation to give in, to cast herself into his arms and allow herself to be carried away, without further thought. She needed him so much, his strength and his man's warmth. Despite the mildness of the evening, she felt chilled to the heart. Yet, perhaps just because she had suffered so much to win this love, her pride restrained her on the very verge of yielding.

The worst of it was that she could not really blame him. From his man's point of view, he was right. But neither could she retract, or not without telling him the whole. And even then? Jason's feelings towards Napoleon had grown so very bitter!

Miserably unhappy, Marianne chose, none the less, the course that came most naturally : to fight.

She put up her head and met her lover's gaze squarely.

'I have given my word,' she said. 'It is my duty to go. If I abandoned my mission now, you might still love me as much – but you would have less respect for me. In my world, and in yours too, I think, we have always placed duty before happiness. My parents died for that belief. I will not disgrace it.'

It was said quite simply, not boasting. Merely a statement of fact.

It was Jason's turn to pale. He made as if to go to her but

checked himself and bowed slightly, without a word. Then, crossing the room in a few swift strides, he opened the door and called:

'Lieutenant Benielli.'

The lieutenant appeared promptly, accompanied by Jolival, whose eyes went straight to Marianne. She avoided his anxious glance. Signor Dal Niel's grappa had evidently been to the lieutenant's taste. His face was noticeably more flushed than on his previous appearance, although he had lost none of his rigidity.

Jason studied him from his superior height with a cold and barely contained anger.

'You may return to the Duke of Padua with a quiet mind, Lieutenant. I sail at dawn tomorrow for the Bosphorus where I shall have the honour to convey the Princess Sant'Anna.'

'I have your word on that?' the other said, without emotion.

Jason's fists clenched in a visible effort not to drive them into the little Corsican's arrogant face, which must have recalled, all too clearly, another that was out of reach.

'Yes, Lieutenant,' he ground between his teeth. 'You have. And you can have something else, as well. A piece of advice. Get out of here before I give way to my inclinations.'

'Which are?'

'To throw you out of the window. It would not be good for your uniform, your fellows or your own comfort on the journey. You've won. Don't try my patience too far.'

'Oh, please, go!' Marianne breathed, terrified that the two men would come to blows.

Jolival was already laying a discreet hand on Benielli's arm. The lieutenant, while clearly dying to hurl himself at the American, had the sense to look closely at the faces of the other three. He saw that Marianne was on the verge of tears, Jason tense and Jolival anxious, and he realized that something was seriously amiss. His stiffness showed the faintest relaxation as he bowed to the young woman.

'I shall be privileged to report to the Duke that the Emperor's trust was not misplaced. May I wish your serene highness a successful voyage.'

'Accept my good wishes for your own journey. Good-bye, monsieur.'

In a moment she had turned back, imploringly, to Jason but even before Benielli had quitted the room, Jason too was bowing coldly.

'Your servant, madam. My ship will weigh anchor at ten o'clock tomorrow morning, if that suits you. It will be ample time if you are on board half an hour before that. Allow me to wish you a good night.'

'Jason! Have pity . . .'

She held out her hand to him, begging for him to take it, but he was encased in his anger and resentment and either did not or would not see it. Without a glance, he strode to the door and went out, letting it swing shut behind him with a bang that echoed in the very depths of Marianne's heart.

Slowly her hand fell and she threw herself sobbing on the sofa.

There, a moment or two later, Jolival found her, half-choked with tears, as he came hurrying back, sensing disaster.

'Good God!' he cried. 'Has it come to this? Whatever happened?'

With much difficulty, a good many tears and hesitations, she told him while he busied himself with a handkerchief and some cold water in trying to calm her sobs and restore her face to something like the appearance of a human being.

'An ultimatum!' Marianne hiccupped at last. 'A – a beastly b-bargain! He told m-me – told me I m-must choose . . . And he said it was . . . for my own good!'

She turned suddenly and clung to Arcadius's lapels, saying beseechingly :

'I can't . . . I can't bear it! Oh, my friend, for pity's sake, go and find him. Tell him . . .'

'What? That you've given in?'

'Yes! I l-love him . . . I love him s-so very much . . . I c-can't . . .'
Marianne was beyond knowing or caring what she was saying now.

Jolival gripped her shaking shoulders with both hands and forced her to look at him.

'Yes, you can. I am telling you that you can, because you

are right. Jason is abusing his power by offering you such a choice, because he knows how much you love him. Not that, from his point of view, he isn't right. He has little enough cause to love the Emperor.'

'He – he doesn't love me!'

'Of course he loves you. Only, what he hasn't understood is that the woman he loves is you, as you are, with all your inconsistencies and follies, all your enthusiasms and revolts. Change, make yourself into the cool, submissive person he seems to want and I wouldn't give him six months to stop loving you.'

'Truly?'

Gradually, by dint of much persuasion, Jolival was beginning to penetrate to the slough of despond where Marianne was floundering, letting in a little air and daylight to which, unconsciously, she was already turning.

'Yes, truly, Marianne,' he said seriously.

'But, Arcadius, think what will happen at Constantinople! He'll leave me. He'll go away and I shall never see him again, never!'

'It's possible ... but before that you will have lived with him, almost on top of him, in the confined space of a ship's quarters for quite a long time. If you aren't able to drive him out of his mind in that time, then you're not Marianne. Play his game for him. Let him enjoy his bad temper and the blow to his masculine pride. If anyone goes through hell, it won't be you, I promise you.'

As he talked, the light came back, little by little, to Marianne's eyes, while that other light of hope was reborn within. Meekly she drank the glass of water with the little cordial in it which he held to her lips, then, leaning on his arms, she managed to walk as far as the window.

It was dark by this time but everywhere lights shone like points of gold reflected in the dark water. A smell of jasmine floated in, along with the sound of a guitar. Down below, by the waterside, couples were drifting slowly along, pairs of dark shapes, moving close together, that melted into one. A decorated gondola passed by, steered by a lithe figure like a dancer. Light streamed golden from behind the drawn curtains, and with it came the happy note of a woman's laughter. Away beyond the Dogana di Mare, the masthead lanterns of the anchored ships swayed gently.

Marianne sighed and her hand tightened a little on Jolival's sleeve.

'What are you thinking?' he asked softly. 'Feeling better?'

She hesitated, not quite knowing how to phrase her thought, but with this one faithful friend she had no need to dissemble.

'I was thinking,' she said, somewhat regretfully, 'that it is a beautiful night for love.'

'That's true. But remember that one night lost may add to the joy of others still to come. The nights in the east are unrivalled, my child. Your Jason doesn't know yet what he is in for.'

Whereupon, closing the window firmly on the swooning night outside, Jolival led Marianne into the little rococo salon where supper awaited them.

Part Two
Perilous
Isles

Chapter Six
Currents

At some point the bed started to sway. Only half-awake, Marianne turned over and buried her nose in the pillow, trying to shake off a disagreeable dream, but the swaying persisted and slowly her brain cleared, and she realized that she was awake.

Then something creaked somewhere in the body of the ship and she remembered she was at sea.

She considered the round brass porthole in the further wall with a jaundiced eye. The daylight that filtered through it was grey with big white patches that were dollops of sea water. There was no sunshine, and, outside, the wind was blowing strongly. The Adriatic, this stormy July, wore the colours of a dismal autumn.

'Just the weather to begin a voyage like this!' she thought morosely.

Contrary to Jason's original announcement, they had not left Venice until the evening of the previous day. The privateer had suddenly felt again the lure of the unofficial cargo which had nearly cost him so dear in France and he had spent the day loading a small consignment of Venetian wines. It consisted of a number of casks of Soave, Valpolicella and Bardolino from which he anticipated making a handsome profit on the Turkish market where there was not always strict adherence to the laws of the Koran, and where foreign residents were known to be excellent customers. The Grand Signior himself was said to possess a pronounced taste for champagne.

'That way,' the privateer had explained to Jolival, who was inclined to be less shocked than amused at the deliberate vulgarity, 'I shan't have the voyage for nothing.'

As a result, they had gone aboard at nightfall, just as Venice was lighting her lamps and making ready for her nocturnal revelry.

Jason Beaufort was waiting at the head of the ship's gangway to welcome his passengers aboard. The bow he gave them was sufficiently formal to send a chill through Marianne's heart but at the same time acted as a spur to her anger, hardening her determination to fight back. Seeing that this was how he wanted it, she tilted her pretty nose insolently and considered him with an ironic concern.

'Surely, Captain, we are a little later than arranged? Or am I mistaken?'

'You are perfectly correct, madam.' Jason's voice was clipped but his evident annoyance did not go to the length of 'Serene Highnessing' her. 'I was obliged to delay our departure for commercial reasons of my own. I must ask you to excuse me, but you must remember, at the same time, that this brig is not a ship of war. If you wanted punctuality, you would have done better to apply to your Admiral Ganteaume for a frigate.'

'Not a ship of war? Yet I see cannon there. At least twenty of them, surely. Do you employ them going after whales?' Marianne asked sweetly.

From the set of his jaw and the whitening of his knuckles, this little exchange seemed to be putting a severe strain on the captain's nerves but his politeness did not falter, in spite of his very evident desire to send his passenger to the right about.

'You may not be aware, madam, that, as matters stand today, even the smallest merchant vessel must have some means of defence.'

But the lady appeared determined to push him to his limit.

'There is a great deal I am not aware of, Captain, but if this is a merchant ship, then I'll be hanged! Even a blind man could see she's built for speed, not for lumbering about the sea with a hold full of merchandise.'

'She is a privateer, certainly,' Jason said fiercely, 'but a neutral vessel. And if a neutral privateer wants to get a living these days, with your confounded Emperor's damned blockade, then there's nothing for it but trade! And now, if you have no more questions, allow me to show you to your cabin.'

Without waiting for a reply, he led the way across the scrubbed decks, their brasswork gleaming in the lantern light, and in his haste almost knocked over a thin man of middle height, dressed in black, who was coming round the corner of the deck house.

'Oh, is that you, John? I didn't see you there,' he apologized with a smile which did not quite reach his eyes. 'Come and be introduced. Princess, this is Doctor Leighton, our surgeon. Princess Corrado Sant'Anna,' he added, laying a slight, deliberate stress on the first name.

'You have a medical man on board?' Marianne exclaimed in genuine surprise. 'You take good care of your men, Captain. I congratulate you. But how is it that you said nothing of there being a follower of Aesculapius on board?'

'Because there wasn't. But the absence of a surgeon is a thing I have long regretted. So much so that I engaged the services of my friend Leighton some months ago.'

Friend? Marianne studied the doctor's pale face to which the lantern light had imparted a yellowish tinge. He had light, deeply-sunken eyes of no very clearly defined colour, calculating eyes which seemed to be weighing her up in some cold scale of his own.

Marianne thought with a little shudder that Lazarus might have looked like that when he rose from the dead. He said nothing but merely bowed, unsmiling, and Marianne had the sudden, instinctive feeling that not only did the man not like her, he disliked everything about her very presence on the ship. She made up her mind that she had better avoid Dr Leighton in future as far as possible. She had no wish to encounter that death's head. It remained to see, however, what degree of friendship really existed between Jason and this sinister little man.

While Jolival went off to take up his quarters in the poop and Gracchus settled in with the crew forward, Marianne took up residence with Agathe in the deck house.

On first entering her cabin, she had been conscious of a little pang: the room had so obviously been refurbished for a woman's occupation. The waxed mahogany floor was covered with a fine Persian rug; there was a toilet table adorned with a number of pretty knicknacks, and sea-green damask was used for the curtains over the portholes and the coverings on the soft feather bed. It all spoke so clearly of the tender care of a man in love that Marianne was touched. This room had been made ready for her, so that she should feel at home there, to be a frame for her happiness. Bravely she put the thought aside, although promising herself to thank the master of the vessel for his courtesy next day, for neither Marianne nor her maid left the cabin again that evening. They spent the time unpacking their trunks and settling themselves in, which was by no means the work of a moment.

Agathe, for her part, took possession of a tiny cabin next-door to that of her mistress. It contained a bunk, a toilet table and a porthole, but its new owner was more than a little suspicious of it, being unashamedly terrified of the sea.

Marianne lay in bed and stretched, yawned and finally sat up, wrinkling her nose. The inside of the ship had a strange smell, faint, it was true, but in some indefinable way, disagreeable. She had noticed it when she came aboard and it had surprised her a little because the slight aroma, reminiscent of something ancient and unclean, seemed out of keeping with the holystoned appearance of the ship.

She glanced at the clock set in the panelling, saw that it was ten o'clock, and considered getting up. Not that she particularly wanted to but she did feel very hungry, for she had eaten nothing before coming aboard the night before.

She was still hesitating when the door opened to admit first a laden tray and then the person of Agathe, as prim and starched as if they were at home in Paris, followed in turn by Jolival in a dressing-gown. He appeared in excellent spirits.

'I came to see how you had passed the night,' he said cheerfully, 'and how you were settling in. But I can see you lack nothing. Well, I never! Damasks and carpets! Our captain has looked after you very nicely.'

'Are you not comfortable, Arcadius?'

'Oh, I'm well enough. Much like himself, which is to say plain but wholesome. And the cleanliness of the ship is beyond praise.'

'It's clean, I agree, but there's a funny smell ... I can't precisely pin it down. Don't you notice it? Or haven't you got it where you are?'

'Oh, yes. I've noticed it,' Jolival said, seating himself on the foot of Marianne's bunk and helping himself to a piece of bread and butter and some cakes from the tray. 'I noticed it, although it is very faint ... but I couldn't believe it.'

'Not believe it? Why ever not?'

'Because ...'

Jolival paused to finish his bread and butter before he went on with unexpected seriousness :

'Because I have smelled something like it once before in my life, only much, much stronger, a truly unbelievable stench. It was at Nantes, in the harbour there ... near a slave ship. The wind was blowing from the wrong direction.'

Marianne's hand remained poised, in the act of pouring herself a cup of coffee. She stared incredulously at her friend.

'It was the same smell? You are quite sure?'

'It's not a smell you forget if you've once met it. I tell you, it haunted me all night.'

Marianne set down the coffee-pot with a hand that shook suddenly, so that a large brown stain spread over the tray-cloth.

'You aren't suggesting Jason is engaged in that frightful trade?'

'No, because then the smell would be much stronger, in spite of any amount of scrubbing and fumigating. But it makes me wonder if he hasn't had something to do with that kind of – of transport at some time or other.'

'It's quite impossible!' Marianne cried vehemently. 'Don't forget, Arcadius, that six months ago the *Witch* was lying in Morlaix roads, where Surcouf took her and sailed her to our rendezvous. If Jason had been engaged in that foul trade, *he* would have smelled the smell, and I can't think he would have run the risks he did for the master of that sort of vessel. Anyway, when Jason does carry contraband, let me remind you, it's wine not human beings!'

She was trembling with indignation, so that when she put down her cup it rattled nervously in the saucer. Jolival smiled soothingly.

'No need to get so excited. In a minute you'll be accusing me of calling our friend a dirty slaver! I said nothing of the kind. Although, at the risk of disappointing you, if Surcouf had noticed anything, he wouldn't have objected. He's carried "black ivory" in his own vessels before now. A good shipowner can't afford to be over-nice. All the same, like you, I find this odd smell very surprising.'

'Perhaps it's not what you think. After all, you only smelled it once.'

'It's not the kind of thing you forget,' Arcadius said grimly. 'Nor the kind that can be got rid of by washing, and unless this vessel has had an epidemic of yellow fever aboard her—'

'That's enough, Arcadius. You're upsetting me. You're probably imagining things. I expect it's just a dead rat somewhere. Where is Jason at the moment?'

'Forward in the chart room. Are you wanting to pay him a call?'

There was a faintly anxious note hovering somewhere at the back of the light, ironic voice but Marianne poured herself another cup of coffee calmly enough. The rich scent of the scalding beverage filled the tiny cabin, overcoming the insidious odour.

'Should I?'

'Not necessarily. Unless you want to edify the ship's company with another passage of arms like last night's. Our skipper would appear to be in an extremely bad temper. Before retiring to shut himself up forward he rocked the poop with an astonishing tirade on the subject of the defective stowing of a cask.[1]

Marianne wiped her mouth with unusual concentration, a proceeding which enabled her to keep her long curling lashes prudently lowered, yet there was a lift to her brows that struck Jolival as more insubordinate than ever. However, her voice, when she answered, was miraculously soft and gentle.

'Then I have no intention of putting myself in his way. All I want to do is stretch my legs on deck and get a breath of air.'

'The weather's overcast, it's raining and there's a sea running.'

'So I saw. But I must have air. We'll take a stroll together, Jolival, if you'll be kind enough to come and collect me here in half an hour's time. I can see by your face that you're going to find some other horrid reason to stop me going out – such as that Agathe and I are the only women aboard among a hundred men! Well, the last thing I mean to do is to spend all my time cooped up in this hole, particularly when I know quite well that Jason will never so much as cross the threshold. Am I right?'

Jolival refrained from answering. Delivering himself of a fatalistic shrug, he began to steer an erratic course towards the door, negotiating the half-open trunks with their overflow of ribbons and furbelows.

When he had gone, Marianne looked round for her maid but Agathe had disappeared. Her call was answered only by a feeble groan. Stepping quickly to the communicating door, she found the wretched Agathe collapsed on her bed, retching spasmodically into her starched apron. All her prim flirtatiousness had vanished and there remained only a little girl, very green in the face, who looked up at her mistress out of hollow eyes.

'Good gracious, Agathe! Are you as ill as this? Why didn't you tell me?'

'It – it came over me all of a sudden. When I was bringing your tray ... I didn't feel very well and then, just as I got here ... It must have been the smell of the fried eggs and bacon – oooooooh!'

The mere mention of these items was enough to bring on another spasm and the little abigail disappeared again into her apron.

'Well, you can't go on like this,' Marianne said firmly, substituting a basin for the apron as a start. 'There's a doctor on board this beastly vessel and I'm going to find him. He's a Friday-faced creature but surely he can do something to help.'

She bathed Agathe's face briskly with cold water and eau-de-Cologne, gave her a bottle of salts and then, having first buttoned a close-fitting coat of honey-coloured cloth securely over her night-gown, she tied a scarf round her head and sallied forth in the direction of the companion-way leading up to the main deck. Climbing the steps to the deck proved something of a problem but eventually she emerged into the deck-housing between the mainmast and the mizzen.

At that moment, the brig encountered a squall. The sea fell

away from the bows and she had to cling to the steps to keep herself from sliding down again on her face. When she came out on deck she found the wind astern and the strength of it took her unawares. The loosely-tied scarf was whipped from her head and her long, dark locks writhed about her like some wild creeping plant. The empty deck rose and fell. She turned towards the poop and received the wind full in her face. The ship was running before the squall. There were white caps to the waves and all around was the singing in the shrouds and the crack and murmur of the sails. She saw the helmsman on the poop, which was reached from the lower level of the deck by a flight of steep, ladderlike steps. In his heavy canvas jacket, he looked like a part of the ship, standing there with legs braced wide apart and big hands anchored firmly on the wheel. Looking up, Marianne saw that the better part of the duty watch were perched on the yards, frantically engaged in taking in topgallants, topsails and mainsail, hauling down the main jib to bear away down wind under foresail and fore staysail, according to the orders that came booming through the loud-hailer from the poop.

Without warning, a dozen or so barefoot monkeys dropped from above and began running about the deck. One of them cannoned into her so sharply that she was sent reeling towards the poop ladder. She flung out her hands and managed to grab hold of it in time to prevent herself from sprawling headlong, while the sailor pursued his way aft without a backward glance.

'Your ladyship must forgive him. I do not think he saw you,' said a deep voice gravely in Italian. 'Are you hurt?'

Marianne hauled herself upright, flinging back the hair that blinded her, and stared with a kind of shocked surprise at the man before her.

'No,' she said automatically, 'no, thank you.'

He moved away at once, with an easy gait that seemed to fit itself effortlessly to the irregular pitching of the ship. Marianne watched him go, petrified, for some reason she could not explain, but with a curious mixture of fear and admiration. Her season in hell was still too fresh in her mind for the sight of a black skin to inspire her with anything but alarm, and the sailor who had spoken to her, though not so dark as Ishtar and her sisters, was black, like them. Damiani's three slaves had been the colour of ebony whereas this man seemed to have been moulded in a kind of golden bronze, and despite an instinctive shudder based chiefly on the association of remembered fear and dislike, Marianne readily admitted that she had rarely beheld a more splendid figure of a man.

He was barefoot, like all the crew, his lower limbs encased in tight canvas trousers, and he had the disturbing physical perfection of the great cats. To see him springing up the shrouds to stow a sail with all the lithe grace of a bronze leopard was an unforgettable experience. Nor did a brief glimpse of his face in any way disgrace the whole.

She was still lost in these reflections when a hand grasped her arm and hauled rather than helped her up the steps to the poop.

'What are you doing here?' yelled Jason Beaufort. 'What the devil do you mean by coming out in such weather? Do you want to be swept overboard?'

He sounded furious but Marianne noted, to her private satisfaction, a note of real concern underlying the rebuke.

'I was looking for the doctor. Agathe is dreadfully ill and must have help. She was very nearly sick bringing me my breakfast.'

'Then why was she bringing it? Your maid has no business in the galley, Princess. There are servants on board, thank God, whose duty it is to attend to such matters. Ah, there is Toby, now. He has orders to see that you want for nothing.'

Another black man had emerged from the galley regions, carrying a pailful of vegetable peelings. This one had a cheerful moon face surmounted by a circle of wiry, grizzled hair from the midst of which his bald crown rose in well-polished nakedness to confront the elements. His face split open in a beaming smile at the sight of his master, revealing a snowy crescent of white teeth.

'Go and tell Dr Leighton there's a patient for him in the deck house,' Beaufort called.

There was a faint frown in Marianne's eyes and she was unable to stop herself asking: 'Have you many negroes on board?'

'Why? Don't you like them?' Jason snapped back, for her look had not escaped him. 'There are plenty of them where I come from. I thought I had told you that my own nurse was black. It's not something people in France or England are accustomed to, I grant you, but in Charleston and anywhere in the South it's perfectly normal and natural. But, to answer your question : I have two, Toby and his brother Nathan. No, I was forgetting. I've three, now. I took on another at Chioggia.'

'At Chioggia?'

'Yes, an Ethiopian. The poor devil had been a slave of your friends the Turks and had escaped. I found him adrift in the port when I was taking on water. You can see him up there astride the tops'l yard.'

A creeping chill which had nothing to do with the weather, though it was cool for the time of year, stole over Marianne. The man whose appearance had made such an impression on her – was she dreaming, or did he really have light eyes? – was a runaway slave. And, runaways apart, what of the other two, the servants Jason had spoken of? Jolival's words returned unbidden to her mind, and because she could not bear the smallest cloud on her love she could not help asking the question that rose to her lips, although she phrased it with a little circumlocution :

'Yes, I had noticed him. Your "poor devil" is a fine-looking fellow – and very different from him.' She nodded at Toby, now engaged in emptying his bucket overboard. 'Is he another runaway slave?'

'There are as many different races of blacks as there are whites. The Ethiopians claim descent from the Queen of Sheba and her son by Solomon. Their features are in general finer and more aquiline than those of other Africans, and they have a fierce pride which does not take easily to slavery. Some of them are much lighter-skinned, too, like this one. But why should you think Toby and Nathan are runaways? They were born into my family's service. Their parents were very young when my grandfather bought them.'

The chill turned to ice. It seemed to Marianne that she was moving into a new and unfamiliar world. It had never occurred to her that Jason, a free American citizen, might regard slavery as something perfectly normal. She knew, of course, that the trade in 'black ivory', as Jolival had called it, illegal in England since 1807 and frowned on, although not actually banned, in France, still flourished in the American south where the country's wealth was largely built on black labour. She knew, too, that as a southerner, born in Charleston, Jason had been brought up among the negroes of his father's plantation. He *had* talked to her once, with some affection, about his black nurse, Deborah. But the problem which faced her now, in all its brutal realism, was one that she had not previously considered except in an abstract, almost disembodied light. Now she was looking at Jason Beaufort, slave-owner, discussing the buying and selling of human beings as dispassionately as if they were cattle. Obviously, this state of affairs seemed perfectly natural to him.

As things stood between them just then, Marianne might have been wiser to conceal her feelings, but she had never learned to resist the impulse of her heart, especially where the man she loved was concerned.

'Slaves! How strange to hear that word on your lips,' she murmured, instinctively abandoning the superficial, hurtful formality which had subsisted between them. 'You have always seemed to me the very image and symbol of liberty. How can you even bring yourself to say it?'

For the first time that morning, she beheld a genuinely arrested look in the faint widening of the blue eyes turned on her, but the smile which followed that unguarded expression was sardonic as ever, and neither candid nor even remotely friendly.

'I should imagine your Emperor can say it readily enough. He reintroduced slavery and the slave-trade as First Consul, after it had been abolished by the Revolution. He shuffled off the best part of the problem with Louisiana, I grant, but I've never heard that the folks of San Domingo had much cause to bless him for his liberalism.'

'Let's leave the Emperor out of this. I am talking about you and only you.'

'Are you condescending to criticize my way of life, and the ways of my people? That's rich! Well, let me tell you something. I know the blacks better than you. They're fine fellows for the most part and I like them, but you can't alter the fact that they're still no more sophisticated than children. They laugh and cry as easily, and they have the same unpredictability and the same warmth of heart. But they need guidance.'

'With a whip? With chains on their legs and treated worse than cattle! No man, whatever his colour, was put on this earth to be a slave. I wonder what the Beaufort who left France under Louis XIV, after the Revocation of the Edict of Nantes, would have thought of your reasoning. I daresay he knew freedom was worth any sacrifice!'

A certain tightening of the lines round Jason's mouth might have warned Marianne that his patience was wearing thin, but she herself was spoiling for a fight. She would a hundred times rather face up to a good row between them than this frigid politeness.

There was a black look in the privateer's eyes and a scornful curl to his lip but he answered with no more than a shrug:

'My poor idiot, it was that very ancestor who started our plantation at La Faye-Blanche and bought the first slaves. But the whip has never been in use with us, and our blacks have had no cause to complain of their treatment. Ask Toby and Nathan! If I'd tried to give them their freedom when the estate was burned they would have lain down and died at my door.'

'I didn't say that you were bad masters, Jason—'

'What did you say then? Was I dreaming when I heard you referring to chains and men treated like cattle? Not that I'm surprised to find you such a staunch supporter of liberty! It's not a word much in use among women of your kind. The majority prefer, I might even say insist on a form of sweet servitude. You don't like the word? But then you, perhaps, are not altogether woman! You're quite at liberty, though, madam! At liberty to ruin everything, to smash everything around you, beginning with your own life and other people's! Oh, there's nothing to touch a truly liberated woman! She's capable of anything! Give woman freedom and they turn into dear little puppets, clinging like crazy to their crowns and peacock feathers!'

The arrival on the scene of Jolival cut short this diatribe. Jason, now quite beside himself, was shouting loudly enough for

the whole ship to hear him. He had contained himself too long
and now his pent-up anger was released. Catching sight of the
little vicomte's amiable features, he barked furiously :

'Take this lady back to her cabin. Treat her with the respect
due to a free ambassadress of a liberal Empire! And don't let me
see her here again. The quarterdeck is no place for a woman,
however liberated! Nor am I obliged to endure her. I too am free!'

And turning on his heel Jason went swiftly down the ladder
and strode forward to shut himself up in the chart room.

Jolival made his way to Marianne who was gripping the rail
with both hands, struggling with the wind and a violent desire
to cry.

'What have you done to him?'

'Nothing! I was only trying to explain to him that slavery is
an abomination and how shocking it is that there are poor
wretches on this ship without the right to call themselves men!
And you saw how he spoke to me!'

'Oh, so now you're fighting about the condition of mankind,
are you?' Jolival said helplessly. 'Good God in heaven, Marianne! Haven't you enough to quarrel about, you and Jason,
without adding things that are no concern of yours? Upon my
word, anyone would think you actually enjoyed tearing yourselves to pieces! He's dying to take you in his arms and you're
ready to throw yourself at his feet, yet put you together and
you're at each other like a pair of fighting cocks. And in front of
the hands!'

'But, Jolival, have you forgotten the smell?'

'Did you mention that to him?'

'No. He didn't give me time. He got angry straight away.'

'And just as well! My dear child, what do you think you're
doing? When will you learn that men have their own lives and
will live them as they think best? Come along now, let me take
you to your cabin. I'm damned if I'll let you out alone again!'

Marianne went with him meekly, accepting the arm he offered
to escort her back to the deck-house. This time they had to make
their way past the members of the crew who had now descended
from the shrouds. The wind being aft had enabled them to follow the quarrel with interest, and Marianne caught a number of

broad grins, which covered her with confusion. However, she pretended not to notice them and to be absorbed in conversation with Jolival who was discoursing fluently upon the weather.

They were about to descend the stairs leading below when she saw the dark-skinned fugitive leaning against the mainmast. He had seen her, too, but he did not smile. His eyes, actually of a kind of bluish tint, held a rather melancholy expression. Half-unwillingly, Marianne took a step towards him.

'What is your name?' she asked, a little nervously.

He abandoned his indolent pose and stood up to answer her. Once again, she was struck by the savage beauty of the man's face and the strangeness of his light eyes. Except for his dark skin, the runaway slave had nothing at all negroid about him: the nose was finely chiselled and there was no thickening about the firm, well-shaped lips. He bowed slightly and said softly:

'Kaleb ... at your service.'

A profound pity, the outcome of her recent dispute with Jason, swept over Marianne for the poor wretch who was, after all, no better than a hunted animal. She tried to find something to say to him and, recalling what Jason had told her, she asked:

'Do you know that we are going to Constantinople? I am told that you have escaped from the Turks. Are you not afraid—'

'Afraid of being recaptured? No, madame. If I do not leave the ship, I have nothing to fear. I am a member of the crew now and the captain will not allow anyone to touch one of his men. But I thank you for your kind thought, madame.'

'It was nothing. Was it in Turkey that you learned to speak Italian?'

'Just so. Slaves there are often given a good education. I speak French also,' he added in that language, after only the faintest hesitation.

'I see.'

With a little nod, Marianne at last followed Jolival down the dark companion ladder.

'If I were you,' Jolival remarked humorously, 'I should be careful how you talk to the men. Our dear captain is quite capable of deciding you are inciting them to mutiny, and probably clapping you in irons without more ado.'

'Quite capable, I agree. But, Arcadius, I can't help feeling sorry for that poor man. A slave – and a runaway slave at that – it's so dreadfully sad. And it's terrifying to think what might happen to him if he were recaptured.'

'Oddly enough,' Jolival said, 'I don't feel in the least sorry for your bronze sailor. Possibly on account of his physique. Any master, however cruel, if he had the smallest regard for his money, would think twice about killing such a valuable property. Besides, he told you himself, he has nothing to fear. He has the American flag to protect him.'

As Marianne entered her cabin, the smell caught her by the throat. There was no doubt about it, Agathe was very ill indeed. However, as she came in, Dr Leighton was in the act of closing the door to the maid's tiny chamber.

He told Marianne that, dosed to the eyebrows with belladonna, the girl would sleep off her miseries, and went on to add that she should not be disturbed. Marianne, however, did not like his tone, any more than she liked the look of her cabin.

Soiled towels were strewn about everywhere and right in the middle of her dressing table was a basin part-full of a yellowish liquid which slopped to and fro uninvitingly. The smell which greeted her left Marianne in no doubt of its contents. All this was quite clearly deliberate and gave her a very good idea of what kind of cooperation she might expect from Dr Leighton.

'The stench in here!' Jolival exclaimed, hurrying to open the porthole. 'That's the best way to get seasick.'

'Sickness is very rarely agreeable,' Leighton retorted sourly, making for the door. Marianne stopped him with a gesture to the damask curtains round her bed.

'I trust you had enough towels, doctor,' she said with heavy irony. 'You appear to have missed these, and my dresses, too.'

The thin, parchment-coloured face was rigid but there was a cold glint in the man's eyes and an extra tightness about his lips. In his dark clothes, with the lank hair falling to his collar, John Leighton was as stern and unbending as a Quaker. Perhaps, indeed, that was what he was, for the look he bestowed on the elegant Marianne bordered on revulsion. She wondered again how such a man could be Jason's friend. He would have got on much better with Pilar!

Furiously Marianne thrust away the disagreeable thought of Jason's wife. It was bad enough to know the woman was still alive, even though in the depths of some Spanish convent, without having to think about her!

Leighton, meanwhile, had mastered his evident spurt of anger. He bowed with, if possible, a greater coldness and contempt than before and went out, followed by a look from Jolival suggestive of feelings strongly divided between laughter and indignation. In the end he shrugged it off and merely remarked:

'Can't say I'm much taken with that fellow. I hope to God I shan't need his services. Being doctored by him can't be much fun. To think we've got to face that at mealtimes!'

'Not me!' Marianne declared. 'Since I'm forbidden to set foot on the quarterdeck, I'll not enter the cabin either! I shall take my meals here ... and I shan't object if you do the same.'

'I'll see. In the meanwhile, come and take another turn on deck. I'll send for Toby to clean up this mess, or else your appetite will suffer. But, if I were you, I'd not go to earth. You won't get anywhere by skulking in your tent, you know. Show yourself! Let him see you in all your glory. The sirens never went back to their caves until they'd made sure of their victims.'

'You may be right. But how can I make myself look beautiful when I'm being shaken about like a cork in a saucepan of boiling water?'

'It's only a summer squall. It won't last.'

He was right. Towards the end of the day, the wind and the sea subsided. The gale became a pleasant breeze, just enough to swell the sails. The sea, which had been so grey and turbulent throughout the day, was now smooth and flat as shimmering satin, laced with little white flecks. The tall blue lines of the Dalmatian coast were now to be seen in the distance, while in the foreground lay a chain of islands coloured green and amethyst in the light of the setting sun. It was warm outside and Marianne indulged in the melancholy luxury of musing alone at the rail, watching the changing shore and the red-sailed fishing boats heading for home.

For all the beauty of the evening, her heart felt heavy, sad and lonely. Jolival was somewhere else, probably in the company of the first-officer, with whom he seemed to have struck up a friendship.

The first-officer was a convivial soul, an Irishman by birth, whose red nose betrayed a fondness for the bottle and who could not have been a greater contrast to the chilly Leighton. Since he knew something of France and a good deal more about the produce of her vineyards, it did not need many words to assure him of the vicomte's regard.

But it was not the absence of Arcadius which troubled her, as Marianne privately admitted. Her temper had subsided with the squall and she felt in her heart a vast longing for peace and quiet and tenderness.

From where she stood, she could see Jason standing on the poop, next to the man at the wheel. He was smoking a long clay pipe, as tranquilly as though there were no lovely woman in love with him on board his ship. She wanted, oh so very much, to go to him! Already, earlier in the day, when the bell had rung for luncheon, it had cost her a struggle to stay firm in her decision to eat alone, solely because there would have been nothing between them but the width of the table. Her throat had ached so that she could barely touch the meal Toby had brought to her. Tonight it would be even worse. Jolival was right. It would be nice to make herself beautiful and then to take her seat opposite him and see if she could still exercise some power over that unshakeable will. She was burning to go to him but her pride refused without a formal invitation. After all, he had banished her from his private territory and in such a way that she could scarcely go to him now without loss of face.

A foreign body interposed itself between her and the happy poop. She had no need to turn her head to know that it was Arcadius. He reeked of Spanish tobacco and Jamaica rum. Perceiving that she was still wearing her day dress, he clicked his tongue reprovingly.

'Why aren't you changed?' he asked quietly. 'The bell will go soon.'

'Not for me. I am staying in my cabin. Tell Toby to bring my dinner to me.'

'This is nothing more than a fit of the sullens, Marianne. You are simply sulking.'

'Perhaps I am but I shan't budge from what I told you before. I'm not setting foot in there – not unless I'm asked as clearly as I was thrown out.'

Jolival laughed.

'I've often wondered what Achilles did in his tent while all the other Greeks were away fighting the Trojans. And especially what he thought. It looks as though I'm going to find out. Very well then. Good night, Marianne. I shan't see you again because I've promised that fire-eating young Irishman I'd teach him how to play chess! Do you want me to carry your ultimatum to the captain, or will you?'

'I forbid you to mention me to him! I am staying in my cabin. If he wants to see me, he knows where to find me. He knows me well enough – and he's no coward! Good night, Arcadius. And don't fleece your young Irishman. He may drink like a fish but he looks as green as a girl.'

To say that Marianne slept well would be an exaggeration. She tossed and turned in her cot for hour after hour. How many hours, she had no difficulty estimating, thanks to the regular chiming of the ship's bell. She felt stifled in the narrow space, filled with the sound of Agathe's snoring penetrating the thin partition which divided them. It was almost dawn before she fell into a dreamless sleep from which she woke to dismal reality and a cracking headache round about nine o'clock, when Toby tapped discreetly on her door.

Hating the whole world and herself most of all, Marianne was on the point of dismissing both the negro and his tray when he picked a large letter off the cup on which it had been balanced and held it out to her silently between finger and thumb, while she glared up at him through the tangles of her hair.

'This from Massa Jason,' he said, grinning. 'Ver' ver' important.'

A letter? A letter from Jason? Marianne snatched it eagerly and ripped open the seal, stamped with a ship's figurehead, while

Toby stood with his tray on his arm and the grin broadening on his round face, making a careful study of the ceiling.

The note was not a long one. It took the form of a brief, formal apology from the captain of the *Sea Witch* to the Princess Sant'Anna, begging her to overlook his lapse from good manners and to reconsider her decision to take her meals alone in her cabin and honour his table in future with the feminine charm of her presence. Nothing more. Not one word of affection. Precisely the kind of excuses he might have sent to any distinguished passenger with whom he had exchanged words. Part disappointed, part relieved because at least he was offering her the necessary bridge, she addressed herself to Toby who was still gazing heavenwards, apparently lost in a beatific vision of his own.

'Put it down here,' she said, pointing to her lap, 'and tell your master I shall dine with him tonight.'

'Not at luncheon?'

'No. I'm tired. I wish to sleep. Tonight.'

'Ver' good. He sho' gonna be pleased.'

Pleased? Would he really? Still, the words had a comfortable sound to the self-imposed recluse and she rewarded Toby with a lovely smile. She liked the old negro. He reminded her of Jonas, her friend Fortunée Hamelin's butler, both in his rolling accent and his infectious good humour.

Marianne dismissed him, with orders that she was not to be disturbed for the remainder of the day, a command which she repeated a few minutes later to Agathe, who appeared, yawning, in the doorway, looking heavy-eyed and still rather sallow.

'Stay in bed if you don't feel well, or otherwise please yourself, only don't wake me before five o'clock.'

She did not add 'because I want to look my best' but that was the real reason for this sudden urge to sleep. A glance in her mirror had shown her a turned-down mouth and dark rings under her eyes. She could not show herself to Jason looking like that. So, after swallowing two cups of scalding hot tea, she snuggled down again, curled herself into a blissful cocoon and fell fast asleep.

That evening, Marianne dressed herself for a simple meal with all the elaborate care of an odalisque about to try her luck with the sultan. Her own natural good taste warned her that too much splendour would be out of place on what was practically a ship of war but, for all its deliberate simplicity, her final appearance was none the less a miracle of graceful elegance. However, miracles take time to achieve and a good deal more than an hour was required before Marianne was bathed, scented, her hair dressed and herself finally inserted into a clinging robe of white muslin with no other ornament than a spray of pale silk roses nestling in the deep decolletage. More of the same flowers were tucked into her hair on either side of the chignon which was worn low on the nape of her neck in Spanish fashion.

It was Agathe, whose attack of sea-sickness had apparently stimulated her imagination, who conceived the notion of this new arrangement. She had brushed and brushed her mistress's hair again and again until it shone satin-smooth and then, instead of dressing it high, after the mode in Paris, had arranged it in gleaming bands which hung in heavy coils on her neck. It was a style that did full justice to Marianne's long, slender throat and delicate features and gave to her green eyes, with their faint, upward slant, an added touch of mystery and exotic charm.

'Oh, my lady, you look a dream, and not a day more than fifteen!' Agathe declared, evidently well-pleased with her handiwork.

Arcadius, when he knocked on the door a few minutes later, shared her opinion, but advised the addition of a cloak for the short walk across the deck.

'It is the captain who is to be the dreamer, not the crew,' he said. 'We can do without a mutiny on board.'

His advice was sound. When Marianne, wrapped in a cloak of green silk, crossed the deck to the poop, the men on watch, who were engaged in shortening sail for the night, stopped work with one accord to watch her pass. All of them were clearly intrigued by the presence of the beautiful woman on board, and probably most were envious as well. There was more than one gleam in the eyes that followed her. Only the cabin boy, sitting on a coil of rope mending a sail, gave her a cheery grin and an easy unselfconscious: ' 'Evening, ma'am. Fine day.' And he received a friendly smile for his pains.

A little farther on, Gracchus, now apparently quite wedded to a life at sea and on the best of terms with everyone on board, greeted her with unaffected enjoyment.

She saw Kaleb, too, rubbing up the barrel of one of the guns on the main deck under the watchful eye of the master-gunner. He glanced up, like the others, but his serene gaze was devoid of all expression, and he returned to his work at once.

Then Marianne and her companions were entering the after cabin where Jason Beaufort, his first-officer and the doctor were already gathered by a table laid for dinner, engaged in drinking glasses of rum which they all promptly put down in order to bow as she came in.

The cabin and its mahogany panelling were illuminated by the fires of the setting sun which flooded through the stern windows, filling every corner and rendering unnecessary the candles placed on the table.

'I hope I have not kept you waiting,' Marianne said, with a little smile which took in all three men impartially. 'It would be a poor return for your kind invitation.'

'Military precision was not designed for ladies,' Jason said, adding in a tone which he did his best to render agreeable : 'To be kept waiting by a pretty woman is always a pleasure. Your health, ma'am.'

The smile lingered on him for no more than a moment but, beneath the downcast lashes, Marianne's eyes did not quit his face. To her profound and secret joy, hugging the knowledge to her as a miser hugs his gold, she was able to observe that her efforts had not been wasted. As Jolival helped her off with her cloak, Jason's tanned face took on an ashen hue and his fingers whitened suddenly on the stem of his glass. With a high crack, the heavy crystal snapped and the pieces smashed on to the carpeted floor.

'You should watch how you drink,' Leighton rallied him caustically. 'Your nerves are on edge.'

'When I need your professional advice, Doctor, I'll ask for it. Shall we eat?'

The meal passed in almost total silence. The company ate little and talked less, oppressed by the atmosphere of tension which had descended on the cabin.

The gloom which was spreading over the sea seemed to have extended to those in the ship. Jolival and O'Flaherty began by exchanging various reminiscences of their travels, with a kind of forced gaiety, but the conversation soon lapsed. Marianne, seated on Jason's right, was too much occupied in observing him to have much energy left for conversation. But Jason, at the head of the table, like the inhibited Benielli on some earlier occasions, studiously avoided letting his eyes rest on his neighbour, and especially not on that delicious and all too provoking expanse of bosom.

Marianne could see his long, brown hands on the white cloth, not far from her own, fiddling nervously with his knife. She had an impulse to put her own hand over those restless fingers and soothe them into peace. God alone knew what would happen if she did!

Jason was as taut as a bowstring stretched to breaking point. The momentary loss of control which had made him snap at Leighton had brought no relief. Head bent, his eyes fixed on his plate, he was glum, irritable, obviously ill at ease and furious with himself for being so.

Marianne knew him well enough to be fairly sure that at that moment he was bitterly regretting that he had ever invited her to his table.

Moreover, slowly his mood was infecting her. She had John Leighton opposite her and the antipathy between the two of them was so strong as to be almost tangible. The man had the knack of making her hackles rise with every word he spoke, even when not specifically directed to her.

When Jolival inquired how the vessel, on her way to Venice, had managed to navigate the Straits of Otranto where the English squadrons based on St Maura, Cephalonia and Lissa were continually harassing the French forces from Corfu, Leighton grinned wolfishly.

'If we're at war with England it's the first I heard. Or with

Bonaparte, either, come to that. We're a neutral nation. Why should we worry?'

The disparaging reference to the Emperor as 'Bonaparte' made Marianne quiver. Her spoon clattered against her plate. Sensing, possibly, that it was a sign that she was ready to give battle, Jason intervened, but with an ill grace.

'You're talking like a fool, Leighton,' he said harshly. 'You know quite well our trade with England ceased on 2 February. We are neutral now only in name. And what have you to say of the English frigate which gave chase to us off Cape Santa Maria di Leuca? If by some miracle a French ship-of-the-line hadn't turned up to distract her attention, we should have been obliged to fight. As it is, there's no guarantee we shan't have to fight our way out of that damned channel.'

'If they knew who we had on board, the English would be bound to chase us. An – er – friend of the Corsican! It would be too good to miss!'

Jason's fist crashed down on the table, making the cutlery jump.

'There is no reason why they should know, and in that case we should fight! We have guns and, praise God, we know how to use them! Any objections, Doctor?'

Leighton leaned back in his chair and spread his hands pacifically. His smile broadened, but smiles were not becoming to that sallow face.

'No, by no means. Although it's possible the men might have. Already there are murmurs that two women on board will bring bad luck.'

Jason did look up at this and his eyes blazed on the rash speaker. Marianne saw the veins swell in his temples but he kept a rein on his temper. His voice, when he spoke, was icy cold.

'The men will have to learn who is master on board this ship. You, too, Leighton. Toby, you may bring the coffee now.'

The fragrant brew was served and drunk in dead silence. Toby, for all his bulk, flitted round the table with the airy efficiency of a domesticated elf. No one uttered another word and Marianne was on the verge of tears. She felt miserably that everything on board this ship, which had meant so much to her, rejected her. Jason had not wanted to bring her, Leighton hated her and she had not even the satisfaction of knowing why, and now the crew looked on her as a Jonah! She curled her cold fingers round the thin china cup to get a little warmth from it. Then she swallowed the hot coffee at a gulp, and rose.

'Pray excuse me,' she said, in a voice whose trembling she could not control. 'I should like to return to my cabin.'

'One moment,' Jason said, rising also. The others followed suit. He glanced round at them and said curtly: 'Do not leave yet, gentlemen. Toby will bring rum and cigars. I shall escort the Princess.'

Before Marianne, still unable to believe her good fortune, could utter a sound, he had picked up her cloak and placed it round her bare shoulders. Then he opened the door for her and stood aside to let her go first. They were absorbed into the summer night.

It was dark blue and full of stars. They glittered softly and because the surface of the sea was pricked with little phosphorescent wavelets it seemed as if the ship were sailing through the starry sky. The deck was in darkness but men were gathered on the forecastle, squatting on the deck or standing, leaning on the rail, listening while one of their number sang. The man's voice, slightly nasal but agreeably pitched, reached easily to the man and woman moving slowly down the short flight of steps.

Marianne held her breath, her heart pounding. She did not know why Jason had suddenly felt the need to be private with her but hope welled up tremblingly inside her and she dared not be the first to speak for fear of breaking the spell. She walked slowly ahead of him, oh, so very slowly, with her head a little bent, wishing that the deck was ten miles long. At last, Jason spoke.

'Marianne!'

She stopped at once but without turning. She waited, paralysed with hope now that he had used her name once more.

'I wanted to tell you ... that on my ship you are quite safe. While I am in command, you need have no fears, either of the

English or of my own men. Forget what Leighton said. It is unimportant.'

'He hates me. Is that, too, unimportant?'

'He does not hate you. Not you specifically, I mean. He feels the same way about all women. He dislikes and resents them, not altogether without reason. His mother did not care for him and the girl he loved and was to have married left him for another. Since that time, he has fallen back on a general detestation.'

Marianne nodded and turned, slowly, to look at Jason. He was standing with his hands clasped behind his back, as though he did not know what to do with them, staring out to sea.

'Why did you bring him?' she asked. 'When you knew what this voyage was to be? You were coming for me and yet, on your own admission, you brought with you a man who hates everything to do with women.'

'Because . . .' Jason seemed to hesitate for a moment before going on, in something of a hurry: 'He was not to make the whole voyage with us. It had been agreed that on the way home I was to set him down at a place arranged between us. You must remember that Constantinople was not then included in our plans,' he added, with a touch of bitterness that betrayed his hurt.

Marianne was stabbed by it to her very soul. Her own gaze went sadly to the sea, where it fled in ripples of blue and silver away from the side of the ship.

'Forgive me,' she murmured. 'Duty and gratitude can be heavy burdens to carry, but that is no reason to disown them. I wish with all my heart it could have been different for us. I'd dreamed for so long of this voyage, wherever it took us. For me, it was not the end that mattered but being together.'

In an instant, he was close to her, pressed hard against her. She could feel his hot breath on her neck as he implored her, with a passion near to desperation:

'It's not too late. The course we are on is still – our course. It's not until we're through the straits that we must choose . . . Oh, Marianne, Marianne, how can you be so cruel to us both! If you would only . . .'

His hands were touching her. Weakly she shut her eyes and relaxed against him, aware to the point of agony of the moment's closeness.

'Am I the one who is cruel? Did I offer you an impossible choice? You thought it only a whim, some kind of attempt to keep alive a past that is gone, a past I don't even want ...'

'Then prove it, my love! Let me take you away from all this. I love you to death and you, of all people, know it! You made that dinner hell for me. I've never seen you look so lovely ... I'm only a man! Can't we forget the rest of the world?'

Forget? It was such a beautiful word and how Marianne longed to be able to utter it with the same conviction as Jason. A nasty, insidious little inward voice would keep whispering that the forgetfulness was to be all on her side. Was he going to wipe the slate clean of all his own past memories? But the present moment was too precious and Marianne did not want to lose it yet. Perhaps, after all, Jason was going to give way? She wriggled round in the circle of his arms and brushed his lips briefly with her own.

'Can't we forget as easily on the way to Constantinople as on a course for America?' she murmured, kissing him. 'Don't torture me. You know I have to go ... but I need you so! Help me!'

There was a little silence, momentary but complete. Then, all at once, Jason's arms fell.

'No,' he said.

He stepped back. Between the two bodies which, a moment before, had been touching, ready to melt together into the same fusion of joy, the curtain of refusal and incomprehension had dropped coldly into place once more, the captain's tall figure bowed sharply, outlined against the blue vault above.

'Forgive me for asking you,' he said icily. 'This is your cabin. Allow me to wish you a good night.'

He had turned away, he was going further perhaps now than before, just because of love's weakness which had made him cry out in his distress. Pride, that terrible, unapproachable masculine pride, was uppermost once more. As the virile figure vanished into the night, Marianne cried after him:

'Your love is nothing but lust and obstinacy! But I'll always

love you, whether you like it or not ... in my own way, because it's the only way I know! You liked it well enough before ... It's you who cast me off.'

That went home. He checked, fractionally, as though he would
have turned back, then he stiffened and went on towards the
after-cabin where, safe from feminine wiles, those other men, his
brothers, waited for him.

Left alone, Marianne turned towards her own cabin. She was
about to open the door when she had the odd feeling that someone was watching her. She swung round abruptly and as she
did so a dark shadow detached itself from the foremast and
slipped away forward. It was silhouetted for an instant, lithe
and dark, against the yellow glare of the prow lantern. Marianne
knew, from the supple way he moved, that it was Kaleb and
the knowledge annoyed her a little. Apart from the fact that
she had other things on her mind just then than the fate of the
black people of America, she could not at that moment see the
runaway slave as anything other than a source of discord between Jason and herself.

The door banged to behind her and she hurried to the haven
of her bed to mull over in solitude possible ways of defeating
Jason's obstinacy. Whatever else had happened, that evening
she had won a victory, but she strongly doubted whether Jason
would grant her the opportunity of winning any more. Instinct
told her that he would probably avoid her like the plague. It
might perhaps be wise to deprive him of that satisfaction by
keeping out of his sight for a while, even if only to give him
time to start asking himself a few questions.

The *Sea Witch* sailed on through the night, regardless of the
hopes and fears she carried with her, while on the forecastle
the sailors continued their singing.

Chapter Seven
The Corfu frigates

On the morning of the eighth day at sea, as they were approaching the coast of Corfu, a vessel appeared out of the sun, bearing down on the brig under her full spread of canvas, a tall white pyramid to eastward which was signalled by the masthead look-out with a hail:

'Sail on the port-bow!'

From the poop deck, Jason Beaufort's voice spoke like an echo: 'Let her come. Steady as she goes.'

'An English frigate,' Jolival announced. He had a telescope to his eye and was studying the approaching vessel. 'I can see the red ensign at her peak. Looks as though she means business, too.'

Marianne, standing by him at the port rail, hugged her big cashmere shawl about her and shivered. There was something new and disturbing in the air. Pipes shrilled all around her, calling all hands on deck. Jason, standing beside the helmsman, was watching the Englishman. There was tension in every line of his body, a tension reflected in the crew, both on deck and aloft.

'Are we in the Straits of Otranto already?' Marianne asked.

'Yes. That Englishman must be out of Lissa. But he turned up very promptly ... almost as if he was expecting us.'

'Expecting us? But why?'

Jolival shrugged helplessly. Jason had given an order to O'Flaherty who responded with a loud 'Aye aye, sir!' and clattered down the steps calling men to him. In a moment, weapons were being taken from chests and handed out among the sailors as they filed quickly past the first-officer, selecting swords, cutlasses, pistols, dirks or musketoons according to their abilities and preferences. Within the space of a very few seconds, the brig had been cleared for action.

'Are we really going to fight?' Marianne whispered anxiously.

'So it seems. Look, the Englishman has put a shot across our bows.'

A puff of white smoke had come from the long black hull banded with yellow, and was followed by a dull report.

'Hoist our colours!' Jason yelled. 'Show them we're neutral. The damned fool's coming straight at us.'

'A battle!' Marianne exclaimed softly, more to herself than to Jolival. 'That's all we needed! Maybe the men are right and I do bring bad luck.'

'Don't talk rubbish,' growled the vicomte. 'We all knew this might happen and the men have never looked on a fight as a disaster. This is a privateer, don't forget.'

But the thought lingered uncomfortably. For a week now, not a day had passed without some incident or accident to the ship. The vessel seemed to be fated. It had begun with half the starboard watch going down with some form of food poisoning, of unknown origin, and lying groaning in their hammocks for twenty-four hours. Then, a man slipped on the main deck, when the ship pitched suddenly, and split his head open. The next day, two of the seamen came to blows over some trivial matter and had to be put in irons. Finally, only last night, fire had broken out in the galley and, although it had been put out very quickly, Nathan had narrowly escaped being burnt alive. On the rare occasions when she left her cabin for a breath of air, she would look the other way if she caught sight of John Leighton's pale face and the mocking challenge in his eyes. Once already, she had seen the boatswain, an olive-skinned Spaniard with the pride of a hidalgo and the grossness of a drunken monk, extend the back of his hand with two fingers towards her in the traditional gesture to ward off the evil eye.

Meanwhile the frigate was still coming on and in answer to the brig's signals had hoisted a flag of truce, indicating that she wanted to parley.

'Let him come alongside,' Jason snapped. 'We'll see what he wants. But have the men standing by, all the same. I don't like the look of things. The moment I caught sight of his tops'ls, I got the feeling he was after us.'

He began calmly stripping off his blue coat, unwinding his

stock and rolling up his sleeves. Nathan, who was very nearly the image of his brother Toby, stood at his elbow ready to hand him his cutlass. Jason tested the edge against his thumb before stowing it in his belt. Urged on by the boatswain's pipes, most of the men were already at action stations.

'I'll have the guns loaded and run out,' Jason ordered.

Clearly, the privateer was not going to be taken by surprise. The frigate was very close now. She was the *Alcestis* of forty guns, a well-found vessel under the command of an efficient captain, Commodore Maxwell. Those on board the *Sea Witch* could see the marines ranged in perfect order on her deck, but no barge was being lowered. That meant communication would be by loud-hailer; not a good sign.

Jason picked up his own voice trumpet.

'What do you want?' he called.

An English voice came back, a trifle distorted but clear and menacing.

'To visit your ship. We have excellent reasons.'

'I'd like to know them. We are an American vessel and therefore neutral.'

'If you're neutral, you shouldn't have Bonaparte's envoy aboard. You have a choice: hand over the Princess Sant'Anna or we send you to the bottom!'

Marianne held her breath and something icy seemed to trickle down her spine. How had the Englishman known that she was on board? And more than that, how did he know that she was on a mission for Napoleon? She was dreadfully aware, suddenly, of the enemy's power. The mouths of the cannon protruding from her gun ports looked enormous. Marianne was conscious of nothing but the guns and the matches, flaring a little in the morning breeze, in the hands of the gun crews. But there was no time to think about the future, for already Jason's voice was answering boldly:

'You can try!'

'Do you refuse?'

'Would you agree, Captain Maxwell, if someone asked you to hand over your honour? My passengers are sacred. Ladies especially.'

The stiff figure on the frigate's quarter-deck bowed.

'I anticipated that would be your answer, sir, but it was my duty to put the question. We fight it out, then.'

The two ships drew apart, each loosing their first broadside before they were out of range. But they fired before the crews had got the guns properly laid and neither hit the target. Drawing off again, they reloaded and returned to the charge, like two knights in the lists.

'We can't win,' Marianne wailed. 'Go and tell Jason to give me up. The English will sink us. They are much better armed than we are!'

'Your friend Surcouf wouldn't think much of that for an argument,' said Jolival. 'The next time you see him, you must ask him to tell you about the *Kent*. A duel between two ships at sea is more a matter of seamanship and winds, and of stout hearts if it comes to grappling. And I've an idea our men are stout enough at heart!'

There was no doubt that the faces of the men about them on the deck were alive with the excitement of the coming fight. The seamen had smelled powder and it made their eyes shine and their nostrils flare. Marianne caught sight of Gracchus among them: armed with a pistol and clearly as happy as a king, the young coachman was preparing to do battle with the best. Up in the rigging, men were busy with the sails as, amid a flow of orders, the brig heeled round with a proud and stately grace into the wind. The Englishman, less easily manoeuvrable, had barely begun to turn but a fresh volley rent the air and white puffs dotted the air between them as the *Alcestis* let go her stern chasers.

Craig O'Flaherty came hurrying up to Marianne.

'Captain's compliments, ma'am, and will you go below. No need to expose yourself. We're going to try and capture his wind.'

The flush on his face owed nothing to drink this morning. If Jason had ordered rum all round for the crew to hearten them for the coming action, he had taken care to pass over his first-officer. O'Flaherty made a move to take Marianne's arm to lead her below but she hung back, clinging to the rail like a child that would not go to bed.

'I don't want to go below! I want to stay here and see what happens. Jolival, tell him I want to see!'

'You can watch from the portholes. You'll be safer there, although you may not see so well,' Jolival told her.

'It's an order, ma'am,' the first-officer added. 'You must go down.'

'An order? To me?'

'Well, to me, actually. I'm afraid my orders are to see you to safety, by force if necessary. The captain went on to say that if you insisted on exposing your life it was scarcely worth him risking the lives of his men.'

Tears welled up in Marianne's eyes. Even now, with death threatening them both, Jason was sending her away from him. She surrendered, acknowledging defeat.

'Very well. In that case, I'll go alone. You are needed, Mr O'Flaherty, I believe.' She glanced significantly towards the poop where Jason, apparently having dismissed her from his mind, was absorbed in his strategy. His eyes were fixed on the enemy and a stream of orders issued from his lips.

The *Alcestis* was showing her elegantly carved and gilded stern windows as the *Witch* came across on an oblique course to windward, neatly cutting the wind from her sails. Then, as her canvas flapped helplessly, the *Witch*'s carronades roared. Smoke billowed over the brig's deck but through it came a shout of triumph.

'A hit! There goes her mizzenmast!'

It was echoed grimly by the voice from the masthead:

' 'Nother vessel coming up astern, sir! She's opening fire on us!'

The last words were drowned in the noise of another report, a little farther off.

The newcomer had slipped out from behind the small green island called Phanos and was bearing down on them under every stitch of canvas, flying the unmistakable British flag. Jolival blenched and seizing hold of Marianne began to drag her towards the companion.

'It's a trap!' he cried. 'We'll be caught between two fires. Now I see why the *Alcestis* let us take her wind so easily.'

'Then we're lost? In that case—'

Tearing herself from his grasp, Marianne made a dash for the poop, determined at all costs to get to Jason and die with him. But Kaleb was before her, barring her way.

'Not that way, madame! It's dangerous.'

'I know! Let me go! I must go to him!'

'Stop her!' Jason bellowed. 'If you let that lunatic woman up here, I'll have you in irons!'

The end of this speech was lost in the smoke and din as part of the rail disintegrated and the shot sliced through the shrouds and ploughed on into the deck-house roof.

Instantly, Kaleb had flung Marianne to the ground, hurling himself on top of her and pinning her to the deck with all his weight. The noise was deafening and visibility down to no more than a few feet. The guns' crews were firing almost before they had finished reloading. Fire belched from every one of the brig's gun ports but her decks were rent with agonizing screams and the groans of injured and dying men.

Coughing and choking, Marianne fought vigorously to free herself from the smooth and powerfully muscled body holding her down. At last, with the energy of desperation, she managed to push him off and struggle to her knees.

Without so much as a glance of gratitude for the man who had saved her life, and who, in any case, was already returning to his duties, she peered through the smoke in search of Jason. She could not see him, the entire after part of the ship being enveloped in a thick fog, but she heard his voice yelling, with an inexpressible note of triumph, in response to another shout from the masthead:

'Reinforcements are coming! We'll make it yet!'

Staggering to her feet, Marianne began to run towards the sound and literally fell into the arms of Gracchus who, his face blackened with powder, loomed ghostlike out of the reeking smoke.

'What is he saying, Gracchus?' she gasped, clinging to him. 'Reinforcements? Where?'

'Come with me. I'll show you. There are more ships coming. French ships. They're coming from the big island. And in the

nick of time too. We were in a bad way between these two misbegotten Englishmen!'

'You're not hurt?'

'Me? Not a scratch. In fact, I'm almost sorry it's all over so
soon. Battles are good fun!'

Marianne allowed herself to be towed to the rail. The smoke
was thinning now and, with a broad sweep of his arm, Gracchus
indicated the three vessels which could be seen rounding the
small islet of Samothrace. They were three frigates, their sails
bellying in the sun, and looking as unreal as three icebergs advancing through the blue morning. Their colours fluttered gaily
at their peaks. They were the *Pauline*, Captain Montfort, the
Pomone, Captain Rosamel, and the *Perséphone*, Captain Le
Forestier.

All sails set, the three ships came swooping to the American's
rescue, their sleek keels cleaving through the blue water.

On board the *Sea Witch*, the men greeted their appearance
with a frantic cheer. Caps waved in the air.

But already the two English ships were drawing off, abandoning the fight. One after the other, they rounded the rocky coast
of Phanos and, knowing themselves safe from pursuit in those
dangerous waters, sailed away slowly into the morning haze,
followed by a last, defiant broadside from the brig.

Marianne stared after them, frowning. It had all happened so
quickly ... far too quickly. The two ships appearing one at a
time, as though they had been lying in wait behind their two
islands, and then the fight which was over after a few shots
fired: it was all very strange and unlikely. Above all, the question remained: how had the English learned of her presence on
board an American brig and, more important still, of the secret
mission given her by Napoleon? Hardly anybody knew, and
those few could be trusted absolutely because, apart from the
Emperor and Marianne herself, they were limited to Arrighi,
Benielli, Jason and Jolival, all of whom were above suspicion.
Who, then?

Jason meanwhile had embarked on an inspection of his ship.
The damage, in general, was not serious and would be easily
repaired when they came to port. There were some wounded

lying on the deck with John Leighton already busy attending to them. Coming to where Marianne was kneeling by a young seaman with a splinter in his shoulder, the privateer bent down and took a quick look at the wound.

'That's nothing to worry about, my lad. Wounds heal fast at sea. Dr Leighton will deal with you soon.'

'Have we ... any killed?' Marianne asked, too busy stanching the flow of blood with her handkerchief to look up, but conscious of his eyes on her.

'No, none. It's lucky. But I'd like to know who the bastard was who gave you away. Or have you been chattering indiscreetly, my dear Princess?'

'I? Chattering? Are you out of your mind? I'd have you know the Emperor is not in the habit of putting his trust in chatterboxes!'

'Then I can think of only one answer.'

'What's that?'

'Your husband. You escaped from him and he gives you away to the English to get you back. I can understand it, in a way. I'd have been capable of doing something of the same sort myself to stop you going to that damned country!'

'That's impossible!'

'Why so?'

'Because the Prince is—' Marianne stopped suddenly, realizing what she had been about to say, and turned a flushed face back to her patient before concluding: '... is incapable of anything so vile. He is a gentleman.'

'While I'm a brute, is that it?' Jason's lip curled. 'Very well. We'll leave it at that. And now, with your permission, I am going to welcome our rescuers and tell them we intend to put in at Corfu for repairs.'

'Is there much damage?'

'No, but enough to need attention. You never know, we may well meet up with a few more of my friend Prinny's ships before we get to Constantinople.'

A few minutes later, Captain Montfort, Commodore of the squadron, was piped aboard the *Sea Witch*. Jason, who had resumed his coat and stock, was waiting on the deck to greet him. There followed a brief, courteous exchange during which Captain Montfort assured himself that the American vessel had suffered no disabling injury or loss of life, and invited the privateer to accept his escort to Corfu where the superficial damage to the *Witch*'s superstructure could readily be put right. Jason thanked him and expressed his gratitude for the frigates' prompt and unexpected intervention.

'It was a godsend, sir. But for your help we'd have been lucky to pull through.'

'Godsend nonsense! We were told to look out for you and to make sure your vessel negotiated the Straits of Otranto without interference. The English squadrons are on continuous patrol.'

'You were *told*? By whom?'

'By special messenger from the Italian foreign minister, Count Marescalchi, who is at present in Venice. He warned us that a noble Italian lady, the Princess Sant'Anna, a personal friend of the Emperor's, would be travelling on an American ship. We were to watch out for you and to provide you with an escort until you were through the Cerigo Channel and into Turkish waters. I dare say you may not know it but you are running a twofold risk.'

'Twofold? Apart from having to run the gauntlet of the English base at Santa Maura* . . .'

Montfort drew himself up, aware that what he had to say did not redound to his nation's credit.

'The English also hold Cephalonia, Ithaka, Zante and Cerigo itself. Our strength was insufficient for the defence of all the Ionian Islands which Russia ceded to us by the Treaty of Tilsit. But it is not only the English we have to fear. There are also the flotillas belonging to the Pasha of the Morea.'

Jason laughed.

'I think I have enough fire power to deal with a few fishing smacks!'

'Do not laugh, monsieur. The Pasha is the son of the formidable Ali Pasha of Yannina. He's a powerful man, as well as a shrewd and devious man. We can never be sure if he's for us

* Levkas.

or against us, and he's busy carving himself an empire behind the backs of the Turks. The Princess would be a nice prize for him, too, especially if she should chance to be beautiful . . .'

Jason made a sign to Marianne, who had been observing the commodore's arrival from a conveniently secluded vantage-point behind Jolival and Arcadius.

'Here is the Princess. Permit me to present Captain Montfort, to whom we owe, if not our lives, most certainly our freedom.'

'The danger is much greater even than I feared,' the captain said, as he bowed over her hand. 'No ransom on earth could wrest from Ali such a prize.'

'You are very gallant, Captain, but this pasha is a Turk, I suppose, and I am related to the Haseki Sultana. He would not dare—'

'He is not Turkish, madame, but Epirote, and he would undoubtedly dare. He conducts himself in this world as an independent monarch, knows no law but his own. As for his son's ships, do not scorn them, monsieur. They are manned by devils and, if they once succeed in boarding you, which they may do very readily because their small ships are able to slip close in under the guns, they will give your men such a fight as they will not easily repel. You will be well advised to accept our escort – unless slavery holds any charms for you.'

Two hours later, preceded by the *Pauline* and followed by the other two frigates, the *Sea Witch* entered the narrow northern passage between Corfu and the wild mainland of Epirus. On their right lay the long green island rising at its north-eastern end to the sun-drenched mass of Mount Pantocrator. It was late afternoon before the four ships entered harbour and dropped anchor in the shelter of the Fortrezza Vecchia, the old Venetian citadel now transformed by the French into a strong modern fortress.

Standing on the poop deck with Jason and Jolival, wearing a cool dress of lemon-yellow jaconet and a Leghorn hat trimmed with wild flowers, Marianne watched Nausicaa's isle draw nearer.

Jason, bareheaded and dressed in his most respectable blue coat and a snowy shirt which emphasized his darkly sunburned features, had his hands clasped behind his back and was clearly brooding with deep and growing resentment on the realization that Napoleon had now left him no choice : like it or not, he was bound to carry Marianne to Constantinople. When she looked at him with eyes filled with tender hopefulness and murmured : 'You see, there was nothing I could do. The Emperor knows how to ensure his orders are obeyed. There is no escape,' Jason had growled back through his teeth :

'There is, if you really want it. Dare you tell me that you do?'

'With all my heart! When I have accomplished my mission.'

'You're more stubborn than a Corsican mule!'

The tone was still aggressive but renewed hope had sprung up in Marianne's heart. She knew that Jason had too much honesty, where both himself and others were concerned, not to admit the inevitable. From the moment that Marianne's will ceased to be her own and became the prey of external forces, he was able to silence his masculine pride and return to her without losing face in his own eyes. Moreover, when her hand had brushed his, timidly, he had not withdrawn it.

Corfu harbour presented a smiling picture which went well with Marianne's new mood. The black hulls and gleaming brasswork of the warships of the French fleet mingled with the brightly painted Greek boats, decorated like antique vases, with their curiously shaped sails.

Beyond rose the flat white houses, shaded by ancient fig trees, lying within the circling arm of the Venetian ramparts, grey and hoary with age, which went none the less by the hopeful name of the New Fort. The old fort, the Fortezza Vecchia, was at the other end of the harbour, a heavily fortified peninsula attached to the mainland by a steeply sloping esplanade and looking frowningly out to sea. Only the tricolor flag flying from the keep provided a touch of gaiety.

The quayside was enamelled like a meadow in springtime with a cheerful motley crowd in which the brilliant reds of Greek costumes mingled with the light dresses and pastel-shaded parasols belonging to the wives of officers of the garrison. There was a joyous hubbub of talk, laughter and song and sporadic outbursts of applause from the throng, all backed by the mewing of the gulls.

'What a delightful place!' Marianne exclaimed softly, wholly won over. 'How happy they all look!'

'A bit like dancing on the edge of a volcano,' Jolival said. 'Too many people would like to get their hands on the island for the people to be quite as happy as they look. But it's a land made for loving, that I grant you.'

He helped himself to a pinch of snuff, then added, with elaborate casualness: 'It was here, wasn't it, that Jason – the Argonaut, I mean – brought Medea and married her after he had stolen her away from her father, the King of Colchis, along with the Golden Fleece?'

This apt allusion to classical mythology earned him a scowl from the American Jason and a short answer.

'That's enough classics for one day, Jolival,' Jason warned him curtly. 'I don't care much for legends unless they end happily. Medea was an atrocious female, murdering her own children in a fit of jealousy!'

The vicomte, elegantly flicking a grain of snuff from the revers of his cinnamon coloured coat, was unperturbed by the brusqueness of his tone, and merely laughed.

'Who can tell where jealousy may lead? Wasn't it St Augustine who said that the measure of love is to love without measure? Great words, and how true! As for legends, there is always a way round them. To have a happy ending it's often enough to want one – and to alter a few lines.'

The brig had no sooner come alongside than she was mobbed by a noisy, colourful throng who swarmed aboard, all anxious to get a look at the new arrivals from the other side of the world. It was not often that the American flag was seen in the eastern Mediterranean. Furthermore, the word had gone around that there was a grand court lady on board and everyone was eager to see her. Jason had to post Kaleb and two more of his strongest men in the ship's company at the foot of the poop ladder to save Marianne from suffocation.

He did, however, allow up one gentleman, elegantly attired in a coat of sky-blue superfine and fawn-coloured pantaloons for whom Captain Montfort was doing his best to make a way through the crowd, although even then the gentleman's magnificent cream-coloured neckcloth came very near to suffering irreparable damage. After them, like a splendid shadow, came the colonel of the 6th Regiment of the Line.

Shouting to make himself heard above the din, Montfort managed to present the newcomers, Colonel Pons, who came to welcome her on behalf of the Governor, General Donzelot, and Senator Alamano, one of the principal personages of the island, who had a request to make to her. In a flowery speech which lost much of its elegance through being shouted at the top of his voice, the senator invited Marianne 'and her suite' to go ashore and accept the hospitality of his house for as long as the *Sea Witch* remained in harbour for repairs.

'I assure your ladyship that you will find it vastly more comfortable than remaining on board ship, agreeably as I am sure you are accommodated, and offering much more protection from vulgar curiosity. If you remain here you will have neither rest nor quiet, and Countess Alamano, my wife, would be grieved to be denied the pleasure of entertaining your ladyship.'

'If I may add my word to what the senator has said,' Colonel Pons put in, 'I should add that while the Governor would be most happy to offer her the hospitality of the Fort, he feels that the senator's house is much more suited to the accommodation of a young and lovely lady.'

Marianne hesitated. She had no wish to leave the ship because that would mean leaving Jason, and just at the moment when he was showing some signs of weakening. On the other hand, she could not very well disappoint these people when they were giving her such a kindly welcome. The senator was a plump, smiling man whose bravely curling whiskers did their utmost to impart an air of ferocity to his good-natured face.

She glanced at Jason and saw him smile for the first time in many days.

'Loath as I am to part with you, ma'am, I believe that these gentlemen are right. While we are undergoing repairs – a matter of three or four days I should think – your life on board would be exceedingly uncomfortable, quite apart from the curiosity you would arouse. This will enable you to rest and relax.'

'You will come and visit me ashore?'

His smile broadened, lifting one corner of his mouth with the familiar irony, but the eyes which met hers had recovered nearly all their old tenderness. He took her hand and kissed it quickly.

'Most certainly. Unless the senator forbids me his house.'

'I? Why, my dear Captain, my house, my family and all I have are yours! You may move in for weeks at a time with your whole crew if you've a mind. It would make me the happiest of men.'

'Then you must be the owner of vast estates, indeed, sir,' Jason answered him, laughing. 'But I fear that would be to impose on you rather too much. If you'll go ashore, ma'am, I'll see that your maid follows with such baggage as you require. For the present, then, good-bye.'

A brief order, a twittering of pipes and the crew had cleared the deck for Marianne and her escort to leave. She took the senator's proffered arm and accompanied by Arcadius and by Agathe, who was evidently delighted at the prospect of setting foot on dry land again, made her way to the gangway to cross the plank linking ship to shore. The senator went first, holding her hand with the satisfied air of King Mark presenting Isolde to his people.

Marianne descended graciously to the cheers of the crowd delighted by her beauty and her smile. She was happy. She felt beautiful and admired and marvellously young and, more than all this, she did not need to turn her head to know that she was watched by one pair of eyes whose regard she had almost despaired of ever regaining.

And then, just as her foot, in its yellow silk slipper, touched the warm stone of the quay, it happened; precisely as it had happened before, one night at the Tuileries, over a year ago. Then it had been in the Emperor's cabinet, after that concert when she had braved his anger by walking off the stage right in the middle of a song, without a word of explanation . . . after the terrible quarrel which had taken place between herself and the master of Europe. Without warning, the white town, the blue sea and green trees and the multi-coloured crowd all merged into an insane kaleidoscope. Marianne's eyes swam and her stomach heaved wildly.

Just before she slipped into unconsciousness and the arms of the senator, who opened them in the nick of time, there was an instant's realization that happiness was not to be, not yet. The evil consequences of her Venetian nightmare were not yet done.

Senator Alamano's house was situated not far from the village of Potamos, a couple of miles from the town. It was simple, white and spacious, and the surrounding garden was a perfect earthly paradise in miniature – a paradise in which nature, almost unaided, had played the role of gardener. Orange and lemon trees, citrons and pomegranates, bearing flowers and fruit together, alternated with arbours of vines, all tumbling headlong down to the sea. The heady scent of flowers was lightened by the freshness of a spring that tumbled down a bed of mossy rocks to form a tiny stream whose clear waters played mischievous hide-and-seek about the garden with the myrtles and the huge sprawling fig trees contorted with age. House and garden nestled in the hollow of a valley whose slopes were silvered over with hundreds of olive trees.

The woman who ruled over this miniature Eden, and over the senator as well, was small, busy and irrepressibly gay. Much younger than her husband who, although he would never have admitted it, was well on the way to a youthful fifty, Countess Maddalena Alamano had a real Venetian head of hair, made of fire and honey, and a true Venetian way of speaking, fast, soft and slurred, and by no means easy to follow until one got used to it. She was pretty rather than beautiful, with small, delicate features, an impudent tiptilted nose, eyes bright with mischief, and the prettiest hands in the world. Besides being kind, generous and hospitable, she also possessed a busy tongue, capable of diffusing an incredible amount of gossip in the shortest possible space of time.

The curtsy with which she greeted Marianne on her jasmine-covered terrace was stately enough to have satisfied a Spanish *camarera mayor*, but she spoilt it immediately by running forward to embrace her with a spontaneity that was wholly Italian.

'I am so happy to see you,' she explained. 'I was so afraid that you would sail right past our island! But now you are here and everything is all right. It is such a pleasure ... such a real happiness! And how pretty you are! But so pale ... so very pale! Are you—'

But here her husband broke in. 'Maddalena, you are tiring the Princess. She needs rest rather than chatter. She was unwell leaving the boat. The heat, I daresay.'

The Countess snorted.

'At this hour of day? It's practically dark! More likely that abominable smell of rancid oil that's always hanging over the harbour! When are you going to admit it, Ettore, that the oil warehouse ought to be moved. It makes everything smell horrible. Come, dear Princess. Your room is quite ready for you.'

'I am putting you to all this trouble,' Marianne said with a sigh. She smiled in a friendly way at the vivacious little woman. 'It makes me quite ashamed to arrive here and go straight to bed. But it's true. I do feel rather tired tonight. Tomorrow I'll be better, I'm sure, and we shall be able to improve our acquaintance.'

The room which had been made ready for Marianne was pretty and picturesque and very welcoming. The bright red hangings, embroidered in black, white and green by the women of the island, stood out cheerfully against the plain white painted walls which showed up the fine Venetian furniture, in striking contrast to the rustic simplicity of the setting. A touch of comfort was added by the warm red Turkish rugs scattered on the white marble floor, the Rhodes pottery on the dressing-table, and the alabaster lamps. The windows, framed with jasmine, were wide open on the darkened garden but were fitted with fine-mesh screens as a barrier between the mosquitoes outside and the people inside the house.

There was a bed for Agathe in the dressing-room and Jolival, after a flowery exchange of compliments with his hostess, found himself assigned to a room nearby. He had made no comment when Marianne had come to herself again in the senator's carriage but from that moment, his eyes had not left her, and Marianne knew her old friend too well not to discern the anxiety underlying his lighthearted courtesy to their hosts.

After a dinner eaten with the senator and his wife, he came up to Marianne's room to bid her good night, and she saw by the way he quickly extinguished his cigar that he had guessed the real reason for her faint.

'How do you feel?' he asked quietly.

'Much better. I have not felt faint again.'

'But you will do, I think ... Marianne, what are you going to do?'

'I don't know.'

Silence fell. Marianne stared down at her fingers, fiddling nervously with the lace edging on her sheet. The corners of her mouth turned down a little, in the way they had when she was going to cry. All the same she did not cry, but when she looked up suddenly her eyes were dark with pain and there was a little roughness in her voice.

'It's so unfair, Arcadius! Everything was going to be all right. Jason was beginning to understand, I think, that I couldn't shirk my duty. He was going to come back to me, I know he was! I could feel it! I saw it in his eyes. He still loves me!'

'Did you doubt it?' Jolival exploded. 'I didn't! You should have seen him just now, when you fainted. He nearly fell in the sea, jumping straight from the stern rail to the quay. He literally tore you out of the senator's arms and carried you to the carriage to get you away from the crowd, who were sympathetic but horribly curious. Even then he would only agree to let the carriage go after I assured him that it was nothing. That quarrel of yours was only a misunderstanding brought about by his pride and obstinacy. He loves you more than ever.'

'Well, misunderstanding won't be the word for it if he ever finds out about – about my condition! Arcadius, we've got to do something! There are drugs, ways of getting rid of – of it.'

'They can be dangerous. These things often end in tragedy.'

'As if I cared! Can't you understand I'd rather die a hundred times than give birth to this – oh, Arcadius! It's not my fault but it disgusts me! I thought I'd washed it all away, but it is too strong. It's come back and now it's taking possession of me! Help me, my friend ... try and find me some potion, anything ...'

Her head on her knees, cradled in her folded arms, she had begun to cry soundlessly, and to Jolival that silence was worse than any sobs. Marianne had never seemed to him more wretched and defenceless than she was then, finding herself a prisoner of her own body, the victim of a mischance which could cost her all her life's happiness.

After a moment, he sighed. 'Don't cry. It does no good and will only make you ill. You must be brave if you are to overcome this new ordeal.'

'I'm tired of ordeals,' Marianne cried. 'I've had more than my share.'

'Maybe so, but you've got to go through with this one, all the same. I'll try and see if it's possible to find what you want on this island but it's not going to be easy and we haven't much time. The language they talk in these parts nowadays hasn't much in common with the Greek of Aristophanes that I learned at school, either, but I'll try, I promise you.'

Feeling a little calmer now that she had shared some of her anguish with her old friend, Marianne managed to get a good night's sleep and woke the next morning so completely refreshed that she was seized with doubts. Perhaps, after all, her faintness had been due to some quite different cause? There was certainly a most unpleasant smell of oil about the harbour. But in her heart she knew that she was trying to deceive herself with false hopes. There was the physical proof whose presence, or more precisely absence, corroborated all too surely her own spontaneous diagnosis.

As she got out of her bath, she stood for a moment staring at herself in the mirror with a kind of horrified disbelief. It was much too soon as yet for anything to show. Her body looked the same as ever, just as slim and unmarked, and yet she felt for it the kind of revulsion inspired by a fruit that looks perfect outside yet is eaten away by maggots within. She almost hated it. It was as though, by admitting an alien life to enter and grow there, it had somehow betrayed her and become something apart from herself.

'You're coming out of there,' she threatened under her breath. 'Even if I have to have a fall or climb the masthead to do it.

There are a hundred ways of getting rid of rotten fruit, as Damiani knew when he tried to keep his eye on me.'

With this object in mind, she began by asking her hostess if it were possible to have the use of a horse. An hour or two's gallop could have amazing results for one in her condition. But when she asked the question, Maddalena looked at her with eyes wide with astonishment.

'Horse riding? In this heat? We have a little coolness here but the moment you are out of the shade of the trees—'

'I'm not afraid of that, and it is so long since I was on horse-back that I'm aching for a mount.'

'You're a perfect amazon,' laughed the Countess. 'Unfortun-ately there are no riding horses here, apart from those belonging to the officers of the garrison. Only donkeys and a few mules. They are all very well for an airing, but if it's an intoxicating gallop you're after, you'd have a job persuading them to do more than a sedate trot. The ground here is generally too steep. But we can go out in the carriage as often as you wish. The country is very beautiful and I should enjoy showing it to you.'

Disappointed in this direction, Marianne agreed readily to everything her hostess had to offer in the way of distraction. She went with her for a long drive through narrow valleys covered with bracken and myrtle where it was deliciously cool, and along the sea shore on to which the Potamos valley and the Alamano's garden debouched. She saw with delight the tiny island of Pontikonisi in its dreamlike bay and the tiny monastery of Blachernes, looking like a small white ink-pot left lying on the surface of the water, with a huge cypress, like a black quill, be-side it. They paid a call on the Governor, General Donzelot, at the Fortezza Vecchia and he took them on a tour of inspection and gave them tea.

Marianne inspected the old Venetian cannon and the bronze statue of Schulenburg who had defended the island against the Turks a century before, flirted mildly with a number of young officers of the 6th Regiment of the Line who were visibly dazzled by her beauty, and was generally charming to everyone pre-sented to her, promised to attend the next performance at the theatre which was the garrison's chief amusement, and finally, before returning to Potamos where the Alamanos were holding a grand dinner party in her honour, knelt for a few moments before the sacred relics of St Spiridion.

St Spiridion had been a Cypriot shepherd who rose, by reason of his virtue and ability, to be Bishop of Alexandria. His mummified body had been acquired from the Turks by a Greek merchant who gave it as a dowry with his eldest daughter on the occasion of her marriage to an eminent Corfiot named Bulgari.

'And ever since then, there has always been a priest in the Bulgari family,' Maddalena concluded in her vivacious way. 'The one who showed you the relic and took some money from you is the latest.'

'Why? Have they still such reverence for the saint?'

'Well, yes, of course. But it's more than that. St Spiridion represents the greater part of their income. They didn't give him the Church, they only, as it were, hired him out. Rather a come-down for a great saint, don't you agree? Not that he doesn't answer prayers just as well as any of the rest. He's a splendid saint, for he doesn't seem to bear a grudge at all.'

Even so, Marianne dared not ask the one-time shepherd to intercede for her. Divine aid was not for her in the deed she contemplated. That was more a matter for the devil.

The grand dinner at which she was the guest of honour in white satin and diamonds seemed to her quite the longest and most boring she had ever sat through. Jolival had departed that morning first thing for the other end of the island to inspect the excavations which General Donzelot was undertaking there. Jason and his officers had been invited but had declined, pleading the urgency of the repairs to the ship, and Marianne, having waited all day in eager anticipation of the evening which would bring her reluctant lover to her, was hard put to it to conceal her disappointment and maintain a smiling face and an air of interest in what her neighbours were saying to her. The left-hand neighbour, at least, for on her right she had General Donzelot who was a man of few words. Like most men of action, Donzelot hated wasting time in conversation. He was polite and friendly but Marianne could have sworn that he shared her own opinion of this dinner as nothing but a tiresome duty.

Her other neighbour, by contrast, was indefatigable. He was a local notable whose name she had already forgotten, and he entertained her, in the most gruesome detail, with an account of the epic battles he had fought in his younger days against the ferocious troops of the Pasha of Yannina during the Souliot rising. Now, if there was one thing Marianne loathed, it was listening to people recounting their experiences of war. She had had more than enough of that at Napoleon's court where there was scarcely a man without a tale to tell.

Consequently it was with a sense of relief that she regained her own room when the evening came to an end at last and delivered herself up to Agathe's hands to be divested of her finery. Enveloped in a lace-trimmed wrapper of fine lawn, she was settled on a low chair to have her hair brushed for the night.

'Monsieur de Jolival is not back yet?' she asked Agathe who was busy with two brushes shaking out the hair which had been bound up all day long.

'No, my lady. At least, that is to say he came in while you were all at dinner, just to change. And I must say, he needed to! His clothes were all white with dust. He said not to disturb anyone on his account because he was going straight out again and would get his dinner down at the harbour.'

Marianne closed her eyes, satisfied, and abandoned herself to her maid's deft fingers with a deep sense of reassurance. Jolival was doing his best for her, she was certain. He had not gone down to the harbour for the sake of entertainment.

After a few minutes she told Agathe that she might stop now and go to bed.

'Don't you want me to plait your hair for you, my lady?'

'No, thank you, Agathe. I'll leave it loose tonight. I've a trifle of a headache and would rather be alone. I shan't go to bed yet.'

When the girl, who was accustomed to asking no questions, had dropped a curtsy and left her, Marianne went to the long window opening on to a small balcony and, taking down the screen of mosquito netting, stepped outside. She felt stifled and in need of air. The screens were a good protection against the insects but they also seemed to prevent the free circulation of air.

Tucking her hands into the wide sleeves of her wrapper, she moved across the balcony. It was much warmer than it had been the night before. Not a breath of wind had come at nightfall to cool the parching atmosphere. Earlier, at dinner, she had felt as if her satin dress were sticking to her skin. Even the stone balustrade on which she was leaning was still warm.

Out of doors, though, the night was glorious : an eastern darkness, rich with stars and heavy with perfume, ringing with the rhythmic note of cicadas. Down below, thousands of glow-worms made a second firmament of the dark shapes of trees and shrubs, while at the foot of the valley the sea gleamed softly, a silvered triangle framed by the tall spires of cypress trees. Except for the plaintive scraping of the cicadas and the faint swish of the sea on the pebbled shore, there was not a sound to be heard.

That little patch of water shining at the bottom of the garden suddenly began to exercise a magnetic effect on Marianne. It was so hot that she longed to bathe. The water would be cool and heavenly, soothing away the fever of impatience which had been growing on her all through that dreary dinner.

She hesitated. Not all the servants would be in bed yet. Some were probably still engaged in tidying the rooms which had been used for the party. If she went down and announced her intention of going for a swim they would probably quite certainly think her mad, while if she merely said that she was going for a walk they would probably follow at a discreet distance to make sure that no harm came to such a distinguished visitor.

A preposterous idea occurred to her. In the old days at Selton Hall she had had her own way of leaving her room without anyone's knowing, with the aid of the ivy that covered the walls. The little balcony here was only on the first floor and there were climbing plants rampaging all over it.

'It remains to be seen whether you are still as athletic as you used to be, my girl,' she told herself, 'but anyway it's worth trying.'

Her spirits soared at the thought of the escapade and of a cool swim. Childishly excited, she scampered to her wardrobe, dragged out the simplest dress she could find, a simple lavender print with a ribbon sash, and slipped it on over a pair of drawers. She added a pair of flat-heeled slippers and thus equipped made her way back to the balcony, replacing the mosquito screen carefully behind her. Then she began the descent.

It was divinely simple. She had lost nothing of her old skill and in a few seconds her feet touched the sanded path and she was swallowed up in the overgrown darkness of the garden. The path that followed the course of the stream down to the tiny beach passed quite close to her balcony and she found it without trouble. She was hot after her climb and she sauntered unhurriedly down the sandy slope to the water beneath an over-hanging canopy of leaves. The path was like a tunnel, filled with exotic scents, with a lighter patch at the far end, but underneath the trees it was pitch dark.

Suddenly, Marianne came to a stop and listened, her heart beating a little faster. She thought she had caught the sound of a light, furtive footfall behind her. It occurred to her that someone might have seen her come out and followed her and she was tempted to turn back. She waited a few seconds, un-certain what to do, but she heard nothing more and the sea seemed to beckon to her, cool and inviting. She walked on, keeping her ears open and treading as softly as she could but there was no further noise.

'I dreamed it,' she told herself. 'My nerves must be all on edge.'

By the time she got down to the beach, her eyes had grown accustomed to the darkness. There was no moon but such a multitude of stars that the sky was filled with a milky radiance that threw a faint light on the sea. Quickly she slipped off her clothes and clad only in her long hair, ran straight into the sea. As she plunged forward into the water, she almost cried aloud for joy as the blessed coolness enveloped her. Her parched body seemed to melt and liquefy. She had never known such a de-licious bathe. When she remembered swimming as a child in the river that ran through the park at Selton, or from some empty cove on the Devon coast, it was in much colder water, cold enough, frequently, to bring the tears to her eyes. This was just cool enough to be life-giving and caressed her skin like silk. It was clear, too, so limpid that, splashing like a puppy dog, she could see her legs moving under water like a paler shadow.

She rolled over on to her stomach and set out to swim towards the middle of the little bay. Her arms and legs fell automatically into the remembered rhythm and she moved easily through the water, pausing from time to time to float for a moment on her back with eyes half-closed, revelling in her delight. She decided that she would swim until she was tired, a healthy, physical tiredness after which she would sleep like a child.

It was during one of these periodic rests that she became aware of a soft, regular splashing. It was coming closer and she identified the sound at once. Someone else was swimming in the bay. Raising herself up out of the water she peered through the darkness and made out a shadowy figure coming towards her. There was someone there, someone who had followed her, perhaps. She remembered the footsteps she had thought she heard earlier, on the way down. Realizing suddenly the foolishness of coming down to bathe alone like this in the middle of the night in a strange country, she turned to swim back to the shore, but the mysterious swimmer changed direction to cut her off. He was swimming fast and powerfully, clearly seeking to intercept her, and if she continued on her present course in a few more minutes he would have succeeded.

In sudden panic she reacted idiotically and in an attempt to frighten off what she thought must be some unknown enemy, she cried out in Italian:

'Who are you? Go away!'

Her voice died in a gurgle as she swallowed a mouthful of salt water, but the stranger did not pause. He came on silently towards her, in a silence that was the most frightening part of the whole thing. Then Marianne lost her head completely and tried to escape by swimming straight ahead, making for one of the points of the bay in the hope of reaching land and so eluding her pursuer. Such was her terror that it did not even occur to her to wonder who it was. It crossed her mind that he was probably only a Greek fisherman who could not understand her and might have thought she was in danger, but she dismissed the idea at once. When she had first caught sight of him he had been swimming slowly and quietly, making as little noise as possible, advancing on her almost stealthily.

The shore was closer now but the distance between the two swimmers had also diminished appreciably. Marianne was beginning to tire. Her movements were growing sluggish and her heart was thumping painfully in her breast. She knew that she was nearly at the end of her strength and that she had no choice now but to sink or let him overtake her.

Suddenly, she saw, directly in front of her, a minute crescent-shaped opening, paler than the surrounding rocks. Summoning up her last, remaining strength, she forced her limbs into one last effort but the man was gaining on her. He was close behind her now, a great black shadow with no distinguishing features. Terror stopped her breath and, at the very instant two hands reached out towards her, Marianne went under.

She returned to consciousness and to an awareness of strange sensations. She was lying on the sand in inky darkness and a man was holding her in his arms. He, too, was naked for she could feel the texture of his skin next to hers, smooth and warm but strongly muscled. She could see nothing at all, except perhaps a thickening of the darkness before her face, and when she stretched out her arms, instinctively, they touched rock to the side and above her. She was in some kind of low, narrow cave in the rocks. She tried to cry out, seized with a sudden terror at finding herself immured in this crevice in the rocks. A firm and burning mouth stifled her cries. She tried to struggle but the arms tightened round her, holding her still as the unknown man began to caress her.

Sure of himself, he made no attempt to hurry. His hands were gentle but subtly experienced and she knew that he was seeking to rouse her to the pitch where love becomes an irresistible fever. She tried to set her teeth and stiffen her muscles but the man had an extraordinary knowledge of the female body. Her fears had evaporated long ago, and now Marianne could feel long, shuddering waves of pleasure stealing up through her body. Still the kiss went on, that, too, strangely skilled, and Marianne found her breath sucked from her and her spirit weakening ... It was so strange, this making love with a shadow.

Little by little, she felt the weight of a tall body, full of strength and life, and yet it seemed to her that in some curious way she was making love with a ghost. Witches in the olden days who claimed to have had intercourse with the devil must have felt like this. She might have thought that it was nothing but a dream if that other flesh had not felt so warm and solid and but for the faint yet altogether earthly smell of mint which clung about the person of her unknown lover. Moreover, he was gradually attaining his ends. Possessed by the most primitive desires, Marianne was moaning now in his arms. The insistent waves of pleasure were mounting within her, higher and higher, overwhelming her ... When, at last, the man allowed his long control to break, she burst like a red sun.

Two voices cried out together. That, and the chaotic beating of his heart was all that Marianne heard of her invisible lover. The next instant, he had risen, gasping, and was gone.

She heard the pebbles shifting under his running feet and raised herself quickly on her elbow, in time to see a tall figure dive into the sea. There was a tremendous splash, then nothing more. The man had not uttered a single word.

When Marianne crept out of the hollow in the rocks which the stranger had chosen to shelter them, she felt light-headed but physically curiously calm. It astonished her that she should feel so happy. She felt no shame or guilt for what had happened, perhaps just because the man had vanished so swiftly after making love to her, and had vanished so completely. No trace of his presence remained. He had simply melted into the night and into the sea whence he had come, as the morning mist is dissipated in the first rays of the sun. Who he was and where he came from, Marianne would probably never know. He was most likely a Greek fisherman, as she had first thought. She had seen many since landing on the island, beautiful and untamed as clouds in the sky, and still carrying about them a little of the aura of the old gods of Olympus who had been skilled at catching mortals unawares. He must have seen her go down to the beach and enter the water and it had been instinctive for him to follow her. The rest had been inevitable.

Perhaps it was Jupiter ... or Neptune? she thought, amused

in a way that astonished even herself. In the ordinary way, she would undoubtedly have felt outraged, baffled and indignant, and heaven knew what else, but she felt none of these things. More than that, she was honest enough to admit to herself that those fleeting moments of passion had been not disagreeable and would linger rather pleasantly in her memory. She would be able to look back on it all simply as an adventure, a distinctly nice adventure!

The little inlet was not nearly so far from the beach as she had feared. She had been so frightened before that she had not been properly conscious of the direction. The moon, which was now rising beyond the point, sent a thin sliver of silver over the water, and it was suddenly much lighter, although just as hot.

Hoping that this time no one would see her, Marianne slid back into the water and swam to the beach, pausing when her toes touched the sandy bottom to take a cautious look up and down. Then she hurried out of the water and put on her clothes as fast as she could manage, without bothering to dry herself, only wringing the water out of her hair. Carrying her shoes to keep them from getting full of sand, she made her way up the beach to the dense shadow of the trees.

She was just stepping into it when she was frozen where she stood by the sound of a laugh. It was a man's laugh but this time Marianne was not in the least afraid. Anger and exasperation were uppermost. She was growing a little tired of this night's surprises. Besides whoever had laughed was probably the same ... She felt her temper rising. She had been inclined to find her adventure rather charming, yet if he could laugh ...

'Come out!' she cried. 'And stop laughing.'

'Good was it – your bathe?' came a mocking voice in execrably uncertain Italian. 'Good to watch, yes. Beautiful lady!'

As he spoke, the man emerged from under the trees and came towards Marianne. The white flowing robes he wore gave him a faintly ghostly appearance and the turban wound round his head made him seem to her to be very tall. She did not stop to think that this turbaned figure might belong to a henchman of the terrible Ali against whom she had been warned. She only thought that the man's words and his laughter had been an insult. Instantly, she darted forward and dealt him a ringing box on the ears, almost before she could see him.

'You ill-mannered lout!' she abused him. 'You were spying on me! How dare you!'

The slap had one good thing about it, in so far as it told her that this Turk or Epirote or whatever else he might be was not her erstwhile ravisher. Her hand had encountered a bearded cheek, whereas the other's face had been smooth. But far from resenting her attack, the stranger had begun to laugh.

'Why you angry? I have done wrong? I walk here every night – see no one. Sea, shore and sky, nothing else. Tonight I see a gown on the sand and someone who swims. I wait.'

Marianne was regretting the slap. He was only someone out for a late stroll, after all. Probably, his house was nearby. He had not been guilty of anything so very dreadful.

'I beg your pardon,' she said. 'I thought it was something else. I did wrong to hit you.' Then, as a new idea came to her, she added: 'But since you were on the beach, did you see anyone come out of the water before me?'

'Here? No, no one. A few minutes ago ... was someone swimming – out there, by the point. That's all.'

'Oh. Thank you.'

Evidently her elusive lover must have been Neptune. Seeing that the man had nothing more to tell her, she prepared to go on her way. She supported herself with one hand against the trunk of a cypress while she put on her shoes, but the stranger, it seemed, did not intend to leave matters there. He came closer.

'You not angry now?' he said, and again there was that laugh which Marianne was beginning to think sounded a little simple. 'We ... friends?'

He had both hands on her shoulders, trying to pull her towards him. It was a bad move, for Marianne, furious, pushed him away so fiercely that he was caught off balance and fell headlong on the sand.

'You—'

There was no time to search for a suitable adjective. The shot had been fired at the precise moment Marianne pushed the man away and the ball passed between them. She felt the wind of its passing and instinctively flung herself to the ground. A second shot followed almost at once. Someone was firing at them from beneath the trees.

The man in the turban wriggled towards her.

'Not move ... not be afraid ... shoot at me,' he whispered.

'You mean someone is trying to kill you? But whatever for?'

'Ssh!'

He was slipping dexterously out of his flowing white garment. Next he took off his turban and hung it on a bush. It was immediately made the target of two shots in quick succession.

'Two pistols. No more balls, I think ...' the stranger said softly, almost gaily. 'Not move ... Assassin come to see me dead ...'

Realizing what he meant, Marianne flattened herself as best she could among the undergrowth, while her companion drew a long, curved knife silently from his belt and crouched, ready to spring. He did not have long to wait. In a little while, cautious footsteps crunched on the sand and a dark shape came gliding through the trees. It came forward a little way, then stopped, then, evidently reassured by the silence, came on again. Marianne had barely time to glimpse a thickset, remarkably energetic-looking figure moving with knife in hand, then, with a bound like a wild beast, the stranger was upon him. They rolled together on the ground, locked together in a desperate struggle.

The shots, meanwhile, had aroused the household and Marianne saw light approaching through the trees and the inhabitants of the Alamano estate turned out with lanterns and, no doubt, guns. They were led by the senator himself in his night-shirt and cotton nightcap with a pom-pom on the top, a pistol in each hand. After him came a dozen or so servants, variously armed. The first person they saw was Marianne, standing in the middle of the path.

'Princess!' the senator exclaimed. 'Is it you, here, at this hour? What is happening?'

For answer, she stood aside and let him see the two men still grappling one another furiously on the ground, uttering ferocious animal grunts. The senator gave one anguished howl and, stuffing his pistols into Marianne's hands, dashed forward to separate them. His servants rushed to help and in a few seconds the two adversaries had been parted by main force. But while the man with the turban was treated with the utmost solicitude, the other was instantly bound and flung on the ground with a roughness that made it quite clear he, at least, could look for no sympathy from the senator.

The Venetian was hastily assisting the stranger to resume his flowing robe and turban.

'You are not hurt, lord? You are quite sure you are not hurt?' he asked several times over.

'Not in the least, I thank you. But my life I owe to this young lady. She throw me down, just in time.'

'Young lady? Oh, the Princess, you mean? Lord!' This time the wretched senator was seen to be invoking his maker. 'Lord, what a business! What a business!'

'Perhaps if you were to introduce us?' Marianne suggested. 'It might make things a little clear. To me, at any rate.'

Still suffering somewhat from shock, the senator launched into a series of introductions and explanations which rapidly became hopelessly involved. All the same, Marianne was able to gather that she had just prevented a highly unfortunate diplomatic incident and succeeded in saving the life of a noble refugee. The man in the turban was now revealed as a youth of about twenty, who without his pointed beard and long black moustache would probably have looked a good deal younger. He was Chahin Bey, the son of one of the Pasha of Yannina's latest victims, Mustapha, Pasha of Delvino. After Ali's janissaries had taken their city and murdered their father, Chahin and his younger brother had sought refuge in Corfu where they were given a hospitable welcome by the governor. They were living in a pleasant house higher up the valley, overlooking the sea, where they were in sight of the watch at the fort. In addition, two soldiers were constantly on guard at their door, but even so, it was scarcely possible to prevent the young princes from walking abroad whenever they wished.

The attacker, apparently one of Ali's agents, was one of the

fierce Albanians from the Chimera Mountains whose arid peaks
could be seen across the northern channel. So much was clear
from the red scarf he wore round his head. The remainder of
his costume was made up of baggy trousers with a short skirt
of heavy linen, silver-buttoned waistcoat and a pair of espa-
drilles. From the wide red belt that cinched his waist in tighter
than any stays, the senator's servants took an astonishing
selection of weapons. The man was a walking arsenal. Once
bound, however, it proved impossible to get another word out
of him. He was tied to a tree and remained there in brooding
silence, guarded by a number of armed servants, while Alamano
sent a messenger hurrying to the fort.

On learning the real identity of the woman whom he had
taken for some pretty local girl out for a spree, Chahin Bey
displayed just the right amount of confusion consonant with
good manners. The sight of Marianne's face, revealed in the
light of the lanterns, afforded him a degree of pleasure that
was evidently enough to overcome all merely social considera-
tions. Seeing his gaze fixed brilliantly on herself all the way up
to the house, Marianne realized that she had awoken in him
sentiments no whit less primitive than those which she had
aroused in the unknown man in the water. The thought gave
her no satisfaction whatever. She had had enough of the primitive for one night.

'I hope the story will not get about,' she confided to Maddalena, who had emerged from her chamber, clad in an abundantly
frilled dressing-gown, to provide the heroes of the occasion with
sustaining drinks on their return.

'It was quite by accident that I was able to thwart the
attacker, you know. I had gone down to the beach to bathe. It
was so dreadfully hot! And then, as I was coming back, I
bumped into the Bey and had the good fortune to knock him
down just at the very moment the assassin fired. It is really
nothing to make a fuss about.'

'But that is what Chahin Bey is certainly doing. Listen to him.
He is already comparing you to the houris of paradise! Besides
declaring that you have the courage of a lioness. You are in a
fair way to becoming a heroine to him, Princess.'

'Well, I've no objection to that, so long as he keeps his feelings to himself. And if the senator will say nothing about my part in the affair.'

'But why? You have done a very fine thing which does great honour to France. General Donzelot—'

'Need never know,' Marianne wailed. 'I am really a very retiring person. I don't in the least care to be talked about. It is so embarrassing.'

What was particularly embarrassing, just then, was the knowledge that if Jason heard of what had taken place that night on the beach, he was likely to draw very different conclusions from the real truth. His nature was too jealous to allow him to overlook the smallest thing. But how was she to explain to her hostess that she was madly in love with her ship's captain and his opinion mattered more to her than anything?

Maddalena's brown eyes, which had been observing Marianne's slowly reddening cheeks, were alight with laughter as she murmured:

'It all depends on how the story is told. We'll do our best to restrain Chahin Bey's enthusiasm. Otherwise, the governor might conclude that you – er – collided with our young friend while endeavouring to dissuade him from seeing himself as Ulysses meeting Nausicaa. And you wouldn't wish the governor to think . . .'

'Not the governor or anyone else! The truth is, I feel a trifle foolish and even my friends—'

'There is nothing particularly foolish in wishing to bathe when the weather is as hot as this. But then, I have heard that Americans are exceedingly strait-laced, and even prudish.'

'Americans? Why Americans? I am certainly travelling in a vessel of that nation but I don't see . . .'

Maddalena slid her arm quietly through Marianne's and walked with her to the staircase that led to her room.

'My dear Princess,' she said softly, selecting a lighted candle from among those placed on a side table, 'let me tell you two things. One is that I am a woman and the second that, although I do not know you very well, I like you a great deal. I shall do all I can to shield you from the slightest inconvenience. If I spoke of Americans, it was because my husband told me of your captain's alarm when you were unwell at the harbour, and also what an excessively charming man he is! Don't worry. We'll try and ensure that he knows nothing. I will speak to my husband.'

As it turned out, Chahin Bey's enthusiasm was not of a kind to be stemmed. Alamano was silent about the part played by Marianne when handing the would-be assassin over to the island's police force, but as soon as it was light a procession of the Bey's servants entered the senator's garden bearing gifts for the 'precious flower from the land of the infidel caliph' and settled themselves outside the front door, waiting with the inexhaustible patience of the east until they could deliver their messages.

These, in addition to the presents, consisted of a letter couched in the most flowery Greek vernacular in which Chahin Bey declared that since 'the splendour of the princess of the sea-coloured eyes has put to flight the black-winged angel Azrael', he was her knight for all the days allotted to him by Allah on this sinful earth and meant to devote to her and to his oppressed people, groaning under the heel of the infamous Ali, the remainder of a life which, but for her, would already be no more than a memory too brief for glory.

'What does he mean?' Marianne asked uneasily, when the senator had concluded his somewhat halting but adequate translation.

Alamano spread out his arms in a gesture of ignorance.

'My dear Princess, I assure you I have not the least idea. That kind of phraseology is typical of oriental politeness. Chahin Bey means, I take it, that he will no more forget you than he will forget his own lost people.'

Maddalena, who had been following the reading of the letter with a good deal of interest, put down the big fan of woven reeds with which she had been trying to mitigate the heat and smiled at her new friend.

'Unless he is declaring his intention of offering you his hand as soon as he has recovered his domains? It would be quite in keeping with his romantically chivalrous nature. My dear, that boy fell head over ears in love as soon as he set eyes on you!'

What Chahin Bey actually meant was not made plain until that evening, with the arrival of Jason Beaufort, white with rage. He stormed on to the terrace where the two women were stretched in long chairs taking some refreshments and watching the sunset and it was all he could do to remember the ordinary observances of civility due to his hostess. As he made his bow to Maddalena, Marianne could tell from the frowning glance he cast in her direction that he had something to say.

The usual polite exchanges took place in an atmosphere so charged with electricity that Countess Alamano could not fail to notice it, and she took the first opportunity to excuse herself gracefully, on the score of being obliged to speak to her cook, realizing that the other two wished to be private together.

Almost before her dress of lilac muslin had vanished through the french window leading into the house, Jason turned on Marianne and accused her roundly:

'What were you doing down on the beach last night with that crazy Turk?'

'Good God!' Marianne exclaimed faintly, subsiding despairingly on to her cushions. 'The gossip on this island flies faster than in Paris!'

'This isn't gossip. Your admirer – there is no other word for the fellow – came on board just now and told me that you saved his life last night in circumstances which are to say the least obscure – as obscure as the jargon he talks!'

'But why should he go and tell you that?' Marianne said, mystified.

'Ha! You admit it, then?'

'Admit what? I have nothing to admit. Nothing that signifies, at least. It's true I did happen to save the life of a Turkish refugee last night, quite by chance. It was so hot that I could not bear to stay in my room and I went down to the beach for a breath of fresh air. At that hour of night I thought I should be quite alone there—'

'So much so that you thought you could bathe. You took off your clothes – all your clothes?'

'Oh, so you know that, too?'

'Of course. I gather the memory of it kept your exotic swain awake all night. He saw you emerge from the sea in the moonlight, as naked as Aphrodite, it seems, and by far more beautiful! What have you to say to that?'

'Nothing!' Marianne cried, stung by Jason's accusing tone, especially as she was beginning to feel slightly more guilty and a trifle less nostalgic about the passionate scene of the previous night. 'It's quite true I took my clothes off. My goodness, what's wrong with that? You're a sailor yourself. Don't tell me you never swam in the sea? Would you put on a dressing-gown and slippers and a nightcap to get into the water?'

'I'm a man,' Jason snapped. 'It's not the same.'

'I know!' Marianne flashed bitterly. 'You are creatures apart, demi-gods to whom all is permitted, while we poor females are only allowed to enjoy the water all bundled up in shawls and overcoats! The hypocrisy of it! When I think that in the days of King Henry IV the women used to bathe stark naked in the middle of Paris in broad daylight, right below the Pont Neuf, and no one thought a penny the worse! And now I'm committing a crime because I try to forget the heat for a little while on a dark night on an empty beach on what is practically a desert island! Well, I was wrong and I'm sorry. Will that do?'

Something of the venom in her tone must have penetrated, because Jason stopped striding up and down the terrace, hands behind his back, much as he was used to do on his own deck, although rather more furiously and came instead to stand before Marianne. He looked at her for a moment and then said on a note of vague surprise:

'You're angry?'

She stared up at him with flashing eyes.

'Is that wrong of me, as well? You come here steaming with rage, you rant at me, determined to find me guilty, and then when I object you are surprised! You always make me feel halfway between a hysterical bacchante and the village idiot!'

The privateer's set face relaxed for an instant into a fleeting smile. He held out his hands and plucked her from her cushions, drawing her up to stand within the circle of his arms.

'Forgive me. I know I've been behaving like a brute again, but I can't help it. As soon as it is anything to do with you, I see red. When that blundering idiot came along, all smiles, and told me about your exploit, incidentally describing how he'd seen you coming out of the water all glistening in the moonlight, I very nearly throttled him.'

'Only nearly?' Marianne said nastily.

This time Jason laughed outright and held her closer.

'Are you sorry? If it hadn't been for Kaleb – you remember the runaway slave I found – who got him away from me, I'd have done Ali Pasha's work for him after all.'

'The Ethiopian?' Marianne said thoughtfully. 'Did he dare to come between you?'

'He was at work on the planking close by, and on the whole, just as well,' Jason said indifferently. 'Your Chahin Bey was squealing like a stuck pig and people were beginning to notice.'

'He's not my Chahin Bey!' Marianne broke in with annoyance. 'And you still haven't explained what made him go off and tell all this to you, of all people?'

'Didn't I tell you? For the simple reason, my angel, that having made up his mind to go with us to Constantinople he came to ask me to take him on board with his household.'

'What? He wants—'

'To go with you, yes, my darling. The boy seems to know what he wants. His plans for the future are quite cut and dried: to go to Constantinople and complain to the Grand Signior of the wrongs done to himself and his people by Ali Pasha, then set off home with an army – oh, and yourself – and when he has reconquered his province to offer you the position of first wife to the new Pasha of Delvino.'

'And – and you agreed?' Marianne cried, appalled at the idea of trailing the young Turk after her for weeks to come.

'Agreed? I told you, I nearly strangled him. After Kaleb got him away from me, I told him to see him ashore, and I informed your admirer that under no circumstances would I have him set foot on board my ship again. I've no use for would-be pashas. For one thing I didn't like him, and for another I'm beginning to think there are a deal too many people aboard the *Witch* as it is. You don't know how much I long to be alone with you, my love ... Just you and me, the two of us, day and night. I think I must have been mad to think I could ever part from you! Ever since Venice, I've gone through hell, just wanting you. But that's all over now. We sail tomorrow—'

'Tomorrow?'

'Yes. The repairs are almost done. By working all night we'll be able to leave in the morning. I'm not leaving you here much longer, not with that besotted ape on your doorstep. Tomorrow I'll take you away. Tomorrow our new life will begin. I'll do anything you want – only for pity's sake don't let's hang about in Turkey! I can't wait to get you home – to our home. Only there will I be able to love you as I want to ... and I do want to, so very much.'

As he spoke, Jason's voice had dropped until it was no more than a deep, passionate murmur, punctuated by kisses.

Around them, dusk was falling and the glow worm lights were springing up about the garden. Yet to Marianne, in the arms of the man she loved, there came, oddly enough, none of the joy she would have imagined, only a few minutes earlier, from such a signal victory. Jason was surrendering, he was admitting defeat: she ought to have been wild with delight. But while her heart melted with love and gladness, her body had no share in it. In fact, she was not feeling at all well. She had the impression she was going to faint, as she had the other day, getting off the boat ... Perhaps it was the faint tobacco smell that clung to Jason's clothes, but she was almost sure that she was going to be sick ...

He felt her slump suddenly and start to slip from his arms. He caught her just in time. In the last glimmer of daylight, her face was deathly pale.

'Marianne! What is it? Are you ill?'

As he spoke, he picked her up and laid her down gently in her nest of cushions, but this time Marianne had not lost consciousness altogether. Gradually, the dreadful sick feeling passed off and she managed to smile.

'It's nothing ... the heat, I expect.'

'No, you are not well. This is the second time you've swooned like that. You must see a doctor.'

He stood up as though to go in search of Maddalena but Marianne clutched his arm and pulled him back.

'It's nothing, I tell you. I'm quite sure I don't need a doctor. I know what it is.'

'You do? Then what is it?'

She cast about desperately for a plausible lie and said at last with an assumed carelessness:

'Nothing – or almost nothing. It's just that my stomach is a little delicate these days. It's – it's since – since I was a prisoner.'

Jason studied the pale face for a moment, mechanically chafing her icy hands as he did so. He was clearly only half convinced. Marianne was not the kind of woman to faint for nothing, swooning over the scent of a flower or the slightest emotion. Something about it worried him. However, he had no time to ask further questions.

The sound of approaching footsteps evidently indicated the return of Maddalena. Marianne sat up quickly and, evading his instinctive move to prevent her, got to her feet.

'What are you doing?'

'Oh, please, don't say that I was ill. I hate to have people fuss over me. Maddalena would only worry, and then I should have to put up with her cosseting.'

Jason's protests were lost in the click of heels as the Countess reappeared, bearing an oil-lamp with a thick glass shade. Warm yellow light spilled over the terrace and gleamed on her red hair and gently teasing smile.

'Would you rather it were dark?' she said. 'But here come my husband and Monsieur de Jolival. We are just going to dine. You'll stay, of course, Captain?'

The American inclined his tall person in an apologetic bow.

'I'm truly sorry, Countess, but I must return to my ship. We sail tomorrow.'

'So soon?'

'My repair work is finished and we have to reach Constantinople as quickly as possible. It grieves me to be obliged to rob you of the Princess so soon, but the sooner we are there the better. The frigates that are to escort us have many other calls on their time. I should not wish to detain them too long. You will have to excuse me.'

As though in haste, suddenly, to be gone, he said his farewells and bowed over the hands of both ladies, letting his blue gaze dwell for a moment, with a faintly troubled look, on Marianne's. Then he went away through the garden, just as the voices of Jolival and Alamano made themselves heard inside the house.

'A strange man,' Maddalena remarked, looking thoughtfully after the captain's tall figure as it vanished into the darkness. 'But certainly attractive! Perhaps, all things considered, it's just as well he's not staying here too long. Every woman on the island would be mad for him. There is something masterful about his eyes that suggests he doesn't take kindly to being crossed.'

'You're quite right,' Marianne said, her mind elsewhere. 'He hates to be contradicted.'

The Countess smiled. 'That wasn't altogether what I meant,' she said. 'Shall we join the gentlemen indoors?'

Jolival was the very person Marianne needed to see just at that moment. This second spell of faintness had seriously alarmed her, for if she were to have many more like it life on board ship promised to become almost impossible. Meanwhile, Arcadius had practically disappeared. She had scarcely seen him since the night of her arrival and that, too, had worried her because it was not a good sign.

She sat through dinner with her anxieties undiminished. Jolival looked tired. He was making an effort, visible only to those who knew him well, to respond to his hostess's bright conversation, but his light easy chatter was belied by the troubled look in his eyes.

'He's failed,' Marianne thought. 'He hasn't been able to find what I need. He wouldn't look like that if he had.'

Even Maddalena's witty account of Marianne's nocturnal adventures failed to smooth the lines of care wholly from his face.

When he came to her room for a few moments, before retiring to his own, Marianne learned that he had indeed drawn a complete blank.

'I did hear of an old Greek woman, some kind of witch who lived in a hut on the side of Mount Pantocrator, but when I managed to find the place at last, this afternoon, there was nothing but a few mourners and an aged *papas* about to conduct her funeral. But don't despair,' he added, quickly, seeing her face fall. 'Tomorrow I'll go back to the Venetian tavern where I got the information and—'

Marianne sighed wearily.

'It's no good, Jolival. We are leaving tomorrow morning. Didn't you know? Jason came just now to tell me. He's in a hurry to leave Corfu ... largely, I think, on account of my ridiculous adventure with Chahin Bey.'

'He knows of that?'

'The idiot wanted to go with us. He went and told Jason the whole story.'

There was a silence, occupied on Jolival's part by restless fiddling with the crystal rose-bowl on the table.

'How do matters stand between you?'

In a few words, Marianne described their last encounter on the terrace and the manner in which it had ended.

'He gave in sooner than I expected,' was Jolival's comment when it was done. 'He loves you very deeply, Marianne, in spite of all his temper and his rudeness and his fits of jealousy ... I wonder if you wouldn't be better advised to tell him the truth.'

'The truth? About my condition?'

'Yes. You are not well. I was watching you at dinner. You're pale and nervous and you scarcely ate a thing. You'll suffer dreadfully on board ship. And there's that doctor, Leighton. He never takes his eyes off you. I'm not sure why, but you've made an enemy there who'll stick at nothing to be rid of you.'

'How do you know?'

'Gracchus tipped me the wink. Your coachman, in case you didn't know it, is beginning to discover his vocation as a seaman. He lives with the crew and he's found a friend who can speak French. Leighton has a few supporters among them who are always grumbling at the presence of a woman on board. Besides, he's a doctor. He may discover the truth about your illness.'

'I thought doctors were bound to secrecy by the rules of their profession,' Marianne said bluntly.

'So they are, but as I said, this one hates you and I'd judge him capable of a good deal. Listen to me, Marianne. Tell Beaufort the truth. He is capable of understanding, I'm sure of it.'

'And what do you think he'll say? I can tell you. He won't believe me! I'd never dare to tell him such a thing straight out.'

Like Jason on the terrace, earlier that evening, Marianne was pacing up and down her room, kneading a tiny lace handkerchief between her hands. In imagination she was picturing the scene she had conjured up of herself facing Jason, telling him that she was pregnant by her steward. Enough to make him shun her like the plague!

'You, who are always so brave, are afraid to have it out?' Jolival reproached her softly.

'I'm afraid of losing the man I love for ever, Arcadius. Just as any woman in love would be.'

'How do you know you would lose him? I've told you, he loves you, and perhaps—'

'There, you see!' Marianne interrupted him with a little hysterical laugh. 'You said perhaps. Perhaps that's what I don't want to risk.'

'And suppose he finds out? Suppose he guesses somehow?'

'Then he does. Let's say I'd rather play all or nothing, if you like. In a little more than a week, if all goes well, we'll be in Constantinople. I'll do what's necessary there. Until then, I'll try and hold out.'

With a sigh of resignation, Jolival rose from his chair and went to Marianne. Taking her face between his hands, he deposited a fatherly kiss on the forehead which was set just now in an obstinate frown.

'You may be right,' he said. 'I've no right to compel you. But – I suppose you wouldn't, well, accept the notion of letting me deal with the explanations that frighten you so much? Jason likes and, I believe, respects me. I expect he would believe me.'

'He'd believe that you are very fond of me and would stand up for me at all costs – and that I had spun you an enormous yarn! No, Arcadius, I won't let you. But I thank you from the bottom of my heart.'

He bowed, smiling a little sadly, and went to his own room, while for Marianne there began a sleepless night haunted, para- doxically, by the shadow hanging over the days to come and by the strange sense of quietude left over from the night before. The sense of fulfilment which had come to her in that fan- tastic interlude, outside time and ordinary reality, was still strong enough to engender in her a kind of private exultation, free from any feelings of shame or false modesty. In the arms of her anonymous lover, she had experienced a moment of ex- ceptional beauty, made beautiful by the very fact that she still did not know who he was.

The next day, as she leaned on the *Witch*'s rail and watched the white houses and the old Venetian fortress of Corfu fade into the golden morning mist, she could not help giving one more thought to the man who was somewhere in that jumble of rock and tree, and who, it might be, would return sometimes to cast his nets or tie up his boat in that little inlet where, for one unknown Leda, he had been, for a little while, the embodi- ment of the ruler of the gods.

Chapter Eight
Cythera

For two days the *Sea Witch* sailed southwards, escorted by the *Pauline* and the *Pomone*. The three vessels negotiated the English possessions of Cephalonia and Zante without incident and followed the coastline of the Morea, standing far enough out to sea to avoid the pasha's flotillas.

The weather was glorious. The blue waters of the Mediterranean shone like a fairy's mantle. Even the heat was not unendurable, thanks to the steady breeze that filled the great square sails, and the three ships made good speed under their majestic piles of white canvas, their colours flying jauntily.

The enemy was lying low, wind and sea were ideally favourable, and to the fishermen who looked up from their lobster-pots to watch the passing of the tall white pyramids, the two frigates and the brig presented a perfect picture of serene and graceful power.

Yet on board the American brig nothing seemed to go right.

To begin with, Marianne was ill, just as Jolival had foretold. Ever since they had passed through the southerly channel between Corfu and the mainland and headed for the open sea, she had been obliged to keep to her cabin. Calm though the sea was, she had not stirred outside but had remained stretched on her bunk, suffering tortures every time the boat rolled, even slightly, and wishing over and over again that she were dead.

Nor did the faint smell which still persisted in the interior of the ship do anything to improve matters. It had begun to seem almost intolerable. Marianne lived in a hideous nightmare of sea-sickness for no apparent reason, unable to think two consecutive thoughts. There was only one fixed idea which haunted her, firm and unalterable, and that was at all costs to keep Jason out of her cabin.

Agathe was horrified to see her mistress, whose health was usually robust enough for anything, in this condition. To her, Marianne decided to tell the truth. She had complete confidence in her maid, who had always been unfalteringly loyal, and in her present state she desperately needed a woman's help. Agathe proved worthy of her trust.

Instantly the flighty, scatterbrained and timorous girl became transformed into a kind of dragon, a watchdog with a totally unexpected bite. Jason was the first to feel it when, in the evening after they sailed from Corfu, he came and tapped on the door, confident of his welcome. Instead of the smiling, deferential and mildly conspiratorial Agathe he was expecting, he was confronted, behind the mahogany panel, by an impeccably starched abigail who informed him with the utmost formality that her highness the Princess was indisposed and quite unable to receive visitors. After which, having delivered herself of an apology worthy of an ambassador, Agathe shut the door in his face.

Dr Leighton met with no more success when he presented himself some minutes later to examine the invalid and offer his services. Agathe, more frigid than ever, assured him that her highness had just gone to sleep, and categorically refused to interrupt such a beneficent slumber.

Arcadius de Jolival, taking the hint, did not appear. This abstention left him to bear the full brunt of Jason's hurt surprise. Considering, with some justification perhaps, that he need not expect to be treated like an ordinary visitor, Beaufort was already lashing himself into a temper by the time he came to discuss Marianne's inexplicable behaviour with Jolival.

'Does she think I don't love her enough to stand the sight of her in bed ill? How the devil does she mean to go on when we're married? Shall I have to leave the house, or resign myself to getting news of her from her abigail?'

'But there is just one thing you're forgetting, my friend. At present you are not yet married. And even if you were, it wouldn't surprise me overmuch if things were as you say. You see, Marianne is too much a woman, too proud and it may be too much of a coquette as well, not to know that there are limits to the degree of intimacy that can exist in even the greatest love. No woman in love wants to be seen looking low and ugly. She's always been the same, even with her best friends. Whenever she was ill in Paris, her door was always kept tight shut – even to me,' Arcadius lied superbly, 'who am like a father to her.'

Then Leighton took a hand. Assiduously filling his long clay pipe – an operation which made it unnecessary for him to look up as he spoke – he produced a thin smile which made no alteration to his cheerless face.

'Such feelings are natural to a pretty woman, but a doctor ought not to be regarded as a man, or as an ordinary visitor. I find it hard to understand why the Princess should show reluctance to submit to my examining her. When her maid was ill, she came in search of me at once with, I flatter myself, excellent results.'

'What makes you think she was reluctant?' Jolival retorted frostily. 'I understood you to say the Princess was asleep? Surely sleep is the best possible cure?'

'Well, let us hope it will prove sufficiently efficacious for the Princess to be well again tomorrow. I shall call upon her again in the morning.'

The doctor's tone was smooth, even conciliating, but Jolival did not like it. There was a vague threat underlying the apparently harmless words which made him uneasy. The man was quite determined to see Marianne and examine her, precisely, perhaps, because she did not seem to want it. The devil only knew what conclusions he might jump to if she refused to admit him again. Jolival lay awake all night trying to think of some way to avert the danger. He could not help looking on Leighton's interest as a very real danger: the man was malevolent enough to guess precisely what it was they wished to hide.

As it happened, the doctor did not prosecute his plan and Agathe was not called upon to invent a fresh excuse to keep him out. Considerably to Jolival's surprise, he divided his time that day between his own cabin and the crew's quarters, where a sudden outbreak of dysentery had occurred, and appeared to have lost interest in their passenger.

When Jason tapped on the cabin door again that afternoon, Agathe told him merely that her mistress was still feeling too far from well to see anyone but that she hoped to be better soon.

This time, Jolival heard no complaint from him but the crew bore the brunt of Jason's black mood. Pablo Arroyo, the boatswain, had to endure some scathing criticisms of the state of the decks and Craig O'Flaherty was hauled over the coals for the flushed condition of his nose and the smell of wine on his breath.

Meanwhile, Marianne lay in bed and suffered, swallowing the endless cups of tea, brought by Toby, which was all her stomach could support. She felt weak, ill and incapable of the smallest effort. It was like nothing she had ever experienced in her life.

It was after dark when Agathe, who had gone out at her mistress's insistence to get some air on deck, returned, all smiles, carrying a dumpy bottle from which she proceeded to pour a dose into a glass.

'That doctor may not be as bad as you think, my lady,' she said. 'I met him just now and he gave me this. He said you should feel better very quickly.'

'He doesn't know what's the matter with me,' Marianne said faintly. 'How can he make me better?'

'I don't know but he assured me it was a certain cure for the seasickness and disorders of the stomach. You never know ... the medicine might do you good, my lady. You ought to try it.'

Marianne hesitated for a moment, then she dragged herself painfully upright among her pillows and held out her hand.

'Give it to me, then,' she sighed. 'You may be right. In any case, I feel so ill that I'd be glad to accept poison from the Borgias themselves! Anything rather than go on like this!'

Agathe made her mistress as comfortable as she could and sponged her clammy forehead with a cloth soaked in eau-de-Cologne before putting the glass to her lips.

Marianne sipped cautiously, half-convinced that she would not be able to keep the potion down for five minutes. She drained the glass to the last drop, all the same, and, amazingly, felt no trace of nausea.

It had a queer taste, faintly bitter yet sweetish, but not unpleasant. There was some kind of spirit in it which burned a little as it went down but revived her. Gradually, the spasms of nausea that had racked her for the past two days diminished and finally ceased altogether, leaving only a profound sense of exhaustion and a longing for sleep.

Marianne's eyelids drooped irresistibly but, before she closed her eyes, she smiled with sleepy gratitude at Agathe, who was watching her anxiously from the foot of the bed.

'You were quite right, Agathe. I feel much better. I think I'll sleep now. You get some rest as well, but go and thank Doctor Leighton first. I must have misjudged him, you know, and now I'm ashamed.'

'Oh, there's nothing to be ashamed about,' Agathe said. 'He may be a good doctor but I'll never manage to bring myself to like him. Besides, it's his job to tend the sick. But don't worry, my lady, I'll go.'

Agathe found John Leighton on the forecastle in low-toned converse with Arroyo. Since she liked the boatswain no better than the doctor, she waited for him to go away before delivering her message. When she thanked the doctor on her mistress's behalf, she was bewildered to see him laugh.

'What's so funny about that?' she demanded indignantly. 'It's very nice of my lady to say thank you! You were only doing your job, after all!'

'As you say,' Leighton agreed. 'I was only doing my job. I do not need her thanks.'

Turning his back upon the abigail, he went away aft, still laughing. Agathe flounced back to the cabin to tell her mistress but found Marianne sleeping so peacefully that she had not the heart to wake her. So she tidied the cabin, let in some fresh air and then went to bed herself, with the satisfaction of a job well done.

Dawn was just breaking when there came a violent hammering on the cabin door, waking Marianne with a start. Agathe, who had taken the precaution of leaving her own door ajar, woke also. Although in general a heavy sleeper, she had been sleeping remarkably lightly since coming on board and now she tumbled out of bed in a moment, still half in a dream, and crying out in terror: 'What is it? What's happened? Oh, Lord, we're sinking!'

'I don't think so, Agathe,' Marianne said calmly, propping herself up on her elbow. 'It is only someone banging on the door. Don't open it. It's probably some drunken sailor.'

The blows were redoubled and in a moment they heard Jason's voice shouting furiously:

'Are you going to open this damned door or do I have to break it down?'

'Oh, Lord, my lady!' wailed Agathe. 'It's Monsieur Beaufort! He sounds ever so angry, too ... What do you think he wants?'

Jason undoubtedly sounded beside himself with fury and there was a note in the harsh, thickened voice which sent a thrill of fear down Marianne's spine.

'I don't know, but we'll have to let him in, Agathe,' she said. 'He'll do as he says and if we let him break the door down it will only make matters worse.'

The shivering Agathe put a shawl over her nightgown and went to open it. She had barely time to flatten herself against the bulkhead before it was flung back in her face and Jason burst into the room like a cannon shot. At the sight of him, Marianne let out a scream.

In the red glow of the rising sun, he looked like a devil. His hair was standing on end, his neckcloth hanging loose and his shirt unfastened to the waist, and he had the brick-red complexion and glassy eyes of a man in the last stages of drunkenness. Drunk he certainly was, and Marianne's nostrils quivered at the heavy odour of rum that filled the cabin.

Yet she was suddenly too frightened to have any thought to spare for being ill. Never had she seen Jason in such a state. There was madness in his eyes and he was grinding his teeth as he advanced on her with terrible slowness.

Agathe, equally terrified but ready to defend her mistress at all costs, tried to fling herself between them. One glance at his tensely-working fingers had convinced her that he meant to strangle Marianne, a conviction that her mistress fully shared. But Jason seized her ruthlessly by the shoulders and propelled

her, heedless of her protests, out of the cabin and locked the
door on her. Then he turned back to Marianne who was shrinking back against the wall behind her cot, trying desperately to
press herself bodily into the silk and mahogany furnishings. She
read her death in Jason's eyes.

'You, Marianne . . .' he snarled, 'you are with child?'

She uttered a cry of terror, denial springing automatically to
her lips:

'No! No, it's not true . . .'

'Come, come! That was it, wasn't it? Your fainting and your
sickness and your upset stomach! You're big with child, by
God knows who! But I mean to know . . . I'm going to find out
whose bed you've wallowed in now! Who was it this time,
eh? That Corsican lieutenant of yours? The Duke of Padua?
Your phantom husband, or your Emperor? Answer me! By
God, I'll make you speak!'

He had one knee on the bed and his hands round Marianne's
throat were forcing her back among the tumbled sheets, but his
grip had relaxed.

'You're mad!' she croaked at him in terror. 'Who told you
this?'

'Who? Why Leighton, of course! You felt better, didn't you,
after his potion? But you don't know what it was he dosed you
with. It's what they give to pregnant negresses on board the
slavers to keep them alive until the voyage ends. They can't
afford to let them die, you see, not when it's two lives for the
price of one!'

Marianne was filled with an overriding horror that made her
forget her fear for a moment. It was Jason saying these horrible
things, using these foul words! With a supple movement, she
jerked herself free and crouched back in the corner of the
alcove, hands up to protect her throat.

'On board the slavers! Are you telling me you've dealt in
that filthy trade?'

'Why not? It's hugely profitable!'

'So – that smell?'

'Aha! You noticed it? It's true, it clings. There's no amount
of scrubbing can quite get rid of it. Yet I only carried black

ivory the once – to oblige a friend. But we weren't talking of what I've done, but of you. I swear to you I mean to make you talk!'

He pounced on her again, dragging her out of her refuge, trying to get his hands round her neck once more. But by now anger and disappointment had come to Marianne's aid. She hit him, hard, sending him staggering back off the bunk, the alcohol in his system impairing his balance, to crash heavily into a chair which broke under his weight.

There was a fresh knocking on the door and Jolival's voice made itself heard. Marianne guessed that Agathe must have run to him for help.

'Open up, Beaufort!' called the Vicomte. 'I must speak to you.'

Jason struggled to his feet and went over to the door but he did not open it.

'Well I don't want to speak to you,' he snarled. 'Take yourself off! My business is with the lady!'

'Don't be a fool, Beaufort! And don't do anything you'll be sorry for afterwards! Let me in—'

There was fear in his voice, the same fear that gripped Marianne, but Jason only laughed again, with that dreadful laughter that was not his own.

'Why should I let you in? So that you can tell me how she got herself pregnant? Or is it your own part as pander you want to explain?'

'You're drunk! You're out of your mind! Why not open the door?'

'Oh, but I will, my dear friend, I will ... when I've dealt with this drab here as she deserves!'

'She is a sick woman! You aren't normally a coward, have you forgotten?'

'I've forgotten nothing!'

He swung round from the door and sprang at Marianne so suddenly that she was taken by surprise. Hurled violently to the deck, she screamed aloud, as much from terror as from hurt.

In another moment, the door burst open under the combined attack of Jolival and Gracchus. They almost fell into the room, Agathe on their heels, and snatched Marianne away from Jason, who appeared to have the fixed intention of strangling her. At the same time, Agathe seized a big water jug and flung the contents full in his face. He spluttered and shook himself like a dog, but slowly a spark of life began to show in his glazed eyes.

Sobered, to some extent at least, he tossed back the black hair dripping in his eyes and glared bitterly at the little group. Agathe had helped Marianne to her bed and after a brief, compassionate glance at the motionless form, Arcadius turned to Jason, shaking his head sadly at the ravaged face where the marks of suffering had bitten deeper than anger.

'I should have made her tell you the truth,' he said quietly, 'but she would not. She was afraid, horribly afraid of what you would say.'

'Was she?'

'Judging by what has just happened, she had every reason to be! But I give you my word of honour as a gentleman, Beaufort, that she was in no way to blame for what occurred. She was raped, appallingly. Will you let me tell you the whole dreadful story?'

'No! I can easily imagine your fertile imagination will have invented a splendid tale, calculated to appease my anger and to make me more her slave than ever. Unfortunately I do not want to hear it.'

Before Jolival could utter another word, Jason had taken the whistle he wore on a chain round his neck and blown three sharp blasts. At once, the boatswain appeared, framed in the broken doorway. Other men were visible behind him so that it seemed probable that half the crew had been listening eagerly.

Jason indicated Jolival and Gracchus.

'Put these men in irons, until further orders.'

'You have no right!'

Marianne had come to her senses and, despite Agathe's efforts to restrain her, had sprung to her friend's side. She was overpowered in a moment.

'I have every right,' the American retorted. 'I am sole master after God aboard this ship!'

'If I were you,' Jolival observed, moving calmly to the door, a seaman on either side of him, 'I should leave God out of this.

The real winner here is the devil ... and your friend the doctor, of course. Honest, honest Iago – as Shakespeare so aptly puts it.'

'We'll leave Dr Leighton out of this.'

'Indeed? Even though he broke his Hippocratic oath by betraying Marianne's condition?'

'He was not called to attend her. Therefore she was not his patient!'

'A nice, specious bit of reasoning – that did not come from you. Suppose we say he laid a trap, the basest kind of trap, concealing it under charity, and you applaud him for it! It's not like you, Jason.'

'Take him away, I said,' Jason roared. 'What are you waiting for?'

Gracchus fought like a tiger as the crew dragged them away but he was heavily outnumbered. Even so, as he was hustled past Jason, he managed to wrench them to a halt for a moment and looked straight into his eyes, his own hot with indignation.

'To think I once loved and admired you!' he said in a voice in which bitterness and desperation vied with anger. 'Mademoiselle Marianne would 'a' done better to 'ave left you to rot in prison at Brest, for if you didn't deserve it then, you deserve it now!'

Then, having spat on the ground to show his contempt, Gracchus let them take him away. The cabin emptied, leaving Jason and Marianne face to face.

In spite of himself, the privateer's eyes had followed the departing figure of Gracchus. He had paled under that furious outburst, and clenched his fists, but he had made no other move. Yet it seemed to Marianne that his eyes had darkened for a moment with a shade of regret.

The violent scene which had just taken place in her cabin had succeeded in restoring all her courage at a stroke. She was a natural fighter. It was her element and she felt at home in it. In a way, too, however disastrous the consequences, it was a relief to her to be done with the stifling atmosphere of lies and deceit. Jason's blind and jealous rage was after all a kind of loving, even though he might have rejected the idea with loathing, but it was a devouring and, perhaps, an all-consuming fire. In a few moments the love by which she had lived for so long might be reduced to nothing more than ashes – and her own heart with it.

Agathe had remained crouching by the bed. Like an automaton, Jason went to her and taking her by the arm, quite gently, took her to her own cabin and locked her in. Marianne watched him in silence, hugging round her the thick shawl which she had flung over her thin nightgown. He turned and saw her standing facing him, her head held high. There was anguish in her green eyes but they met him squarely.

'Now you can finish what you have begun,' she said steadily, letting the shawl drop just sufficiently to disclose the darkening bruises on her slender neck. 'All I ask is that you get it over quickly. Unless you'd rather hang me from the yard-arm in sight of all the crew?'

'Neither. I meant to kill you just now, I admit. I should have been sorry all my life. One does not kill such women as you. As for hanging you from the yard-arm, I fear I lack the appetite for melodrama which you, no doubt, picked up in treading the boards. In any case, you must be aware that while my crew might well enjoy the sight, it wouldn't please your watchdogs quite as much. I've no wish to be sunk by a brace of Napoleon's frigates.'

'Then what do you propose doing with me and my friends? You might as well put me in irons along with them.'

'Unnecessary. You'll stay here until we drop anchor at Piraeus. I'll put you ashore there, with your friends, and you can find yourself another vessel to take you on to Constantinople.'

Marianne's heart quailed. If he could talk like this, then his love for her must be dead indeed!

'Is that how you keep your promises?' she said. 'Didn't you engage to carry me to a proper port?'

'One port is much like another. Piraeus will do very well. From Athens you will have no difficulty in reaching the Turkish capital – and I shall be well rid of you, once and for all.'

He spoke quite slowly, without apparent anger, but in a heavy, exhausted voice in which to the thickening caused by drink was now added a note of disgust. In spite of all her anger and her grief, Marianne felt her heart moved with a kind of desperate pity. Jason looked like a man wounded to death. Very softly she asked:

'Is that really all you want? Never to see me again ... never? For our ways to part ... never to meet again?'

He had turned away from her and was looking out of the porthole at the sea, its deep blue struck into a myriad flashing sparks by the sun's fire. Marianne had an odd feeling that her words, penetrating, only served to harden him.

'That is what I want,' he said at last.

'Then, dare to look me in the face and tell me.'

He came to her, slowly and stood looking at her. The sunlight, entering the cabin, bathed her in light. The red shawl clutched about her shoulders was a garment of flame and the heavy masses of dark hair that fell about her pale, strained face, accentuated its almost transparent whiteness. With the bruises on her throat, she was as beautiful and tragic as sin. Beneath the folds of red cashmere, the breasts rose and fell with her emotion.

Jason said nothing but his eyes, as he studied the slender form before him, grew clouded and their expression was transformed slowly to one of impotent rage.

'Yes,' he said at last, reluctantly, 'I do still desire you. In spite of what you are, in spite of the revulsion I feel, I do have the misfortune to desire your body, because you're lovelier than any man could bear. But that, too, I shall overcome. I'll learn how to kill my desire ...'

Marianne felt a thrill of joy and hope. Was it possible, after all, to round this tricky point? Was there victory to be won from the impossible?

'Wouldn't it be easier ... and more sensible, to let me tell you everything?' she murmured. 'I swear by my hopes of salvation to conceal nothing of what happened to me ... not even the worst! But give me a chance ... only give me one single chance!'

She was longing now to plead her own cause, to tell him of all the suffocating horror built up in those past weeks. She sensed that she could still win him back to her. It was clear from the tormented, famished look on his face, the agony it revealed. She still possessed enormous power over Jason – if only he would listen.

But he refused to listen. Even now, the words she said did not seem to pierce through the armour he had built around himself. He was looking at her, yes, but with eyes that were strangely devoid of expression. Her voice did not reach him, and when at last he spoke, it was to himself, as though Marianne had been no more than a lovely statue, an effigy standing there.

'Oh yes, she's beautiful,' he said broodingly, 'beautiful and venomous, like the flowers of the Brazilian jungles that feed on insects and whose brilliant hearts smell only of rottenness. Nothing could be brighter than those eyes, or softer than that skin ... those lips ... nothing purer than that face or more captivating than that form ... And yet it is all false ... all vile! I know ... and even now I cannot bring myself to believe it because I have not seen ...'

While he spoke, his trembling hands were touching Marianne's face, her hair, her throat, but there was no light in his eyes, they were like the eyes of a dead man.

'Jason!' Marianne implored him. 'For pity's sake, listen to me! I love you, I have never loved anyone but you! Even if you were to kill me, my soul would not forget to love you. I am still yours, still worthy of you – even though you can't believe it for the present.'

She was wasting her breath. He did not hear her, lost as he was in a waking nightmare, where his dying love fought for survival.

'Perhaps if I had seen her in another's arms, seen her give herself to another man ... vile, and contemptible ... perhaps then I should be able to believe it.'

'Jason,' Marianne begged, almost in tears. 'Jason, stop ... have pity!'

She was trying to grasp his hands, to get close to him and penetrate the icy fog which lay between them, but he shook her off and the colour darkened in his face under the pressure of a fresh wave of anger.

'I know,' he cried, 'I know how to combat the sirens' song! And I know how to destroy your power, too, she-devil!'

He sprang to the door and dragged it open, calling in a powerful voice:

'Kaleb! Come here!'

In the grip of an irrational terror, Marianne hurled herself at the door and tried to slam it shut but he flung her back into the room.

'What are you going to do?' she asked. 'Why are you calling him?'

'You'll see.'

The next moment, the Ethiopian entered the cabin and, despite her fear, Marianne was struck again by the splendour of that bronze face and body. He seemed to fill the narrow space with a kind of kingly majesty.

Unlike the other coloured men he did not bow to the white master. In response to Jason's order, he closed the door and then stood with folded arms before her, waiting quietly, but his light eyes went quickly from the privateer to the white-faced woman.

'Look at her, Kaleb,' Jason said, brutally, pointing. 'Tell me what you think of her. Is she beautiful?'

There was a moment's silence before Kaleb answered gravely: 'Very beautiful. Very frightened also.'

'A sham! That face is used to play-acting. She's an adventuress disguised as a princess, a singer trained to do anything for applause! She'll sleep with any man she fancies, but you're a handsome fellow – no reason why she shouldn't fancy you! Go on, take her! I give her to you!'

'Jason!' Marianne cried, horror-struck. 'Are you mad?'

The slave started and a quick frown creased his brows. Then his face hardened, giving him the look of some stern, basalt image of an ancient pharaoh. He shook his head and turned to go but pulled up short at a cry from Jason.

'Stay where you are! That's an order! She's yours, I said, so take her – here and now! Look!'

He reached out swiftly and snatched the cashmere shawl roughly from Marianne's shoulders. The light nightgown she wore was anything but concealing and a slow flush mounted to her cheeks as she crossed her arms over her breast to cover herself.

No trace of emotion was visible on the impassive features of the Ethiopian as he moved towards her.

Marianne shrank back, sensing a threat and terrified that the slave was going to obey. But Kaleb did not touch her. He merely bent and picked up the shawl as it lay on the deck. As he did so, his strangely blue eyes met hers for an instant. There was no bitterness in them, as might have been expected after the way she had recoiled from him, but only a kind of melancholy amusement.

With a rapid movement, he replaced the soft woollen stuff round her shivering shoulders. Marianne seized it and hugged it to her as though to glue it to her body. Then, turning to the captain who had watched frowning, Kaleb said simply :

'You gave me shelter, lord, and I am here to serve you – but not as your executioner.'

Jason's eyes flashed wrathfully but the Ethiopian met them without flinching, without insolence either, but with a dignity which Marianne found impressive. Then Jason waved him to the door.

'Get out. You're a fool!'

Kaleb smiled briefly.

'Am I? I'd not have left this room alive, had I obeyed you. You would have killed me.'

It was not a question. Simply a statement of fact and Jason did not offer to contradict it. He let the seaman go without another word, only his frown deepened. He seemed to hesitate for a moment, glancing at the girl who had her back to him now so that he should not see her tears. She was deeply hurt by what had happened, for her pride as well as her love was wounded. A man's jealousy might carry him so far but to be abused like this left bleeding scars in the very heart's tissue, scars which might never fully heal.

The sound of the door slamming violently told her that Jason had gone but there was small comfort to be had from the fact that it was followed by no click of the key turning in the lock.

Now that he had judged her, Jason would hardly consider it worth while to lock her in. For one thing, the mere fact of being on a ship at sea constituted imprisonment enough, and for another, he must know that Marianne had no desire to leave him, that she was dreading the moment when the Athenian coast would rise above the horizon, bringing with it what looked like being an irrevocable parting. For whatever her grief, or possibly because of it, Marianne was determined not to utter another word in her own defence. The abominable treatment meted out to Jolival and Gracchus forbade it.

The day dragged endlessly, with no other company than Agathe's. The only person to cross her threshold was Toby, who brought her meals, but the old negro seemed as out of spirits as the two women. His eyes were reddened, as though with tears, and when Agathe asked him gently what was wrong he only shook his head unhappily and muttered that the master was not himself, not himself at all.

'He walk de deck all night long, like some sick wolf, and in de day, he don' seem to hear what no one say to him.'

There was nothing more to be got from him but this observation, from a servant so devoted, was enough to make it clear how great was Jason's suffering, and Marianne thought with anguish that the discovery of her condition had unleashed forces for evil in him quite unsuspected even by those who had known him from childhood.

Fortunately, Leighton's potion, which she continued taking in small doses, maintained its beneficent effects and, freed from the dreadful nausea, Marianne had at least the consolation of being able to think straight. It was a dubious advantage as she lay awake, with eyes wide open, staring into the shifting darkness, counting every hour by the ting of the ship's bell that timed the wretched progress of her thoughts.

In her own corner, Agathe was not sleeping either. Her mistress could hear her praying softly and the occasional little sniffing sounds that showed that she was crying.

When dawn came, it found them both equally pale and wretched.

Even though the door was not locked on the outside, Mari-

anne dared not leave the cabin. She was afraid that her appearance might provoke Jason to another of the unpredictable fits
of rage which she had learned to fear. God alone knew what his
state of mind might be by this time, or whether Jolival and
Gracchus might not have to suffer for her imprudence. It was
safer to stay where she was.

But when Toby appeared, in a state of abject terror and
shaking in every limb so that the breakfast things he brought
clattered on the tray, Marianne forgot all these prudent resolu-
tions. He told her that Kaleb had attempted to kill the doctor
during the night and had been sentenced to a hundred lashes
as punishment, to be witnessed by the whole crew.

'A hundred lashes! But he'll die!' Marianne cried, appalled.

The whites of Toby's eyes rolled. 'He mighty big fellah,' he
pronounced. 'But one hund'ed lashes sho' is plenty. He go for to
kill dat doctor, sho 'nuff, but ah ain't never known Massa Jason
flog no poh darkie afoh!'

'But, Toby, he can't have tried to kill the doctor! Why should
he?'

Toby nodded his woolly head. Fear had given his skin a curious
greyish tinge.

'Maybe yes. Dat doctor, he bad man. Trouble all de time evah
since he come aboa'd! Nathan, he say he gwine sell Kaleb fo' a
high price in de market at Candy.'

'You say the doctor means to sell Kaleb? But Monsieur Jason
found him and saved him when he was a runaway slave. He
would never sell a man who had trusted him!'

'Not in de o'dinar' way, no. But Massa Jason, not hisself no
moh . . . He quite, quite diffe'ent! De bad times is comin' foh us
all, ma'am! De good times is all gone now, all'long o' dat Doctor
Leighton!'

Toby dragged his feet wearily to the door, his head sunk between his shoulders, wiping away a tear on his white cotton
sleeve. There was something deeply moving about the old man's
unhappiness. It must be dreadful to him to see a man whom he
had loved and served all his life reduced suddenly to the state of
a wild beast. Perhaps he even feared for himself . . .

Marianne detained him just as he was going.

'When – when is it to be?' she asked.

'Now. De hands jus' comin' on deck now.'

Marianne became aware of the patter of dozens of pairs of bare feet on the deck and of the boatswain's voice uttering unintelligible commands. Toby was scarcely out of the cabin before she had leaped out of bed.

'Hurry, Agathe! Get me a dress and some shoes, and a scarf.'

'Oh, my lady, what are you going to do?' the girl wailed, not moving. 'I'm sure you'd much better not get involved! Monsieur Beaufort's taken leave of his senses, my lady, and you must never cross a madman!'

'Mad or not, I'll not let him kill a man who was only trying to defend his freedom, and perhaps his life! Least of all in this barbarous fashion! That Leighton creature isn't worth it! Hurry, now!'

'But what if he's angry with you, my lady?'

'As things are, Agathe, I don't think I've anything to lose! Besides, the two frigates are still with us, I suppose. I can have nothing to fear.'

By the time Marianne came on deck, the crew was already drawn up, facing aft, in a silence broken only by the ghastly sound of the lash biting into unprotected flesh. Punishment had already begun. Swiftly she forced a way through the tight-packed ranks of men. The barrier they formed was almost impenetrable, but Marianne got far enough to see a sight which froze the blood in her veins. Kaleb was triced up to the mizzen rigging. Standing alone, between the rows of seamen on either hand, Pablo Arroyo, armed with a long whip made of thongs of plaited leather, was administering the flogging. In contrast to the assembled men whose faces bore witness to how little they relished the scene and who winced visibly at every stroke of the lash, the boatswain was quite evidently enjoying his revolting office. With his sleeves rolled back from his wiry arms, he was laying into his victim with all his strength, delivering his blows with a slow relish that was clearly aimed at inflicting the greatest possible degree of pain, while his face was twisted into a hideous expression of sadistic cruelty. He was not hurrying. He was savouring every moment, and now and then his tongue appeared between his teeth, as though the man were literally licking his chops.

Blood was already dripping from the lacerated flesh. Kaleb's face, pressed against the wooden mast, was a mask of suffering. His eyes were closed but he did not cry out. Only the faintest groan escaped his set lips each time the lash bit. Drops of blood, bright red in the sunshine, were beginning to splash on to Arroyo's face, but Jason stood impassively on the poop, presiding over the punishment.

He still wore the same, curiously blank expression and the lines in his face were graven deeper than ever. His left hand fidgeted nervously with his neckcloth, while the other was hidden behind his back.

Leighton, at his side, affected a modest demeanour which was belied by the sheer triumph that shone through every line of his pale face.

Suddenly it was clear that the victim was no longer conscious. His body slumped in its bonds and the muscles of his arms stood out with the strain, while his grey face drooped against the mast.

'He's fainted,' said a voice which Marianne recognized as O'Flaherty's. It was harsh with indignation and it acted like a signal on Marianne.

Spurred by the same sense of outrage, she threw herself forward, forging through the packed rows of the crew which parted to let her pass. So great was her impetus that she fetched up close to Arroyo and but for the lieutenant who dragged her sharply back, would have received the lash full in her face.

'What's that woman doing there?' barked Jason, whom the sight of Marianne had apparently roused from his torpor. 'Take her back to her cabin!'

'Not before I've told you what I think!' she screamed, struggling in O'Flaherty's arms. 'How can you stand there and watch a man being done to death before your eyes!'

'He is not being done to death. He's receiving well-deserved punishment.'

'Hypocrite! How many blows like that do you think he can bear and live?'

'He attempted to kill the doctor. He deserves to hang. My only reason for not hanging him is that Dr Leighton interceded for him.'

Marianne gave a crack of laughter.

'Interceded for him, did he? I'm not surprised! I daresay he thought it a shame to kill a man who'd fetch a good price in any of your loathsome markets in human flesh!'

Jason's face darkened with rage and he was about to make a violent reply, when Leighton's cold voice cut in like a knife:

'Precisely. Such a slave is worth a fortune and I am the first to deplore this punishment.'

'I did not bring him from Venice to sell him again,' Jason snapped. 'I'm only carrying out the law of the sea. If he dies of it, so much the worse. You may go on, Arroyo.'

'No! I won't let you! Coward! You're nothing but a coward and a bully! I won't let you!'

The boatswain was already raising his whip again but uncertainly. Anger had given Marianne an added strength which made it almost impossible for the lieutenant to hold her. Around them the men stood staring, fascinated by the raging, wild-eyed woman, too dazed to intervene.

Jason, beside himself, was already springing down from the poop to go to his lieutenant's assistance, when the voice from the masthead cried:

'Captain! The *Pomone* is asking what's amiss. What'll I tell her?'

'Punishment, tell 'em!'

'They must have heard the Princess screaming,' O'Flaherty muttered breathlessly. 'With a telescope they can see all that's going on here. Better belay, Captain. Short of knocking her unconscious, we can't keep her quiet, and it's not worth risking a fight, two against one.'

'It's not that I don't want one,' Jason snarled, clenching his fists. 'How many lashes now?'

'Twenty-five.'

Sensing victory within her reach, Marianne had stopped struggling, and was conserving her breath to scream the louder if Jason did not give in.

For a moment, their eyes met, both filled with an equal rage, but it was the privateer's that were the first to fall.

'Cut him down,' he ordered curtly, swinging on his heel. 'But put him in irons. If Dr Leighton is willing to attend him, he can have him.'

'I hope you're proud of yourself, Jason Beaufort!' Marianne cried scornfully. 'I don't know which I admire most : your hospitality or your sense of honour!'

Jason had already turned away, but he paused beside the mizzenmast where two men were engaged in cutting down the Ethiopian's motionless figure.

'Honour?' he said, with a weary little shrug. 'It's not a word you know the meaning of! As for my hospitality, as you call it, I'd have you know that on board this ship it's called discipline. Those who flout the common law must take the consequences. And now, go back to your cabin. You have no business here, and I may yet forget that you're a woman.'

Marianne turned without a word and laid her hand with dignity on the arm which O'Flaherty was holding out to her uneasily, waiting to escort her to her cabin.

As they went, she saw that the ship was now sailing past a dark and desolate-looking coast, in sombre contrast to the bright blue sea and sparkling sunshine. It was a land of stark, black rock, bare hills and sharp, menacing reefs. In the clear Greek light it seemed a place designed for storms and darkness and shipwreck. A place for murder, too. The thought made her shiver a little and she turned to her companion :

'Do you know what land that is?'

'The island of Cythera, ma'am.'

Marianne exclaimed in surprise :

'Cythera! You can't mean it? Surely, you are joking? Cythera? Those gloomy, barren rocks!'

'Yes, indeed it is. The island of love! It's a sad disappointment, I agree. I can't imagine anyone wishing to embark for such a dismal spot.'

'No ... but isn't that just what we all do? We embark, full of joy and eagerness, for our dream Cythera, only to arrive here, on a harsh rocky isle where everything is smashed. That's what love is, Lieutenant. It's a trap, like the fires lit by wreckers on an empty shore to entice lost ships in to shatter themselves on the cruel rocks. Love is a shipwreck, a wreck made all the worse because it happens just when you think a haven is in sight.'

Craig O'Flaherty drew in his breath. His naturally cheerful face bore a look of distress that sat uneasily on it. He was silent for a moment and then said quietly:

'You mustn't despair, ma'am. You aren't wrecked yet.'

'No? In two or three days we'll reach Athens. What can I do then but take passage on some Greek vessel going to Constantinople, while you set a course for America.'

There was another silence. The lieutenant appeared to be having some difficulty in breathing but, as Marianne glanced in surprise at his flushed face, he seemed to make up his mind with an immense effort, like a man reaching a decision he has been putting off for a long time.

'No,' he said abruptly. 'Not for America. Or not at first, at any rate. We're bound for Africa.'

'Africa?'

'Yes. For the Gulf of Guinea. We're expected on the island of Fernando Po, in the Bight of Biafra, and – and the slave depots of Old Calabar. That is why the doctor was so much against this voyage to Constantinople – and your own presence on board.'

'What are you trying to tell me?'

Marianne uttered the words in a strangled shriek and O'Flaherty grasped her hastily by the arm and hurried her onward, casting uneasy glances around him.

'Not here, ma'am! Go back to your cabin. I have my duty.'

'But I want to know—'

'Later, I beg you! When I am free – this evening, for instance. I'll come to your door and tell you everything then. In the meanwhile, try not to blame the captain too much. He has fallen into the clutches of a devil who aims to drive him mad.'

They had reached Marianne's door by now. O'Flaherty was bowing briefly and, much as she longed to know the truth about the things that had been kept from her, she realized that for the present it was useless to insist: better to wait and let the lieutenant tell her in his own good time.

Yet, as he turned to go, she called him back:

'Mr O'Flaherty, just one thing more. How is the man who was flogged?'

'Kaleb?'

'Yes. I know the thing he did was very bad but – that terrible punishment . . .'

'He was spared the greater part of it, thanks to you, ma'am,' the lieutenant said gently, 'and a man of his strength doesn't die of twenty-five lashes. As for the thing he did – well, I know two or three more'd be glad to do the same. Until this evening, then, ma'am.'

This time, Marianne let him go. She entered the cabin thoughtfully, to be greeted with something not far short of rapture by Agathe who had evidently been expecting Jason Beaufort to hang her mistress at the yard-arm for daring to interfere.

Marianne told her in a few words what had taken place and then withdrew into a silence which lasted until evening. Her brain whirled with such a confused multitude of thoughts that it was all she could do to sort them out. There were so many questions that she did not give up until her head was aching. Overcome at last by weariness and the pain in her temples, she decided to try and sleep. It would help to build up her strength and, in any case, sleep was quite the best way of making the time pass quickly when one was consumed with curiosity.

She was roused from her sleep by the sound of gunfire which sent her dashing breathlessly to the porthole, fearing an attack. But it was only the frigates of their escort firing a farewell salute. Cythera had vanished. Westwards, the sun was low in the sky and the two warships, their mission accomplished, were going about for the return journey to Corfu. They could not go any further for fear of offending the Sultan, who was not friendly to France. The British squadrons were equally cautious, to avoid damaging the recently improved relations between their own government and the Sublime Porte. In the normal way of things the *Sea Witch* should have been able to make Constantinople without further trouble – if her captain had not decreed that the voyage was to end at Piraeus, whence he would set a course for Africa.

It was this mention of Africa that tormented Marianne more even than her own predicament. O'Flaherty, if Marianne had understood him correctly, had implied that Jason intended to sail for the Bight of Biafra to pick up a cargo of slaves. Yet that could not possibly be true, since Jason's one object in going to Venice had been to meet the woman he meant to make his wife and take her with him to Charleston. It was to be a lovers' trip, almost a honeymoon. A cruise on board a slave ship could scarcely be expected to appeal to a young woman, and certainly no man worthy of the name would inflict such a voyage on the woman he loved. Then, what?

She remembered suddenly what Jason himself had told her on their first day out. Leighton was not to make the whole voyage with them. They were to put him ashore somewhere. Was it only the sinister doctor who had business at Old Calabar – or was it Jason who had not dared to tell her the whole truth? The bond between him and Leighton was not one of friendship, or not of friendship alone. There was something else. Pray God it was not a plot between them!

As the afternoon drew on to evening, Marianne waited for O'Flaherty with growing impatience. She prowled about her cabin, unable to sit still, and continually asking Agathe what time it was. Still the lieutenant did not come, and when she tried to send her maid for news, she found that this time she was really a prisoner. Her cabin door was locked on the outside. A fresh period of waiting began, a time of nervous fears that grew worse with every hour that passed.

Still the lieutenant did not come. Nerves stretched to breaking point, Marianne could have screamed, banged, clawed, anything to relieve the anger and alarm which threatened to choke her. There was no reason for it that she knew but, like a wild creature, she sensed the approach of some new danger.

What came, at last, when dawn was not very far off, was the sound of the key being turned in the newly-mended lock. John Leighton entered, with a group of seamen at his back amongst whom Marianne recognized Arroyo, carrying a lantern. Contrary to his usual habit, the doctor was armed to the teeth, and an extraordinary expression of triumph, which he seemed unable to hide, shone through his livid countenance, giving it a sinister vitality. Clearly this was the great moment of his life, a moment for which he had been waiting for a long time.

Marianne reacted instantly. Reaching for a wrapper she slid out of bed and faced them.

'Who gave you leave to enter here?' she demanded with dignity. 'Oblige me by getting out at once!'

Ignoring this, Leighton came further into the cabin. The seamen crowded into the doorway, craning their necks eagerly to get a glimpse into the unfamiliar prettiness of the women's cabin.

'I'm desolated to disturb you,' the doctor said, with heavy sarcasm, 'but I fear that it is you who must get out. You must leave this ship at once. A boat awaits you.'

'Leave the ship? In the middle of the night? Are you mad? Where do you expect me to go, may I ask?'

'Where you like. We are in the Mediterranean, not the Atlantic. Land is not far off, and it will soon be dawn. Prepare yourself.'

Marianne folded her arms, hugging her wrap more closely round her, and looked at him, unmoving.

'Fetch the captain,' she said. 'I am not stirring until I hear it from his own lips.'

'Indeed?'

'Yes, indeed! You have no authority, Doctor, which entitles you to give orders on board this ship. Least of all such orders as that.'

Leighton's smile grew, acquiring an added venom.

'I fear,' he said, with horrid smoothness, 'that those are the captain's orders. Unless you wish to be put into the boat by force, you will obey at once. I repeat: make your preparations. Put on a dress, a cloak, what you will, but do it quickly.' He glanced round the cabin. 'You cannot, of course, be permitted to take your trunks, or your jewels. You will not need them at sea and they would only be useless clutter in the boat.'

There was a pause while Marianne digested this astonishing

speech. What did it all mean? Was she to be robbed of all her baggage and set adrift on the open sea? It was incredible, horrible and unimaginable, that Jason should have decided suddenly to get rid of her, in the middle of the night, after relieving her of everything she possessed. It was still more inconceivable that he should have chosen Leighton for his messenger. It was so unlike him ... it must be so unlike him, surely? Yet even as she asked herself the question, the seeds of doubt were planting themselves in her anguished mind, reminding her of another night, long before, the dreadful night of her wedding to Francis Cranmere, when Jason had left Selton Hall, taking with him every penny of Marianne's fortune.

Seeing that the man before her was showing signs of impatience, she turned her rage on him.

'I thought this vessel was an honest privateer,' she said, with all the scorn at her command. 'I see now that I have fallen among thieves! You are no better than a common pirate, Doctor Leighton, and the worst kind of villain, for you attack defenceless women with force. Well, I'm too weak to oppose you. Pack our things, Agathe. That is, if this gentleman will kindly tell us what we are allowed to take.'

'I did not say,' Leighton countered blandly, 'that you might take your maid. How should you need an abigail in a boat? Any more than you will need your fine dresses? Whereas she may be useful here. You look surprised? Did I omit to tell you that you were to go alone? I must ask your serene highness to forgive me.' Then, with an abrupt change of tone, he added: 'Jump to it, you men. We've wasted too much time already. Take her away!'

'Villain!' Marianne screamed wildly. 'I forbid you to lay hands on me! ... Help! ... Help!'

But already the men were swarming into the cabin, transforming it in an instant into a miniature hell. Marianne fought bravely, hemmed in by eyes that gleamed like red-hot coals, foul breath that reeked of rum and greedy hands that pawed at her furtively under the guise of dragging her away, but resistance was useless. Yet she redoubled her efforts at the sound of frantic screams from Agathe who was being held down on the bed by two seamen while a third ripped off her nightgown. There was a gleam of plump, white flesh that quickly vanished into the curtained recesses of the bunk, hidden beneath the body of the man who, urged on by his companions, was now energetically raping her.

Meanwhile, although she kicked and scratched with all her might, Marianne was overpowered and with a gag thrust in her mouth to stifle her cries, was manhandled out on to the deck.

'You see,' Leighton told her piously, 'this is what comes of not being sensible. It is your own fault that we have been obliged to use force. Nevertheless I hope you will do me the justice to admit that I have held my men in check. I might easily have let them deal with you as they have with that girl of yours. These good fellows do not love you, Princess. They blame you for changing their captain into a spineless weakling, but they'd be quite willing to enjoy your dainty person, all the same. So thank me properly, instead of spitting like a wild cat. Away with her, you men!'

If sheer blind rage could kill, the doctor would have dropped dead on the spot, or else Marianne herself might well have died. Driven half out of her mind by the sound of Agathe's shrieks, feebler now but still audible, so beside herself with anger as to be scarcely conscious of what was happening to her, Marianne fought with such fury that they had to tie her hands and feet to carry her to the side. There a rope was slung under her armpits and she was lowered with a bump into the open boat bobbing gently on a line from the ship's side. As she made contact with the wooden thwart, uttering an involuntary cry of pain, someone severed the line. The sea carried the boat away at once and, looking up, Marianne saw, far above her, a row of heads gazing down. Leighton's voice sounded mockingly in her ears:

'Happy landings, your highness! You'll have no trouble freeing yourself. The ropes are not too tight. And there are oars in the bottom of the boat, if you can row. You need not worry about your friends and servants – I'll take care of them!'

Sick with fury, with a burning head and a sharp pain in her back, Marianne watched the brig sail past her boat, veer gently and then draw away, still hardly able to realize what had happened to her.

Soon, before her wide, tear-drenched eyes, appeared the graceful, brightly-lit stern windows, surmounted by their three lanterns. Then the vessel went about and altered course. Gradually the tall pyramid of sails receded and was lost in the surrounding darkness, until it was nothing but a vague shape marked by tiny twinkling lights.

Only then did Marianne begin to grasp the fact that she was alone on the wide sea, set adrift without food or water, practically without clothes, and doomed, coldly and deliberately, to die unless a miracle occurred.

There was the ship, hull down on the horizon, taking her only friends with it, the ship that belonged to the man she loved and to whom she had sworn to devote her life, and who not so long ago had vowed that he loved her above all else. Yet he had not been able to forgive her for concealing her misery and shame from him.

Chapter Nine
Sappho

True to Leighton's mocking assurance, Marianne was able to free her hands and feet and get the gag from her mouth without a great deal of difficulty but, except for the small satisfaction to be gained from the unrestricted use of her limbs, she did not find herself very much better off.

All round her was the empty sea. It was still dark, with the awesome, impenetrable blackness of before dawn, but it was a moving darkness, lifting and tossing her as a child plays with a toy in its hand. She was cold as well, for her thin cambric night-gown and light wrapper offered little protection against the early morning chill. A white mist was gathering, thick, penetrating and horribly clammy.

Her groping hands found the oars underneath the thwart but, although she had learned to row as a child, she knew that her efforts would be useless in the absence of anything to steer by. She could only wait for daylight to dispel the darkness and the mist. Pulling her thin garments round her as best she could, she huddled in the bottom of the boat and let it drift, choking back her tears and forcing herself not to think of the others she had left on that fatal ship : Jolival and Gracchus in irons, and Agathe at the mercy of the drunken seamen ... and Jason. God alone knew what had become of Jason by now. O'Flaherty had said that he was in the power of a demon, but for Leighton to be so obviously master of the brig, backed up by that handful of brigands, Beaufort must surely be a prisoner, or worse. As for the jovial Irishman, he had probably shared his captain's fate.

To stop herself thinking too much about them, and in a desperate effort to help them, if there were still time, Marianne started to pray as she had never prayed before, with a frantic, terrified earnestness. She prayed for her friends and for herself, abandoned to the mercy of the sea with no other protection than a flimsy boat, a few yards of cambric and her own courage and fierce instinct for survival. In the end, she fell asleep.

She woke, chilled to the bone, with an aching back and her inadequate clothing wet and clammy from the mist. It was light, although the sun had not yet risen, and the mist had thinned. The sky was faintly blue except in the east, where it was dyed a pinkish orange. The sea lay calm as a millpond, extending in an unbroken expanse as far as the eye could see, without a sail or sight of land. There was hardly a breath of wind. The breeze would get up later in the morning, reaching its peak at about ten o'clock.

Marianne stretched her cramped limbs and set herself to consider her position as calmly as she could. She concluded that, though bleak, it was by no means desperate. The study of geography had formed part of the broad education planned for her as a child by her aunt Ellis, and geography, in England, had included the use of the globes. She had laboured for hours, too, over boring maps of mountains, rivers, seas and islands, loathing it all because outside the sun was shining and she was longing to be free to enjoy a good gallop across country on her pony, Harry. She had never been fond of drawing, either. Now, in her trouble, she sent up a prayer of thanks to her aunt's ghost, thanks to whose efforts she had been able to follow approximately the course taken by the *Witch*, so that she now had some vague idea of where she was.

This was in the region of the Cyclades, the constellation of islands which makes the Aegean Sea a kind of terrestrial milky-way. If she went on in an easterly direction, she was almost bound to come across one or other of the islands before very long and there was always the possibility of encountering a fishing boat. After all, as the unspeakable Leighton had said, this was not the dreaded Atlantic Ocean, where she would have faced certain death.

As much to warm herself and provide a distraction from the terror induced by the vast loneliness around her, as with any very real hope of hastening her salvation, Marianne got out the pair of oars from the bottom of the boat, fitted them to the thole-pins and began to row energetically. The boat was heavy and so were the oars, designed for the calloused hands of seamen, not for the soft palms of a lady, but the physical exercise did provide a kind of comfort.

As she rowed, she did her best to sort out in her mind what must have happened on board the *Sea Witch*. When they had carried her on deck, she had certainly been blind with rage, but not so blind that she had not registered the fact that Leighton had only a handful of the men with him : not more than thirty or so out of a hundred or more who made up the crew. Where were the others? What had the doctor done with them? A strange kind of doctor, who seemed as well able to make men sick as to cure them! Were they prisoners under hatches? Drugged ... or worse? The villain must have had a whole arsenal of diabolical potions at his disposal to enable him to get the better of normally strong, intelligent men. Her own experiences in Venice had taught her how a potion, a philtre, or whatever such devilish brews should be called, could break the will and unleash buried instincts, bringing a human being to the verge of madness. There had been a strange look in Jason's eyes during those last hours on the ship.

That there had been mutiny aboard, Marianne was now quite certain. Leighton and his supporters had made themselves master of the ship. She refused to believe that Jason, however hurt or angry he might be, could have changed in an instant, so radically, into a rapacious freebooter, scheming to take both her jewels and her life. No, he must be a prisoner, and powerless. Everything in Marianne's mind rejected the idea that Leighton could have struck at the life of a man who was his friend and who had welcomed him aboard his ship. In any case, Jason's skill as a seaman must make him indispensable to the navigation of such a vessel. He could not possibly be dead. But ... what of his lieutenant? And the prisoners?

As she thought of Jolival, Agathe and Gracchus, Marianne's heart contracted. The evil doctor could have no pressing reason to spare their lives, the Vicomte's and the young coachman's at least, unless he suffered from any qualms about adding further needless crimes to an already overburdened conscience.

As for poor Agathe, the use they had for her was all too clear. Kaleb, who since his attempt on Leighton had been numbered by Marianne among her own people, had, because of his commercial value, nothing immediate to fear beyond the prospect of being sold back into slavery at the first opportunity. Yet that was bad enough, and Marianne felt an overwhelming pity for the dark and splendid being. His nobility and generosity had made a deep impression on her, and now, once again, he was to know the chains of slavery, the cruel whips and fetters of men who differed from him only in the colour of their skin.

Marianne rested breathlessly on her oars. The sun was up now and beat down on the sea with a glare that hurt her eyes. It was going to be a hot day, and she had nothing to protect her from the burning rays.

To guard against sunstroke, she tore off a strip from her wrapper and wound it round her head like a turban, but this did nothing to shade her face which was already starting to burn. In spite of it, she rowed on doggedly, eastwards.

There was worse to come. By midday, thirst was beginning, slowly and inexorably, to make itself felt. At first it was no more than a dryness of the lips and mouth. Then, little by little, the dryness spread to her whole body. Her skin grew hot and parched. She made a feverish search of every corner of the boat in the hope that food and water might have been stowed aboard in case of shipwreck, but there was nothing, only the oars : nothing to quench the thirst which was becoming a torment, nothing ... only the blue immensity of water which mocked her.

She sought some relief by taking off her scanty clothing and hanging it over the side to scoop sea-water over her body. It revived her a little and she moistened her lips and even tried to drink a few drops of cool water, but this only made things worse. The salt smarted on her lips and merely accentuated her thirst.

Hunger came later, and was not so bad. Marianne would gladly have gone without food for two days for the sake of one glass of fresh water, yet a time came when she could no longer ignore the gnawing of her stomach. Her condition, the fact that there was a new life dependent on her own, only made her body more demanding. It was not long before she was suffering badly from fatigue. The sun was merciless. With a last effort she managed to ship the oars and lay them in the bottom of the boat, then she lay down, shielding herself from the killing rays as best she could. Still there was no land in sight, not even another boat, and if help were not forthcoming soon, she knew that she would face death – the slow, appalling death that she no longer doubted had been meant for her by Leighton. Yet, the man was a doctor and must, at some stage in his life, have sworn a solemn oath to succour anyone threatened by sickness and death.

The fact that she had not so far encountered any other human being, nor even caught a glimpse of a sail, suggested that the *Sea Witch* had already deviated from her course before setting her adrift. They must have put her overboard somewhere in the midst of the broad stretch of open water that lay between the Cyclades and the island of Crete. Leighton's purpose had not simply been to get her off the ship : he had condemned her, quite cold-bloodedly, to death.

She very nearly cried as the cruel reality of her situation came home to her, but she forced back the tears with all the feeble strength left to her, knowing that she could not afford to waste a drop of the precious water that remained in her exhausted body.

Evening brought some relief from the heat but the dehydration that seemed to be draining her body, like a vampire, only grew worse. Soon even her bones seemed to be crying out their torturing need for water.

As she had done earlier, she scooped sea water over herself and knew a momentary relief. With it came the temptation to let herself slide into the blue water and seek a final end to all her sufferings. But the instinct of self-preservation was stronger, that and the odd little flicker, like the night-light burning in a sick-room which keeps the shadow of death at bay, which still flared up in her and bade her live, if only for the sake of revenge.

The temperature dropped unexpectedly after dark and, after suffering from the heat all day, Marianne shivered all night long in her thin lawn, without a wink of sleep. Not until the sun had risen once more over the empty sea, did she manage to drop off and forget her parched and aching body. But the awakening was all the more painful. She was stiff and sore and desperately weak.

Even so, at the cost of an almost superhuman effort, she succeeded in sitting up, only to fall back motionless into the bottom of the boat, at the mercy of the sun which now increased her torment.

After that, the mirages began to occur. She seemed to see land on the burning horizon, and fantastic shapes of ships, and great sails racing towards her, bending over her, but when she stretched out her arms to seize them in her delirium, she touched only the empty air and the wooden sides of the boat, and was left weaker than before. The day passed with infinite slowness. In spite of the little she had managed to contrive in the way of shelter, the sun beat down on her with hammer strokes, and her tongue, which seemed to have swollen to three times its normal size, had grown too big for her mouth and was threatening to choke her.

The boat drifted gently: in what direction Marianne had no means of telling. For all she knew, or cared, it might have been moving in circles. She was lost, and she knew it. She could hope for no help, now, but death. Opening her burned eyes painfully, she dragged herself to the side, determined now to drop into the water, if she could find the strength, and make an end of this inhuman torture. But her body had become like a baulk of dead wood and she could not raise it.

Something red passed through her misted field of vision. Her hands touched water. She thrust harder. The rough wood scraped her chest but she did not feel it, insensible now to any pain but the vast fire that was consuming her whole being. Another little effort and her hair was trailing in the sea. The boat tipped gently and Marianne slipped over into the blue water which closed, mercifully cool, over her head.

Too weak and too indifferent to swim, asking nothing but to get it over as quickly as possible, she let herself sink. Her mind shook free of the real world and consciousness receded.

Yet the terrible need for water which had tormented her

seemed to pursue her into death. She was haunted by water, it invaded her, she was dissolving in it. Sweet, life-giving water was flowing over her, as spring water wells up and covers dry stones. It was no longer the bitter, salt sea-water but a fresh draught, light as rainfall on the grass in a parched garden. Solaced, Marianne began to dream that the Almighty, in His mercy, had decreed that she should spend eternity drinking sweet water, and that she had gone to the paradise of those who have died of thirst.

If so, it was a singularly hard and uncomfortable paradise. Her disembodied spirit was actually hurting quite savagely. Her swollen eyelids parted painfully and she saw a heavily bearded face bending over her, out of which looked a pair of questioning black eyes. Something red flapped in the background which she was soon able to identify as a sail rippling in the wind.

Seeing that she had regained consciousness, the man slipped an arm beneath her head and supported her while he held something rough and cool to her cracked lips. It was the rim of an earthen jar. He let a little more of the blessed water trickle down her throat. As he did so, he said something incomprehensible, evidently speaking to someone Marianne could not see. Weak as she was, she struggled round and saw a black figure standing outlined against the red sail. He made a sinister impression standing there in the fiery glow of the setting sun : there was a Greek priest on board. Although himself heavily bearded and by no means clean, he was looking at her with evident disapproval. He said something clearly unflattering in reply and pointed an accusing finger. Instantly the man holding Marianne drew a piece of sailcloth over her, while the priest tucked his hands in his sleeves and turned away to stare at the horizon. Marianne remembered suddenly that her flimsy nightclothes must be in ribbons.

She tried to smile her thanks to her rescuer but her parched lips would only form an agonized grimace and she winced at the pain of it.

The man, apparently a fisherman, then reached behind him and produced a small phial of olive oil, which he smeared generously over her face. After this, he drew a basket towards him and took out a bunch of grapes, some of which he fed cautiously to his patient. Marianne took them eagerly : they were white and sweet and it seemed to her that she had never tasted anything so delicious.

Then he finished wrapping Marianne in her cocoon of sail-cloth, slipped a rolled-up fishing net under her head, and signed to her to go to sleep.

At the other end of the boat, against the red sail whose colour faded with the fading light, the priest stood in an impassive and hieratic pose, eating black bread and onions, washed down by frequent draughts from a pot-bellied jar that he had beside him. When he had finished, he embarked on a lengthy prayer involving various ritual prostrations which, on the moving boat, called for considerable acrobatic skill. By the time this was over, it was quite dark and, curling himself into a ball with his strange-looking mitre tipped over his eyes, he settled himself into his corner and began to snore, without another glance at the creature whom his companion had fished out of the water.

Tired as she was, Marianne felt no desire to sleep. She was exhausted but the thirst, the terrible thirst, had gone; the oil on her face had soothed away some of the pain and she felt almost better. The heavy canvas protected her from the chill of night-time, and above her the stars were coming out, one by one. They were the same stars she had seen the night before, as she lay in the bottom of her boat, but then they had seemed cold and hostile. Tonight there was something friendly about them and from the bottom of her heart Marianne offered up a prayer of thanks to the God who had sent a saving hand to her just at the very moment when she had abandoned hope and decided to put an end to her existence. She could hear the man humming now, through closed lips, as he steered his little craft. She could not understand the language, she did not know to what land he was taking her, nor even where she was, but she was alive, and the sea that bore them up was the same sea that carried the American brig and the pirate who had taken possession of it. Wherever she was taken now, Marianne knew that it was only the first step towards her revenge. She knew, too, that she would know no rest until she had tracked down John Leighton and made him pay the price of his crimes in blood. Every sailor, friend or foe, who sailed the Mediterranean, must be pressed into service to pursue the slaver, so that Leighton might be hanged from the yard-arm of the ship he had stolen!

Towards midnight, the moon rose, a thin crescent giving scarcely more light than the stars. A light breeze sang in the sail, and the sea slid past the vessel's hull with a noise like silk. The fisherman's voice sank to a low, faintly melancholy chant, so low and soothing that Marianne dropped off to sleep at last. She was sleeping too deeply to see the island, with its tall black cliffs, or hear the whispered colloquy between the priest and the fisherman, nor did she feel the hands that carried her ashore, wrapped in the sail.

When she woke, there was nothing but the absence of tormenting thirst to prove that she had not dreamed her rescue. She was lying in the shadow of a rock and a few stunted bushes on a shore of black sand strewn with silver weed. In front of her a sea the colour of indigo lapped at a fringe of black and white pebbles. The piece of sailcloth that had been wrapped round her had gone, like the boat, priest and fisherman, but her thin cotton rags were dry, and when she looked round she saw two bunches of golden grapes laid out neatly on a big flat stone. Automatically her hand crept out towards them. She felt incredibly weak and tired.

Raising herself on her elbow, she nibbled a few of the sweet, juicy grapes. They tasted real enough to assure her that this was not all part of some fantastic dream. She was dizzy and ill, but there was no time to ponder why her fisherman rescuer had apparently changed his mind and abandoned her again on a deserted shore, for at that moment the shore ceased to be deserted.

At the far end of the beach, where a path led down through the rocks, a white procession was emerging, so unexpectedly anachronistic in appearance that Marianne could only rub her eyes to ensure they were not deceiving her.

Led by a tall dark woman, as beautiful and queenly as Athena herself, and a pair of flute-players, came a file of young girls dressed in the many-folded antique chiton, their black hair bound with criss-crossing white fillets. Some carried branches, others bore an amphora on one shoulder, and they walked two by two, slowly and gracefully, like the priestesses of some ancient rite, singing a kind of chant to the piping notes of the flutes.

This curious procession was coming towards her. Marianne dragged herself over the sand until she felt that she was safely hidden by the rock, and with its help managed to stand upright. Her head was swimming and she was still very weak, far too weak to run away from this apparition from the past, which made her feel that she had taken a leap back over about two thousand four hundred years.

However, the women had not seen her, and so took no notice of her. The procession swung away towards a fig tree, in whose shade Marianne could make out a figure, a statue of Aphrodite, mutilated but undoubtedly ancient. The left arm was missing but the torso was undamaged and the right arm bent in a graceful attitude of welcome. The head, whose profile was turned to the girl by the rock, was perfect in its beauty and purity.

The flutes continued playing while the offerings were laid before the statue. Then the other girls prostrated themselves, and the tall dark woman stepped forward and addressed the goddess in the noble tongue of Demosthenes and Aristophanes, to the amazement of Marianne who still stood clinging breathlessly to her rock. Forgetting her own wretched plight for a moment, Marianne listened, wonderingly, to the language she had learned as part of Ellis Selton's plan for her niece's education, letting the woman's warm, grave tones sink into her being:

Deathless Aphrodite, on your shining throne,
Beguiling daughter of Zeus, to you I pray.
Do not with pain and anguish like a stone
Crush my poor heart.

But come to me, as you would come of old,
Hearing my cries of passion from afar,
Leaving your father's dwelling-house of gold,
To bear my part.

The bright-winged sparrows harnessed to your car,
Flew swift from heaven through the midway air,
A myriad flutterings brought you from afar
To this black earth.

Soon, soon they came. And you, O Blessed One,
Your glorious face illumined with a smile,
Would ask what new grief, what insane desire
Consumed my heart.

What was it made me call to you again?
Whom must Persuasion lead back to your love?
Who is it, Sappho, who now gives you pain?
Who wrongs your heart . . . ?

The music of the words, the inexpressible beauty of the Greek
language, entered into Marianne and took possession of her
already half disembodied spirit. She felt as if the burning prayer
were pouring from her own heart. She too was in anguish; she
too was suffering from wounded love, a love debased, dis-
figured and deformed. The passion by which she lived had
turned against her and was rending her with its claws. The
woman's complaint made her fully conscious of her own unhappiness which had been almost driven from her mind by
her physical ordeal and by the violence of her hatred for John
Leighton. Now she was brought face to face once more with
the realities of her own situation: a very young woman, abandoned, grieving and bitterly hurt, and tortured by the childish
need to be loved. She had been maltreated by life and by men,
as though she were strong enough to stand up to their cruelty
and selfishness. Everyone who had loved her had tried to make
use of her, to dominate her, all of them, except perhaps the passionate, enigmatic lover of that night in Corfu. He had asked
nothing but pleasure he had rendered back a hundredfold. He
had been gentle . . . gentle, and tender. Her body remembered
him with gladness, as in the torments of thirst it had remembered all the sweet water it had known. She had a sudden curious
intuition that happiness, plain ordinary happiness, had come
near to her and passed away again with the stranger.

The tears were pouring down her hollow cheeks. She lifted her arm in its ragged sleeve to brush them away and, loosing her hold on the rock, fell to her knees. Then she saw that the girls had paused in their invocation and were looking at her.

She tried to run away, to hide herself in terror in the shadow of the bushes, for to her bruised spirit any human creature seemed an enemy, but she was too weak to stand and could only sink back on to the sand. Already the girls were all around her, bending over her curiously and talking rapidly in a tongue which bore little resemblance to ancient Greek. The tall woman approached more slowly, and the chattering circle parted respectfully before her.

Bending over the castaway, she put aside the tumbled mass of dark hair, sticky with sand and sea-water, and lifted the waxen face down which the tears still coursed. Marianne did not understand the question put to her but she murmured, without much hope:

'I'm French . . . lost . . . be kind to me . . .'

A gleam shot through the kneeling woman's dark eyes and, to Marianne's astonishment, she whispered quickly in the same language:

'Good. Be quiet now. Do nothing. We will take you with us . . .'

'You speak—'

'Be quiet, I said. We may be watched.'

Swiftly unfastening the golden fibula that clasped the classical peplos of white linen that she wore over her pleated tunic, she put it round the other woman. Then, still in the same low voice, she issued a number of orders to her companions and they lifted Marianne, silently now, and held her upright, supported by the shoulders of two of the strongest of their number.

'Can you walk?' the woman asked, and answered her own question at once:

'No, of course you can't. Your feet are bare. You would not get past the first bend in the path. We'll carry you.'

All the girls set to with remarkable speed and efficiency and constructed a kind of litter made of interlaced branches tied together by the fillets from their hair. They laid Marianne upon it, and then six of her new friends raised her on their shoulders, while the rest plucked trails from a wild vine that grew nearby, and asphodels, and some of the strange silvery weed that straggled all over the beach, and arranged these over her just as if it were a funeral bier. When Marianne's eyes turned inquiringly to the strange priestess, she smiled briefly.

'It is best that you should feign death. It will save us from the possibility of awkward questions. The Turks think us mad and fear us on that account ... but moderation in all things!'

As a further precaution, she laid a fold of the peplos over Marianne's face, without giving her time to protest. All the same, the latter's curiosity impelled her to whisper:

'Are there Turks here?'

'They are never far off when we come down to the shore. They wait for us to leave before they steal the jars of wine we put by the goddess. Now be quiet or I'll leave you here.'

Marianne took the hint and made herself lie as still as possible as the procession of women returned by the way they had come, chanting another hymn, this time with all the solemnity of a funeral dirge.

The journey was a long one, over a route that seemed remarkably steep and difficult. Lying on her uncomfortable stretcher of branches, with her head often lower than her feet, and the cloth over her face making breathing difficult, Marianne felt one of her attacks of nausea coming on. Her bearers, however, must have had unusual stamina because they did not once falter in their pace in all that interminable ascent, nor interrupt their singing. All the same, she could not help a sigh of relief when at last they put her down.

A moment later she was lying on a mattress covered with some rough fur which seemed to her the height of comfort, and the linen cloth was removed from her face. At the same time the heat that beat down out of doors gave way to an agreeable coolness.

The room in which she found herself was long and low, and a pair of narrow windows opened on to a blue vista that might have been the sky or the sea or both. It seemed to have undergone a good many vicissitudes down the centuries. Two sturdy

Doric columns supported a cracked ceiling on which were traces of old gilding, radiating outwards from the central figure, probably representing a saint, with a thin, bearded face, a halo and huge, staring eyes. Fragments of old frescoes still clung to the brick walls, as incongruous as the pictures on the ceiling. On one side the remains of a pair of ephebes pranced, long-legged, towards a row of flaking Byzantine angels, stiff and unbending in their striped robes and all squinting atrociously. On the other side was a whitewashed wall with a simple niche containing a magnificent funerary vase of black and white on which a wistful god in a green cloak with a lance sat brooding on a slate-blue throne. A gilt bronze masque lamp with multicoloured glass hung from the ceiling, just below the beard of the hollow-cheeked saint. Besides the bed covered with goatskins on which Marianne was lying, the furniture consisted of a few stools, and a low table holding a big earthenware bowl heaped with fat grapes.

Standing in the midst of all this, the worshipper of Aphrodite, in her long white tunic, no longer looked quite such an anachronism.

Her arms were folded over her splendid bosom and she was considering her find with obvious perplexity. Marianne sat up and saw that the two of them were quite alone. The girls had gone. The woman saw her staring about her and interpreted the look.

'I sent them away. We have to talk. Who are you?' The tone was hard and far from friendly. The woman was suspicious of her.

'I told you. A Frenchwoman. I was shipwrecked and—'

'No. You're lying. Yorgo the fisherman left you on the beach before dawn. He told me he had found you last night, just as you went into the water from a boat. You were half dead from thirst and exposure. What were you doing in that boat?'

'It's a long story...'

'I've plenty of time,' the woman said, pulling up a stool and sitting down.

It was strange, like talking to an antique statue come to life by magic. The woman was herself the epitome of her extraordinary room. To begin with, it would have been hard to tell her age. Her skin was smooth and unwrinkled but her gaze was that of a mature woman. More than anything, she looked like an incarnation of Athena, yet her almond eyes were almost as disproportionately huge as those of the Byzantine face on the ceiling. She had said that she was reputed mad, and yet there emanated from her a quiet strength and assurance that impressed Marianne and certainly did not strike her as in any way alarming.

'I was in that boat,' she said simply, 'dying of thirst, as you yourself said, and the reason I let myself slip into the water was to make an end the sooner.'

'You had not seen Yorgo and his boat?'

'I was past seeing anything. There was something red, but I thought it was only another mirage. Do you know what it means to die of thirst?'

The woman shook her head but there had been a revealing tremor in Marianne's voice on the last words, and she lay back, white-faced. The stranger frowned and rose quickly.

'Are you still thirsty?'

'And hungry . . .'

'Wait, then . . . You shall talk afterwards.'

A few minutes later, after swallowing a little cold fish, some goat cheese, bread, grapes and a cup of a remarkably heady wine, Marianne felt restored to life and able to satisfy her hostess's curiosity, in so far as that was possible without running into fresh perils.

The woman was Greek, an inhabitant of a country under Turkish occupation, and she herself was an envoy sent to those same Turks with the object of reviving the ties of friendship between their two nations. Marianne hesitated a moment, not knowing quite how to begin her story. In the end, she asked a perfectly natural question which, besides allowing her more time for thought, would also test the ground a little.

'Can you tell me, if you please,' she asked softly, 'where I am? I have no idea . . .'

But the woman refused to be drawn.

'Where did you come from, with your boat?'

'From a ship bound for Constantinople, from which I was set adrift on the open sea a little before dawn. That must have been three days ago.' Marianne sighed. 'We had sailed past Cythera that morning . . .'

'Of what nationality was this ship? And what had you done to make them set you adrift like that? And in your nightgown?'

The woman's tone was deeply suspicious and Marianne thought wretchedly that her story was really rather improbable and it would not be easy to make anyone believe it. However, the truth was always likelier to ring true than any made-up tale, however well-intended.

'The vessel was American. A brig, out of Charleston, South Carolina. Captain – Captain Jason Beaufort.'

It was all she could do to utter the name. It came out as a kind of strangled sob, but had at least the unexpected advantage of making the woman's stern face relax a little. The heavy eyebrows, so dark they might have been drawn in Indian ink, rose slightly.

'Jason? A fine Greek name for an American. But it seems to cause you pain. Are you by any chance the Medea to this Jason? Was it he who abandoned you?'

'No – not him!'

The cry of protest sprang straight from Marianne's heart. Her face clouded and she went on in a deadened voice : 'There was a mutiny on board ... I think Jason is probably a prisoner – but he may be dead, and my friends with him.'

Omitting only her own adventures in Venice which could do nothing but add to the unlikelihood of her whole situation, she told the story of the *Sea Witch*'s fatal voyage as best she could. She told how Leighton, to obtain possession of the ship for use in the slave-trade, had done his utmost to set Jason against her, how, in so far as she had been able to reconstruct the course of events, he had succeeded in getting hold of the ship and, finally, how he had set her adrift in an open boat, without food or water, and with no possible hope of rescue. She told of her fears for those she had left on board : for Jolival, Gracchus, Agathe, and for Kaleb who had been flogged for trying to rid the vessel of the devil who coveted it.

She must have put enough real passion into her account of the experiences of those dreadful days for it to carry conviction, because, as she talked, the look of suspicion faded from the other woman's face and was replaced by curiosity. She sat with her long legs crossed, her elbow on her knee and her chin resting on her hand, listening with the deepest interest but in complete silence.

At last, unnerved by this lack of speech, Marianne ventured to ask :

'Does it – does it seem to you very improbable? I know my story must sound like a novel – but it is the truth, I swear it.'

The woman shrugged.

'The Turks have a saying that the truth floats and will never be put down. Yours has a strange sound, like all truth, but do not be alarmed. I have heard far stranger stories than this of yours. You have only to tell me now what is your name, and what was your business at Constantinople?'

The difficult moment had come, when the choice must be made that might have dire consequences. From the beginning of this conversation, Marianne had been reluctant to reveal her proper identity. She had considered giving a false name, explaining her presence on board the American vessel as the flight of a woman in love, anxious to put the greatest possible distance between her guilty joys and a husband's anger, but she had been studying her hostess's grave face while she talked and found herself increasingly disliking the idea of handing her a fabrication which, love story or not, was more than likely to disgust her. In addition, Marianne knew herself to be a bad liar, and a clumsy one, like any woman not in the habit of lying. She was not even very good at keeping her feelings to herself, as the recent catastrophic end to her love had proved all too clearly.

She remembered, quite suddenly, something that François Vidocq had said to her as they journeyed back together from the coast of Brittany. 'Life, my dear, is a vast ocean strewn with reefs. We can expect to strike one at any moment. It is best to be prepared. In that way, there is often a chance of escape . . .'

The reef was there before her, hidden behind that broad, impenetrable brow, those enigmatic features. Telling herself that she had nothing more to lose, except for a problematical revenge, Marianne decided to drive straight at it. After all, whatever happened, it did not matter very much now, and if the woman believed that she was an enemy and killed her, it would not be so very terrible. She said clearly and steadily :

' 'I am called Marianne d'Asselnat de Villeneuve, Princess Sant'-Anna, and I am going to Constantinople, at the command of my master, the Emperor Napoleon, in order to persuade the Sultana, to whom I am related in some degree, to break off the alliance with England and resume friendly relations with France – and also to pursue the war with Russia. There, now I think you know all about me.'

The effect of this candid statement was astonishing. The woman sprang to her feet, became very red and then, as the redness faded, was left as pale as ever. She stared at the castaway, open-mouthed, as though to speak, but then shut it again without a word. After which she turned abruptly on her heel and made for the door as though she had suddenly been faced with a heavy load of responsibility which was more than she could bring herself to deal with. She stopped dead at the sound of Marianne's voice :

'May I remind you that, while I have told you everything you wished to know, you, on your side, have not answered my perfectly natural question. Where am I? And who are you?'

The woman swung round and stared at Marianne out of the black eyes which looked larger than ever.

'This is the island of Santorini, known to the ancients as Thera, the poorest of all Greek islands, where one is never sure of living until tomorrow, or even until nightfall, because it rests on the primeval fire. As for me, you may call me Sappho. I am known by that name.'

Without adding another word, the strange woman hurried from the room, stopping to lock the door carefully behind her. Marianne shrugged, resigned already to this new kind of prison. Then she picked up the peplos which Sappho – since Sappho she was – had left behind and, wrapping it round herself, lay down again on the goatskins and prepared to recoup her strength properly by a really good sleep. The die was cast now. It was out of her hands.

The early evening found her still locked in the chapel, sitting by the window, without having set eyes on a living soul. The view before her was a strange one, consisting of an expanse of ruins and ashes, in which each object seemed to partake of a peculiar silvery quality. The stumps of broken columns and fragments of walls rose from a fine dust made up of every shade of grey. All this jutted out from a wide plateau one side of which was under cultivation. The labour of the peasants had carved out great terraces which were planted with low vines, sheltered by fig trees twisted by the wind and silvered over with the ubiquitous dust. On the far side, beyond a dilapidated stone windmill with tattered sails, the plateau seemed to drop straight down into the sea.

Here and there in the distance was the white cube of a house or the shape of a donkey, so grey and still that it might have been turned to stone like everything else in that depressing landscape which, although scarcely likely to raise the spirits of one who had every reason to regard herself as a prisoner, nevertheless exerted a curious fascination over Marianne : so much so that she jumped when she heard Sappho's calm voice behind her.

'If you would care to join us,' the voice was saying, 'this is the time for us to salute the sun . . . Dress yourself.'

She held out a tunic like the ones Marianne had already seen on the other girls, with a pair of sandals and a fillet for her hair.

'I should like to wash,' Marianne said. 'I have never felt so dirty.'

'Of course. Wait, I will bring water for you.'

She was back in a moment with a full bucket which she set down on the worn flagstones. In her other hand she had a piece of soap and a towel.

'I cannot let you have any more,' she said, apologetically. 'Water is very scarce here because we must rely on the rain to fill our cisterns, and when summer comes, the level drops very quickly.'

'The people here must suffer greatly then . . .'

Sappho gave her the quick smile which conferred such charm on her rather austere face.

'Less than you think. They are not over fond of washing and, as for drinking, we have plenty of wine. It would not occur to anyone to drink water. Hurry, now. I will wait outside. By the way, do you speak any tongue besides your own?'

'Yes. I speak English, German, Italian, Spanish, and I was taught ancient Greek . . .'

Sappho grimaced. Evidently, she would have been far better pleased by even the roughest Greek dialect. She thought for a moment and then said:

'It would still be best for you to say as little as possible, but if you must speak, speak Italian. These islands long belonged to Venice and it is a language which is still understood. And don't forget to use the familiar form to everyone – we are not very formal here.'

Marianne washed quickly, achieving miracles with the small amount of water allotted to her. She even managed to wash her hair and having dried it as best she could, plaited it, still damp, and wound it round her head. She felt amazingly better. The sunburn on her face and arms was no longer sore, thanks to the fisherman's oil, and by the time she had put on the pleated tunic, she felt almost as fresh as if she had just come out of her own elegant bath in Paris. At last, she pulled open the heavy wooden door of her temporary lodging and found Sappho waiting for her, seated on the coping of a well. She had a lyre in her hand and the girls whom Marianne had seen that morning were grouped about her.

Seeing Marianne, Sappho rose and pointed to a place between two of the girls, who did not even glance at her. Then the white procession moved off towards the edge of the plateau, the whole extent of which now became visible to Marianne.

To the east, it fell away in a gentle slope towards the sea, dotted with vines and plantations of tomatoes; to the west it rose to a ridge, on top of which stood a big solidly-constructed white building which, but for the protruding belfry, might have been a fortress. Behind this building, the sun was going down. As for the place where Marianne had spent the day, it was in actual fact a small half-ruined chapel, on whose ochre-coloured dome was a curious thing like a lightning conductor which might once have been a cross. All around it were the crumbling porticoes of an old Byzantine villa, with the well at its heart.

Singing another of its strange archaic hymns, the procession made its way to a high point overlooking the blue expanse of the sea. Here the grey dust was replaced by a block of lava carved into the semblance of a throne. Sappho stepped up to it majestically, clutching her lyre to her breast with her folded arms, while the girls knelt at her feet. All turned to face the setting sun, endeavouring to imitate the ecstatic look which illumined their mistress's face. Marianne might have found it all rather absurd if she had not realized that all this was nothing but a front and that there was something else, infinitely powerful and respectable, concealed behind this continuous masquerade to which all the women were committed.

'They think us mad,' Sappho had said, and she was certainly doing her utmost to convey that impression. She had remained for a moment in thought, her head resting on her hands, and then, striking a few chords on her lyre, she began to sing in a strong voice some kind of long hymn to the sun. As music it was not bad, but Marianne very soon came to the conclusion that it was by far too long and boring to be worth the trouble of trying to translate the words.

In a little while some of her companions got up and began to dance. The dance was a slow, ceremonial one and yet oddly suggestive, as though the strong young bodies revealed by the folds of linen in the movements of the dance were being offered up to the dying sun.

Before very long this strange concert acquired an even stranger counterpoint. Three black figures in tall headdresses appeared on the steep slope leading up to the white fortress-like building on the ridge, three very angry figures, shouting and waving their fists at the dancers. Marianne gathered that the building must be a monastery and that her companions' choreographic exercises were not to the liking of the holy men who lived there. Remembering the monk in Yorgo's boat and his evident disapproval of herself, she could not be surprised, but felt some alarm when the three protesters started to throw stones. Happily, the distance was considerable and their aim singularly bad.

At all events, neither Sappho nor her followers seemed to take much notice. Nor did they show any sign when one of the monks ran down the road and accosted two passing Turkish soldiers, a pair of janissaries in felt hats and red boots. He gesticulated furiously towards the women but the Turks scarcely bothered even to look round. After one bored glance at the dancers, they shrugged their shoulders and went on their way northwards.

By this time, moreover, Sappho had finished her song. The sun had disappeared below the ridge, and it would soon be dark. The women formed up as before, in silence, and retraced their steps towards the old villa, with the poetess and the flute-players in the lead, looking more exalted than ever.

Marianne, walking in their midst, sought in vain for answers to the questions that filled her mind. She was so deep in her thoughts that she did not see a clump of mastic growing in the path, and tripped over it. She would have fallen if the girl next to her had not put out a strong hand to steady her – a hand so strong, in fact, that Marianne found herself looking at its owner with rather more attention.

She was a tall, lithe-limbed creature who carried herself proudly, and the face below the mass of black curls gathered on her neck was fine-featured and keen. Like most of her companions, she was tall and well-built, not in the least fragile, yet not without a certain gracefulness. Her dark eyes smiled briefly as they met Marianne's, and she held her for a moment before letting her go; then she resumed her steady walk as though nothing had occurred. But she left yet another question-mark in Marianne's mind: Sappho must make her girls train like young Spartans, because the body of the girl who had supported her had felt as hard as marble.

The procession broke up when it reached the villa. One by one, the girls passed in front of Sappho and went through the gate, but when it came to Marianne's turn, the poetess took her and led her to the chapel.

'It will be best if you do not mix with the others tonight. Stay here and I will bring you your supper in a little while.'

Marianne obeyed meekly and closed the painted wooden door behind her. Inside, it was almost dark and there was a strong smell of fish which had not been there when she went out. She tried to discover where it came from and thought that she had found it when she saw a small flat fish gleaming on the floor beside the bed. She picked it up, automatically, and was still staring uncomprehendingly at it and wondering how it could have come there when Sappho reappeared, carrying on her head a basket containing food and an oil-lamp which she took out and placed on the table, lighting it at once.

When she saw what Marianne was holding, she frowned, and took the fish from her.

'I shall have to scold Yorgo,' she said, and the lightness of her tone rang a little false. 'He *will* leave his baskets in here when he comes back with his catch, because it is nearer than the kitchen.'

Marianne smiled. 'It doesn't matter,' she said. 'I was only wondering how the fish came here.'

'In a perfectly natural way, you see ... it couldn't be more natural. Now you may eat.'

She had been setting the table swiftly, with a helping of roast kid, some tomatoes, bread, cheese and the inevitable grapes, but now her hands seemed to linger a little over the bowls and other everyday things she had arranged, as if she were putting off the moment when she would have to say what she had come to say. Suddenly she seemed to make up her mind.

'Don't go to sleep after you have eaten,' she said. 'I will come for you when it is quite dark.'

'What for?'

'Ask no questions. Not now. Later, you will understand much that must have seemed to you strange, even insensate. You need know only that I do nothing without a good reason, and it has cost me much thought, all day, before I made up my mind what I should do about you.'

Marianne's throat felt suddenly dry. The woman's voice held a veiled but horrid menace. It occurred to her that perhaps she was really dealing with a lunatic who, like all those in that condition, refused to recognize her own madness. Nevertheless, she refused to show her fear and merely said quietly :

'Ah! ... And you have decided?'

'Yes, I have decided ... to trust you. But woe to you if you are deceiving me! The whole of the Mediterranean will not be big enough to save you from our vengeance. Eat now, and wait for me. Oh, I nearly forgot ...'

She took a bundle of black material from her basket and tossed it on to the bed.

'Put this on. Darkness is a fine concealment if you know how to melt into it properly.'

This Sappho was a strange creature, Marianne thought. She was still wearing her absurd classical garb but she was a very different person now from the one she had been hitherto. It was as though she had suddenly decided to throw off a mask and reveal her real face, and that face had something implacable about it that could be disquieting. Yet she had said that she had chosen to trust her, although there had been such a menacing note in her voice as she said it that it was almost as though she regretted her decision, or as though her attitude were not of her own choosing, to say the least, and she was merely bowing to circumstances.

Whatever the truth of it, Marianne felt that it was best to do as she was told, since her fate depended on it, but at the same time to be on her guard. As she regained her strength, so she was regaining her appetite for life.

She sat down at the table and began to eat, quite calmly and with relish. She even found herself enjoying the strong, heady wine which was the island's pride, and the agreeable sense of well-being it sent coursing through her veins. She had slept so well that she felt quite rested now and almost ready to face up to whatever new obstacles fate seemed to be taking a malign pleasure in putting in her way.

Darkness had fallen long before Sappho returned to the chapel, and Marianne had long been ready and waiting, without impatience, sitting on a stool with her hands hugging her knees. She had put on the costume given to her, which turned out to be of the kind commonly worn by the peasant women of the Greek islands, consisting of a full black cotton skirt with a thin band of red round the hem, a tight-waisted bodice to match, and a large, black scarf covered with fine red embroidery which was worn over the head, completely hiding the hair.

The other woman was dressed in almost identical fashion and she cast an approving glance over Marianne.

'What a shame you don't speak our language! You might easily be taken for one of our girls. Even your eyes are as fierce as if you'd been born here! Now, put out the lamp and follow me, without a sound.'

The darkness swallowed them. Marianne felt Sappho's hand take hold of hers in the blackness and draw her forward. Outside, the night seemed inky black and carried on its breath the scent of thyme and myrtle with a faint whiff of sheep. Without that guiding hand, Marianne would undoubtedly have fallen flat within a few steps, because she was walking blind, feeling the ground ahead with her foot before she put it down.

'Come on!' Sappho whispered impatiently. 'We'll never get there at this rate.'

'But I can't see,' Marianne protested. She refrained from inquiring where she was being taken in such haste.

'That will pass. Your eyes will grow accustomed.'

They did, far more quickly than Marianne would have thought possible. At the same time she understood the reason for Sappho's precautions in dressing her in dark clothes and enjoining her to keep silent. A few furlongs from the villa, and hidden from it until they were outside the broken wall, a fire was burning. The light came from outside a formless white building, something between a mosque and a barn, and illuminated the weird, mustachioed figures of a number of Turkish soldiers who were gathered round it, cooking something in a big copper cauldron suspended over the fire.

The firelight also served to show Marianne that the path Sappho had taken passed close by this guard post, but already the poetess had put her finger to her lips and was leading her noiselessly behind a piece of ruined wall which must have belonged to some ancient fortification. The two women were engulfed at once in a thicket of tamarisk and juniper and, with the aid of this twofold cover, were able to move forward slowly, bent almost double and taking care to avoid the smallest snap of a twig underfoot. With this precarious shelter, they passed close enough to the Turks to smell their food cooking. Marianne felt the clutch of fear. At last the perilous part was over, and the two women walked on a little farther and then joined the path which was now winding through what must have been an ancient cemetery, dotted with antique steles and the empty stone troughs of what might once have been sarcophagi. At that point, Sappho turned sharp left up a stony sloping path, like nothing more than a mule track, which climbed precipitously towards the summit of the ridge.

By now Marianne's eyes had grown sufficiently used to the dark for her to make out some details of the landscape, even distinguishing the white blurs of the cistus flowers that grew in patches along the path. It became clear that, for all its winding to and fro, this path was leading them to the hostile white walls of the monastery.

Marianne pulled gently at her companion's sleeve as the other woman climbed ahead of her.

'Surely we aren't going there?' she said as Sappho looked round, and she pointed to the ridge.

'Yes, that is where we are going. To the monastery of Ayios Ilias.'*

'Judging from what I saw earlier on, you aren't exactly on the best of terms with the monks there.'

Sappho paused for a moment, hands on hips. She was breathing hard, for the climb was a tough and tiring one, even for someone who was used to it.

'There is appearance,' she said, 'and reality. The reality is that the higoumenos Daniel is expecting us at eleven o'clock. What you witnessed at sunset was nothing more than a conventional exchange. My song required an answer – and the answer was forthcoming.'

'With stones?' Marianne said, bewilderedly.

'Precisely. Eleven stones were thrown. That meant eleven o'clock. It's time you should know, stranger, that all of us here,

* St Elias.

and on every other island in the archipelago, and throughout Greece, have sworn to devote our lives to shaking off the Turkish yoke which has oppressed us for centuries. We are all vowed to the service of freedom: rich and poor, peasants, brigands, monks ... and madmen! But we must stop talking and press on, because the way is steep and it will take us a good quarter of an hour to reach Ayios Ilias.'

In fact it was twenty minutes later when Marianne and her companion stood beneath the monastery's tall white walls. Marianne, still barely recovered from her recent ordeal, was breathless and thankful that it was night: by day, in the glare of the sun, the climb must be intolerable, for there was not so much as a tree or a blade of grass. She was sweating under her black cotton skirts and knew how to value the draught that swirled under the big entrance portico, a massive semicircular arch surmounted by an open pediment hung with bells. An iron gate, adorned with the two-headed eagle of Mount Athos, to which Ayios Ilias belonged, creaked open. A shadow stepped out from among the thick dark shadows of the doorway, but there was nothing alarming in it. It was the plump shadow of a fat little monk, bearded and pigtailed, who, to judge from the odour of sanctity that emanated from him, was not inclined to waste the island's precious water supply unnecessarily. He said something in an undertone to Sappho and then rolled away like a little ball on his short legs, leading the two women along a terrace by a white wall, past a stone-built cistern and elegant Byzantine basin, before plunging into a maze of passages, curved bays opening on to empty vestibules and stairways which, in the light of the smoky torches that burned here and there, looked as if carved out of snow. At last he opened a painted door into the monastery chapel.

Two men were standing in the light of the great bronze lamp in front of a massive eighteenth-century iconostasis, carved and painted in a primitive style, like a child's picture book. But if there was something primitive about the chapel, with its silver-mounted icons and white walls decorated with the two-headed eagle of the Holy Mountain, its two occupants had nothing of the freshness and innocence of childhood about them.

One, wearing a long black robe and gleaming pectoral cross, was the higoumenos Daniel. He had the narrow, emaciated face of the ascetic, made to look still longer by his grey beard, and his eyes were those of a visionary and fanatic. He had the power to annihilate time, and as she crossed the chapel towards him, Marianne had the unnerving feeling that he could see right through her, as though she had no real substance or personal identity.

The other man was almost a giant. He was of bear-like proportions, and to his muscular figure was added a face strong to the point of savagery. His eyes were fierce and commanding, his long hair hung down his back from beneath a round cap with a silken tassel, his moustaches were arrogant, and stuck in the red belt which he wore under his sleeveless goatskin jacket there protruded the butt of a silver-mounted pistol and the hilt of a long knife.

Sappho, meanwhile, having apparently forgotten all about her prayers to Aphrodite, had moved forward humbly to kiss the abbot's ring.

'Here is she of whom I told you, most holy father,' she said, speaking in a Venetian dialect. 'I believe that she may be of great use to us.'

The Greek priest's eyes looked straight through Marianne but his hand made no move towards her.

'If she so wills it,' he said slowly, and the habits of monastic life, with its eternal whispering, had given a curiously muffled, toneless quality to his voice. 'But does she?'

Before Marianne could answer, the giant flung himself impulsively into the conversation.

'Ask her rather if she would live or die! Or moulder here until the flesh shrivels from her bones. Either she helps us, or she never sees her own land again!'

'Be quiet, Theodoros,' Sappho said quickly. 'Why should you treat her as an enemy? She is French and the French are not our enemies, far from it! Think of Korais! Besides, I know that refugees are given asylum in Corfu, and that is what she is here, a refugee. It was the sea brought her to us, and I believe with all my heart that it was for our good.'

'That remains to be seen,' the giant growled. 'Did you not say she was cousin to the Haseki Sultana? That ought to teach you caution, Princess!'

Marianne looked round, startled at the title which was clearly addressed to her companion. The worshipper of Aphrodite smiled at her surprise.

'I belong to one of the oldest families in Greece. My name is Melina Koriatis,' she said, simply but not without pride. 'I told you that I was going to trust you. As for you, Theodoros, you are wasting precious time. You know quite well that Nakshidil is a Frenchwoman carried off by Barbary pirates as a girl and given to old Abdul Hamid for his harem.'

Seeing that the giant was still frowning obstinately, Marianne decided that she had remained silent long enough. It was time she took a hand.

'I do not know yet what you want of me,' she said, 'but before you come to blows about it, would it not be simpler to tell me? Or must I agree without hearing? I owe you my life, I know – but it might occur to you that I have other things to do with it besides devote it to your affairs.'

'I have told you the choice before you,' Theodoros said.

'She is right,' broke in the abbot. 'And it is also true that we are wasting time. You agreed that she should come here, Theodoros, and you have a duty to listen to her. And you, young woman, listen to what it is we ask of you. You shall tell us afterwards what you feel but before you answer, beware. We are in a church and God's eye is on us. If your tongue is ripe for falsehood, then you had better go now. You do not seem very willing to aid us.'

'I have no love for lies, or for dissimulation,' came the answer. 'And I know that if you have need of me, then I also have need of you. Speak.'

The priest appeared to think for a moment. His head dropped on his breast and he closed his eyes briefly, before turning to the silver icon of St Elias, as if in search of counsel and inspiration. Only then did he begin.

'You, in your western lands, know very little of Greece, or

rather you have forgotten because, for centuries now, we have not owned the right to freedom, to live our own lives.'

In his strange, flat voice, which could still show flashes of bitterness, anger and grief, the higoumenos Daniel gave Marianne a rapid summary of his country's tragic history. He described how the land that had produced the purest light of civilization had been ravaged successively by Visigoths, Vandals, Ostrogoths, Bulgars, Slavs, Arabs, the Normans of Sicily, and then by the crusaders from the west brought by the Doge, Enrico Dandolo, who after the capture of Byzantium had carved up the country into a multitude of fiefs. These fiefs, in turn, had fallen to the Turks and for almost two hundred years Greece has ceased to breathe. Abandoned to the mercy of despotic Ottoman governors, she had been reduced to slavery, ground beneath the heel of the pashas, who were never the sort to let the post of executioner go unfilled. The only freedom left to the Greeks had been freedom of worship, since the Koran displayed a fair degree of tolerance in this respect, and the one person who had to answer to the Sublime Porte for the behaviour of the enslaved nation was the patriarch of Constantinople, Gregorios.

'But we have never lost hope,' the abbot went on, 'and we are not yet quite dead. For fifty years, the corpse of Greece has been stirring and struggling to rise. The Montenegrins of Epirus rebelled in 1766, the Maniots in '69, and the Souliots, more recently, in 1804. The scurvy dog, Ali, crushed them as bloodily as others had been crushed before them, but the harvest is raised from the blood of martyrs. More than ever we are determined to shake off the yoke. Look at this woman—'

His thin hand, with the bright ring gleaming on it, rested affectionately on the so-called Sappho's arm. 'She comes from one of the wealthiest families of the Phanar, the Greek quarter of Constantinople. For a hundred years her people have been compelled to give pledges to the Turks and have occupied exalted positions. More than one has been hospodar of Moldavia, but the youngest among them chose freedom and made their way to Russia, our sister in the Faith, and are at this moment fighting the enemy in Russia's ranks. Melina herself is rich, powerful, and a cousin of the patriarch. She could have chosen a carefree life in her palaces on the Bosphorus or the Black Sea. And yet she has chosen to dwell here, in the guise of a madwoman, in a half-ruined house on this god-forsaken island ravaged every now and then by fire, for the very reason that Santorini, beneath which the volcano never wholly slumbers, is of all Greek islands the one least watched by the Turks, who have no interest in it and consider it a shame even to be sent here.'

'Why do you do this?' Marianne asked, looking at her strange companion. 'What do you hope to gain by this weird life?'

Melina Koriatis shrugged and smiled in a way that made her seem suddenly much younger.

'I act as an agent and a clearing house for information between the Archipelago, Crete, Rhodes and the ancient cities of Asia Minor. The news comes here and is passed on. Others come here, also, who need help and can be comparatively safe. Have you noticed the girls who live with me? No, of course, you were too exhausted and you had too much to worry about on your own account. Well, if you look at them more closely, you will see that, except for the four or five girls who came here out of loyalty to me, all the rest are boys.'

'Boys!' gasped Marianne, recollecting even as she spoke the unusual strength of the women who had carried her and the hard muscles of the one who had walked at her side earlier that evening. 'But what are you doing with them?'

'Making soldiers for Greece,' the Princess answered grimly. 'Some are the sons of men who have been killed, whom I have brought here to prevent their forcible enlistment as janissaries. Others were carried off by the pirates who haunt the islands, for unfortunately we also suffer from an accursed plague of traitors and renegades working on their own account, like Ali. I or my agents purchased them in the markets of Smyrna or Karpathos. In my house they are themselves again, forgetting the shame but not the hatred. I train them for war, in the caves of the island, as the warriors of Sparta were once trained, or the athletes of Olympia. And then, when they are ready, Yorgo or his brother Stavros takes them wherever good fighters are needed ... and brings me others. I am never short. The Turks are never tired of executions, nor do the traders tire of profit.'

Marianne stared wide-eyed, overwhelmed by feelings of mingled pity and horror at this fresh revelation of the infamous traffic in human flesh. She was staggered by the woman's daring. There was a Turkish post only a few furlongs away from the refuge she had created! For the first time, she felt a genuine rush of friendship towards her and she smiled warmly, how warmly even she herself was not aware.

'I cannot help admiring you,' she said, with sincerity, 'and if I can help you I will do so gladly, although I do not see how. As this man has said, my mission from the Emperor is to the Sultana, to try and recreate the ties of friendship which have lapsed ...'

'But he also gives shelter to thinking men of our nation. One of our greatest writers, Korais, who has devoted himself with all his might to our rebirth, lives in France, at Montpellier; and our poet Rhigas was put to death by the Turks because he wanted to meet Bonaparte and win his support for us.'

Here the man addressed as Theodoros interrupted. He had evidently had more than enough of history lessons and was eager to get down to immediate practicalities.

'Napoleon wants the war between Turkey and Russia to continue,' he said abruptly. 'Tell us why? We, too, wish it to continue, naturally, until the Porte is defeated, but we should like to know your Emperor's reasons.'

'I do not really know them myself,' Marianne answered, after only the faintest of hesitations. In fact, it did not seem to her that she had any right to reveal Napoleon's plans, especially when these were still secret. 'I think he is chiefly anxious to remove the Sultan from the English influence.'

Theodoros nodded. He studied Marianne as though he meant to pierce her very soul, and then, apparently satisfied, he turned to the abbot.

'Tell her everything, father. She seems to be honest, and I'm willing to put it to the test. If she should betray me, she'll not live long enough to boast of it. Our friends will see to that.'

'I've not the least intention of betraying anyone!' Marianne broke in hotly. 'I'm tired of this everlasting suspicion! Say what you want and have done with it!'

The priest's hands moved pacifically.

'Some night soon, you will leave here in Yorgo's boat. This man,' he indicated the giant, 'will go with you. He is one of our chief people and a good leader of men. Because of that, five years ago, the Turks drove him from his home in the Morea and he has been forced to live in hiding, never staying long in one place. He moves constantly about the Archipelago, always on the run but still free, breathing fire into lukewarm hearts to ignite the torch of revolt and, with his courage and faith, doing all he can to help those who need his help. Today it is in Crete that he is needed, only he could do no good there, whereas there is much that he could do on the Bosphorus. Last night, at the same time as he brought you here, Yorgos brought a monk from the monastery of Arkadios in Crete. There is bloodshed there and the cries of the oppressed rise to heaven. The pasha's janissaries will plunder, burn, torture and impale on the slightest suspicion. This must stop, and Theodoros thinks that he has the means to stop it. But to do so, he must go to Constantinople, which for him is equivalent to throwing himself into the jaws of the wolf. With you, he has a chance not only to get in but also of getting out again alive. No one would think to question a great lady of France travelling with a servant. He will be that servant.'

'He? My servant?'

Marianne stared incredulously at the ferocious-looking giant, with his fiercely curling whiskers and his picturesque garb, thinking that nothing could be less like the conventional Parisian idea of a respectable butler or servant of a great household.

Melina smiled. 'He won't look quite like that,' she said with amusement. 'And he shall be an Italian servant of yours, since he speaks no French. All that we ask of you is to take him with you and get him into Constantinople in your company. You will be staying at the French embassy, I imagine?'

Remembering what General Arrighi had told her about the repeated appeals for help on the part of the ambassador, Comte de Latour-Maubourg, Marianne could not doubt for an instant that she would be warmly welcomed.

'I can't think of anywhere else,' she admitted, 'that I could go.'

'Excellent. No one would think of looking for Theodoros in the French embassy. He will remain there for a little while and then, one day, he will simply vanish and you can forget all about him.'

Marianne frowned. Her mission to the Sultana was delicate and complicated enough already; she did not see how she could afford to risk bringing worse trouble on herself by taking under her protection a proscribed rebel leader who was probably quite well known, since he dared not enter Constantinople openly. It was enough to wreck her entire mission and to ensure that she herself spent the rest of her life, assuming she was allowed to live, in meditating on her indiscretion on the mouldy straw of a Turkish gaol.

'Is it essential,' she asked, after a moment's thought, 'that he goes there himself? Would it not be possible for me to do his work for him, somehow?'

The giant's sharp, white teeth showed a ferocious grin and his hand stroked the chased silver handle of his knife.

'No,' he said, with a curl of his lip, 'you cannot do my work for me. You are nothing but a foreign woman and I do not trust you enough. But you have the choice of refusal, if you wish. After all, no one knows that you are here . . .'

Beyond a doubt, if she refused, this brute was capable of slitting her throat on the spot, church or no church. Moreover, she had a real desire to accomplish her mission and to escape from this rat hole so that she could find the brig again, with the piratical doctor and, more than all else, Jason and her friends. If it were fated that, after the joy of rendering a signal service to Napoleon, the only happiness left to her in this world was to see John Leighton hanged, then she did not mean to let slip even the smallest chance of bringing it about; and no such chance existed on Santorini.

'Very well,' she said at last. 'I agree.'

Princess Koriatis exclaimed delightedly but Theodoros was not yet satisfied. He clamped his big hairy hand round Marianne's wrist and drew her close to the iconostasis.

'You are a Christian, yes?'

'Certainly I am, but—'

'But your Church is not ours, I know that. But God is the same for all his children, in whatever fashion they pray to him. So, you will swear, here, before these holy images, to perform faithfully everything that is asked of you in order to assist me to enter Constantinople and to stay there. Swear!'

Unhesitatingly Marianne stretched out her hand toward the images, their silver mountings glinting with points of gold in the flickering lamplight.

'I swear,' she said firmly. 'I will do it to the best of my ability. But—' She let fall her hand and turned slowly to look at the woman who called herself Sappho. 'I want you to know that it is not for your sake, or because I am afraid of you. I will do it for her, because she has helped me and I should be ashamed to fail her now.'

'Your reasons do not matter. But may you be damned to all eternity if you break your word! Now, father, I think we may go.'

'Not yet. We still have something to do. Come with me.'

They followed the abbot's black robe out of the chapel and through the white stairways and passages until they emerged at last on the topmost terrace of the monastery. Under the rising moon, it looked as white as a field of new-fallen snow. At that elevation the wind blew incessantly and Marianne shivered in her thin clothes, but the prospect before her was an amazing one.

From that height it was possible to see the whole of Santorini: a long crescent-shape of accumulated lava and volcanic slag, dotted with straggling white villages. Its deep bay was almost entirely enclosed by a chain of rocky islands that marked the rim of the old crater, now sunk beneath the waves. From Palaia Kaimeni, one of the two largest of these, Marianne could see a faint drift of smoke, and the wind brought a tang of sulphur to her nostrils. At the site of the monastery itself, the ground fell away sharply in a dizzy precipice dropping straight down, two thousand feet or so, into the black waters of the sea. Not a tree was visible in the cold moonlight. It was an apocalyptic landscape, a waste of stone to which man clung only by some miracle of stubbornness, in peril of his life. Those wisps of smoke looked ominous to Marianne, and she stared at them fearfully. The greater part of her life had been spent amid the green English countryside, a far cry from this scorched land.

'The volcano is breathing,' Melina said, hugging her arms across her chest as though to keep herself from shivering. 'Last night, I heard him grumble. Pray God, he does not wake.'

But the abbot Daniel was not listening. He had walked on to the far end of the roof, where there was a small pigeon house. With Theodoros' help, he took out a large pigeon, fastened something to one leg, then let it go. The bird circled for a moment above the monastery and then flew off in a north-westerly direction.

'Where is he going?' Marianne asked, her eyes still on the vanishing white speck.

Melina tucked her arm comfortably through her new friend's and drew her back to the steps.

'To find a vessel worthier of the French Emperor's ambassadress than Yorgo's fishing boat,' she said. 'Yorgo will take you no farther than Naxos. Come, now. We must go in. It is past midnight and soon the bell will ring for the first of the night offices. We must not be seen here.'

The two women bade farewell to the higoumenos and followed the fat monk back to the monastery door. Theodoros, with a brief good night, had vanished into the depths of the building where he had been living for some days past. The night was much brighter now and on the long terrace with the cistern, even the smallest details stood out with chiselled clarity in a bleached universe.

As they stepped outside, under the porch with the belfry, the echoes wakened in the monastery, solemnly calling the monks to prayer. Muttering a hasty blessing, the fat monk swung the iron door to, and Marianne and her companion hurried away down the steep path to the villa.

The return journey was accomplished much more speedily than the outward one, and they passed the guard post without trouble. The fire was dying down and only two guards remained, sleeping up against their long-barrelled guns. The women's light tread was in no more danger of waking them than the faint rustle of the undergrowth. A few minutes later, Melina shut the door of the old chapel behind them and lighted the lamp.

They stood for a moment, looking at one another without speaking, as if they were really seeing one another for the first time. Then, very slowly, the Greek princess moved closer to her new friend and kissed her on the brow.

'I want to thank you,' she said simply. 'I know what it must have cost you to agree to take Theodoros with you, and I want you to know that even if you had refused, I should not have let him kill you.'

'He may still do so when we are far away from here,' Marianne muttered, unable to repress a certain resentment against the giant.

'Of course not. First of all, he needs you – and then he has a strict sense of honour. He is rough, violent and passionate but, from the moment that you are travelling companions, he will die for you if you are in danger. That is the law of the mountain klephts.'

'Klephts?'

'The mountaineers of Olympus, Pindus and Taygetos. They live by brigandage, of course, but they are really much more like your Corsican bandits than ordinary robbers. Theodoros, like his father Constantine before him, was their chieftain. There is no more valiant fighter for Greek freedom . . . As for you, you are one of us now. The service you are rendering gives you the right to ask aid and protection from any one of us. Go to sleep now, and peace be with you.'

Peace? In spite of all her heroic efforts, Marianne did not find it again that night. What lay before her was not conducive to peace of mind; in fact she had never found herself in a worse mess. For the first time since leaving Paris, she began to long for her quiet, comfortable house in the rue de Lille, the roses in her garden, and her cousin Adelaide's sardonic, reassuring presence: Adelaide who must be waiting there quietly, dividing her time between the gossip of the neighbourhood, the services at the church of St Thomas Aquinas, and her interminable little snacks, for the letter which would summon her to America, to join Marianne and her old friend Jolival . . . A letter that would

never come. Unless the threads of destiny were to sort themselves out at last, which did not look like happening!

'I'll make you pay for this, Jason Beaufort!' Marianne exclaimed suddenly, anger reviving in her at the memory. 'If you
are still alive, I'll find you, wherever you are, and make you
pay for all I've suffered on your account, through your stupid
obstinacy! And now it's all your fault I'm mixed up in this insane business, putting to sea with a boatload of dangerous
rebels . . .'

She was within an inch of echoing Antigone's anguished cry:
'I was made for love, not for hate.' Yet it did her good to be the
old Marianne again, with her hopeless rages, her miseries, quar-
rels and follies, just as she had derived comfort from the thought
of her home and her cousin, even if it was only the comfort of
regret.

So much had happened to her already, she had suffered such
a variety of experiences, that her present situation was not really
so much worse than it had been on other occasions in the past.
Even the fact that she was pregnant by a man she loathed had
ceased to matter so very much. That was now the least of her
problems. A slightly philosophical note began to creep into her
angry thoughts.

'All I need now,' she thought, 'is to find myself becoming a
brigand chief! But with Theodoros perhaps that won't be so
very far off!'

In any case, the important thing for the moment was how
they were to get to Constantinople, wretched place! She had
lost all her papers, passports, credentials, of course; everything
had gone that could prove her identity. However, she knew herself to be equal to persuading the ambassador, at least, to recognize her, and there was a small inner voice which whispered to
her, stronger than all the reason and logic in the world, that at
all costs, somehow, she had to reach the Ottoman capital, if
she had to travel on a fishing boat, or even swim! And Marianne
had always placed great faith in her inner voices.

Chapter Ten
The island where time stands still

Yorgo's boat cast off, slid over the dark water in the shadow of the cliffs and put to sea. The white figure of Melina Koriatis, standing in the entrance to the little cave that served as a discreet landing stage, receded and her waving hand was lost in shadow. Soon, even the cave mouth itself had disappeared.

Marianne sighed and huddled in the big black cloak given her by her hostess, seeking what shelter she could find from the spray in the lee of the heavy canvas that was laced across from side to side of the vessel to protect the cargo, in this case jars of wine.

The fisherman's boat was a scaphos, one of those curious and rather badly-built Greek vessels that have nothing essentially Mediterranean about them, save their gaudy sails: a jib and a big gaff mainsail rigged up to a yard of inordinate length. She rode very low in the water, amply justifying the expanse of canvas, especially at times like the present when there was a heavy sea running. It must have been blowing a gale somewhere, for the night was cold, and Marianne blessed the warm wool they had bundled her up in, over her tattered gown.

She had felt a little sad at parting from the woman called Sappho. She had liked the revolutionary princess with her strangeness and her courage, recognizing in her something akin to herself and to those other women she had known with the capacity to grasp life with both hands: women like her cousin Adelaide and her best friend Fortunée Hamelin.

Their good-byes had been brief.

'We may meet again, perhaps,' Melina had said, shaking her

hand with a firm grip, like a man's. 'But if our paths should not cross, then go with God.'

That was all, and then she had gone with them down the dark narrow staircase cut in the rock beneath the floor of the chapel in which Marianne had been housed.

The sight of Yorgo lifting up the heavy stone and sliding into the lightless hole with the ease of long practice had told Marianne all that she needed to know about how she had come to find a fish by her bed, but Melina had coolly furnished her with the details. It appeared that whenever Yorgo and his brother were landing contraband articles such as guns, powder, shot or similar items, they were in the habit of carrying it in their baskets, hidden under a batch of fresh fish, and bringing it up the steps under the chapel. These led down by means of a long and fairly gently sloping chimney cut in the rock to a cave, half-filled with water, where a fishing boat could tie up out of sight of anyone.

Running before a southerly wind that filled the sails and whipped up the sea, the scaphos made good speed along the east coast of Santorini, before heading straight out to sea. No one had said a word since they left the cave. The passengers sat apart from one another, as though in mutual distrust, and gave themselves up to the rhythm of the ship. Only Theodoros took his turn at the helm.

When he had turned up, earlier, with Yorgo, Marianne had scarcely recognized him. He was dressed in rags, much like those in which she herself had been decked, but his were half-concealed under a rough woollen blanket, and with his face covered by a flowing beard that joined his hair and obscured his moustache, he looked like some mad prophet. His appearance was certainly an unlikely one for the servant of a fashionable Frenchwoman, but it fitted perfectly the part of a recent castaway.

The story which had been concocted to explain Marianne's return to her ordinary life was a fairly simple one. On his way to Naxos with a cargo of wine, Yorgo was supposed to have found the Princess Sant'Anna and her servant adrift, clinging to a few spars, in the water between Santorini and Ios, the ves-

sel in which they were travelling having been sunk by pirates —
who apparently abounded in the islands and were perfectly
capable of sinking any vessel which came in their way.

Once arrived in Naxos, where there was a considerable popu-
lation of Venetian origin and where the Turks tolerated the existence of a number of Catholic communities, the fisherman
would take the two 'castaways' to a cousin of his, a man called
Athanasius, who acted in the ill-defined capacity of gardener,
steward and man-of-all-work to the last descendant of one of
the old ruling families of the island, a Count Sommaripa. He,
naturally, could not do otherwise than offer the hospitality of
his house to an Italian princess who found herself in difficulties,
until such time as a vessel should put in at Naxos that could
carry her to Constantinople. If the pigeon from Ayios Ilias had
done its job properly, that ship should not be long in coming.

This business of the ship that was to come for her made
Marianne uneasy. In her view, any vessel would have done as
well, even a Turkish xebec. All she wanted was to get to the
Ottoman capital as soon as possible, since that was the only
place from which to begin her search for the *Sea Witch*. She
did not see at all why it was necessary for her to arrive in a
Greek vessel, unless her mysterious new friends had some
ulterior motive. In which case, what was it?

Melina had told her that there was a Greek merchant fleet,
based on the island of Hydra, which even the Turks would hesitate to attack. The men who manned it were trustworthy, and
strangers to fear. They covered the islands and were able to
drop anchor with impunity off the quays of Phanar, and they
carried, as well as grain, oil and wine, many of the conspirators'
hopes. Hydra had been the pigeon's goal.

In other words, Marianne told herself, they are almost certainly pirates got up as merchants. She was beginning to wonder
if her name was going to be used to cover not just one rebel
with a price on his head, but a whole ship's crew of them. By
this time she was seeing rebels everywhere.

There was, in fact, another passenger who had embarked at
the same time as herself and the alarming Theodoros, and
Marianne was not unduly surprised to see beneath the fisher-

man's cap the face of the tall dark girl who had steadied her on the way back from the rock where Sappho sang her hymn to the setting sun.

Released from his classical draperies, the young guest revealed himself as nature intended: a slim, energetic boy with a keen face, who had smiled at her with cheerful complicity as he handed her into the boat. She now knew that he was a young Cretan called Demetrios whose father had been beheaded a year earlier for refusing to pay a tax, and that he was going now to take up a prearranged position in one of the mysterious places where the rebellion, which no Greek ever doubted would soon come, was slowly ripening to fruition.

The voyage passed off without incident. The sea subsided towards morning and, although as a result the wind abated somewhat, there remained enough of a steady breeze to bring the scaphos, by about midday, into line with the opening of the bay of Naxos. Directly ahead, beyond the dunes covered with long rippling grasses and a species of tall greenish lily, a little town lay glaring white and dozing in the sun, clinging to the sides of a conical hill on whose summit the inevitable Venetian fortress crumbled slowly beneath the disillusioned folds of the Sultan's green flag with its triple crescent.

On a tiny island just outside the harbour the white columns of a small abandoned temple also seemed to droop dispiritedly.

For the first time since they had set sail, Marianne approached Theodoros.

'Are we landing now? I thought we should have waited until nightfall?'

'What for? At this time of day, everyone's asleep – and sleeping much more deeply than at night. It's too hot for anyone to put their nose out of doors. Even the Turks are having a siesta.'

The heat was certainly intense. It was reflected back from the white walls with a ferocity that was almost unbearable and all other colours were bleached into the general all-prevailing whiteness. The air vibrated as though with the humming of invisible bees, and there was not a living soul to be seen on the baking quay. Every house was closely shuttered against the glare, and whenever they did catch sight of a human being it was of someone fast asleep on the ground, back against a wall and cap or turban pulled well down over his eyes, in the shade of a rose trellis or a dark doorway. It was the Sleeping Beauty's island. The entire harbour lay under a spell of sleep and every single creature in it was firmly resting.

The scaphos eased up to her moorings, melting into the multi-coloured mass of masts and hulls: Turkish chektirmes and caiques mingling with the Greek scaphaï and sacolevi. The whole port stank indescribably from the quantities of refuse putrefying in the sun on the surface of the water, and, as they drew nearer to the white town which had looked so glorious in the sunlight from afar, Marianne saw that dirt and neglect reigned everywhere. The splendid white walls were cracked and the grand houses clustered round the citadel at the top of the hill were falling into ruin, almost as certainly as the fortress itself and the white temple collapsing slowly out in the bay.

'Hard to believe that this is the richest island in the Cyclades, isn't it?' Theodoros muttered. 'There are oranges and olives in plenty inland, but they were allowed to grow wild. We will not work for the Turks.'

They went ashore quietly, without attracting any attention. Only a cat, disturbed from its sleep, squawked, spat and then fled to find a more peaceful spot. Marianne, in her black cloak, and Theodoros, in his blanket, were both sweating profusely, scarcely able to breathe for the heat. But they did not have to endure it long. A few steps over the scorching hot stones brought them to a white house in fair condition with an arched doorway overshadowed by a dusty vine. This was the house of Yorgo's cousin Athanasius.

He was not at home. The newcomers found only an old woman muffled in black draperies, who poked a wrinkled face cautiously through the minute crack which she let appear in the door before starting to shut it in their faces. Yorgo began to argue with her in a rapid, breathless dialect but the old woman behind the door only shook her head and stood her ground. It was obvious that she wanted nothing to do with them. Thereupon, Theodoros pushed past Yorgo and advanced on the door. It yielded to a thrust of his hand and the old woman fled to the end of the passage, squeaking like a frightened mouse.

'I don't know whether or not we were expected,' Marianne said quietly, 'but I don't think we are very welcome.'

'We shall be,' the giant assured her.

He strode down the passage and spoke a very few words in rough, commanding tones. The effect was magical.

The old woman came back, looking as delighted as a condemned sinner reprieved from hell to heaven, and before Marianne's astonished gaze she knelt and kissed Theodoros' great hand with fanatical respect. He pulled her, none too gently, to her feet, whereupon she launched into a spate of voluble explanations and, opening a door, ushered her visitors into a low, cool room smelling strongly of sour milk and aniseed. Then she vanished in a swirl of black cotton petticoats, having first set on the rough wooden table a bottle, some wine cups and a dewy water-jar, as fresh as if it had that moment come from the well.

'She is Athanasius' mother,' Theodoros remarked. 'She's gone to fetch her son to take us to the Venetian.'

He poured water neatly into one of the cups and offered it to Marianne. Then, throwing back his head, he let the water flow in a cool stream from the jar straight down his throat.

Yorgo had prudently returned to his boat. Thieves might not be deterred even by the sacred siesta hour and he had his cargo of wine to think of.

Young Demetrios had gone with him and, for the moment, Marianne and her supposed servant were alone, he leaning up against the small barred window, she seated on a stone bench, whose hardness was not greatly lessened by a thin cushion stuffed with dry grass. She was fighting off sleep. She had slept little on the boat, kept uneasily wakeful by the heavy seas running the night before. Nor were her spirits particularly high. It might have been because she was tired and lonely, but she came to fancy that she was doomed to wander, like Ulysses on his way home from the Trojan Wars, from island to island amid people who were strangers to her and events that were foreign to her way of life. The east, which she had pictured to herself in the glowing colours of a honeymoon, now seemed arid and inhospitable. She longed again for her garden, where the roses must just now be at the height of their beauty. Where now was the scent that used to mingle so gloriously with the honeysuckle on summer evenings?

The old woman's return broke into this melancholy train of thought just as she was beginning to reflect miserably that as things stood she could not even ask to be taken to Athens and put on the first ship back to France. Quite apart from the trouble she might expect from Napoleon if she returned with her mission unfulfilled, she was now saddled with this great fellow to drag about with her, and he was watching her as closely as a good housewife watched a pan of milk over the fire!

The man now accompanying the old woman did a good deal to reconcile her to existence. Athanasius was a tubby, smooth-skinned little man with the face of a cherub under a cluster of grey curls, and the pleasantly rounded figure of the verger of a Norman cathedral. He welcomed the enormous, ragged Theodoros like a long lost brother, and the dirty, dishevelled gipsy that was Marianne like the Queen of Sheba in person.

'My master,' he announced, bowing as low as his stomach would permit, 'is eager to offer your most serene highness the hospitality of his palace. He begs you to forgive him for not coming himself to greet you, on account of his great age and rheumatism.'

Her most serene highness thanked Count Sommaripa's steward, thinking meanwhile that she must be giving the poor man a very strange idea of grand Franco–Italian ladies in general. At present she would look distinctly out of place in a nobleman's residence. All the same, she could not help looking forward to a temporary return to the comforts and luxuries of an aristocratic household, and it was with a lighter step that she set out with the obliging Athanasius for this promised paradise, Theodoros following at her heels.

They passed through a maze of steep cobbled alleys, where the big round stones were painful to the feet, through strange medieval streets, tortuous and evil-smelling, and by vaulted passages that offered a brief, welcome coolness, until at last they reached the summit of the hill and the Venetian quarter built round the citadel and the ancient ramparts. Here there were indeed some western religious houses, showing the Roman cross : the Brothers of Mercy side by side with the Ursulines, together with an austere cathedral that seemed oddly out of place, and one or two noble façades that still displayed some dim reflection of the former glories of the dukes of Naxos and the Venetian court. The once-lordly houses with their crumbling armorial bearings seemed to crowd up against the ramparts as though in search of some last reserves of strength, but as she crossed the worn threshold of the Sommaripa palace, with its Latin inscription, Marianne realized that the worthy Athanasius' notions of what a real palace ought to be were not so very well-formed either.

This was only the ghost of a palace, an empty shell where echoes lived and, by amplifying the smallest sound, attempted to bring back some semblance of life to the place. Marianne stifled a regretful sigh : it was not here that she would find the comforts of civilization.

An old man appeared in the doorway of a huge empty room which was furnished only with stone benches and a vast cedar-wood table, with a red geranium spilling out of a round earthenware pot on the sill of a dear little arched window. He should, she felt, be the familiar spirit of this timeless place. He was a tall, blanched individual with a vacant gaze, and his flowing garments looked for all the world as if they had been woven out of the cobwebs hanging from the ceiling. He was so pale that he might have lived for years in a cavern underground, away from light and air. He must have lived long in the shadow of these ancient stones, turning his back on reality. He could never have felt the touch of the sun or the sea winds.

He, too, seemed unconscious of Marianne's appearance. He bowed over her hand with all the dignity of a Spanish grandee receiving an infanta, assuring her of the honour done to his house, and proffering a hand as knotty and wrinkled as an olive kernel to lead her to the apartment set aside for her.

It might be the siesta hour, but the passage of two ragged strangers through the streets of Naxos had not gone unobserved by the Turkish watch, and the Count was just leading Marianne towards the uneven stone staircase when a dozen soldiers in red leather boots and red and blue striped turbans marched into the porch. Commanding them was an odabassy wearing a kind of white felt mitre with a green crown. His rank corresponded roughly to that of artillery captain, but he also had authority over the inns on the island. The new arrivals seemed to interest him.

He was waving a fly-whisk, languidly, and his evident bad temper betrayed clearly enough the irritation he felt at having been dragged out of the cool shade of the fortress just when the afternoon was at its hottest. It showed, too, in the tone he used to address Count Sommaripa, which was that of a master to a disobedient servant.

Possibly because there was a woman present, and a foreign woman at that, the old man appeared to rouse himself. He gave a round answer to the odabassy's contemptuous speech and, although Marianne did not understand a word of the Ottoman language, she was still able to grasp the gist of what was being said. She heard her own name mentioned several times, and the name of Nakshidil Sultan, and gathered that the Count was informing the Turkish officer, with some hauteur, of the identity of the unfortunate traveller and the importance of leaving her in peace.

The odabassy showed no disposition to persist. His sneer was transformed into a smile and he bowed to his Empress's cousin as agreeably as he knew how, before departing with his troop.

The rebel, Theodoros, had remained standing rigidly, three steps behind his supposed mistress, while all this perilous explanation was going on. In all that time, he had not flinched, but judging from the long breath he let out as they turned back to the staircase at last, Marianne guessed that he had suffered a nasty moment, and smiled to herself, thinking that, for all his great size, the mighty warrior was only human after all and subject to the same anxieties as ordinary men.

The room to which the old Count led Marianne could not have been in use since the days of the last dukes of Naxos. A bed that could have sheltered an entire family behind its curtains of faded brocade reigned in splendid isolation between four walls proudly adorned with tattered and rust-spotted banners, while a selection of broken stools huddled together in the corners of the room. But there was a magnificent mullioned window with a view of the sea.

'We were not prepared for such an honour,' the old Count was saying apologetically. 'But your servant shall bring you what you need and we will send to the Mother Superior of the Ursuline convent for a suitable gown – since our own size is somewhat different . . .'

The use of the plural form was bizarre but no more so than the rest of the Count's person or his rather toneless voice and Marianne did not dwell on it.

'I should be most grateful for the dress, my lord Count,' she said, smiling, 'but for the rest, I beg you will not put yourself out. I am sure that we shall have no difficulty in finding a ship—'

The old man's curiously vacant gaze seemed to light up at the word.

'The larger vessels do not often call here. We live in a forgotten land, madame, a land passed over by the hubbub and the glory and the recollections of the great ones of the earth. It is enough to keep us alive, fortunately, but you may find that your stay is longer than you imagine. Come with me, my friend.'

The last words were addressed to Theodoros, who had already been drawn to the window, as though to a lover, and was gazing out hungrily at the empty sea. He dragged himself away unwillingly and followed the Count, as befitted his role of the perfect servant. He returned in a short while with Athanasius, the two of them carrying a heavy table which they placed in the window. This was followed by a variety of toilet articles and linen, slightly but not impossibly worn.

While he busied himself making the room more or less habitable, Athanasius chatted away, thoroughly enjoying the sight of new faces and the opportunity of having a foreign lady to serve, but the more expansive he became, the more Theodoros withdrew into his shell.

'Almighty God!' he cried at last, when the little man urged

him to come and help in making up the bed, 'we are only staying a few hours, brother! One would think from the way you are going on we were to stay for months! Our brother Tombazis in Hydra should have got the pigeon and the ship may come at any moment now.'

'Even if your ship were to appear at this minute,' Athanasius responded peaceably, 'it would still be advisable for madame to play her part – you and she have been shipwrecked. You must be tired, exhausted. You need at least one night's sleep. The Turks would not understand it if you flung yourselves on board the first vessel, without so much as pausing for breath. Odabassy Mahmoud is stupid – but not as stupid as that! Besides, it makes my master happy. Madame the Princess's coming here is to him a reminder of his youth. He has travelled in the west, you know, long ago, and visited the doge's court in Venice and the king of France.'

Theodoros gave a disgusted shrug.

'He must have been rich then! He doesn't seem to have much left.'

'More than you might think,' said Athanasius with a smile, 'but it is not good to tempt the enemy's greed. The master has known that for a long time. Indeed, it is the only thing he does remember clearly. And now,' he finished, beaming at Marianne, 'I am going to the Ursulines for a gown. It would be best if you came with me. No servant worthy of the name would remain with his mistress when she desires to rest.'

But the giant's patience was evidently at an end. With a furious gesture he flung the faded silk counterpane, which he had just taken off the bed, across the room.

'I was not made for this!' he shouted. 'I'm a klepht! Not a lackey!'

'If you shout like that,' Marianne observed coolly, 'every soul in the place will soon know it. You not only agreed to play the part – you actually asked for it. Personally, I should be very glad to part with you. You are a thorough nuisance!'

Theodoros glared at her from under his bushy brows, like a dog about to bite. She expected for a moment to see him bare his teeth, but he only growled:

'I have a duty to my country.'

'Then do it quietly. Did you notice the motto carved over the entrance as we came in? *Sustine vel Abstine*.'

'I don't know Latin.'

'Roughly speaking, it means: Stay the course or stay out. It's what I have been doing myself and I'd advise you to do the same. You are forever grumbling. Well, fate's not a matter of choice; it's something you put up with. Think yourself lucky if it offers you something worth fighting for.'

Theodoros flushed darkly and his eyes flashed.

'I've known that long enough,' he boomed, 'and no woman is going to teach me how to act!'

Under the shocked gaze of Athanasius, who clearly could not believe that anyone could be so rude to a lady, he rushed from the room, slamming the door thunderously behind him. The little steward shook his head and made his own way to the door but, before going out, he turned and bowed and there was a smile in his eyes.

'Your highness will agree with me that servants nowadays are not what they were.'

Marianne had been half afraid that Athanasius would come back with a monkish habit, but when he returned he brought a cloth-wrapped package, with the compliments of the Mother Superior, containing a pretty Greek dress made of a natural woven stuff embroidered in multicoloured silks by the nuns. With it, there was a kind of shawl to go over the head, and several pairs of sandals of various sizes.

It was all very different from Leroy's elegant creations, packed away in Marianne's trunks and now sailing somewhere in the hold of the American brig, destined to be sold for the benefit of John Leighton, along with the ancestral jewels of the Sant'-Annas, but by the time she was washed, brushed and dressed, Marianne felt much more like her real self.

Furthermore, she felt almost well. The sickness which had made her suffer so horribly on board the *Sea Witch* had virtually disappeared and, but for the pangs of hunger which consumed her almost incessantly, she might almost have been able to forget that she was expecting a child and that time was not on her side. For, unless she got rid of it very soon, it would soon become impossible to do so without grave risk to her own life.

The room was afire with the glow of the setting sun. Down below, the harbour had come to life again. Boats were putting out for the night's fishing, and others returning, their decks armoured in shining scales. But they were all only fishing boats. There was no 'great ship worthy to carry an ambassadress', and as she leaned on the stone mullion, Marianne was conscious of a growing impatience, like that which devoured Theodoros. Him she had not set eyes on since his tempestuous exit a little while before, and she guessed that he was down by the waterfront, mingling with the people of the island — the island on which Theseus had abandoned Ariadne — scanning the horizon for the masts and yards of a big merchant vessel.

Would it ever come, this ship which a white pigeon had sped away to summon for her, to carry her to that almost legendary city where waited the golden-haired Sultana, on whom, unconsciously, she had begun to fasten all her hopes?

A hundred times over, since her reawakening to life and awareness in Melina's house, Marianne had told herself what she would do when she got there. She would go at once to the embassy and see Comte de Latour-Maubourg, and through him obtain an audience with the Sultana. Failing that, she would, if necessary, batter down the doors to carry her complaint to someone with the decency and power to scour the Mediterranean for the pirate's brig. The people of the Barbary coast were, she knew, great seamen; their swift-sailing xebecs and their means of communication were almost as efficient as anything possessed by Napoleon's highly-valued Monsieur Chappe. If they acted quickly, Leighton might find himself arrested off any port on the Mediterranean coast of Africa, hemmed in by a pack of hunters who would make him sorry he was ever born, while his unwilling passengers might yet be saved — if only there was still time.

Marianne's eyes grew moist at the remembrance of Arcadius, Agathe and Gracchus. She could not think of them without a deep sense of loss. She had never realized, when they were with her every day, how fond of them she had become. As for Jason, whenever he came into her mind – which was all too often – she exerted every ounce of will-power she possessed to drive him out again. How could she think of him without giving way to grief and despair, with all the torments of regret tearing at her heart? She no longer blamed him for his cruelty to her, or for the hurt that he had done her, admitting loyally that she had brought it on herself. If she had only trusted him more, if she had not been so terribly afraid of losing his love, if she had dared to tell him the truth about her abduction from Florence, if only – if only she had just a little bit more courage! If 'ifs' and 'ans' were pots and pans . . .

She ran her slender fingers caressingly over the warm stone, as though it could bring her some comfort. It must have seen so much, this old house with its austere device proclaiming the acceptance of suffering. How many times must the setting sun, going down flaming into a sea splashed all over with its golden spume, have shone on this same window; on what faces, what smiles and what tears? The solitude about her was peopled suddenly with faceless shadows, with insubstantial forms wreathing in the amber dust raised by the evening breeze, as though to comfort her. The departed voices of all the women who had lived, loved and suffered between those venerable walls whose glory had now crumbled into ashes whispered to her that this was not the end, here in an ancient palace perched like a melancholy heron on the rim of an island, a palace which had wakened for a moment but would soon fall back into the nothingness of sleep.

For her there were days yet to come when Love might have its say.

'Love? Who was the first to call it Love? Better to have named it Agony . . .'

Marianne remembered hearing those lines somewhere once and they had made her smile. That was a long time ago, in the first flush of her seventeen years, when she had thought herself in love with Francis Cranmere. Whose were they? Her memory, usually so reliable, failed that night to give her the answer, but it was someone who knew . . .

'If your highness would be good enough to step downstairs, his lordship will do himself the honour of dining with you.'

Athanasius had not spoken loudly but Marianne started as though at the sound of the Last Trump. Brought abruptly back to earth, she smiled at him vaguely.

'I'll come . . . I'll come at once.'

She left the room, while Athanasius remained to close the window and shut out demoralizing fantasies behind thick wooden shutters. He caught up with her at the head of the stairs, when her hand was already poised on the white marble balusters polished by years of contact with innumerable human hands.

'If I may warn your highness, do not be surprised at anything you may see or hear during dinner,' he murmured. 'The Count is very old and it is long now since anyone came here. He is sensible of the honour done him tonight but – but he lives with his memories. He has done so for so long now that – that they are to some extent a part of himself. They are with him always. Your highness may have noticed his use of the plural form . . . I don't know if I make myself clear . . .'

'You need not worry, Athanasius,' Marianne said gently. 'Nowadays I am not easily surprised.'

'But your highness is so young—'

'Young? Yes . . . perhaps. But older than I look, I daresay. Don't worry. I shan't hurt your old master – or drive away his familiar spirits.'

Yet, for all that, the meal left her with a curious feeling of unreality. This was due not so much to the old-fashioned suit of green satin which her host had donned in her honour, and which he must have worn long before at the doge's court in Venice, as to the fact that he spoke hardly a word to her.

He greeted her gravely at the door of a large room where suits of rusty armour stood guard round the walls beneath the flaking frescoes, and led her down the whole length of an endless table set with old silver, to a seat placed on the right hand of the chair of state at its head, where he took his own place.

Another place was set at the foot of the table, before a chair identical to that of the master of the house. Only there a half-opened fan of painted silk and mother of pearl lay on the plate of old blue Rhodian ware, and beside it a rose in a crystal vase.

Throughout the meal, it was to the invisible mistress of the house rather than to his youthful neighbour that the old gentleman addressed his remarks. Occasionally he would turn to Marianne, exerting himself to conduct the conversation as if it were actually being directed and initiated by the ghostly countess, and he gave to it a turn of delicate and outmoded gallantry that brought tears to his young guest's eyes. She was overcome with emotion at the sight of a love so faithful that it could transcend the grave and recreate the loved one's presence with this touching persistence.

She learned that the countess's name was Fiorenza, and so strong was her husband's evocation of her presence that he almost made it seem an objective reality. Twice Marianne thought she saw the silken fan quiver delicately.

Now and then she let her eyes wander past the crested back of her host's chair to meet those of Athanasius, standing there in his everyday black suit with the addition of a pair of white gloves. She was not much surprised to note that they seemed abnormally bright.

The food was good and plentiful but in spite of the appalling hunger that was always with her these days, reminding her very much of Adelaide's, Marianne could not do justice to the meal. She nibbled a little, forcing herself to maintain her part in the ghostly conversation and uttering anguished mental prayer that it would soon be over.

When the Count rose at last and, bowing, offered her his arm, it was all she could do not to sigh aloud with relief. She allowed him to lead her back to the door, suppressing a crazy urge to break into a run, and even went so far as to smile and curtsey to the empty chair.

Athanasius followed three paces behind them, bearing a torch.

At the door, she begged the Count not to accompany her further, insisting that she had no wish to disturb his evening, and it wrung her heart to see how he brightened and hurried back into the dining-room. As the door shut behind him, she turned to the steward who was looking at her absently.

'You did right to warn me, Athanasius. It's frightening! Poor man!'

'Your highness must not pity him. He is happy so. For many, many evenings, now, he will talk of your highness's visit, with the Countess Fiorenza. To him, she is still living. He sees her come and go, take her seat facing him at table and sometimes, in the winter, he will play for her on the harpsichord that he had brought here once, at great expense, from a town called Ratisbon in Germany, for she loved music.'

'Was it long ago she died?'

'Oh, she is not dead, or if she is now, we shall never know. She left here, twenty years ago with the Ottoman governor of the island, who had seduced her. If she still lives, it must be in a harem somewhere . . .'

'She ran away with a Turk?' Marianne gasped with amazement. 'Was she mad? Your master seems such a good man, so gentle . . . and he must have been quite handsome at that time . . .'

Athanasius made a little movement of his shoulders which precisely expressed his opinion of the logic of the female mind, and confined himself to a vaguely apologetic statement which excused nothing:

'Mad, no. She was only a pretty, feather-headed woman for whom life here was not very amusing.'

'I daresay she must have found it infinitely more amusing in a harem,' Marianne said with sarcasm.

'Bah! The Turks are not such fools. There are plenty of women who were made for that kind of life. And there are others who cannot bear to be put on a pedestal. It makes them lonely and afraid. Our countess belonged to both kinds at once. She adored luxury and idleness and sweetmeats, and thought her husband a poor kind of man because he loved her too much. It was after she left that something went wrong with him. He's never accepted the fact that she's gone away, and he has gone on living with the memory of her as if nothing had happened. And what with wanting so much to see her, I think in the end he really came to it, and now he's reached a kind of happiness that's greater, maybe, than he would have had if she'd stayed with him, because the years have not changed the thing he loves ... But I'm boring you. Your highness must wish to retire.'

'You aren't boring me, and I'm not tired. Only a little upset. Tell me, where is Theodoros? I haven't seen him.'

'At my house. Since he can't tear himself away from the harbour, I thought best to send him there. My mother will look after him. But if you require his services ...'

'No, thank you,' Marianne said, smiling. 'I think I can manage without the services of Theodoros. Let us go up, if you please.'

The first thing she noticed on entering her bedchamber was a small tray placed near her bed, on which was bread and cheese and fruit.

'I thought,' said Athanasius, 'that madame might not have much appetite for dinner, but that perhaps a little something during the night ... ?'

This time Marianne went straight up to him and, taking his plump hand in both of hers, shook it warmly.

'Athanasius,' she said, 'if you weren't about the only thing your master has left to him, I'd ask you to come with me. A man-servant like you is a gift from heaven!'

'I love my master, that is all ... I am sure your highness has the capacity to arouse a devotion as great, or greater than mine. May I wish your highness a good night – and no regrets.'

The night might well have proved every bit as good as the worthy man had hoped, if only it had been allowed to run its proper course. But Marianne was still in her first sleep when she was shaken vigorously awake by a rough hand on her shoulder.

'Hurry! Get up!' said Theodoros' hurried voice. 'The ship is here!'

Marianne peered through half-open eyes at the big man's face, tense in the wavering light of a candle.

'What?' she asked, sleepily.

'You must get up, I tell you. The ship is here and waiting! Get up!'

By way of extra encouragement to her to hurry out of bed, he laid hold of the covers and flung them back, discovering what had evidently been the last thing he had thought of in his haste :

a female form clad only in a tumbled mass of dark hair and touched to warm gold by the candlelight. He stood literally rooted to the spot while Marianne, wide awake now, flung herself on the sheet with a howl of rage.

'How dare you! Are you mad?'

He stirred with difficulty and passed a shaking hand over his bearded chin, but his eyes still stared at the place in the now empty bed where the girl's body had lain an instant before.

'I'm sorry . . .' he managed to say at last. 'I did not know – I didn't think—'

'I'm not interested in what you thought. I gather you have come in search of me? Well, what is all this about? Are we leaving now?'

'Yes – at once. The ship is waiting. Athanasius came to tell me.'

'This is ridiculous! It's the middle of the night! What time is it?'

'Midnight, I think – a little after.'

He was still standing in the same place, speaking like a man in a dream. From her refuge behind the bedcurtains, Marianne watched him uneasily. He seemed to have forgotten his haste. Almost he seemed to have forgotten why he had come there, but there was a softness about that ferocious countenance which Marianne had never seen there before. Theodoros was in the process of succumbing to a kind of witchcraft that must be dispelled at once.

Without quitting her refuge, she reached out towards a small brass bell that Athanasius had left with her in case she should need anything in the night, but she was still reluctant to wake the echoes of the sleeping house.

'Go back to bed,' she advised. 'It is an excellent thing that the boat has come, but we can hardly leave like this, without telling anyone.'

Before the Greek could answer, even supposing that he was going to, Athanasius crept softly round the half-open door. He took in the scene before him at a glance. It was certainly an unusual one: the Princess huddled behind the bed curtains with only her head and her bare shoulders showing, and Theodoros staring at the bed as though about to fall into it.

'Well?' Athanasius said in a reproachful whisper. 'What are you doing? Time is short.'

'Then it's true what this man says?' Marianne asked, not moving. 'We are leaving now?'

'Yes, madame, and you must do so quickly if you would avoid serious trouble. The risk we run here, with the Turks, is nothing compared to it. The master of the polacca sent from Hydra has heard that three vessels belonging to the Kouloughis brothers, renegade pirates, are on a course for Naxos. If they sight the island before you have left it there is a good chance that you will never reach Constantinople but end up in Tunis, where the Kouloughis' sell their slaves.'

'Sla—! I'm coming! Only get Theodoros out of here so that I can get dressed. He seems to have been turned into a pillar of salt!'

There were some words capable of making Marianne rise above herself, and slavery was one of them. When Athanasius had dragged Theodoros bodily out of the room, she dressed herself hurriedly and joined the others on the dark landing outside the bedroom. By the time she appeared, carrying the candle, Theodoros seemed to have recovered his wits. He threw her a smouldering glance, suggesting that it would be a good while before he forgave her for being the cause of his moment of weakness, or what he regarded as such.

Athanasius, however, smiled encouragingly and took her hand to help her down the stairs.

'I don't like leaving like this,' Marianne objected. 'So furtively, like a thief! What will the Count say?'

The little servant's eyes met hers above the candle flame.

'Why, nothing. What can he say, other than "very good" or "an excellent notion", when I tell him your highness has gone to explore the island in the company of the Countess Fiorenza? It is as simple as that.'

Guided by Athanasius, who seemed to have cat's eyes, Marianne and Theodoros made their way down through the maze of narrow streets leading to the harbour. When they reached the waterfront, they went on, making for the side nearest the isle with the ruins of the little temple.

A big three-master with a tapering prow, like a swordfish, was at anchor off the spit of land. Her impressive rigging was an odd mixture of fore and aft and lateen sails. No light was showing on board and she looked like a ghost-ship floating on the calm waters of the harbour.

'The longboat is waiting just here, close by, in front of the chapel of the Knights of Rhodes,' whispered Athanasius.

The nearer they got to the vessel, the sulkier Theodoros seemed to become.

'That's not Miaulis's ship, nor Tombazis',' he growled. 'It's not even a true polacca. Whose is this vessel?'

'It belongs to Tsamados,' Athanasius said, a trifle irritably. 'It is, in fact, a polacca-xebec, his latest prize and very fast, it seems. What difference does it make to you? It's the ship Hydra has sent. Of course, if you don't want to go aboard——'

The giant's big paw came down soothingly on the little steward's shoulder.

'You are quite right, friend, and I apologize. I'm more nervous than I've ever been.' He showed his teeth. 'That's what it is to travel with a woman.'

The ship's longboat was waiting by a short flight of stone steps. Two dark figures loomed up from it: the figures of the two seamen sent to ferry the passengers aboard.

In spite of herself, Marianne could not help tightening her grip on Athanasius' hand. She felt suddenly that all was not well, although she could not have said why. Perhaps it was the dark night and the unknown vessel but she felt that in saying good-bye to her guide she would be leaving her last remaining friend and plunging into a strange and menacing new world. The thought chilled her.

The steward must have sensed her alarm because he whispered to her.

'Do not be afraid, your highness. The men of Hydra are fine, brave fellows. You will have nothing to fear with them. All that remains for me to do is to thank you for visiting us and wish you a safe journey.'

Calmed by those few words, she answered:

'Thank you, Athanasius. Thank you for everything.'

The farewells were brief. With the help of one of the seamen, Marianne slithered and groped her way down the steep steps, expecting every moment to pitch head-first into the harbour. However, she arrived safely in the dipping wooden boat and Theodoros leaped in after her. Someone fended the boat off with a gaff and then they were away, with the oars, wielded by two pairs of powerful arms, dipping soundlessly into the dark water. On the quay, Athanasius' dumpling figure dwindled, and soon even the houses had receded.

Not a word was spoken on the way out to the ship. Theodoros stood in the bows, one foot on the gunwale, clearly burning with impatience to get aboard, and almost before they touched he had swung onto the companion ladder and, swarming up it with an agility almost incredible for one of his giant size, had vanished over the side.

Marianne followed more slowly, but with sufficient ease and agility to need no help from the seamen, and, when she reached the top, strong hands took hold of her to lift her on to the deck. Only then did it suddenly occur to her that something was dreadfully wrong.

Theodoros was there, standing facing a dark, silent knot of men who seemed to her menacing because of their very silence; they reminded her too much of the shadowy figures standing on the deck of the *Sea Witch*, watching without a word as she was lowered into the boat in which Leighton had doomed her to die.

Theodoros was speaking in the Romaic tongue she did not understand, but there was an odd break in his voice, which was that of a man accustomed to command, suggesting that there was fear somewhere, underlying his anger. He was the only person speaking and that in itself was alarming, for not a soul answered him.

The two sailors from the longboat had climbed up after her

and Marianne could feel them close behind her, so close that she could hear them breathing.

Then, without warning, someone uncovered a dark lantern and held it by a face, so that it seemed to spring out of the darkness in the shadow of the mainmast. It was that of a sallow-skinned, strong-featured man, his nose jutting arrogantly above a bristling, horizontal moustache and his eyes hard under the high, deeply-lined forehead. But what was most terrible of all was that the face was laughing, laughing still in silence but with a cruelty that made Marianne shudder.

On Theodoros the apparition of this demonic head had acted like the vision of a gorgon. He uttered one cry of sheer fury and then turned to Marianne a chalk-like countenance on which, for the first time, she could read fear.

'We are betrayed!' he said. 'This ship belongs to the renegade Nicolaos Kouloughis!'

He had no time to say more before the silent crew of pirates seized them and thrust them down into the bowels of the ship.

The last thing Marianne saw, before she was swallowed up by the terrifying black hatchway, was a bright star shining, high up through the ratlines. Then a sail was hoisted suddenly, blotting it out, as a hand might cover a gigantic eye to hide its tears.

Chapter Eleven
Between Scylla and Charybdis

Between decks it was dark and stiflingly hot, with a stench of filth and rancid oil.

From the bottom of the ladder, Marianne had been flung into a corner, without ceremony, while Theodoros was dragged away somewhere else. She had fallen on to something rough that might have been an old sack and had huddled there, not daring to move, half deafened by the row that was going on all round her.

The oppressive silence that had reigned earlier was shattered and, to judge by the din the pirates were making now, the amount of shouting and excited chatter drowning the furious bellowing of their prisoner, it seemed likely that the silence which had struck them on the deck was due in a large measure to sheer astonishment. It was rather as though they had not expected such a prize.

Certainly there was no mistaking one thing : for these men, Theodoros was what mattered and Marianne herself was of very minor interest. She had known as much from the casual way she had been thrown down, like a rather troublesome parcel, but one that might be worth picking up again later, to sell to the highest bidder in the market at Tunis, as Athanasius had warned her.

As she thought of Count Sommaripa's steward, the notion that he might have been responsible for the betrayal Theodoros had spoken of did not so much as cross her mind. Yet he had been the first to sight the polacca, and had been in touch with the crew. Hadn't he said that she belonged to Captain Tsamados? He, again, had been the one to rouse the fugitives and urge them to leave at once, at the risk of his master's being obliged to face some awkward questions from the odabassy. Even so, Marianne simply could not believe in such turpitude on the part of a man who, still, after twenty years, could have tears in his eyes as he watched his master conversing with a ghost.

Possibly the people of Hydra were not as trustworthy as they were thought to be – or, perhaps, after all, it was all nothing but a tragic mistake.

Seeing the great ship come in, Athanasius might quite genuinely have thought her the one they were expecting. The Count himself had told Marianne that sea-going ships rarely put in at Naxos. He could have got in touch with the pirates without having the faintest idea who they were, while they, sensing a profit to be made, would have played their parts well and taken care not to undeceive him. But that was only one possibility among the many churning in the head of their involuntary passenger, and she forced herself not to think of any of them. This was not the moment to ponder whys and wherefores. Now, faced with this new, terrible and wholly unexpected peril, Marianne made herself concentrate her whole mind on the one single idea of escape.

A ray of light fell across the deck and swung round to illuminate the foot of the ladder. The men were on their way back, having stowed their prisoner in a safe place. They were all talking at once, perhaps estimating the profit to be made from Theodoros who, Marianne was now beginning to realize, was a person of considerably more importance than she had imagined, although she did not even know his proper name.

In their midst, as the light from the lantern fell on him, she recognized their chief.

Deciding to strike the first blow, she got up and planted herself at the foot of the ladder, barring the way, and prayed inwardly that the difference of language would not prove an insurmountable obstacle.

It seemed to her that whether or not it would do any good, this was the moment to make use of the French Emperor's name, which appeared to mean something in these barbarous latitudes. It might be only a slender chance, but it was worth

trying. It was therefore in French that she addressed the renegade.

'Don't you think, monsieur, that you owe me some explanation?'

Her clear voice rang out like a clarion. The men fell silent at
once, their eyes on the slim figure in the light-coloured dress
who stood facing them with a pride that could not fail to strike
them, even if they did not understand the meaning of what she
said. As for Nicolaos Kouloughis himself, his eyes narrowed and
he emitted a low whistle that might have been as much admiration as malevolence.

Then, to Marianne's surprise, he answered her, with a vil-
lainous accent, it was true, but nevertheless in the language of
Voltaire.

'Ha! The French lady? I didn't believe it was true.'

'What was not true?'

'This business of a French lady. When we took the carrier
pigeon, I thought it was a cover for something else, more interesting. Otherwise why go to so much trouble for a thing as
trifling as a woman, even a French one? And we were right because we've caught the biggest rebel of them all, the one they
never catch, the one the Grand Signior would give his treasure
for – Theodoros Lagos himself! It's the best prize of my life.
A king's ransom on his head!'

'I may be only a woman,' retorted Marianne, to whom the
name meant nothing at all, 'but my head is not altogether worth-
less. I am the Princess Sant'Anna, a personal friend of the Emperor Napoleon, and his ambassadress to my cousin Nakshidil,
Sultana Haseki of the Ottoman Empire.'

This broadside of impressive titles seemed to make some effect
on the pirate, but only for a moment. Just as Marianne was beginning to think that her gamble had paid, he uttered a strident
shout of laughter, which was instantly echoed in a sycophantic
way by the men around him. The only result of this was to get
them sent back to their work with a few sharp commands.
When they were gone, Kouloughis laughed again.

'I was not aware that I had said anything funny,' Marianne
said frostily. 'I do not imagine that the Emperor, my master,

would appreciate your sense of humour. Nor am I accustomed to be laughed at.'

'Oh, but I'm not mocking, believe me. I admire you! You have a part to play and you're playing it to perfection. You almost took me in.'

'You mean that you do not believe I am who I say I am?'

'No, I don't! If you were an envoy of the great Napoleon, and a friend of his into the bargain, you'd not be roaming the seas dressed as a Greek woman, in the company of a notorious rebel and looking for a ship to carry you to Constantinople for your felonious purposes. You'd be on a fine frigate flying French colours and—'

'I was wrecked,' Marianne said indifferently. 'It happens not infrequently in these waters, as I understand.'

'It happens, as you say, frequently. Especially when the meltemi, our dangerous summer wind, blows, but either there are no survivors – or else rather more than two. Your story won't stand up.'

'Well, believe it or not, that's how it was.'

'I don't believe it.'

Without pausing for breath he went on to address her in Greek, a brief and violent speech of which she naturally understood not one word. She heard him out without a blink and even permitted herself the luxury of a contemptuous smile.

'You are wasting your breath,' she told him. 'I have no idea what you are saying.'

Silence. Nicolaos Kouloughis contemplated the woman before him with a scowl that brought his long nose and jutting chin dangerously close to one another. It was evident that she had disconcerted him. What woman could listen without flinching, even with a smile, to that stream of calculated insult, accompanied as it was by a detailed description of the subtle tortures in store for her to make her speak? It really did look as if this girl had not understood anything of what he had said. However, Kouloughis was not a man to hesitate for long, and he shrugged the doubt away, irritably, like a man getting rid of a tiresome burden.

'Well, you may be a foreigner, after all – that or you have a nerve of iron! Either way it makes no differences. Your friend Theodoros will be handed over to the pasha of Candia, who'll pay well for him. As for you, you look as though you'd be worth keeping until Tunis. The bey might prove generous if you take his fancy. Come, I'll take you where you'll be more comfortable. Damaged goods lose their value.'

He had grasped her by the arm and was dragging her towards the ladder, ignoring her resistance. Not even for the sake of an improvement in her own material surroundings, was she willing to be taken too far away from her companion who, she now found, had acquired a certain value in her eyes. Whatever else he might be, he was a brave man and the victim of the same involuntary betrayal on the part of the little winged messenger. She felt at one with him. But the renegade's sinewy fingers were clamped tightly round her slender arm, giving her as much pain as if they had been made of iron.

As she had feared, it was to the sterncastle that he was taking her. Guessing that he was making for his own quarters, she was preparing to put up an energetic fight, for who could tell whether the pirate would not decide to test his captive personally before putting her on the market? It must happen often enough.

The door he opened and closed carefully behind her was, in fact, that of his own cabin, but the cabin itself was the very opposite of what might have been expected of a Mediterranean pirate. Imagination might have predicted a combination of luxury and untidiness mixed with a kind of oriental squalor.

In fact, with its dark mahogany and brass nautical instruments, the room had the brand of austere and sober elegance that would not have disgraced a British admiral. It was, furthermore, meticulously clean. It was not empty.

As Kouloughis thrust her inside, Marianne beheld a youth reclining on the bunk, amid the purple cushions which provided the single note of colour in the room. His appearance was sufficiently arresting to have attracted the most casual eye. In his way, he was undoubtedly a work of art, but of a somewhat perverse kind.

He was dressed, with calculation, in full trousers of pale blue silk with a kind of matching dolman decorated with immense silken frogs. Thick black curls flowed from under a cap with a long golden tassel, and he stared up languorously out of doe eyes rimmed with kohl and further enlarged by dashing pencil strokes. The rose-bud lips that pouted in a face of milky white-ness also quite clearly owed the better part of their bloom to diligent applications of rouge.

This androgynous creature, undeniably beautiful but with a beauty that was wholly feminine, was occupied in cleaning a statuette of a faun, his long, supple fingers polishing the thing, which was of a quite remarkable obscenity, as lovingly as a mother. Here, presumably, was the fastidious housewife respon-sible for this unexpectedly neat domain.

He showed no sign of being disturbed by Kouloughis' tumul-tuous entry with his captive, but merely raised his exquisitely plucked eyebrows and favoured the girl with a glance that was half-affronted, half made up of sheer distaste. No doubt he would have looked much the same had Kouloughis suddenly thrown a bucketful of slops into his well-ordered world: a new and startling experience for one of the prettiest women in Europe.

The big cabin was well lighted by clusters of perfumed candles. Kouloughis dragged Marianne over to one of these and with a quick movement ripped off the embroidered shawl that covered her head and shaded her eyes. The light shone on the gleaming black mass of her plaited hair, and her green eyes sparkled angrily. She shrank back instinctively from the rene-gade's hand.

'How dare you! What are you doing!'

'Taking a good look at the goods I propose to sell, that's what I'm doing. There's no gainsaying you've a lovely face and your eyes are very fine – but it's hard to tell what may lie under the clothes worn by the women of my country. Open your mouth!'

'What—!'

'I said open your mouth. I want to see your teeth.'

Before Marianne could stop him, he had gripped her face between his hands and forced her jaws apart with a deftness born of long practice. Marianne might rage as she liked at finding herself treated precisely like a horse; she was compelled to endure the mortifying examination which, it seemed, was entirely to the satisfaction of the examiner. But when Kouloughis tried to undo her dress, she sprang away and fled for refuge behind the table in the centre of the cabin.

'Oh, no, you don't!'

The renegade looked vaguely surprised but he only gave a small shrug of annoyance and called:

'Stephanos!'

This was obviously the name of the dainty occupant of the bunk and, no less evidently, Kouloughis was summoning him to help.

Apparently the youth disliked the idea, because he began to shriek alarmingly and wriggled himself further down among his cushions as though defying his master to dislodge him, giving vent to a stream of words, uttered in a shrill tone that grated on Marianne's ears like a rasp, the gist of which was unmistakable: the delicate creature was refusing to sully his hands with anything so repulsive as a woman.

Marianne, who reciprocated his dislike to the full, had a momentary hope that his refusal might earn him a box on the ears, but Kouloughis merely shrugged and smiled, an indulgent smile that sat ill on his face. Then he turned back to Marianne.

Her attention deflected by the little scene, she was not expecting this new attack, but he made no further attempt to open her dress, being content merely to run his hands swiftly over her body, lingering a little over the breasts and acknowledging their firmness with a satisfied grunt. This treatment was not at all to Marianne's liking and she responded by dealing the slave-driver two resounding slaps.

For a brief instant, she tasted the fierce joy of triumph. Kouloughis stood stock still, rubbing his cheek mechanically, while his little friend seemed ready to faint with shock and indignation. But it was only for an instant. A second later, she saw that she would have to pay dearly for her gesture.

The corsair's sallow face seemed to turn dark green before her eyes. The fact that he had suffered this humiliation before the eyes of his minion made him wild with rage and, staring with dilated eyes, he suddenly seemed to her a creature less than human.

Urged on by the boy, who was now screaming excitedly in the nasal whine of a maniac muezzin, Kouloughis seized hold of Marianne and dragged her bodily out of the cabin.

'You'll pay for that, daughter of a bitch!' he snarled. 'I'll show you who's master!'

'He's going to beat me,' was Marianne's terror-stricken thought as she was jerked towards one of the carronades that formed the polacca's armament, 'or worse!'

In a trice she found herself bound to the breech. Two men had covered it first with a tarpaulin but not, it was soon clear, with any idea of sparing her unpleasant contact with the metal.

'The meltemi is coming,' Kouloughis told her. 'We'll have a storm and you shall remain out here on deck until it's over. That may cool your temper. When you're cut loose, you'll have thought better of trying to strike Nicolaos Kouloughis. You'll go down on your knees and lick his boots to spare you further tortures! If you're still conscious!'

It was a fact that an ominous swell was getting up and the ship was beginning to roll. Marianne could feel a queasiness inside that intimated sickness to come, but she forced herself not to blench. She was not going to show this brute that she was ill. He would only think she was afraid. Because of this, she chose to attack instead.

'You're a fool, Nicolaos Kouloughis. You don't know your own interests.'

'My interest is to avenge an insult dealt me in front of one of my men!'

'That? A man? Don't make me laugh! But that's beside the point. You're going to lose a lot of money.'

In no circumstances could anyone utter the word money in Nicolaos Kouloughis's presence without arousing his interest.

'What do you mean?' he said, automatically, disregarding both the fact that only a few moments before he had been on the verge of strangling this woman and the undoubted absurdity of entering into this kind of argument with a prisoner lashed to the breech of a gun.

'It's perfectly simple. You said, didn't you, that you were going to hand Theodoros over to the pasha of Candia and sell me in Tunis?'

'I did.'

'That's why I tell you you are going to lose a lot of money. Do you think the pasha of Candia will pay you as much as the prisoner's worth? He'll try and bargain with you, give you something on account and tell you he needs time to get the rest together ... whereas the Sultan will pay much more, and on the spot, in good solid gold! For me too. If you won't believe who I really am, or listen to reason, you will at least admit I'm worth more than the grubby harem of some Tunisian bey! There isn't a woman in the Grand Signior's harem to match me for beauty,' she declared brazenly.

Her plan was a straightforward one. If she could once get him to alter course for the Bosphorus, instead of taking her off to Africa where she would be lost beyond recall, and the very thought of which appalled her, she knew that this in itself would be something of a victory. The important thing, as she had decided once already in Yorgo's boat, was to get there, no matter how.

She studied the corsair's crafty face anxiously to gauge the effect of her words. She knew that she had touched him on the raw, and very nearly breathed a sigh of relief when he muttered at last:

'You may be right ...' But in a moment the meditative tone had changed to one of anger and resentment. 'But you've deserved your punishment!' he cried. 'And you shall suffer it none the less. When the storm is over you shall know what I have decided – perhaps!'

He went away forward, leaving Marianne alone on the empty deck. Was he going to alter course? Marianne had the feeling suddenly that something was wrong. She had seen how Jason's men had acted during the storm the *Sea Witch* had run into after leaving Venice, and it bore no resemblance to the behaviour of Kouloughis' crew.

The seamen on the brig had taken in all sail, leaving the yards bare of everything but the jib and staysail. The men on the polacca were gathered in the bows in what appeared to be some kind of conference, broken now and then by the roars of their captain. Some, the bravest probably, began taking in the more accessible canvas, without enthusiasm, glancing uneasily at the topsails to see how they were standing up to the weather. No one showed the slightest inclination to brave the perils of the shrouds that were now swinging and lashing with the pitching of the ship.

Marianne, for her part, was feeling increasingly unwell. The ship was tossing now like a cork in boiling water and the ropes binding her were beginning to bite into her flesh. She gasped as a wave broke right over her and ran away, foaming, into the scuppers.

All the same, when Kouloughis staggered past her on his way aft, she could not resist jibing at him:

'A fine lot of seamen you've got! If this is how they behave in a storm . . .'

'They put their trust in God and the saints,' the corsair flung back at her. 'The storm is from heaven; it is for heaven to decide the outcome. All Greeks know that.'

This talk of God was the last thing that might have been expected from a renegade pirate, but Marianne was beginning to form her own idea of the Greeks. They were a strange people, at the same time brave and superstitious, ruthless and generous, and for the most part hopelessly illogical. Consequently she merely raised her eyebrows a little and observed:

'I imagine that is why the Turks find them so easy to defeat. Their method is rather different – but I daresay you must know that, from having decided to serve them.'

'I know. That's why I'm going to take the helm, even if it does no good.'

Marianne was prevented from answering this as another dollop of salt water slapped over her, sweeping the deck from end to end. She was choking for breath, coughing and spluttering to free her lungs. When she could see anything again, she caught sight of Kouloughis gripping the wheel with both hands and glaring wildly at the raging sea. The helmsman was crouched under the lee of a bulwark, clutching his beads.

Daylight had crept up slowly, a grey daylight that revealed a gloomy sea. Like a wanton woman doing penance, it had put off its blue satins for grey rags. The waves were mountainous and the air full of flying spume. For all Kouloughis' efforts at the wheel, the vessel was driving forward blindly on a course known only to herself and perhaps to the Devil, however illogically the pirates might persist in seeing the hand of God in it.

The renegade seemed to regard the prayers of his crew as perfectly normal, and it may have been that he himself was leaving it to the storm to decide the outcome of his private dilemma, whether to continue towards Crete or alter course for Constantinople.

A jib was torn off, its sheets frayed and parted, and sailed away into the murky sky like a drunken bird. It did not seem to occur to anyone to do anything about replacing it; but the clamour of invocations to heaven was redoubled, except when drowned by the spray that came on board or by the howling of the wind. The mastheads were dipping and dancing madly against the clouds.

But soon Marianne was past noticing anything. Soaked to the skin, blinded by spray and deafened by the roar of the water, with the wet ropes tightened cruelly and bruising her flesh, she was discovering that her punishment was worse than anything she had imagined. She longed to lose consciousness but could not, and this rough treatment had at least the advantage of making her forget her sickness. On the other hand, the risk of death by drowning was becoming more real every minute and it was beginning to seem to Marianne that she was bound to die where she was, like a rat in a trap.

The slave-trader may have thought the same, or feared to see his profit slipping through his fingers if he prolonged the ordeal, because when there came a slight lull in the storm he locked the wheel and came slithering down from the poop to cut the ropes that bound her.

It was not before time. Marianne's strength was almost exhausted and he had to put both arms round her to keep her from falling on to the steeply tilting deck as the vessel pitched sharply. Half-carrying and half-dragging her to the hatch, he opened it and lowered her down, letting in a fair amount of water at the same time.

The foetid atmosphere of between-decks and the overpowering stench that filled the place succeeded where the onslaughts of the sea had failed, and Marianne was violently sick. The spasms of retching were painful and prolonged, but when it was over she felt better. She groped her way in the semi-darkness to the sacks where she had lain before and stretched herself out on them.

What with the water that had entered below decks and her own sopping wet dress, the sacks were soon in a fair way to being as wet as the deck above, but Marianne told herself that she must bear her troubles patiently. As least she was no longer cold : in fact it was as hot as an oven down there.

Gradually she came to herself again, assisted by a grinding headache. In that enclosed space the sound of the sea against the hull was like the banging of a drum and it was a little while before she realized that not all the thuds that seemed to go right through her head were made by the storm. At the other end of the deck, someone was knocking.

Suddenly she remembered Theodoros and began to make her way awkwardly, more often than not on all fours because of the rolling of the ship, towards the place from which the knocking seemed to come. There was a door made out of great baulks of timber loosely nailed together, but it was fastened by a massive lock.

Marianne put her ear anxiously to the door, clinging as best she could. After a moment, the sound came again and she felt the door shake under her hands.

'Theodoros!' she called. 'Are you there?'

She was answered by an angry voice that seemed to recede slightly as the vessel climbed, hurling her forward against the door.

'Of course I'm here! The dogs have bound me so tightly that I can't hold on! Every time this misbegotten hulk rolls I'm flung up against this damned bulkhead! If it doesn't stop soon I'll be smashed to pulp!'

'If only I knew how to open the door ... but there's simply nothing here that I can use.'

'What? You're free to move about?'

'Yes ...'

In a few words, Marianne told her companion all that had passed between her and the corsair. Once, she heard him laugh, but his laughter ended in a curse as once again the bulkhead shuddered under the impact of its involuntary human battering ram. Yet it seemed that the collision had been lighter.

'Seems to be easing off a bit,' Theodoros commented after a moment. 'But take a thorough look around the place you're in. There may be something lying about that I could use to free myself. There's room to slip a piece of metal, or a blade or something under the door.'

'My poor friend, I'll do my best, but I'm afraid you're going to be disappointed.'

She was still on her knees, embarking on a detailed exploration of her dimly-lit quarters, when the Greek's voice reached her again.

'Princess!'

'Yes, Theodoros?' It was the first time he had called her that, and it surprised her a little. Up to then, he had not found it necessary to call her anything at all.

'I just want to say ... I'm sorry for the way I've treated you. You're a brave woman ... and a good comrade! If we get out of this ... I'd like to be friends. Will you?'

In spite of the hopelessness of their position, Marianne found herself smiling and a little rush of warmth made her heart beat faster and buoyed up her courage. The manly offer of friendship, a friendship which she knew would not fail her, was the very thing she needed most. From that moment, she felt that she was no longer alone and, unexpectedly, she wanted to cry.

'Yes, Theodoros, I will,' she said, with a catch in her voice. 'I can't think of anything I'd like better.'

'Now then, courage! You sound as if you would burst into tears! ... We'll get out of this, you wait and see.'

A thorough, if uncomfortable, search of the space between

decks yielded nothing, and Marianne returned disconsolately to tell Theodoros that she had failed.

'Never mind,' he sighed. 'We'll just have to wait. Something may turn up. These dogs will have to give us something to eat when the storm dies down. We'll think again then. Meanwhile, you'd better try and get some rest. See if you can wedge yourself into a corner and sleep.'

Marianne did her best but it was not easy. However, as the storm died away, she did manage to doze off.

By evening both wind and sea had subsided. The deck on which she lay was once more reasonably horizontal and she had a moment's peace.

There was not a sound to be heard from the other side of the door and she thought that Theodoros must be asleep. It was now pitch dark between decks. Light was no longer penetrating through the deadlights. The air had grown colder, though, and dank.

Marianne was just wondering if they were not going to be forgotten altogether until the ship reached Candia, or wherever else it was bound, for she now had no means of knowing, when someone opened the hatch.

In the light of a lantern, a pair of legs clad in sea boots and canvas trousers appeared, surrounded by swirling vapour. Outside, the storm had been succeeded by a mist, long trails of which came creeping down the steps like ghostly tentacles.

Marianne, lying stretched out on the deck not far from the steps, did not move. She remained lying in the attitude of a woman in the last stages of exhaustion, hoping that the new arrival would disregard her and so enable her to watch what he was going to do, especially if he went anywhere near Theodoros.

As it turned out, he was carrying two earthenware jugs and two lumps of some dark substance which was probably bread. Kouloughis, it appeared, did not believe in feeding his prisoners too delicately. But behind the seaman, Marianne saw through half-closed eyes, another pair of legs descending, and these were enveloped in the ample folds of a pair of silken trousers which seemed oddly familiar.

What was the fair Stephanos doing between-decks, she wondered?

She did not have to wonder long. While the sailor's heavy tread receded in the direction of the door at the far end, the light footfalls of his companion stopped quite close to the ladder. Without warning, he delivered a vicious kick between the girl's ribs. She let out a low cry and opened her eyes, to see him standing over her, foot poised for another blow. He was stroking the blade of a long, curved knife and he smiled, a smile at once so stupid and so cruel that Marianne's blood froze. His eyes stared at her, the pupils shrunk to minute black specks no bigger than a pin. He had come, so far as she could tell, to deal with a creature he considered abject but possibly dangerous in the way he felt that she deserved.

She did not pause to think. She simply gathered herself, as though shrinking from the second blow, and then sprang, panther-like, for his throat. The movement, half-instinctive reflex, half sheer hate, was irresistible. The youth was taken wholly by surprise. He tried to draw back, bumped into the steps and fell. Instantly, she was on him, grasped his head in both hands and banged it against the ladder with such deadly effectiveness that her exquisite adversary was very soon unconscious.

Marianne seized the dagger as it slipped from his hand and clutched it to her with an extraordinary feeling of triumph and power. Her reflex had been due much more to the sight of the weapon than to the kick. Turning to look along the deck, she saw the seaman had hauled open the protesting door and was about to go inside.

It had all happened so quickly that he had heard nothing, beyond the sound of the fall which had evidently not alarmed him. In a flash, Marianne knew that the door must not be allowed to close again.

Gripping the knife in her hand, she ran towards the opening, which showed clear in the light of the lantern. The man was tall and strong, and he was already bending to enter when, with the speed of lightning, she leaped for his back and struck home.

The sailor made a gurgling sound and dropped like a stone beside the lantern, carrying Marianne with him.

Staggered at what she had done, she got to her feet and stood staring dazedly at the bloodstains on the knife. She had just killed a man, with no more hesitation than on the night she had brained Ivy St Albans with a candlestick, after wounding Francis Cranmere in a duel, leaving him, too, as she had then believed, for dead.

'The third time . . .' she muttered to herself. 'The third . . .'

She was roused from her stupor by the voice of Theodoros, torn between delight and admiration.

'Magnificent, Princess! You're a real amazon! Now cut me loose, and hurry! There's no time to waste. Someone may come.'

Mechanically, she bent to pick up the lantern and by its light saw the giant lying flat on the deck, trussed like a chicken. For all the bruises on his face, which showed what he had endured, and the stubble beard, his eyes were frankly hilarious. Marianne dropped on her knees beside him and set about cutting the ropes that bound him. They were stout and thick but she worked with such a will that it was not long before the first one yielded. After that, it was easy and in a few seconds more, Theodoros was free.

'By God, that's better!' he sighed, stretching his long legs to ease their stiffness. 'Now, let's see if we can get out of here . . . Can you swim?'

'Yes.'

'You really are a remarkable creature. Come on.'

Thrusting the dagger into his belt, regardless of the blood which stained it, Theodoros led Marianne out of the cell, taking care to shut the door behind them with the dead man inside. As he turned round, his eye was caught by the recumbent figure of Stephanos, making a light-coloured blue at the foot of the steps, and he eyed his companion in some amazement.

'Have you killed him, too?'

'No – at least, I don't think so. I only stunned him. It was from him I got the knife . . . He was kicking me . . . I think he meant to kill me.'

'Good lord, you don't have to apologize! You ought to be congratulated! Your only mistake was in not killing him . . . but it's a mistake that can soon be remedied.'

'No, Theodoros! Don't kill him! He's – he's – well, I think the captain is fond of him. If we don't manage to escape, he would certainly kill us without mercy . . .'

The Greek began to laugh silently.

'Aha! It's the beautiful Stephanos?'

'Do you know him?'

Theodoros lifted his shoulders in amused contempt.

'Kouloughis and his fancies are common knowledge all through the islands. But you're right when you say he cares for the little scum. It makes a difference, certainly.'

He was just bending over the inert form, to lift it up, when there was a terrible crash. The vessel shuddered through all her length, and a gaping hole appeared in the hull.

'We've struck!' roared Theodoros. 'A reef, probably. This is our chance!'

A veritable chorus of shouts had broken out above their heads and the ship struck again. There was water coming in. With a strong heave, Theodoros hoisted Stephanos over his shoulder as if he had been a sack of flour, letting his head fall forward on to his chest so that the boy's throat was within reach of the curved blade he had taken from his belt. It was clear that his idea was to force a passage through the pirates by threatening to kill Nicolaos' favourite.

Marianne crawled up the steps after him and peered out. The deck was shrouded in mist through which could be seen the ghostly figures of seamen running to and fro, shouting and waving. No one had any eyes for them.

The clamour was deafening. Theodoros crossed himself, backwards in the Orthodox fashion, with the hand that held the dagger.

'Holy Mother of God!' he breathed. 'It's not a reef. It's another vessel.'

Towering above the polacca's starboard side, visible in the smoky glare of the lanterns burning here and there on the Greek vessel's deck, was what looked like a sheer wall of bristling guns.

Theodoros uttered a muffled shout of joy and dumped his burden on the deck without further ado.

'We're saved!' he muttered softly. 'We're going to climb aboard her.'

He started forward but she held him back, saying anxiously: 'Theodoros, are you mad? You don't know what ship that is. They may be Turks!'

'Turks? A three-decker? No, that's a western ship, Princess. It's only in your part of the world they build these floating fortresses. A ship of the line, that's what she is! Can't even see her yards in this fog – although we stand a fair chance of feeling them!'

The rigging of the two vessels seemed to have become entangled in some way, despite the difference in height, and one way or another there was a good deal of debris falling out of the invisible sky.

'Come on, before we get our brains knocked out!'

Theodoros dragged Marianne through the apocalyptic scene towards the after end of the ship. The pirates were mostly gathered round the place where the polacca had struck, which was fairly far forward, but all the same, the Greek was obliged to knock down two or three who loomed up out of the mist and tried to stand in their way. His great fists could deliver a blow like a hammer.

The light near the stern was much better, mainly on account of the stern lanterns of the other vessel and the tall stern windows which threw an aura of light into the milky fog.

'There's what we want,' said the Greek, who had been looking for something. 'Climb on to my back, put your legs round my waist and hold on tight round my neck. You'd never manage to climb a rope on your own.'

He was already bending to take her up. Close by, no more than arm's length away, a rope was hanging down, its upper end apparently lost in the sky.

'I used to once,' Marianne said, 'but whether I could now ...'

'Well, we've no time to try experiments. Jump on and hold tight.'

Marianne obeyed and Theodoros took hold of the rope. He shinned his way up the side of the ship with what seemed incredible ease, as though his burden had weighed nothing at all.

The panic on board the pirate ship had reached its height. There must have been grave damage to the hull and it was clear the vessel was already going down. The shouts of the seamen getting the boats into the water were overridden by the voice of Kouloughis bellowing frantically: 'Stephanos! Stephanos!'

'Let him look on the deck under his feet,' Theodoros muttered. 'He'll soon find his precious Stephanos!'

On board the big three-decker there was also activity, but a disciplined activity. There was a rapid patter of the seamen's bare feet about the deck but, apart from a single voice speaking in a curiously accented Greek to the men on the polacca and a faint background hum of men talking quietly together, there was no noise.

An order came abruptly from the unknown quarterdeck, amplified by the speaking trumpet. The order itself meant nothing to Marianne, yet at the sound of it she started violently and almost let go her hold of her companion.

'Theodoros!' she whispered. 'This ship – she's English.'

He too was startled. It was not good news. The cordial relations which had existed recently between Britain and the Porte was enough to make her the natural enemy of the rebel Greeks. If he were known, Theodoros would be handed over to the Sultan just as readily as by Kouloughis. The only difference would be that the operation would not cost the Sultan a penny, thus effecting a considerable saving.

The entry-port for which they were making was not far off now. Theodoros paused for an instant in his climbing.

'You are French,' he whispered. 'What will happen if they find out who you are?'

'I'll be arrested, imprisoned. Already, only a few weeks ago, an English squadron attacked the vessel I was travelling in, to capture me.'

'Then they must not know. There's one person at least on board who speaks Greek – I'll say that you're my sister, deaf and dumb, and we were taken by Kouloughis in a raid and ask for asylum. In any case, we've no choice. When you're escaping out of hell, Princess, you don't stop to worry if your horse is running away with you!'

He resumed his climb and a few seconds later the two of them tumbled on to the deck of the English vessel, at the feet of an officer who was strolling along by the side of a man in an impeccable white suit, as tranquilly as though they were enjoying an agreeable cruise.

Neither of them showed any undue surprise at the sudden appearance of two dirty, unkempt foreigners. Their reaction was more of faint displeasure, as if something rather improper had occurred.

'Who are you?' the officer demanded sternly. 'What are you doing here?'

Theodoros launched into a long and eloquent explanation while Marianne, suddenly oblivious of her peril, stared about her in amazement. She was conscious of an indefinable sensation, as if the England of her childhood had risen up before her all at once, and she was breathing it in with a totally unexpected delight. Everything, the two beautifully dressed men, both as neat as new pins, the spotlessly holystoned deck, the gleaming brasswork, it all seemed extraordinarily familiar. Even the face of the officer (who, judging by the amount of gold lace he wore, must be the captain), with grizzled side-whiskers half-concealed by the shadow of his great cocked hat, was oddly like a face she knew already.

The man in the white suit was now deep in conversation with Theodoros, but all this time the captain had said nothing. He was watching Marianne, standing in the light of one of the lanterns, and she felt his eyes upon her as strongly as if he had placed his hand on her shoulder.

The man who had been talking to Theodoros turned to the officer.

'The vessel that struck us belongs to one of the Kouloughis brothers, notorious renegade pirates. This fellow says that he and his sister were carried off by him from Amorgos and were on their way to Tunis to be sold as slaves. They managed to escape in the confusion and are asking for asylum. I gather the young woman is deaf and dumb. We can scarcely throw them back into the sea, can we?'

The captain made no reply. Without a word, he reached out

and, taking Marianne's hand, drew her up on to the quarter-deck, where a powerful lantern was burning. There he fell to studying her face as the light fell on it.

Sticking to her part, Marianne said not a word. Then, suddenly:

'You aren't Greek, nor are you deaf and dumb, are you, my child?'

At the same time, he swept off his cocked hat and revealed a full, high-coloured face in which was set a pair of laughing eyes as blue as periwinkles, a face that surged up so unexpectedly from the depths of the past that Marianne could not help giving it a name:

'James King!' she cried. 'Captain James King! But this is incredible!'

'Not so incredible as finding you here, sailing about on a pirate ship in company with a Greek giant! All the same, I couldn't be more delighted to see you, Marianne my dear. Welcome aboard the *Jason*, bound for Constantinople.'

Whereupon Captain King put both arms round Marianne and kissed her warmly.

Chapter Twelve
An irascible antiquary

To find oneself suddenly, halfway across the world, on board the same vessel as an old family friend who, besides being one's accidental rescuer, has all unwittingly become a wartime enemy is an experience of singular awkwardness.

Sir James King had been a part of Marianne's life as far back as she could remember. In those rare intervals when he was not away at sea, he and his family, whose home lay within easy reach of Selton, were among the few callers permitted to cross the sacred limits of Aunt Ellis's carefully guarded threshold. This fact was probably due to her finding them both estimable and restful.

To the fierce old lady, ruling her vast estates with a rod of iron and tending always to carry about with her a faint aroma of the stables, Sir James's wife Mary, with her pretty dresses and big frothy hats, and her perpetual look of having just stepped out of a portrait by Sir Thomas Lawrence, was a continual source of interest and amazement. Even life's hardest knocks seemed to roll off her, baffled by her charming smile and the exquisite good manners that were second nature to her.

Marianne, giving her all a child's whole-hearted admiration for something perfect in its kind, had seen her come through an epidemic of smallpox, to which her two youngest children had fallen victim, and wait with unfailing constancy for the return of a husband long believed lost at sea, with the serenity of her sweet face apparently quite undisturbed. Only, her eyes had lost a fraction of their delicate blue, and her smile acquired an indefinable tinge of melancholy to betray the anguish she was suffering. She was a woman who would always hold her head high and never give in to circumstances.

Marianne had always been glad to see Lady King, thinking,

as she looked at her, that her own mother, of whom she possessed only a single miniature, must have been very like her.

As ill luck would have it, Lady King had been out of England at the time of her young friend's marriage, having been summoned to Jamaica to the bedside of her ailing sister, where she had been obliged to undertake the management of a large plantation. Her husband, too, had been away, at Malta, and their eldest son at sea. So Marianne had been deprived of the happiness of having those she considered her best friends among the few people present at a ceremony which she was so swiftly to consider a disaster.

Had they been at home, things would almost certainly have been very different and Marianne would not have been forced to seek asylum abroad after the tragic events of her marriage night, since the Kings would have opened their house to her unhesitatingly.

Now and then, in the difficult times which led up to the moment when she had found a haven and a kind of home in her ancestral mansion in the rue de Lille, Marianne's thoughts had gone out to the English family she would probably never see again, now that an impenetrable curtain had been drawn between herself and England. She had continued to think of them a little sadly until, as time went by, they had faded gradually into the mists of her past life, so far back that she had almost forgotten them.

And now, quite suddenly, here they were again, in the person of this elderly naval officer who in so few words had reforged the chain that had been broken.

The rediscovery was not without its problems for Marianne. She knew, of course, that Sir James must have heard of her marriage to Francis Cranmere, but what did he know of the subsequent events?

It was clearly impossible to embark on an explanation of her present prestigious but highly dangerous persona. She knew his forthright nature, his uncompromising sense of honour and deep love for his country. How could she tell such a man that she was the Princess Sant'Anna whom a British squadron had attempted unsuccessfully to capture off Corfu, without placing him in an altogether intolerable position? That Captain King would not hesitate, she was certain. The little girl of Selton Hall would be put firmly out of mind, however much it might cost him to do so and Napoleon's most serene envoy would be instantly incarcerated in a cabin, with the prospect of quitting it only for an equally strict confinement in England.

Thus it came as something of a relief to her to hear him inquire, after the first excitement of recognition had worn off:

'But where have you been, all this time? I learned of your disastrous marriage on my return from Malta, and I know that had my wife been at home she would have advised your aunt most strongly against it. I was told that you had fled from home after gravely wounding Francis Cranmere and killing his cousin, but I could never bring myself to believe ill of you. In my own view, which is that of a good many other sensible people, they came by their just deserts. His reputation seems to have been notorious, and only someone as blind as your poor aunt would have dreamed of matching such a child as you were with a gazetted fortune-hunter.'

Marianne smiled. It amused her that she should have forgotten how talkative Sir James could be, unusually so for an Englishman. It was probably his way of compensating for the long hours of silence at sea. True, he was a good listener too. He seemed to be very well informed about her catastrophic marriage.

'How did you come to hear all this? Was it from Lady King?'

'Good God, no! My wife only came home from Kingston herself six months ago, and in poor health at that. She got a fever out there and she has to watch herself. She don't go gadding a great deal nowadays. No, I heard of your misfortunes from Lady Hester Stanhope, Chatham's niece, y'know. I took her on board last year on the voyage out to Gibraltar. She was pretty badly cut up after her uncle's death and took it into her head to travel about a bit, visit the Mediterranean and all that. Don't know where she is now, of course, though she talked a good deal about the lure of the East. But when she left England this business of your marriage was only some three or four months old and still a good deal talked of. Francis Cranmere came in for some sympathy – he was slow recovering from his wound – and so did you.

'I'd not been long at Portsmouth myself and not much time to spare for gossip while I was there. It was Lady Hester brought me up to date with all the news. She was quite on your side, by the by. Swore that Cranmere had got no more than he deserved and it was a wicked shame ever to have married you to the fellow. But there, I dare swear your poor aunt thought she was doing all for the best, remembering her own youth.'

'I made no objection,' Marianne admitted. 'I was in love with Francis Cranmere – or I thought I was.'

'It's understandable. He's a handsome shaver, by all accounts. D'ye happen to know what's become of him? There's a rumour abroad of his having been taken up for a spy in France and put in prison and heaven knows what else.'

Marianne felt the colour drain from her face as she saw again the red-painted instrument erected in the snowy ditch at Vincennes, and the chained man twitching with the fear of death in his sleep. Once again, the terrible cold of that winter's night seemed to creep into her bones and she shivered.

'N-no,' she managed to say at last. 'No, I've no idea. If you please, Sir James, I'm dreadfully tired. We, my companion and I, that is, have been through a terrible experience.'

'Why, of course, my dear. You must forgive me. I was so happy to see you again that I've kept you standing here in all this bustle. You shall come and rest. We'll talk later. This Greek of yours, by the by – who is he?'

'My servant,' Marianne replied, without hesitation. 'And quite devoted to me. Is it possible for him to be lodged near me? He will be lost otherwise.'

The fact of the matter was that she was not entirely easy in her mind about Theodoros' possible reactions to this total change of plan, and she was anxious to confer with him as soon as possible.

She had drawn no very cheerful conclusions from the heavy frown and general air of mistrust with which he had been following, without understanding, this evidently very friendly exchange between the noble French lady and an officer of His

Britannic Majesty's Navy. Foreseeing trouble, she preferred to face it quickly.

In fact they were no sooner alone in the quarters assigned to them – a cabin with a kind of lobby provided with a hammock adjoining it – than Theodoros opened the subject on a note of suppressed violence.

'You lied!' he said furiously. 'Your tongue is false, like those of all women! These English are your friends—'

'I did not lie,' Marianne interrupted brusquely, it being no part of her plan to encourage him to dwell on his grievances. 'It's true that this particular officer is an old friend but he would become my implacable enemy if he ever found out who I am.'

'How so? He is your friend, you say, and yet he does not know who you are? Do you think I am a fool? You have brought me into a trap!'

'You know quite well that's not true,' Marianne said wearily. 'How could I? I didn't ask Kouloughis to capture us, or bring this ship to this spot. And when I tell you I'm not lying it's the truth. I am French but I was born during the Revolution. My parents died by the guillotine and I was brought up in England. It was there I came to know Captain King and his family. But then something dreadful happened and I fled to France to try and find what was left of my family. Then I met the Emperor and he – that is, we became friends. Soon afterwards, I married the Prince Sant'Anna but the captain does not know that. It's a long time since he saw me. There, you see, it's all perfectly simple . . .'

'Your husband? Where is he?'

'The Prince? Dead. I am a widow and therefore free, which is why the Emperor chose to avail himself of my services.'

The anger had been dying out of the giant's face as she spoke, but suspicion remained.

'What did you tell the Englishman about me?' he asked.

'I said you were my servant and that I had engaged you at Santorini. Then I said I was very tired and would rather talk later. That will give us some time to think, because this meeting has rather taken me by surprise.'

Then, recalling Sir James's first words to her, she added: 'Besides, the most important thing, surely, is that this vessel is on its way to Constantinople? Soon we shall be ashore. What will it matter then how we came there? More than that: aren't we safer on board an English ship of the line than on any Greek vessel?'

Theodoros became lost in thought. So long did he stand there thinking that in the end Marianne went and sat down exhaustedly on her cot to await the outcome of his cogitations. His arms were folded, his head sunk on his chest and his eyes fixed: he must have been weighing every word that she had said. At last he looked up, and held her in a gaze heavy with menace.

'You swore on the holy icons,' he reminded her. 'If you betray me, you are damned to all eternity – and I'll strangle you with my bare hands!'

'Are you there again?' she asked sadly. 'Have you forgotten that I killed a man to set you free? Is that the friendship you promised me so short a time ago? If this had been a Greek ship, or even a Turkish one, we would still be comrades. But because it happens to be English, is all that over?

'Yet I need you so badly, Theodoros! You are the only strength I have left in a world of perils. You have it in your power to ruin me. You have only to tell the truth to that man in the white suit who speaks your language. Perhaps if you saw me kept a prisoner it would change your mind – but by that time it would be too late for my mission and for yours.'

She spoke quite slowly but with a kind of resignation which gradually had its effect on the Greek's stormy temperament. Looking at her, he saw her as both fragile and pathetic in her torn, dirty dress that still clung wetly to her body – that body which even at the height of the storm had still shone radiantly at the back of his mind.

She was looking at him, too, with the great green eyes that fear and exhaustion had now underlined with oddly touching shadows. Never in all his life had he encountered a woman so desirable. He was beset, at one and the same time, by three different and wholly incompatible emotions: he wanted to protect her, and to slake the violence of his desire on her, and then again to kill her to rid himself of his obsession.

He opted for a fourth course. Flight. Without another word, he flung himself out of the tiny cabin, slamming the door behind him, and, deprived of his gigantic form, the room seemed to grow in size.

Marianne beheld his departure speechlessly. Why had he gone without saying anything? Was he going to take her at her word? Had he gone to find the man in white, to tell him the truth about his so-called mistress? She had to know . . .

She made a move as though to rise but she was horribly tired and, spartan as it was, the cot they had given her, with its white sheets, looked softer than a feather bed after the bare boards of the between-decks. All the same, she managed to resist the temptation and forced herself to walk as far as the door and open it. She closed it again at once. Theodoros had not gone far. Like the devoted servant she had called him, he had curled up on the floor outside her door and, overcome with fatigue, was already asleep.

Reassured, Marianne made her own way back to her cot and fell across it, without even taking the trouble to turn back the sheets or snuff the lantern. It was time she had a little untroubled sleep.

Outside, the hubbub was dying down. The British seamen had succeeded with the aid of gaffs in fending off the polacca, which was now sinking slowly, with Kouloughis' men crammed into the vessel's three longboats preparing to make a bid for more hospitable waters.

Captain King's voice, relayed by an interpreter, had warned them to get out of range with all speed unless they wanted to be sent to the bottom, and none of them had shown any great inclination to imitate Theodoros' feat and scale the sides of the floating fortress.

But none of this penetrated to Marianne where she lay deeply and blissfully asleep.

By the time the *Jason* was under way again, she had long sailed away on a dream ship, as swift and white as a seagull, that was bearing her off to some unknown but happy destination. Yet it bore the tragic features of the man she loved as she had seen him last, and, as the white boat sailed on, the face was left behind and sank into the waves crying out piteously. Then it would return, only to recede once more as soon as Marianne stretched out her arms to it.

There was no way of telling how long the dream lasted, reflecting Marianne's unconscious thought which for days had vacillated between hope and despair, between love, bitterness and regrets, but when she opened her eyes to the real world again, the mists had all blown away, taking the renegades with them, and all was sunshine. Yet the impression remained, embedded in her flesh like a poisoned arrow.

Now, finding herself once more back in surroundings that recalled bygone days, Marianne, who through all her dangers had thought of little beyond the fight for life and liberty, became a prey to bitter regrets. The ship's cabin reminded her of another where she still would have preferred to be, for all the agonies that she had suffered there and even if she had known there were still more to endure.

Waking alone in that small, enclosed space, she was made all the more sharply aware of the extent to which she was alone with her shattered dreams in a pitiless world of men, struggling still, like a wounded seagull, to reach a haven where she might find herself a niche to lick her wounds and breathe again.

To think that there were women on this mad earth, which was tossing her back and forth like a bottle in the ocean, who were able to live only for their home and children and the man who provided for them! Women who woke each morning and went to sleep at night with the reassuring warmth of their chosen life's companion! Women who brought their children into the world in peace and joy! Women who were women and not pawns on a chessboard! Who led ordinary lives instead of wandering like gipsies at the mercy of some insane power that seemed to take a malign pleasure in spoiling everything.

Now that she knew she was on her way to Constantinople, where she had dreamed of being, Marianne discovered that she no longer wanted to arrive. She did not want to be plunged once more into an unknown world, peopled with strange faces and strange voices, where she would be all alone, so terribly alone!

And, by one of fate's grim ironies, the ship that was carrying her there bore the name of the man she loved and now believed that she had lost for ever.

'It's my own fault,' she told herself bitterly. 'I tried to force destiny to my own will. I tried to make Jason give in to me, and I didn't trust his love! If it were all to do again, I'd tell him everything, straight out, and then if he still wanted me I'd go with him wherever he wanted, and the farther the better!'

Only it was much too late now and the feeling of powerlessness that swept over her was so overwhelming that she burst into tears and sat sobbing loudly with her head on her knees. It was thus that Theodoros found her when he poked his head round the cabin door, drawn by the noise.

Marianne was so deep in her misery that she did not hear him come in. He stood for a moment, staring at her, not knowing what to do, as awkward as any man in the presence of a woman's grief he does not understand. Then, realizing that her tears were fast becoming hysteria, that she was trembling like a leaf and uttering little inarticulate moans and was almost on the verge of suffocation, he turned up her face and, quite deliberately, slapped her.

The sobbing ceased abruptly. Her breathing also, and for a second Theodoros wondered if he had not struck too hard. Marianne was gazing at him with wide, sightless eyes. She might almost have been turned to stone, and he was just about to give her a shake to rouse her out of her weird trance when she spoke, suddenly, in a perfectly normal voice:

'Thank you. That's better.'

'You frightened me,' he said after a moment, with a sigh of relief. 'I couldn't think what was the matter. You slept well enough. I know because I've been in several times.'

'I can't think what came over me. I was having weird dreams and then when I woke up I started thinking – oh, of things that are lost to me.'

'You were dreaming of this ship. I heard you – you spoke the name.'

'No, not the ship . . . a man of the same name.'

'A man you – love?'

'Yes, and shall never see again.'

'Why? He is dead?'

'Perhaps. I do not know.'

'Then why do you say you'll never see him again? The future is in God's hand and until you have seen your lover's body in the grave you cannot say that he is dead. How like a woman to waste energy on tears and regrets while we are still in danger! Have you thought yet what you are going to say to the captain?'

'Yes. I shall say I'm going to Constantinople to visit a distant relative. He knows I have no near relations left. He will believe me.'

'Then hurry up and get your story straight, because he's coming to call on you in an hour. The man in white told me that. And he gave me these things for you to try and dress yourself. They have no proper women's clothes on board. I'm to bring food for you.'

'I won't have you going to all this trouble on my account. A man like you!'

A swift smile illuminated his craggy face for an instant.

'I am your devoted servant, Princess. I must play my part. These people seem to think it only natural. Besides, you must be hungry.'

In fact, the mere mention of food had been enough to remind Marianne that she was dreadfully hungry. She ate everything that was brought to her, then had a wash and arranged the piece of silk, which Sir James must have bought to take home, in the manner of a classical robe. After this she felt better.

It was a much more self-possessed Marianne who waited for Sir James to make his promised visit and, when he was seated on the only chair, thanked him for his hospitality and for taking such good care of her.

'Now that you are rested,' he said, 'won't you tell me, at least, where I am to take you? As I told you, our course is for Constantinople but—'

'Constantinople will suit me perfectly, Sir James. That is where I was going when – when I was wrecked. I took ship, oh, it seems a very long time ago now, to visit a member of my father's family there. He was French, as you know, and when I fled from England I went to France to try and trace any relatives who might still be living there. There were none, except for one elderly cousin not in very good odour with the present regime. She told me that there was another distant relative of ours living at Constantinople who would certainly be glad to see me, and that after all, travel broadened the mind. So I went, but on account of the wreck I was obliged to spend several months on the island of Naxos. That was where I found my servant, Theodoros. He rescued me from drowning and looked after me like a mother. Unfortunately, the pirates came ...'

Sir James's whiskers twitched in a smile.

'He is certainly devoted to you. It was lucky for you that you had him with you. Very well, then. I'll take you to Constantinople. If the wind holds, we'll be there in five or six days from now. But I'll make a landfall at Lesbos and see if I can get hold of some clothes for you. You can hardly go ashore dressed as you are. Very pretty, I grant, but just a trifle improper. Although, of course, this is the east ...'

He was talking volubly now, made easier by Marianne's half-confidences, and enjoying both the brief excursion into the past and the prospect of a few days' voyage in her company to revive, for both of them, a nostalgic vision of the green lawns of Devonshire.

Marianne was content to listen to him. She was still a little shaken to discover how easily the lies had come to her – and been accepted. She had mingled truth and fiction with a readiness that left her both startled and alarmed. The words had simply come of their own accord. She was even beginning to find that, with practice, she was actually enjoying the part she had to play, even though there was no audience but herself to applaud her performance. Most of all, it was necessary to act naturally, that most difficult of all arts, because failure would be met not with hoots and cat-calls, but with prison or even death. Even in the awareness of her danger there was something exciting that gave a fresh spice to life and made her understand a little of what it was that gave a man like Theodoros his power.

True, he was fighting for his country's independence, but he

also loved danger for its own sake and would seek it out for the
sheer exuberant delight of meeting it and beating it on its own
terms. Even without the call to liberty, he would have flung
himself into perilous adventures for nothing, for the pure joy
of it.

She even discovered suddenly that there was another side to
her mission, apart from the harsh aspect of duty and constraint,
a thrill which, only an hour ago, she would have rejected
fiercely. Perhaps it was because it had already cost her so much
that she could not bear not to finish it.

She learned from Sir James's rambling monologue that the
man in the white suit was called Charles Cockerell and that he
was a young architect from London with a passion for antiqui-
ties. He had come aboard the *Jason* at Athens with a companion,
another architect from Liverpool, whose name was John Foster.
The two of them were on their way to Constantinople to obtain
permission from the Ottoman government to dig for relics of
classical antiquity on the site of a temple which they claimed
to have discovered, since the pasha of Athens, for some obscure
reason of his own, had refused them his consent. Both men
were members of the English Society of the Dilettanti and had
already been exercising their talents on the island of Aegina.

'As far as I'm concerned,' Sir James confessed, 'I'd rather
they'd chosen to travel on any other ship but mine. They're not
an easy pair to get on with, and mighty full of themselves in a
way that could cause trouble with the Porte. But after all the
fuss that was made over those marbles that Lord Elgin carried
back to London from the great temple in Athens, there's no
holding them! They're sure that they can do as well, or better!
As a result, they keep on pestering our ambassador in Constantinople with letters complaining that the Turks won't co-
operate and the Greeks are apathetic. If I hadn't agreed to give
them a passage, I think they'd have stormed the ship.'

Marianne's interests in the ship's other passengers was per-
functory. She had no wish to have anything to do with them
and said as much to the captain.

'It would be best, I think, that I should not leave my cabin,' she said. 'For one thing, it's not easy to know what name you should call me. I'm no longer Miss d'Asselnat and I've no intention of using Francis Cranmere's name.'

'Why not call yourself Miss Selton? You are the last of the line and you've every right to use the name. But, surely you must have had a passport to leave France?'

Marianne could have bitten out her tongue. It was the obvious question and she was beginning to find out that the pleasures of lying had their drawbacks.

'I lost everything in the wreck,' she said at last, 'including my passport ... Besides, that was in my maiden name, of course, but to use a French name on an English ship ...'

Sir James had risen and was patting her shoulder in a fatherly way.

'Of course, of course. But our troubles with Bonaparte have nothing to say to old friendship. You shall be Marianne Selton, then, because you're going to have to show yourself, I fear. Those fellows are as inquisitive as a waggon-load of monkeys, and with an imagination to match! They were very much struck by your romantic arrival and are quite capable of dreaming up some fanciful tale of brigands and God knows what that might well get me into hot water with their lordships at the Admiralty. All ways round, it'll probably be best for both of us if you become thoroughly English again.'

'Do you think they'll believe it? An Englishwoman roaming the Greek islands with a servant like Theodoros?'

'Absolutely,' Sir James laughed. 'Eccentricity isn't a sin with us, you know. More a mark of distinction. Those two scholars are solid citizens enough – and you're Quality. That makes all the difference. You'll have them eating out of your hand. You've excited them enough already.'

'Then, in that case, I'll have to satisfy the curiosity of these architects of yours, Sir James,' she said, with a little, resigned smile. 'I owe you that, at least. I should be miserable if you had to suffer, all through saving me.'

Chapter Thirteen

Night on the Golden Horn

It was a quarter of an hour later that the three-decker dropped anchor off the little port of Gavrion on the island of Andros, and a boat was sent ashore carrying Charles Cockerell, whose knowledge of Greek made him the natural person to undertake the mission of trust which he had, in any case, virtually begged the captain to give him.

He might be an impossible person but he was certainly a man of some resource, for he returned an hour later bringing with him an assortment of female garments which, considering their entirely local origin, were both picturesque and becoming. Marianne, who was beginning to grow accustomed to the fashions of the islands, was delighted with her new wardrobe. Particularly since the gallant architect had thoughtfully included a variety of silver and coral ornaments which did credit both to his own good taste and to the skill of the local craftsmen.

Decked out in a full white gown with triple, floating sleeves, a sleeveless and collarless coat embroidered in red wool, a pair of silver buckled shoes, and even a big red velvet cap, Marianne presided that very evening over Sir James's dinner table, her exotic apparel forming an interesting contrast to the officers' blue uniforms and the plain evening dress of the other two gentlemen.

She provided the only faintly discordant note in what was otherwise a typically English evening. Everything about Sir James's cabin was firmly and unalterably English, from the table silver and the Wedgwood china to the heavy, old-fashioned furniture, the pervading aroma of spirits and cigars – and the lamentably insular cooking.

In spite of the variety of strange dishes she had eaten in the course of her improbable odyssey, Marianne discovered that her stay in France had profoundly altered her taste in culinary matters. She scarcely recognized the dishes she had enjoyed as a child.

Afterwards there were toasts to the King, to the Royal Navy, to Science and to 'Miss Selton', who then made a most affecting little speech, thanking her rescuer and all those who were taking such good care of her.

The two architects were literally drinking in her words, unmistakably impressed by her natural elegance and grace. Both succumbed instantly to her charm – as did all the men present – but each reacted somewhat differently. Whereas Charles Cockerell, a sanguine, rather over-fed young man with an air of regarding life as one enormous Christmas pudding, gazed at her hungrily and lost himself in compliments that tended towards a vaguely Thucydidean turn of phrase, his friend Foster, who proved to be a thin, nervous person whose reddish hair, cut rather long, gave him a disconcerting look of a red setter, said little except in monosyllables, darting quick glances at her out of the corner of his eye. But what little he did say was addressed solely to her, as if none of the others present existed.

After dealing for a while in a general way with the rumblings of revolt that were beginning to be heard in the islands, the conversation soon settled down to a discussion of the exploits of the two colleagues at Aegina and at Phygalia. At this point, the two of them entered frankly into competition with each other, each shamelessly doing his best to claim the greater part of glory for himself at the expense of the other. The only thing in which they were united was their joint criticism of Lord Elgin who, they said, 'had only to bend down to pick up a fortune' with the admirable metopes from the Parthenon.

'At the rate we're going,' Sir James said gloomily as he escorted his guest back to her cabin, 'those two will have come to blows before the voyage ends. Ah, well, I suppose I can always hand them over to the master at arms to ensure fair play. But for goodness' sake, my dear, take care not to smile at one more than the other, or I won't answer for the consequences.'

Marianne laughed and promised, but as time went by she was forced to admit that this lighthearted promise was harder to keep than she had anticipated. For in the few days it took for the *Jason* to reach the Dardanelles, the clash of rivals continued. She could not set foot on deck for a breath of air without one or other, if not both, rushing to keep her company. She began to think they must be mounting guard outside her door. In addition, she soon found their company wearisome in the extreme, since their style of conversation was identical and in both cases revolved around their own magnificent discoveries which they were burning to exploit.

There was another passenger who was sorely tried by the two architects. This was Theodoros. He thought them utterly ridiculous, with their straw hats, their flowing neckcloths, close-fitting white clothes and the green sunshades with which they persisted in shielding their pallid northern complexions – and in the case of Foster, his freckles – from the sun's rays.

'You'll never be able to get rid of them when we get to Constantinople,' he told Marianne one evening. 'They follow you like shadows and they won't give up when we go ashore. How will you manage? Will you take them with you, as escort, to the French embassy?'

'It won't be necessary. They are only interested in me because they are bored and have nothing else to do on board ship. That, and a certain snobbishness. Once we land, they'll be too busy to think of me. All they want is to get their horrid permit and scurry back to Greece.'

'What sort of permit?'

'Oh, I don't know. They've found a ruined temple and they want permission to dig about for buried stones and things. They want to make drawings, too, and study classical architecture – all that sort of thing.'

The Greek's face had hardened.

'There was an Englishman came to Greece once before. He had been ambassador in Constantinople, and he had permission to do all those things. But he wanted more than just to find things and make drawings. He wanted to take the stones with carvings on them away to his own country – stealing the ancient gods of my land. And he did it. Whole cargoes of stone sailed from Piraeus, taken from the temple of Athena. But the first, and most important, never arrived. A curse was on it and it sank. These men long to do the same. I can feel it. I know.'

'Well, we can't stop them, Theodoros,' Marianne said gently, laying a soothing hand on her odd companion's muscular arm, as knotted as an olive trunk. 'Your mission, and mine, are each more important than a few stones. We cannot risk failure, especially as we don't really know. Besides, their ship may sink, too!'

'You are right, but you will not stop me hating these vultures who come to snatch away what little glory my poor people have left.'

Marianne was deeply struck by the bitterness of this man whom she now looked on as her friend, but she had imagined the incident closed and forgotten when events proved her dramatically wrong.

The *Jason* had entered the narrow straits of the Dardanelles and was sailing past the desolate expanse of black earth and sandy waste, with bare hills topped by bleached ruins and the occasional tiny mosque, round which the snowy seabirds wheeled incessantly.

In this corridor of brassy blue, like a broad lazy river, the heat was intense, flung back from bank to bank of treeless, petrified land. In this incandescent universe, the smallest movement became an effort that set the sweat pouring. Marianne lay on her cot, with nothing on but a single shift that clung to her skin, gasping for air despite the open window in the vessel's stern, and taking care not to move. Only her hand waved a fan of woven reed gently to and fro in an attempt to cool an air that seemed to have been breathed straight from a furnace.

It was too tiring even to think, and only one conscious idea floated on the sluggish surface of her mind. Tomorrow they would be in Constantinople. She would not think beyond that. Now was the time to rest, and the ship sailed on in the silence of eternity.

This beautiful silence was shattered abruptly by an angry voice shouting not many feet away. The voice came from the quarterdeck and it belonged to Theodoros. Marianne could not understand what he was saying because he was speaking Greek, but there was no doubt about the fury of his tone. When it seemed to her that the oddly muffled voice answering him was that of Charles Cockerell, Marianne sprang to her feet on the instant, under the remarkably bracing effect of pure terror. She flung on a dress and, without stopping even to put on her sandals, fled out of the cabin. She was just in time to see a pair of seamen literally climbing up Theodoros in their endeavours to prise his fingers loose from the architect's throat.

Horrified, she ran towards them but, before she could reach the Greek, more seamen had come up, in charge of an officer, and Theodoros was borne down by sheer weight of numbers and forced to release his grip. His victim staggered to his feet, gasping and retching, and lurched to the rail, tearing at his neckcloth in his efforts to regain the use of his lungs.

In spite of all that Marianne could do to help, it was a moment or two before he was able to speak. In the meanwhile Theodoros had been overpowered and Sir James had arrived on the scene from his own cabin.

'Good God, Theodoros! What have you done?' Marianne wailed, slapping Cockerell's cheeks to bring him to himself more quickly.

'Justice! I was doing justice! The man is a brigand – a thief!' the Greek said sulkily.

'You don't mean you were trying to *kill* him?'

'Yes, I do say so! And I'll say it again. He deserves to die. Let him look to himself in future, for I shall not abandon my revenge.'

'You may be in no position to do anything else,' Sir James broke in in a voice of ice. His upright figure inserted itself between the horrified girl and the agitated little group who were finding it increasingly difficult to hold the infuriated Greek. 'I'll have that man in irons, if you please, Mr Jones. He'll be required to answer to a court for his attempt upon Mr Cockerell.'

Marianne's horror became blind panic. If Sir James were to

apply the rigid laws of the service to Theodoros, the Greek rebel's career bade fair to finish at the end of a yard or under the lash of the cat-o'-nine tails. She flew to his assistance.

'For pity's sake, Captain, at least hear what he has to say. I know this man. He is good and true and fair! He would not have done this without a good reason. He is not English, remember, but Greek, and he's my servant. I am the only person to answer for him and for his conduct. I am quite willing to do so.'

'Miss Selton is right, sir.' This timid intervention came from the young surgeon who had been fetched to do what he could for Cockerell, an occupation which did not prevent him flying to the help of beauty in distress. 'Won't you at least hear what the fellow has to say? He's always served his mistress faithfully, even if he is a temperamental devil.'

Clearly this new champion of Marianne's was not above suspecting Cockerell of having tried to force his way into her cabin, an offence which in his private scale of values merited no less than hanging. The captain's lips twitched almost imperceptibly but there was no hint of softness in his voice.

'Might I suggest you mind your own damn business, Mr Kingsley. When I need your advice, I'll ask for it. Do what you have to do and then take yourself off. Ha – h'm, I think, all the same, I may as well hear what the fellow has to say for himself.'

It did not take long to tell. In the course of one of the conversations he was inclined to seek out with Theodoros for the purpose of practising his Greek, Cockerell had managed to get round to his favourite subject, his own discoveries. The giant, for his part, happened to find out that the permit coveted by the Englishman was concerned with the ruins of a temple which he, Theodoros, regarded as being in some degree his own private property. This was for the very good reason that he had been born almost in the shadow of its overgrown columns, deep in central Arcadia, which were consequently dear to his savage heart.

'My father told me once that there was a cursed Frenchman came to Bassae some fifty years past. He looked and wondered and made pictures, but he was old, happily, and tired. He went away to die in his own land and we saw no more of him. But this one is young and his teeth are sharp! Left to himself, he will eat up the old temple of Apollo as the other Englishman devoured the temple of Athena. I could not let him do it.'

Never in his career had Captain King found himself confronted with such a motive for attempted murder. Or in such a quandary. Privately, he cursed the architect for his busy tongue and his insatiable appetite for destruction, incomprehensible to his seaman's mind. There was Marianne, pleading earnestly for her servant. Obviously, she would never forgive him if he sacrificed the man to this encroaching civilian. On the other hand, the affair had occurred openly, on board one of His Majesty's ships. He did his best to reach a compromise by reiterating his order that Theodoros be put in irons, but added that nothing was to be decided concerning his case until they reached their destination. The outburst was probably attributable to the effects of heat on an already fiery constitution, he concluded, and he placed perfect confidence in Miss Selton's ability to deal with her own servant as she thought fit. The implication was that in thirty-six hours' time, Theodoros would be free to take himself to the devil any way he chose : at least the architect would be safe from his temper at present.

Marianne breathed again, but this degree of leniency by no means suited Cockerell's book. He had received too great a fright not to have been made exceedingly angry, and he had no sooner recovered his ability to speak than his shrill voice was raised to demand immediate punishment of his attacker. In this he was seconded by his colleague, in whom the affair had suddenly engendered a miraculous solidarity.

'I'm a British subject!' Cockerell shrilled. 'And you, Captain King, as an officer of his Britannic Majesty's Navy, owe me protection and justice! I demand that you hang this man on the spot for his attempt on my life!'

'Well, you haven't died of it, so far as I can see,' the captain replied pacifically. 'And you can hardly call it justice to sacrifice another human life to your very reasonable annoyance. The man is safely stowed in the cable tier by this time, and there he stays until we drop anchor.'

'That won't do. I insist. I command—'

But that, after a lifetime at sea, was too much for Captain King. His patience snapped.

'Here, on this ship,' he said harshly, 'I am the only one who commands. Miss Selton has declared, in your hearing and in mine, that she will assume complete responsibility for her servant. After all your protestations of devotion, that is something you appear to have forgotten. Do you really wish to disoblige her in this matter?'

'I yield to no one in my admiration and respect for Miss Selton, but I also have a good deal of respect for my own life. You may think that a matter of small importance, Captain, but that only makes me the readier to defend it. Either you punish this man as he deserves or I must request you to stop at the first Anatolian harbour and put me ashore. I shall continue my journey to Constantinople on horseback! It is no great distance.'

'Mr Cockerell, this is quite absurd,' Marianne said. 'I am prepared to make any apology you require on my servant's behalf. Believe me, I would not have had this happen for the world and I will see to it that the man is duly punished after we land.'

'It is easy for you to speak of apologies, ma'am,' the architect said sourly. 'But much as I admire you, I cannot look on the matter in quite the same trivial light. With your permission, I repeat what I have already said: either he suffers, or I leave this ship.'

'Then you may go with my goodwill!' Sir James said testily. 'You shall be put ashore, sir, since you insist upon it. Mr Spencer—' he turned to his first lieutenant. 'We will drop anchor at Eregli, if you please. See to it that these gentlemen's baggage is got ashore. I am assuming you will wish to go also, Mr Foster?'

'Most certainly,' came the answer, delivered in a tone of stiff pomposity. 'We Liverpudlians aren't ones to desert our friends in a crisis. I'm right beside you, Cockerell.'

'I never doubted it, Foster. Come, we must see to our preparations. We shall leave no regrets behind us.'

The two of them shook hands with what they evidently considered a most noble and affecting dignity, then went below to their respective cabins to see to the packing of their respective belongings. Captain King, on whom this touching demonstration had produced no more effect than the sardonic lifting of an eyebrow, watched them go, half-angry, half-amused.

'Just take a look at the pair of 'em,' he growled to the still gaping Marianne. 'Pylades consoling Orestes after being spurned by Hermione, shouldn't you say? What those two can't stomach is the fact that their beloved Miss Selton didn't stand up for 'em and offer 'em the Greek's head on a platter! They're furious with me, now, but it's you they won't forgive.'

'Do you think not?'

'Sure of it. They tied themselves in knots to please you and you never melted a fraction. Simply ignored their efforts. They're the kind that makes revolutions. They hate anything that's better than themselves, or won't give in to them.'

'But why leave the ship? Theodoros is in irons. Mr Cockerell is perfectly safe.'

'Why, to reach Constantinople before us, to be sure, and get the ambassador to order his arrest.'

Marianne's heart missed a beat. Theodoros had barely escaped from one peril, thanks to Sir James, before another, yet more serious, reared its head. If he were to be arrested after they dropped anchor, nothing could save him. She remembered all too clearly what Kouloughis had told her. The head of a rebel leader had too high a price on it for any diplomat, anxious to ingratiate himself with a head of state, to let slip such an opportunity. Let the law once get its hand on him, and his fragile alias would soon be broken. And she had sworn before the icons of Ayios Ilias to do her utmost to get her companion safely into the Ottoman capital.

She gazed up at her old friend with tears in her eyes.

'And so all your kindness to my poor servant will be wasted?' she said pitifully. 'For one moment's loss of temper, readily understandable in any man who loves his native land, he must hang! Yet my gratitude to you, Sir James, is none the less. You did all you could. I have been a horrid trouble to you.'

'Come, come! We should all have been bored on this voyage but for you. And I'm not the only one to say so. You have made it a real joy to us all, my dear. And as for that tiresome watch-dog of yours – the best thing he can do will be to slip quietly over the side as soon as we drop anchor in the Bosphorus. He'll have plenty of time. I don't imagine we'll find Stratford Canning – he's our present ambassador, y'know – waiting on the quay-side with an armed guard to greet us. The business is too un-important, and so are the plaintiffs. So, stop worrying your pretty head and come and drink a cup of tea with me. There's nothing like a nice hot cup of tea for refreshment in this con-founded heat.'

For all Sir James's comforting words, Marianne could not feel at ease. There was danger in the two men's anger and resent-ment, whatever their credit with the embassy, but she had known from the glowering looks cast at her by her former ad-mirers that it would be a waste of time and dignity to attempt to reason with them. They had all the inflexible obstinacy of mean little men, and they would regard any such attempt as an unfortunate and incomprehensible sign of weakness on be-half of one whom they certainly felt to be among the dregs of humanity. Her best course was still to trust Sir James's judge-ment and his friendship for herself. Hadn't he as good as told her he would not stand in the way of the culprit's escape? She was even fairly sure that he would let her slip a note to Theodoros in the cable tier, warning him to be ready to escape as soon as he heard the vessel drop anchor.

'I'll have the irons off him as soon as we're under way again,' Captain King remarked as, round about sunset, they came in sight of what had once been the ancient port of Heraclea on the Sea of Marmara. 'That'll make it the easiest thing in the world for him to leave us. Although, you never know. We may be imagining things – painting your two admirers blacker than they are.'

'It's still wise to be prepared,' Marianne replied. 'I can't thank you enough, Sir James.'

Thus it was with a more tranquil eye that she watched the two Englishmen go ashore, amid a welter of baggage slung over the side and the shouts of the boatmen and porters hired to transport them from the three-decker, by means of a caique, to the waterfront, where a bustling, cheerful crowd was welcoming the cool of the evening.

Cockerell and Foster quitted the ship without a word of thanks or farewell, and for a long time their green sunshades could be seen bobbing on a sea of turbans and felt hats. They vanished at last into the compact mass of brightly coloured houses and mosques, riding jerkily on donkeys and surrounded by guides armed with staves and by an eager, screaming throng of small boys.

'The ingratitude of it!' Marianne said. 'They didn't even say good-bye to you. After all you've done for them!'

But Sir James only laughed and gave the order to weigh anchor. The *Jason* heeled over gracefully, almost as though relieved of a disagreeable burden, and resumed her course, while the setting sun turned the sea to amethyst and silvery dolphins played about the golden islets.

This was the last stage. The long exhausting voyage, which had so nearly cost Marianne her life on so many occasions, was drawing to an end. Constantinople was a bare thirty miles away now, and she was half-amazed to think it could be so near.

Gradually, in the dire days that had passed, the city of the golden-haired sultana, from whom she had hoped for so much, and most of all a reason to hope, had come to seem to her like a mirage, a kind of legendary city, eternally receding from her into time and space. Yet now that harbour lay close at hand.

The numbers of sails that studded the darkening sea bore witness to it, as did the lighter trails in the deep blue of the sky, already velvety with oncoming night.

Later that evening, when the wind had dropped suddenly and the ship sailed on under slackened canvas, sliding with a silken rustle through the calm waters, Marianne stood on deck and gazed at the stars of an oriental night that was as balmy as anything she had imagined in the days when the future was still inscribed for her with the name 'Jason Beaufort'. Where was he at that moment? What seas was he sailing in his pride or his grief? Where was the *Sea Witch* spreading her white sails, and whose hand was at the helm? Was he still living somewhere on the face of this earth, the man who only yesterday had claimed in his pride and mastery that there were two things only in this world he loved, the woman he had won only to lose and the ship that bore the likeness of her face.

On that last night of wandering, the onslaught of regrets grew ever more determined. She had trodden a long and painful road to reach the city whose nearness she could now sense, with the aim of doing her utmost to recall its heart – a fragile heart because it beat in a woman's breast, however ardent – to its 300-year-old alliance with France. She had shed on the way all that was true and real in her life: love, friendship, self-respect, fortune, even her clothes, to say nothing of the husband she had never even seen, murdered by the hand of a madman. Would there ever be a harvest? Would she at least return to France with the old alliance renewed? Or would there be failure there also, to match the private tragedy that still lurked in her womb, clinging with such tenacity that nothing, it seemed, could dislodge it?

She remained there for a long time, watching the big bright stars and searching for some sign of hope or encouragement. One in particular seemed to glow more bright and then fell away from the blue vault and plunged like a miniature meteor to extinction.

Marianne crossed herself, hurriedly, and with her eyes fixed on the point where the star had disappeared, murmured the traditional wish into the evening air.

'Let me see him, Lord! Let me see him again, whatever the cost! If he is still alive, let me see him again, just once ...'

That Jason was still alive, in her heart of hearts, she did not doubt. In spite of the cruel way he had treated her, in spite of his raging jealousy and a manner so strange that she had come to wonder if Leighton had not been feeding him secretly with some drug to induce a murderous and frenzied state, she knew that he was too deeply embedded in her heart for her to tear him out without destroying herself; and that even if he were at the other end of the earth, his life could not cease without her being in some way aware of it, through the mysterious vibrations of the soul.

The capital of the Ottoman Empire came in sight just at sunrise. At first it was no more than an outline, seen through a silvery haze on the distant skyline over the pearly sea, made up of nebulous domes and the faint spires of minarets.

On the Asian side the dark green hills, dotted with white villages, tumbled into a sea thick with shipping that looked as if it might have come straight out of some eastern tale : dark brown mahones, driven by the powerful arms of colourfully-dressed oarsmen; caiques gilded and painted like odalisques; shark-nosed xebecs, red and black; antiquated galleys, with their long sweeps lying parallel on the surface, like gigantic water beetles; chektirmes, with angular, skyward-pointing sails – all converging on that unreal city shimmering in the sunlight.

Slowly it grew, until the entire city was spread out before them, flowing away from the ochre-coloured walls strung out between the fortress of the Seven Towers past the Seven Hills and the Seven Mosques, like the arches of some titanic bridge, all the way to the black cypresses of Seraglio Point, in an astonishing jumble of red roofs, translucent domes, gardens and ruins of antiquity, like mighty shoulders braced at the critical moment to prevent the whole edifice of white cupolas ranged between the six minarets of the mosque of Ahmed and the great buttresses of St Sophia from rushing headlong into the sea.

As they rounded the Princes' Island they could see the crenellated line of the sea-wall, and the iridescent pearl began to take on a more precise definition.

The great ship curtsied daintily, her tall white sails dipping to the morning breeze as she came round Seraglio Point and entered the Golden Horn.

This was the great crossroads of the sea, where the hubbub of old Europe met the silence of Asia. The majesty of this three-fold city was overwhelming. It was like stepping into some Ali Baba's cave : your eyes were blinded by the light and brilliance of it all so that you did not know where to look or what to wonder at the most. Then, in the same instant, the sheer seething life of this melting pot of all civilizations took you by the throat and left you helpless.

Clinging to the quarterdeck rail beside Sir James, who was

taking it all in with worldly, unastonished eyes, Marianne stared about her at the vast, pullulating harbour like a blue tongue poked in between two different worlds.

To the left were the colourful picturesque ships of the Ottoman Empire, tied up to the quays of Stamboul. Facing them, at the Galata moorings, were the ranked vessels from the west: black Genoese, Dutch and English, the multicoloured pennons decking their bare yards like so much fruit unpicked by a careless gardener.

On either shore swarmed the busy crowds who, directly or indirectly, won their livelihood from the sea: seamen, customsmen, brokers, scribes, agents of merchants or foreign embassies, porters, stevedores, tradesmen and shopkeepers, and, everywhere, the tall felt hats and military figures of the janissaries of the port police.

Boatloads of men tugged furiously at the sweeps to tow the three-decker ponderously to her anchorage. At the same moment, a barge manned by hard-hatted English seamen put out from the shore and came to meet her. Upright in the stern was a very tall, thin, fair man, dressed with immense elegance. His arms were folded on his chest, and a flowing, light-coloured cloak blew about him.

At the sight of him, Sir James gave a start of surprise.

'Well, God bless my soul! It's the ambassador!'

Marianne was startled out of her own contemplation.

'What?'

'It would seem, my dear, that our two troublemakers must have rather more influence than we thought. The man in that barge is Stratford Canning.'

'Are you trying to tell me he is coming here in person to arrest a poor devil of a Greek who so far forgot himself as to try and choke the life out of a measly architect?'

'It hardly seems likely on the face of it but – Mr Spencer!' The lieutenant appeared at his side. 'Be so good as to ask the midshipman of the watch to step down to the cable tier and cast his eye over it. If the prisoner's still there, heave him out of a gun-port if you must, only get him off this ship. Or I won't answer for the consequences. I trust his irons have been properly filed through?'

The young man smiled. 'No need to fret about that, sir. Saw to it myself.'

'Then all that remains for us to do,' the captain observed, surreptitiously mopping his brow with his handkerchief, 'is to greet his excellency. No, don't you run away, my dear,' he added, as Marianne made a movement to withdraw. 'I'd rather keep you with me. I may need you. He's seen you, in any event.'

This was true. The ambassador, looking up at the little group on the quarterdeck, could not have failed to notice Marianne in her bright costume.

Resigning herself, she watched the diplomat's approach. She was amazed to find him so young. Not even his great height and upright bearing could add many years to an undeniably boyish face. How old was Stratford Canning, she wondered? Twenty-four, twenty-five? Certainly not much more. He was handsome, too. His features might have belonged to a Greek statue. Only the thin, thoughtful mouth and rather long chin were un-mistakably from northern Europe. The deep-set eyes were thoughtful also, and betrayed the poet and dreamer lurking be-hind the correct, diplomatic exterior.

When the barge had hooked on to the chains, he came up the companion ladder with the ease of the born athlete and, as he came forward to where they stood waiting to greet him on the deck, Marianne could see that he was even more attractive than he had looked at first sight. There was an undeniable charm about his person, his manners and his grave, pleasant voice.

Then, as her eyes met his for the first time, something inside her warned her that there was danger also. This man was as hard and bright and clean as a blade of tempered steel. Even his manner, perfect as it was, had something unyielding about it. Furthermore, no sooner was the ceremony of his arrival on board completed and the usual civilities exchanged than he turned from the captain and, without waiting for introductions, made her an exquisite bow and addressed her in a voice of smoothest courtesy:

'Permit me to say how delighted I am to have this opportunity of meeting your serene highness at last. You have delayed so long that we had almost given up hope of your arrival. May I say that for my own part, I am both pleased and – reassured?'

There was no hint of irony in the words and from the total absence of surprise with which she listened to them, Marianne knew, somehow, that she had been expecting them from the moment she had seen the ambassador in the barge. Not for one moment had she believed that a man of his eminence would go to such lengths over a simple matter of a Greek servant.

To Captain King, however, it seemed certain that there was some misunderstanding and he gave a shout of laughter.

'Serene highness?' he exclaimed. 'My dear Canning, you've been misinformed, I fear. This lady—'

'Is the Princess Sant'Anna, ambassadress extraordinary – and extraordinarily discreet also – of Napoleon,' Canning took him up coolly. 'I hardly think she will deny it. So grand a lady does not stoop to lies.'

Marianne felt a slow flush invade her cheeks as the ambassador held her eyes with his own perceptive ones, but she did not let her gaze falter. Instead, she met them with a coolness quite equal to his own.

'It's perfectly correct,' she said. 'I am the person you seek, sir. May I inquire how you found me out?'

'Oh, God, that was simple enough! I was roused up at dawn by a couple of rum fellows demanding justice for some kind of an attack on one or other of them which they said had been committed by the servant of a remarkable and highly aristocratic young lady who had appeared quite suddenly out of the mist one night in the middle of the Aegean. I can't say their misfortunes held much interest for me – but what did interest me more than somewhat was their enthusiastic description of the lady. It corresponded, in every detail, to a description which reached me here some time ago. I had only to set eyes on you, ma'am, for any doubts I might have had to be set at rest. I was told I should have to do with one of the prettiest women in Europe.'

It was not flattery; merely a quiet statement of fact, which drew a rather wistful smile from its subject.

'Very well,' she said with a little sigh. 'Now you know, Mr Canning.' She turned to her old friend, who had been listening to this astonishing exchange with a stunned expression that had altered, gradually, to one of deep disappointment.

'Sir James, forgive me, but I couldn't tell you the truth. I was bound to do my utmost to reach here, and if I have abused your hospitality, please believe me when I say that it was only in the cause of a higher duty.'

'You, an envoy of Bonaparte! Whatever would your poor aunt have said!'

'I don't know. But I like to think she would not have condemned me out of hand. You see, Aunt Ellis always knew that one day my French blood would come out. She did her best to stave it off, but she was prepared for it to happen. And now, your excellency,' she went on, turning back to Canning, 'perhaps you will be so good as to tell me what you mean to do? I do not think you are empowered to arrest me. This is the capital of the Ottoman Empire and France, as well as England, maintains an embassy here. No more – but no less. You were within your rights to try and intercept me on my way here, in fact such an attempt was made by some of your ships off Corfu, but you cannot do so now.'

'Nor should I dream of doing so. We are in Turkish waters, I agree. However ... while on board this vessel, you are on British soil. I have only to keep you here.'

'You mean?'

'You are not to go ashore. You are a prisoner of His Majesty's government, ma'am. Oh, no harm will come to you, of course. I shall simply ask Captain King to ensure that you remain below, in your cabin, during the hours he will remain in port. He will sail tomorrow morning for England, taking you with him under strict surveillance. Once there, you will become the most valuable, and the most charming, of hostages. If that's agreeable to you, Sir James,'

'Perfectly, your excellency.'

Marianne shut her eyes, fighting off the faintness that swept over her. This was the end. She had failed, hideously, on the very edge of success, and for the stupidest of all reasons: the vindictiveness of a pair of silly little men! But her pride refused to let her give way to weakness. Opening her great eyes very wide, she fixed them, sparkling with anger and suppressed tears, on the ambassador's bland face.

'Aren't you rather exceeding your powers, sir?'

'Not in the slightest, ma'am. It's quite within the rules of war – and we are at war. Allow me to wish you a pleasant journey home – for I should be glad to think that England might still feel even a little like home to you.'

'A little, sir. A very little. And now, Sir James, you had better do your duty and shut me up. Good day to you, Mr Canning.'

She turned from the ambassador, and glanced swiftly at the captain as she did so. The set look on his face killed any hope that still remained. Just as she had known when she first came aboard the *Jason*, James King would never let his private feelings interfere with his duty. Possibly he might even feel a certain natural resentment that she had used their old friendship to deceive him.

Sighing, she looked away to cast one final glance over the stern rail at the forbidden city. It was then she saw the *Sea Witch*.

At first she thought it must be an illusion born of her desperate longing to see the ship again, and she paused, brushing her hand uncertainly across her eyes as though unconsciously afraid to destroy the beautiful vision. But there was no mistake. The brig was Jason's.

She was riding easily at anchor, a few cables' lengths away at a little distance from the quay, and pulling gently at her moorings like a dog on a leash. A wave of joy swept over her, welling up from her heart and bringing a tightness to her throat and making her hands tremble as she made out her own image carved on the prow. There could be no further doubt: Jason was here, in this very port, where he had not wished to come but which to her in her abandonment, had been like the promised land.

But how could she reach him?

'Will you step this way, ma'am.'

Sir James's stiff voice brought her back to reality. She was not free to hurry to the man she loved. And, as a final reminder of the fact, two marines fell in on either side of her. She was a prisoner of war now, and that was all.

For a moment, she lost her nerve and gazed wildly up into the elderly captain's expressionless face.

'Where are you taking me?'

'Why, to your cabin, ma'am, as Mr Canning has suggested. Your – serene highness—' his tongue stumbled a little over the unaccustomed words, '– will be asked to remain there, with a guard on the door. Did you think you would be put in irons? We're not in the habit of ill-treating prisoners – not even those who serve Bonaparte.'

Marianne turned her head away so that he might not see that he had wounded her. Her kind old friend had vanished utterly and in his place was now a stern stranger, a British officer who would do his duty even if it meant playing the part of gaoler. It even seemed to Marianne that, in the bitterness of his disappointment, he might not have been sorry to have dealt with her more harshly.

'No, Sir James,' she said after a moment. 'I did not think that. But I wish you would not think too hardly of me.'

Casting one last glance at the brig from which there came no noise or sign of life and which, as she looked, seemed to turn away from her indifferently, she submitted to being escorted back to her own cabin.

The sound of the key turning in the lock grated on her nerves like a file. It was followed by the shuffle of feet and the sound of musket butts striking the deck. From now on, at least so long as they remained in Turkish waters, there would always be a pair of marines on guard outside her door. England was not going to let any friend of Bonaparte's slip through her fingers.

She went slowly to the window and opened it, but leaning out she saw only what she knew already. Her cabin, situated next to the captain's own, was high above the level of the water. Perhaps, in her disappointment, she might even then have made up her mind to the hazardous dive, in a faint hope of escaping from her captors and the fate that lay ahead; but even that desperate course was denied her. All round the stern of the ship as she lay at anchor was clustered a mosaic of little boats, rowing boats, caiques and peramas, thronging round her, as they were round any other ship of any size, like so many baby chicks around their mother hens. More boats were plying back and forth across the water, ferrying passengers and goods from one shore to the other. To jump would have been tantamount to breaking her neck.

Marianne wandered miserably back to her cot and sank down on to it. It was not until then that she noticed they had removed the sheets. Apparently Sir James was determined to take no chances.

That reminded her of Theodoros, and she reflected rather bitterly that he must be a long way off by this time. He had been just in time to benefit from the captain's weakness for the little Marianne he remembered. No one would come and loose her bonds to let her escape.

The Greek had achieved his object. All that she had left was the faint, private satisfaction of having kept the oath that she had sworn on Santorini. In that respect, at least, she was free, if in no other.

The hottest hours of the day slipped by, one by one, each more oppressive than the last, and swifter. There was so little time left for her in Constantinople! And the nearness of the *Sea Witch* made the inevitable prospect of departure more desperate than ever.

Very soon now, with the coming of the new day, the British ship would hoist sail and carry off the Princess Sant'Anna to a dismal future, to be swallowed up in the fogs of England, without even the relieving spice of danger. They would simply put her away somewhere and that would be that. Unless Napoleon remembered her, she would probably be forgotten by all the world.

At sunset came the wailing cries of the muezzins, calling the faithful to prayer. Then darkness came and the tumultuous life of the harbour slackened and died, while the riding lights of the different vessels shone out one by one. With the darkness came a cold wind from the north, which blew into the cabin. Marianne shivered but she could not bring herself to close the window, because by leaning out a little she could still just manage to make out the bowsprit of Jason's ship.

A seaman came in bringing a lighted candle and was followed by another with a tray. These they set down without a word. Probably they were under orders. Their faces were so devoid of all expression as to have become curiously alike. Marianne said nothing, either by word or look, and they went away.

She cast her eye over the tray without interest. A prison is still a prison, however many comforts it contains.

Nevertheless, she realized that she was very thirsty and, pouring herself a cup of tea, she drank it and was in the act of pouring out a second when she heard a heavy thud which made her start and turn her head. There was something on the floor.

Bending, she saw that it was a jagged stone with a thin black thread tied tightly round it. The other end of the thread disappeared through the window.

She tugged it gently, her heart beating fast, and then more strongly. The thread yielded. More of it appeared and was followed by a stout rope knotted on to it. Realizing suddenly what it meant, Marianne hugged the hempen cord to her in a wild access of almost hysterical joy, pressing it to her lips and kissing it as if it were an angel of deliverance. She still had one friend at least!

Hastily snuffing out the candles, she went to the window and leaned out. Down below, in the dense shade of the waterfront, it seemed to her that she could distinguish a human form, but she wasted no time on idle speculation. If she wanted to escape, there was no time to waste. She tiptoed to the door and laid her ear against it. There was not a sound to be heard from the ship, except for the faint creaking of her timbers as she rode at anchor. Even the sentries outside her door were silent.

Moving as silently as she could herself, Marianne fastened the rope's end securely to the leg of her bed. Then she hoisted herself through the window, an operation of some delicacy since it was not very large, and immediately felt the rope held taut by some invisible hand. Slowly, she began the descent, taking care not to look down at the gaping blackness beneath and groping for toe-holds on the vessel's side. Fortunately, none of the windows in the lower decks were open. All the officers except those of the watch must be ashore, enjoying their one night of leave.

The descent was one interminable horror. The rope soon burned her hands raw. Then, at last, she felt arms round her, holding her.

'Let go of the rope,' said Theodoros' voice. 'You've arrived.'

She obeyed and dropped into the bottom of the small boat where he had been waiting for her, and groped in the darkness for his hand. She saw his giant shape loom over her and, at the knowledge that she was free, miraculously, from her floating prison, she was suddenly overflowing with speechless gratitude, struggling at the same time to get her breath and to find the words to tell him what she felt.

'I thought you were far away,' she whispered, 'and now you are here. You came to save me! Oh, thank you ... thank you ... But how did you guess? How did you know?'

'I didn't guess. I saw. I'd just left the boat when the tall, fair Englishman arrived, and I hid on a lighter close by, among a load of timber, to see what I should do. I had a view of what was happening on deck there and when the soldiers took you away, I knew something was wrong. Have they found out who you are?'

'Yes. Cockerell and Foster went to complain and they gave a description of me.'

'I ought to have killed him,' Theodoros muttered. 'Listen, we can't stay here. We've got to get away, fast.'

He unshipped the oars and, softly fending off the perama, began rowing for open water.

'I'm going to row us round Galata point and land by the mosque of Kilij Ali. It's a quiet spot, and not far from the French embassy.'

He was bending vigorously to the oars when Marianne laid a hand on his arm. Not far away, the dark outline of the brig rose out of the black waters. There was only one riding light and from the forecastle a faint, fugitive gleam, but that was all.

'That's where I want to go,' Marianne said.

'There? To that ship? Are you mad? Why there?'

'Because it belongs to a friend – a very dear friend whom I had thought lost. It's the same one on board which the mutiny nearly cost me my life. But I must go.'

'And how do you know it's not still in the hands of the mutineers? Do you really want to reach this city, or only to add to your troubles? Haven't you had enough danger?'

'If it were still in their hands, then it would not be here. The man who stole it didn't want to come to Constantinople. Oh, please, Theodoros! Take me to that ship! It matters dreadfully to me! It's the thing that matters most in all the world because I thought that I should never see him again.'

She was strung taut, like a bowstring, striving with all her might to persuade him. Finally, in a low, breathless voice, as though she were ashamed after all that he had done, she said:

'If you won't take me, I'll go all the same. I'll swim. It's not very far.'

There was silence while the Greek sat with bowed head, thinking, and the little boat drifted gently with no pull at the oars. After a moment he said:

'Is he – the man you call Jason?'

'Yes.'

'Very well. If that is so, then I will take you, and God help us!'

He resumed his work at the oars and the perama began to slide again, silkily, through the water. Very soon, they were in the shadow of the *Witch* and her steep sides loomed above them. Here, too, there was no sound. Theodoros shipped the oars, frowning.

'It's as if there's no one aboard.'

'There must be! Jason would never leave his ship at night in a strange port. She isn't even berthed ... And listen! I think I can hear voices.'

There was, in fact, a murmur of voices from the bows. Forgetting everything in her impatience, Marianne stood up and began groping with her hands along the side of the ship, looking for something to climb.

'Sit still!' the Greek grunted. Like a cat, he seemed as well able to see as in broad daylight. 'There's a companion ladder farther on . . . You'll have us over!'

He edged the perama gently along the hull, but when Marianne tried to catch hold of the ladder, he stopped her.

'Stay where you are. I don't like the look of this. There's something odd about it and I didn't get you away from the English just to let you walk into another trap. You wait here. I'm going up.'

'No! I can't!' Marianne broke out wildly, no longer able to contain her impatience. 'I've waited days and days for this moment when I could set foot on that ship again, and now you want me to stay here in the boat and wait? Wait for what? Everything I want is there, a few feet away! You must see I can't bear it any longer!'

Seeing that no power on earth could restrain her, Theodoros gave in with a bad grace.

'All right, come on then, but try not to make a noise. I may be wrong, but I think they're speaking Turkish.'

In turn, they swarmed noiselessly up the ladder and dropped on to the empty deck. Marianne's heart was thudding so that she could hardly breathe. Everything looked just the same, and yet somehow different. The deck had lost its impeccable whiteness. Odd things seemed to be lying about there; the brass was dull and sheets hung loose, swaying slightly in the night wind. Then there was the silence . . .

She could not explain the apparently deserted condition of the vessel. Someone must surely come . . . a seaman . . . the lieutenant, Craig O'Flaherty . . . or perhaps her old friend Arcadius, whom she missed in his absence almost as much as Jason himself. But no. There was no one. Nothing but that glimmer of light forward. It was towards this that Theodoros was now moving cautiously, one step at a time, only to draw back swiftly into the shelter of the mainmast as two men, carrying long-muzzled guns, came out of the forecastle hatch. Marianne and her companion knew at once what they were, from their red and blue garments, their tall felt hats with the spoon for rice stuck in it, their gleaming weapons and the war-like air. They were janissaries.

'They are guarding the ship,' whispered Theodoros. 'That means there is no crew on board.'

'Maybe, but that isn't to say the captain isn't here either. Let me go and look.'

Unable to endure the uncertainty a moment longer, gripped by a fear she could not have described, and by the same sense of something amiss which had struck Theodoros earlier, she glided like a shadow past the deckhouse, its door swinging crazily off its hinges, and reached the poop and climbed up, taking care to avoid the faint beam from the single stern light.

Eagerly she sprang towards the door that led into the after-cabin and the captain's own sleeping cabin, but there she pulled up short, staring in bewilderment at the boarded-up doorway and, on the planks nailed across it, the great seals of red wax, like drops of blood.

Only then did she look around her, taking in the details she had missed before but which now stood out clearly in the dim light. Everywhere there were traces of a fight : in the splinters of wood torn from the rails and spars, the twisted metalwork and the marks gouged in the deck by cannon shot, and most of all in the dark stains which were most sinisterly evident around the wheel.

At that moment hope abandoned her.

There was nothing more to wait for, nothing to look for, either. Jason's beautiful ship was now a ghost-ship, the battered remnant of the thing she had once been. Someone, certainly, had recaptured her from the mutineers, but whoever that some-one was, it was not Jason, could not be, or why these signs of battle? Why the seals? A Barbary pirate, perhaps, or perhaps some Ottoman rais had come upon the *Sea Witch* far from land, half out of control in the inexperienced hands of Leighton and his crew, and she had fallen an easy prey.

To Marianne's distraught mind, it seemed all too clear what must have happened, from the grim traces left on board. Every-thing proclaimed a battle lost, defeat and death, even down to the bored soldiers keeping guard over the floating wraith, since, for good or ill, it was now obviously the property of some noble person.

As for those she loved and had last seen here, where no echo of their voices now remained, she would never see them more. She knew that now, for certain. They were dead.

Utterly broken by this latest blow, Marianne slid to the deck, oblivious of everything around her, and with her head against the boarded-up door that Jason would never use again, gave herself up to silent tears. It was there that Theodoros found her, huddled against the wood as though trying to become part of it.

He tried to make her stand but could not, for all his great strength. She had become a dead weight, loaded down with an immense burden of misery and despair which were beyond him, as a man, to cope with. She simply lay there, crushed to the ground by the rocklike pressure of grief and disappointment, and he knew that she would make no attempt to drag herself out of it. For her the outside world had simply ceased to matter.

Theodoros knelt beside her and, feeling for her hand, found it cold as if all the blood had already drained away from it. Yet the hand moved, pushing him away.

'Leave me alone . . .' she whispered. 'Go away!'

'No. I'm not leaving you. You are grieving, therefore you are my sister. Come.'

She was not listening. He guessed that she had wandered away from him again, borne on the bitter stream of her own tears, far beyond all reason and logic. Cautiously he raised his head and looked about him.

The janissaries were away up in the bows of the ship and had heard and seen nothing. They were sitting on coils of rope, their guns between their knees, and had taken out long pipes and were smoking placidly, gazing out at the night. The rich scent of tobacco mingled with the smell of seaweed on the breath of the breeze that wafted to them from the Black Sea. Obviously, neither of them suspected there was any other creature on board but their two selves.

Slightly reassured, Theodoros bent over Marianne once more.

'Please, you must try! You cannot stay here . . . it is madness! You must live, you must go on fighting!'

He was using his own terms to persuade her, the things that made up all the world for him. She did not even answer but only shook her head, almost imperceptibly, and he could feel her tears wet on his hand. He was overwhelmed with compassion such as he had never felt before.

He knew that this woman was brave and eager for life, and yet the words of life and battle had no power over her now.

She lay there, as a dog will lie outside the door of its dead master, and he knew that she would never move again unless he did something. All she wanted was simply to lie where she was until death took her. Yet she was so young ... so beautiful.

He was seized with anger against all those who had tried to make use of that youth and beauty, so ill-protected by the re-sounding titles which did not compensate for the load of responsibility they had burdened her with, himself among the rest. He was ashamed of himself, remembering the oath he had wrenched from the castaway before the sacred icons. Not everything was justified in the cause of freedom. And now that she could no longer help herself, this over-tried child who, for all that, had done her best to help him, had even killed for him, he was not going to abandon her.

She had not moved for some time, but when he tried again to lift her, he felt the same refusal, the same resistance which told him that if he persisted she was capable of screaming aloud. Yet they could not stay where they were for ever. It was too dangerous.

'I'm going to make you live in spite of yourself,' he muttered through his teeth, 'but for what I am about to do, forgive me!'

He raised his huge hand. He had learned much about all forms of fighting and he knew how to knock a man out with a single, scientifically-delivered blow to the back of the head. Judging the power of his arm to a hair's breadth, he struck. There was no more resistance. The girl's body slumped instantly and re-laxed. Immediately, he slung her across his shoulder and, bend-ing double so as to be indistinguishable from the bulwark, he made his way back to the entry port where the companion ladder hung.

It was no effort at all. His burden was as nothing to the joy of getting her away.

Seconds later, he had taken the sculls and was steering the perama towards the harbour entrance. A few minutes more and he would have reached the place that he had selected and could carry his companion to the French embassy, which he knew well. Only then would he be able to return to his own battle and to the terrible sufferings of his country. But first he had to return this child to her own place and her own people. She was like a delicate flower that cannot live in strange soil but can only find the nourishment it needs to live and grow in its own ground.

The boat rounded Galata point, past the walls of the old castle, and the minarets belonging to the mosque Kilij Ali lifted their vague white columns to the star-filled sky. They were out on the choppy little waves of the Bosphorus now, and the boat began to dance a little.

Theodoros, still pulling at the oars, began to smile suddenly. Though the wind was cold, the night was clear, calm and beautiful. It was not a night for tragedy. There was some mistake somewhere. What it was he could not tell, but his instinct, the instinct of a man brought up among mountains and used from boyhood to looking at the sky and the stars, told him now that for the woman lying unconscious in the bottom of the boat, the sunshine and the happiness were not gone for good, and Theodoros' instinct had never betrayed him yet. The longest road winds to an end at last, and the longest night must pass and see the dawn.

For the Emperor's envoy, this voyage at least was done and the time come to set foot on the soil of the Grand Signior and the fair-haired Sultana.

With a decisive gesture, Theodoros the rebel sent his boat into the calm waters of a little bay and drove it hard up against the sandy shore.

The Comte de Latour-Maubourg, French ambassador to the Sublime Porte, stared with stupefaction at the scarecrow figure of the giant who had invaded his embassy and dragged him from his bed by thundering on his door, bellowing like a bull, and then pushing his way past the porter.

Next, his perplexed and myopic gaze went to the young woman whom the intruder had deposited, quite unconscious, in a chair, as tenderly as if he had been her mother.

'You tell me this is the Princess Sant'Anna?'

'Herself, your excellency! But this moment escaped from the English vessel *Jason* by whom we were picked up, she and I, on the high sea, but where they were seeking to keep her prisoner. The ship was to have sailed at dawn to take her back to England.'

'A most extraordinary story! Who was attempting to detain the Princess?'

'Your diplomatic colleague from England. He came aboard this morning and recognized her.'

The ambassador smiled thinly.

'Mr Canning is a gentleman who knows his own mind. But you, my friend, who are you?'

'Merely her highness' servant, excellency. I am called Theodore.'

'Damnation! Is she travelling with a retinue? It must be an accomplished one. I notice you speak Turkish. By the way, isn't that faint of hers lasting a rather long time? For I am assuming she has fainted. There hasn't been an accident, I hope?'

'She suffered a shock, excellency,' Theodoros said blandly. 'I greatly regret that I was obliged to – render her unconscious, in order to spare her grief.'

The ambassador's grey eyes looked thoughtful, but not in any way surprised. Years of diplomacy at the Ottoman court had taught him not to be surprised at anything, and especially not at anything that concerned the vexed question of female psychology.

'I see,' was all he said. 'There is water and cognac on that table. See if you can revive your mistress while I go for some salts.'

He returned a few moments later, bringing with him someone else who, as soon as he entered the door, gave vent to a joyful exclamation.

'My God! Where did you find her?'

'So it is she? Canning was not mistaken?'

'No doubt about it, my dear Comte. By God, it makes me wish I hadn't forgotten how to pray!'

Arcadius de Jolival, his eyes bright with tears of joy, hurled himself at the still unconscious Marianne, while the ambassador, following more slowly, began to wave the sal volatile under her nose.

She gave a long shudder, groaned and made an instinctive movement to thrust away the penetrating smell, but she did open her eyes.

They wandered a little at first and then, almost immediately, fastened on the familiar face of Jolival, who was now weeping unashamedly from sheer relief.

'You, my friend? But how? . . . Where am I?'

It was Theodoros, standing very correctly in the background as befitted the servant of a noble house, who answered her.

'At the French embassy, your highness, where I felt it best to bring you after your accident.'

'My accident?'

Marianne's brain was still struggling to catch up with recent events. The comfortable, elegantly furnished sitting-room was reassuring, as was the tear-stained face of her old friend, which was comfortingly real, but what was this accident . . . Then, suddenly, the veil was rent away and once again she saw the battered ship, the door with the red seals on it, the bloodstains and the fierce faces of the janissaries glimpsed in the light of the lantern, and she flung herself against Jolival's chest, and clung to his coat.

'Jason? Where is he? What has happened to him? There was blood on the deck . . . Jolival, for pity's sake, tell me, is he—?'

Gently, he took her hands in his, feeling them tense and very cold still. He held them close to his breast to warm them, but he did not meet her eyes. The beseeching look in them was too much for him.

'Honestly, I don't know,' he said, and there was a break in his voice.

'You don't . . . even know?'

'No. But I am being equally honest when I say that I believe with all my heart he is alive. Leighton could not afford to kill him.'

'But how? . . . Why?'

The questions rose to Marianne's lips so thick and fast that she could not utter half of them coherently.

The ambassador decided it was time to intervene.

'Madame,' he said, 'you are in no state to listen to anything at the moment. You have had a shock, you are exhausted, bruised and very likely hungry. Let me take you to your room and send a little supper up to you. Afterwards, perhaps—'

But Marianne was already on her feet, thrusting aside both the chair and Jolival at once. Only a short while ago, on that empty deck, she had believed that there was nothing in this world left for her to love or hope for, and had felt the life drain away from her like wine out of a leaky cask. She knew now that she had been wrong. Arcadius was here, looking at her, alive and well, and he said that Jason might not be dead.

In a moment all her vitality and fighting spirit was restored to her. It was like a miracle. As though she had been born again!

'I am most grateful to your excellency,' she said in her normal tone, 'for your kind welcome. I shall not hesitate to trespass on your hospitality, I am afraid. But, please, before I go to rest, let me hear what my old friend has to tell me. It is something that matters greatly to me, you understand, and I shall not be able to sleep, I know, until I know what has happened.'

Latour-Maubourg bowed. 'My house and myself are yours to command, Princess. In that case, I shall merely order a light supper to be brought to us here. You will not deny that you could do with it, and so could we. As for your rescuer . . .'

His not imperceptive gaze went from Theodoros' rigidly controlled face to Marianne's anxious one. Ashamed at having thought only of herself, she instantly besought him to see that her 'servant' was properly looked after, whereat the ambassador smiled fleetingly.

'I hoped that I had deserved your confidence, madame. This man is no more your servant than I myself. The French embassy is neutral ground for such as you – Monsieur Lagos. You are welcome to my house, and you shall sup with us.'

'You know him?' Marianne said wonderingly.

'But of course. The Emperor has great admiration for the courage of the Greeks, and has always urged me to keep myself fully informed concerning their affairs. There are few men as popular among the Phanariots as this klepht from the mountains of the Morea. Or few who could answer to his description. A mere matter of size, my friend. You are welcome here.'

Theodoros bowed courteously, without speaking.

Leaving his visitors to recover from their surprise, the Comte de Latour-Maubourg left the room with a dignity not in the least impaired by his Indian dressing-gown of flowing design and the green silk nightcap on his head.

When he had gone, Marianne turned at once to Jolival.

'And now, Arcadius,' she begged, 'tell me everything that has happened since – since our parting.'

'You mean since that villain overpowered us and took possession of the ship, after as good as throwing you into the sea? Seriously, Marianne, I can still hardly believe my eyes. Here you are alive, thoroughly alive, when for weeks now we have hardly dared to think that you could have survived. Can't you see I'm dying to know—'

'And so am I, Jolival! And dying of apprehension, too, because I know you. If you had anything but bad news to tell, you would have been half-way through it by now. Is it – so very dreadful?'

Jolival shrugged and began pacing up and down the room, his hands tucked under his coat tails.

'I don't know. Weird, more than anything. Everything that has happened since the moment I last saw you seems to have been totally irrational. But listen and you'll see.'

Marianne sat curled up in an armchair, listening with all her ears, and as Jolival proceeded, she soon ceased to see or hear anything but the story he had to tell, which was certainly a very strange one.

After criminally abandoning Marianne, the *Sea Witch* had

turned aside from her original course and set sail for Africa. On the following night she was at a point midway between the Morea and the island of Crete when, just as darkness was falling, she was sighted by the corsair xebecs of Veli Pasha, the formidable son of the Pasha Ali of Yannina.

The Epirote's flotilla had easily overcome a vessel in no better or more experienced hands than those of a megalomaniac doctor and a handful of ruffians. At least, so far as the prisoners lying in irons below decks had been able to deduce from the short duration of the fight. One thing, too, they were now certain of, and that was that Jason Beaufort was no longer in command.

'Then how can you think he may be still alive?' Marianne burst out. 'Leighton must have killed him to gain possession of the *Witch*!'

'Killed him? No. But deprived him of his senses, drugged him to the eyeballs. And I don't think that we need look much farther for an explanation of a great deal in his behaviour which seemed to all of us who knew Beaufort well to be utterly unlike him. Not everything can be explained by jealous rage, and I know now that our captain had been in the man Leighton's power ever since Corfu. We were not sufficiently wary of that man.

'O'Flaherty told me in the end that Leighton had long been engaged in the slave-trade and had learned various secrets from the witch-doctors of Benin and Ourdah. After his betrayal of you, he encouraged Beaufort to drink heavily, but what he drank was not honest spirits.'

'Then, if he was not killed, what did Leighton do with him?'

'He escaped with him, in the launch, during the fight. It was pitch dark and everything was in total confusion. A boy who was behind one of the guns saw them go. He recognized the captain who, he said, was like a man walking in his sleep. It was Leighton who took the oars. He also took your jewels, I may add, as a kind of insurance, because we couldn't find them with your things, although we looked.'

'Jason desert his ship when it was in danger! Jason run from a fight!' Marianne said incredulously. 'It's just not likely, Arcadius! He would never get calmly into a boat while his men were being killed.'

'Of course not, but I thought I told you he was not himself. My dear child, if you stick at every piece of unlikelihood in our tale you are going to have a hard time of it. Well, down there in the orlop, we were convinced nothing but death awaited us at the hands of the pasha's devils, that or slavery at best. Nothing of the kind. On the contrary, Ahmet Rais, who was what you might call the commodore of the fleet, treated us with perfect courtesy.'

'Surely that's only natural? You and Gracchus are French, and the Pasha of Yannina daren't quarrel outright with the Emperor. His son must be of the same mind.'

Arcadius gave a lopsided grin.

'If there'd been nothing but the fact of being Frenchmen to save us, I'd not be here today to tell you about it. It was touch and go whether we'd lose our heads when a whole pack of ruffians came bursting into the orlop, foaming at the mouth and waving their scimitars about in a highly dangerous fashion. But – and this is the most extraordinary part of it – Kaleb only had to say a few words to them in their own language to stop them in their tracks. They even bowed to us most politely.'

Marianne was staring at him as if he was delirious.

'Kaleb?'

'You can't have forgotten the bronzed young god you defended so magnificently when Leighton was trying to have him flogged to death? Well, I have to confess that it was he who saved us,' Jolival declared, blandly helping himself to the glass of champagne offered by a servant who wore a curious garb of white flannel below his ordinary French-style coat.

The ambassador had returned a moment or two before and was now sunk in a chair, missing nothing of what Jolival had been saying, or of the impromptu but delicious cold supper which his household staff had been called out of their beds to prepare and serve.

Marianne herself had drained the contents of her glass at a

single gulp, as though the better to assure herself that this was all quite real.

'He saved you?' she cried to Jolival now. 'But, Arcadius, that's absurd. He was an escaped Turkish slave himself!'

'It looks absurd at first sight,' Jolival agreed. 'But to tell you the truth I've been thinking a good deal about our runaway. According to Beaufort, who I must say seems to have been more credulous than one would have expected, this Kaleb was escaping from his Turkish masters on the waterfront at Chioggia, in other words at a respectable distance from Ottoman territory. To further his escape, he then joins the crew of a vessel belonging to a nation notorious for the practice of slavery, and later doesn't turn a hair when he hears that the ship is on its way to Constantinople, of all places. After which, we find out that he possesses a certain influence over the Turks and their associates. It makes you think.'

'You're right. It is very strange. What do you make of it?'

'Either that the man's mad, which I can't believe, or that he is serving the Ottomans in his own way. Don't forget there are plenty of negroes and those of allied races holding important posts around the throne. Even if only in the harem.'

Marianne had a vision of the Ethiopian's lithe figure and his rich, deep voice. She lifted her brows.

'A eunuch? That one? Really!'

'I did not suggest he was. It's only a theory. At all events, he certainly got us out of Veli Pasha's clutches. We barely touched the coast of the Morea, and were not obliged to leave the brig, but allowed to resume our original quarters. Then the xebec escorted us to the Bosphorus, with a prize crew belonging to Ahmet Rais on board.'

'But what became of the remainder of the crew?'

'The mutineers are dead, and the pasha's methods must have made them long for hanging. The rest have no doubt been sold as slaves. O'Flaherty, of course, shared the same clemency as ourselves and we brought him here with us.'

'And – Kaleb?'

Jolival spread his hands in a gesture of ignorance.

'From the moment we dropped anchor at Monevasia in the Morea, we have not set eyes on him, and no one would tell us where he was. The last time we saw him, he said good-bye very politely and then simply vanished, like a genie out of a bottle. Nor would he consent to answer any of our questions.'

'This gets stranger than ever.'

Marianne's thoughts dwelled for a moment on the Ethiopian slave. Had he even been born in the country of the Lion of Judah? Was he ever a slave? He did not look like one. No, Arcadius was probably right and the man was some secret emissary of the Grand Signior's, an agent of some kind, perhaps. But he had been friendly, and she was glad, even if he had been keeping some secret from them, that he was free and safe, and out of Leighton's clutches. Very soon she turned from brooding on Kaleb, with his dark skin and light eyes and his perfect physique, and fell again to pondering the one subject which preoccupied her most passionately: Jason.

Her feelings, she discovered, were queer and complex. The thought of him deep in the power of that evil man was horrifying and revolting, and yet at the same time it brought with it a kind of paradoxical happiness. Now that she knew with what diabolic cunning the doctor had gained possession of his mind, she could forgive him his rages, his injustice and all that he had done to her, because she knew now that he had not been responsible for his actions.

She swept away the past and turned to the future. She had to find Jason, she had to get him away from Leighton and to cure him . . . But where was she to look? And how? To whom should she turn to try and pick up the trail of two men who had vanished in the middle of the night in a small boat, somewhere between Crete and the Morea?

Latour-Maubourg's voice, heavy with sleep and stifling a yawn, brought her the answer:

'With the exception of your jewels, Princess, you'll find all your belongings here, your clothes and your credentials from the Emperor and from General Sebastiani. May I approach the Seraglio in the morning with a view to obtaining an audience for you with Nakshidil Sultana with the least possible delay. Forgive me for seeming to press you like this when you must be in need of a rest, but time presses also, and it may be several days before we hear anything.'

Life was beginning to exert its claims again, and among them that alarming mission the Emperor had charged her with.

Marianne looked up over the rim of the glass into which she had been gazing as though to prise the secrets of the future from its golden depths, and bent on the diplomat a gaze brilliant with hope.

'By all means, Comte. The sooner the better. You cannot be as eager as I am. But will I be admitted?'

'I think so,' Latour-Maubourg smiled. 'I have seen to it, by little rumours spread about, that the Haseki Sultana knows all about the French lady traveller, a kinswoman of her own into the bargain, who was braving great perils to visit her but mysteriously disappeared. She has already expressed a wish to see you, should you by any chance be found. So you will be sure of an audience, for curiosity's sake, if nothing else. It is up to you to make good use of it.'

Marianne's eyes returned to her glass of champagne. It seemed to her that she could see a face now, floating nebulously in the cloud of tiny bubbles. The features were vague, but the face was framed in a cap of golden hair as deep and liquid as the wine itself: the unknown face of one who, long ago in the island of Martinique, had been called by the sweet name of Aimée and now ruled, unseen but all-powerful, over the war-like empire of the Osmanlis. Nakshidil. The French Sultana, the golden-haired, and the one person in the world with power enough to bring her back the man she loved.

Still smiling at the vision, Marianne closed her eyes, in utter confidence.

Juliette Benzoni

A series of glittering fifteenth-century romances in the lusty, turbulent tradition of Angélique.

One Love Is Enough 40p

Violet-eyed Catherine Legoix knew only too well the violence, terror and sensuality of the Hundred Years' War. At twenty-one, a tantalizing and dangerous beauty, she was virgin wife, unwilling mistress, and in love with a man she could not hold.

Catherine 40p

Braving the dangers of war-torn France, Catherine seeks Arnaud de Montsalvy, the nobleman who has scorned her passion – and threatened her life.

Belle Catherine 40p

The tempestuous heroine's search for her lover brings her face to face with torture, lust, imprisonment and the Black Death . . .

Catherine and Arnaud 40p

As the ravishing Catherine seeks vengeance against her arch-enemy, La Trémoille, her beauty is at once her keenest weapon and her greatest danger.

Catherine and a Time for Love 50p

To rescue her husband, Catherine braves the perilous journey from medieval France to Saracen Spain.

Sergeanne Golon

Angélique Book One 40p
The Marquise of the Angels

Only the dazzling and incredible world of Louis XIV could have
produced the passionate Angélique. Married to the sinister Joffrey,
Comte de Peyrac, and installed as Queen in his voluptuous Court of
Love, Angélique enters a life of brutal terror and sublime ecstasy –
an ecstasy soon to be shattered by her husband's enemies.

Joffrey is taken by the Inquisition and sentenced to death for
witchcraft – and Angélique swears to kill the men responsible . . .

Angélique Book Two 40p
The Road to Versailles

Seventeenth-century Paris – for the emerald-eyed Angélique a city
of wild love and vicious hate. Penniless and alone, sworn to kill the
men responsible for her husband's death, Angélique plunges into the
squalid underworld – to the nightmare Court of Miracles, home of
the deformed and the degraded – a world of violence and lust.
Spurred by revenge and ambition, Angélique begins the slow climb
back to Versailles, the glittering court of the Sun King himself . . .

Angélique and the King 40p

Angélique challenges the luxurious and licentious world of Versailles
to win her rightful place at the glittering court of Louis XIV.

But the path to royal favour is beset with treachery, intrigue,
kidnapping and attempted poisonings.

Trapped in the struggle for power between the Sun King's two
famous mistresses, the bewitching beauty from the Paris underworld
becomes the one woman the elegant, libertine King desires but
cannot win . . .

Angélique in Revolt 40p

Emerald-eyed, marble-breasted, with an unquenchable sensuality that makes her beauty irresistible, Angélique flees the silken prison of Louis XIV to become the most hunted woman in his kingdom.

Harried and driven by the King's brutal and licentious cavalry through the forests and marshlands of France, she seeks refuge in the arms of the brave warrior-leader of the rebellious Huguenots.

Angélique and the Sultan 40p

The tempestuous Angélique had known many lovers. But always in her ecstasies of passion, she had been haunted by the memory of her first love, Joffrey de Peyrac.

Now Angélique flees France to risk the perils of Barbary.

In this savage world she learns the horrors of a pirate galley, the degradation of the slave market, the tortures of the seraglio, before being chosen as the beautiful plaything of a lust-crazed Sultan . . .

Angélique in Love 75p

Half-angel, half-devil and wholly woman, Angélique finds herself on board a pirate ship bound for the New World.

An eventful voyage brings murder, lust, storms, mutiny, ice-bergs and hot-blooded excitement. It also reveals the true identity of the implacable buccaneer captain.

What does the future hold for this emerald-eyed beauty — a happiness she does not believe possible, or a life irretrievably ruined?

The Temptation of Angélique Book One 30p
The Jesuit Trap

Spring comes to the wilderness of New France, and Angélique, as lovely and as sensual as Eve, glories in the torment and delight of her passion for Joffrey de Peyrac . . .

Tricked into separation, Angélique finds herself friendless on a frontier ripe for war — a target for Indian attack, Jesuit anger and pirate lust.

The Temptation of Angélique Book Two 30p
Gold Beard's Downfall

Angélique had lain naked in Gold Beard's arms, responding to his caresses, yet remaining faithful to Joffrey de Peyrac.

Now as savage Indians gather for war, she is humiliated, spurned by the one man she loves, scorned by those whose life she had once saved, a prey to Jesuit hatred.

Her heart torn by conflicting emotions, Angélique watches her husband set sail to destroy the blond corsair — Colin Paturel, her desert lover from the past . . .

Angélique and the Demon 75p

Now mistress of the settlement of Gouldsboro, Canada, Angélique feels at peace at last.

But when the man she loves leaves on a mission, Angélique becomes prey to evil forces and unknown strangers — a demon intent on the destruction of her life and her love . . .

Unwilling hostess to the strange but beautiful Duchesse de Maudribourg, Angélique combats poison, intrigue and death — finally to grapple with the unmasked Demon, face to face . . .